PRAISE FOR ELI

'Heartbreaking yet riveting.'

'Tragic and emotional . . . a riveting but heartbreaking read.'
—*Woman's Weekly*

'*The Lines We Leave Behind* is mesmerizing; a deeply affecting story of treachery, deception, sacrifice, and loss. Beautifully written and completely absorbing . . .'
—Karen Dionne, author of the internationally bestselling *The Marsh King's Daughter*

'A fascinating story depicting a part of WWII not often represented: Britain's involvement in fractured Eastern Europe, particularly Yugoslavia. Part spy story, part domestic thriller, *The Lines We Leave Behind* is an emotional journey with a complex heroine who faces danger during the war and psychological consequences after.'
—Emily Winslow, author of *Jane Doe January* and the Keene and Frohmann crime series

'Eliza Graham tells a powerful tale and her characters are well drawn and believable. I enjoyed this book very much.'
—*Historical Novels Review*

'Beautifully descriptive.'
—*Euro Crime*

YOU

LET ME

GO

OTHER TITLES BY ELIZA GRAHAM

YOU

LET ME

GO

Eliza Graham

LAKE UNION
PUBLISHING

Text copyright © 2021 by Eliza Graham
All rights reserved.

Published by Lake Union Publishing, Seattle

www.apub.com

Amazon, the Amazon logo, and Lake Union Publishing are trademarks of Amazon.com, Inc., or its affiliates.

ISBN-13: 9781542017107
ISBN-10: 1542017106

Cover design by Emma Rogers

Printed in the United States of America

For Alison Geary

1

Rozenn fights as the tide ebbs from the creek, slipping away into the sea. The water will sweep back this evening, but if she lets it take her now she will not return again. A flicker of resistance along her neurons, a *non*, and she's pulled herself out of the current. Still here in her own bed in Vue Claire, propped up on pillows so she can see the creek through the window, her son and granddaughters downstairs, her little dog curled at her feet like a medieval tomb carving.

Thinking about those adored granddaughters is pain as much as solace. Rozenn's about to deal their relationship a blow and she can no longer speak or write to explain why. A sister hating a sister is the bitterest of hatreds. She loves that younger granddaughter Morane so fiercely, but Morane's the one who'll hurt the most. All she can hope is that it will only be a matter of weeks, at most months, before Morane understands why her grandmother's done what she's done.

It's not the first time Rozenn has torn her family apart. Something heavy and round presses into her palm. The silver compass. Her guide through the next leg of her voyage? A mist lowers over her eyes. For the last time, she looks out of the window at the water – green, grey and blue all at once, glittering in the sunlight. Even now Rozenn wonders at it. Birds call out, a child laughs on the strip of sand below. Woven through these sounds are the voices of those loved and lost so long ago. *Not yet, I'm not ready*, she pleads. But it's time to go.

The dog whines but doesn't stir. The tide's pull is more insistent now. The mist has completely veiled her eyes. Rozenn surrenders herself to the current, the chain of the silver compass draped around her hand. Guilt for all she's done sweeps through her one last time.

She coughs once. A brief smile softens her face as the waters take her, as though there's someone finally reassuring her that all's forgiven. Everything she is and everything she ever was is drawn into the horizonless sea.

2

When I was small the days and weeks leading to the third Saturday in July would slow to a crawl. I usually packed my rucksack a week ahead of departure, refusing to remove my colouring pens, pyjamas and sponge bag from it. Finally we'd shrug off school and set our alarm clocks for half-five to avoid the holiday traffic heading out of London to the south-west. Dad would worry that we wouldn't fit the rubber dinghy and oars into the boot. My older sister would fret that she hadn't packed enough pairs of shorts and books to read. Mum would fuss about the neighbour forgetting to water the pots on the back patio. I'd be sitting in the back of the car, silently bellowing at them all to hurry. I wanted to be in Cornwall. Now.

Anticipation would weigh down the last mile of the drive through narrow, banked lanes to Helford, crushing me so I felt close to panic. Sometimes I made Dad pull over because I thought I might actually throw up.

'Stop being weird.' Gwen would screw her features into a grimace. 'We're only going on holiday. Can't you just be normal, Morie?'

But staying at Vue Claire was never just a holiday for me. Time spent with my grandmother in her house on a small creek off the Helford estuary on the south coast of Cornwall was the part of the year that mattered more than anything. She'd be waiting for us at the front door, her rare but dazzling smile illuminating her face. *Mes petites.* She'd enfold us into her cashmere- or linen-clad arms, scented faintly with the woody-citrus perfume she'd worn as long as I remembered.

I'd dash through the house, leaving the others to bring in the bags, and out of the back door, over the small lawn that sloped to the water. If it was high tide, I'd lie on the jetty and dip my hands into the water. At low tide, I'd pull off my sandals and jump off the jetty to wade through the pools left behind. Gwen would complain that I wasn't doing my fair share of bringing bags in from the car and I'd have to sever myself from the estuary to help.

I loved the white-walled interior of Vue Claire as much as the outside. Rozenn – for reasons nobody could recall we had always called her this rather than Granny, Grandma or a French version – stored carved animals and puzzles in an old wooden chest. There were games, books, sketching pads, watercolour and oil paints we were encouraged to use. Sometimes I'd catch our grandmother watching us approvingly as Gwen and I sat close together, my auburn head and Gwen's blonde one touching as we played a card game, usually Piquet, which she'd taught us herself. Rozenn would take us to the nearby riding stables for pony trekking and photograph us on sturdy ponies: me beaming, Gwen more wary.

'Stay close to one another,' she urged us as we grew up into such different people. 'Sisters should be part of one another's lives.'

But then she herself had done the thing most likely to rip us apart.

3

Men in heavy boots had arrested the young widow who lived on the floor above them, taking her off in the early hours. Rozenn had heard her ask *pourquoi?* as they stomped past their apartment door, sounding baffled as much as scared. Next morning, when she went out for bread, the concierge told Rozenn that the older woman on the top floor had denounced the widow for listening to the BBC. Jealous of her looks, the concierge added. This might be the well-heeled *seizième* but some women in this *arrondissement* still behaved like alley cats.

Papa came home for lunch as usual and listened as Rozenn relayed all this to him, nodding without comment. While they waited for Maman to serve the fried horsemeat he buried himself in a medical paper on pulmonary developments in Switzerland. When he heard the clink of the plates in the kitchen, he folded the paper up and pushed it away with a sigh. 'I'm losing touch.' Little by little his practice had become less specialist. He'd even added a few middle-aged German officers to his list, now treating not only asthma and bronchitis but fungal infections and dyspepsia.

This lunchtime Maman hadn't burnt the meat and Rozenn could almost imagine it was a piece of beef rather than some old farm-horse. There was spinach too, not usually her favourite accompaniment, but she ate it greedily, Papa nodding approvingly. 'Good source of iron, Rozenn.' She noticed how little her mother now ate, how hollows had formed where her cheeks should be, her skin had grown dry and her nails ridged. They all of them needed more fish, more cheese, more fresh vegetables. More of everything.

Yann bolted the larger portion of meat he'd been given because he was a young male. 'He'll have yours off your fork if you don't eat up,' Rozenn warned Papa, who stared down at his plate as though he wasn't sure what to do with the food.

He managed to take a mouthful and smile.

'François?' Maman frowned at him.

Papa laid down his fork. 'I examined a businessman from Hamburg today. Just the little pin on his lapel to remind you of his loyalty to the party. He's the director of a German construction company.' The words were coming out quickly, as if he'd been storing them up inside. 'But he also works for the Organisation Todt.'

Maman stiffened. Rozenn had heard the name but couldn't remember why.

'It's the organisation the Nazis set up in Germany to build their new roads,' Papa went on. 'But these days it provides labour and resources for all . . . projects over occupied Europe.'

Which now meant Norway to the Pyrenees, as those greeny-grey uniforms had swarmed all over the continent.

'Labour.' Maman said the word quietly.

'So what's wrong with this Todt official?' Yann asked. 'Lingering constipation?'

'Piles,' Rozenn suggested. 'Syphilis?'

Maman seemed too preoccupied even to reprimand her.

'A cough. Exacerbated by the strain of dealing with labour shortages, my patient says. He's lost his German workers to the army.'

'*Le pauvre*,' Yann scoffed.

'He's here to prepare for the fortifications the Germans plan, all the way down the coast from the fjords to south of Biarritz.'

'That's thousands of miles!' Maman sounded incredulous.

'He told me that to do this Organisation Todt will bring in compulsory labour for young men in occupied countries.'

Papa halted. Rozenn stared down at the tablecloth.

'They'll also work in German factories,' Papa said quietly.

The linen needed laundering and there was a rip in it that ought to be darned. Rozenn wanted to put her finger into it and pull the fibres apart.

'People won't stand for it,' she said. 'It's slavery.'

'Herr Braun told me there'd be an exchange: we'd get our POWs back in exchange for over-eighteen-year-olds lent to the Fatherland for a year or two.'

Yann put down his knife. 'I'm not going back there.' After the Fall of France his battalion had surrendered to the Germans and he'd been sent to work at a German plant producing rubber seals. It was where he'd developed appendicitis. Precious days had passed before he'd been taken to a hospital near Hamburg, and weeks had gone by before he'd been repatriated to a clinic in Paris that Papa had organised. The appendix had been removed by then but the infection lingered. Yann's face was still gaunt, if less yellow-looking now that he could walk around the sunny streets and parks.

'They're not taking Yann.' Rozenn pictured him back on some factory line, without natural light, weakened by lack of food, shouted at by some German overseer. She would rip out the heart of anyone who came for her brother.

'They've been filing away the details of every man, woman and child in France,' Papa told her. 'Your friend Theo, you said his family were leaving?'

'It's different for the Monteux family,' Maman answered before Rozenn could. 'They're more vulnerable.'

Poor Maman, with her beautiful apartment, her accomplished friends, her ordered life, her Catholic forbears going back centuries and centuries: she still hadn't grasped her family was vulnerable too, even if it wasn't Jewish.

'Couldn't Yann study something like veterinary medicine?' Maman asked. 'Wouldn't that make him exempt?'

Yann laughed. 'What have the innocent creatures of France done to deserve that fate?'

'Could he get an orderly's job in a German military hospital?' Rozenn's mind was whirring. 'Surely they'd class that as essential labour?'

Papa shook his head. 'If Yann's strong enough to carry stretchers, he's strong enough to handle heavy tools.'

'What about the *Zone Libre*?' The unoccupied southern half of France would be safe, surely? It kowtowed to the Germans, but the Nazis didn't have complete sway there.

'Herr Braun tells me the labour requirement will extend down there too. They aren't really free in unoccupied France, no matter what they tell themselves.' Papa looked at his watch. 'I must go.'

Maman's shoulders slumped. Papa's eyes softened. 'I have an idea, Louise. I can't tell you more now. There's . . . the other matter to attend to first.' The pair of them exchanged glances. 'Expect me back late.' He looked at Rozenn. 'Don't make too many plans for the next few days. You may need to help your mother pack.'

Both his children spoke at once. He raised a hand as he stood up and walked out of the room. 'More later.'

'Where are you going?' Rozenn asked. 'What other matter is this?'

'Don't interrogate your father,' Maman snapped. 'He'll make the decisions that need to be made.'

'We should be honest with them.' Papa paused before picking up his medical bag. 'We had a letter from the convent.'

For whole days, sometimes even a week at a time, Rozenn could forget about the convent.

'There's been illness there. Diphtheria. A death.' He turned to look at Rozenn. Could he read the thoughts racing through her mind? 'I need to see for myself.'

A kinder, better person would have offered to go with him. Rozenn was not that person. She watched Papa close the door behind him. Yann offered a distraction by excusing himself from the table and going to his bedroom to fetch his fold-up easel and box of paints. 'The park again?' she asked.

One of these days he'd have himself arrested for drawing something military or annoying the Germans.

'I can't resist the Bois on an afternoon like this. The trees are such an extraordinary shade of green. And I don't want to miss the last of the chestnuts in flower. I may even have to paint them rather than the people.'

Maman was clearing the lunch table. 'You could put on an apron and help me here, Rozenn,' she called. Yann was male, a convalescing male at that, at liberty, for now, to fill his afternoons as he desired. Rozenn almost wished she was still at the *lycée*. Even the most tedious algebra lesson would be better than acting as skivvy on an afternoon when light poured greeny-gold through the windows.

'Be careful,' Rozenn called to her brother as she went into the kitchen. Last week he'd come home with a bag of croissants and two perfect baguettes: crisp on the outside and pillowy inside, having sketched the shopfront of a *boulangerie* in Passy frequented by women in expensive clothes and their German companions. The female proprietor wanted the sketch for a flyer advertising her baked goods.

Yann might possess an innocence that appealed to most women's maternal instincts, but their German boyfriends hadn't always been as convinced. One of these days he'd be punched or thrown into a black van for offending their sense of proprietorship.

Rozenn rinsed a layer of ill-smelling dish soap off a plate. They called it soap but it didn't seem to do much in the way of cleaning, and left her hands dry and red.

When Maman went into the salon to darn some of the socks in her mending pile, Rozenn crept towards the telephone in the foyer. You weren't supposed to make unnecessary calls so Rozenn didn't telephone as often. Sometimes she heard a little click on the line when she rang Theo Monteux in his family's apartment. And it was no longer their maid who answered, but Madame Monteux herself, sounding guarded.

'Fancy an ice cream?' she asked Theo when he came to the telephone. Not that there would be any ices for sale to native Parisians: the Germans would have scoffed them all. She could do without ice cream but she couldn't do without Theo. The need was pulsing through her veins, probably audible in her voice, she feared.

'Usual place?' he said. 'I bet you my new leather-bound notebook there's no pistachio ice, though.'

'Where did you find a new notebook?'

'Not telling. Half-three?'

Rozenn crept into her room and peered at her reflection in the mirror. A hint of freckles – damn. Last year you could still find lemons and she'd applied the juice to her skin with some success. She dabbed a thin layer of pancake over the freckles and adjusted her hair to ensure a lock hung over each shoulder but the rest of the waves were pinned back. With this blue sateen summer dress and her light silk hat – last year's but still respectable – placed at the correct oblique angle she was presentable, although too much the eager little schoolgirl. She practised raising her eyebrows, trying

10

for an air of amused detachment. Maman had the most delicious raffia clutch bag. Rozenn knew where the creaky boards were under the Persian rug in her parents' room and filched the bag out of her mother's armoire without making a sound. Tucked under an arm it gave her an air of sophistication. Too much the coquette? Better that than looking too innocent.

'Just going out for a breath of fresh air,' she called, closing the apartment door behind her and dashing down the stairs before Maman could question her. They were ridiculously overprotective of her these days. Say this for the Germans, they didn't tend to assault or catcall Parisian women in public – unless they thought you belonged to *certain* groups. She'd seen their soldiers nod politely at blonde-haired girls and then whistle and jeer at a girl of obvious Jewish origins seconds later.

Theo was waiting at their usual place in the Bois de Boulogne: a spot where the tracks crossed and the ice-cream cart was parked. As always his outline – lean but sculptured, impeccably dressed – seemed to turn the postcard-pretty scene into something more stylish and focused. Judging by the way other women glanced at him, they appreciated him too. Theo himself seemed oblivious to the admiration. He turned at her approach. 'Nobody does a brisk walk like you, Rozenn.'

She made a note to approach him less hastily in future. Eagerness wasn't what she was aiming for. He kissed her on both cheeks, took her hands and stood back to look at her, a bashful smile on his face. She knew there'd be just enough pinkness to her cheeks to make her look fresh, but not overheated. 'No ice creams for us this afternoon, though,' he said. 'Pistachio, chocolate, vanilla, all finished.' A fat German sergeant barged past them, carrying a double strawberry cone.

'*Salaud*,' she said in a low tone.

Theo grinned. 'And nobody does elegant swearing like you.' He smiled but it was a smile making an effort to cover something sad.

'What?'

He didn't even try to dissemble. 'We're leaving.' No joke, no ironic quip. Just the words.

She felt coldness sweep through her. This wasn't unexpected: things had been growing harder and harder for the Monteuxs, the father losing his prestigious job in the hospital, all kinds of petty humiliations, threats that private telephones and radios would be forbidden to Jews, that using public facilities would be banned. The Monteuxs were wise to run while they still had resources: money, contacts. But life without Theo . . . She caught a glimpse of his face, creased into sadness. Every time she thought she'd accustomed herself to the Occupation something else happened to remind her how awful it was.

'Will you miss my bad language terribly?' She tucked her arm into his.

'I'll miss all of you, every centimetre.' Rozenn felt the warmth of his dark eyes. Eyes that had admired so much of her body. Eyes whose soft lids she had kissed over and over again.

'When do you go?' A greyness seemed to sweep over her.

'Monday.'

So soon?

'Papa has the papers now.' He lowered his voice. 'Marseilles. He's been promised a job and visas for all of us if we can find our way from there to Lisbon and cross the Atlantic to New York.'

New York. A place where you could still buy an ice cream on a June afternoon. He gave a gentle laugh. 'Sounds like a fairy tale, doesn't it?'

'So this is likely to be our last little promenade.' Rozenn felt her face twist into a scowl as a group of loud German privates walked towards them. She composed herself; when she was out with Theo it was important to do nothing to draw attention. Theo looked like any other French boy. But if they were stopped, his papers would tell the Germans his race. Jews were still allowed to walk in the Bois but subject to insults, sometimes blows.

'Your father was a young medic in the first war, wasn't he?' Theo sounded reflective. To Rozenn's relief they didn't often engage in serious conversations about their families.

'Papa was studying medicine so he worked alongside the doctors in a field hospital.'

'Did he talk to you about it, what it was like, what he saw in those trenches?'

She shook her head.

'My father was at Verdun when he was my age,' Theo continued. 'He said something was crushed in France after that battle. It's why we didn't fight properly last year when the Germans invaded.'

Cut up by metal, their remains left to rot on barbed wire or buried in mass graves. Rozenn knew enough about events a generation ago. When Yann had received his conscription papers last year Papa had gone into the bathroom and closed the door. She'd never heard him cry before.

'This won't do at all. We're only going to talk about amusing things for the next hour.' She gave Theo her brightest smile, the one she'd practised in the mirror, and noted how the look of dejection passed from his face, replaced by hunger. Not for the vanished ice creams, for her. Rozenn relayed the concierge's gossip about the German family in the apartment opposite. *She can buy all the* couture *in Paris she can get her trotters on, but you can't turn a sow into a swan. Those breasts of hers sag like two sacks of flour in her new dress.*

She wasn't going to let Theo remember her as a crumpled emotional mess. Let him pine for her as she'd always been: vivacious, a little acerbic, a distraction. No more talk of Verdun or anti-Jewish measures. No more talk of Theo's departure. He mustn't realise how

13

much she needed him, how much she relied on him to distract her from the Occupation.

'Look at the *derrière* on that one,' she said, nodding at a girl in a pink dress clinging to a field-grey uniformed arm. 'She must remind him of one of the sausages he used to scoff in Frankfurt.'

Theo frowned at the rear of the girl. 'I'm starting to look at plump females with a rumbling stomach.'

'Don't be disgusting.' She tapped his arm with the raffia clutch bag.

A woman walked towards them, pushing a perambulator. Theo licked his lips. 'Mmm, a chubby infant.'

'Gently fricasséed?'

'With some new-season carrots and potatoes and a little parsley. Shame you can't cook, Rozenn. It's one of your only faults.'

She sniffed. 'I'll have you know Maman's teaching me. Now it's her doing it all she wants me to learn so I can help. Neither of us are enjoying the experience. Luckily Yann's a complete pig and will eat anything. Papa looks a bit wistful at lunchtimes, though.'

They reached a bench. 'Let's sit,' he said. He took his cigarette case out and offered her one, lighting it for her.

'You could give me a forwarding address.' She took a casual puff of her cigarette.

'You really want . . . ?' He seemed to need to take a breath. 'I thought you'd find it a bit boring, you know, writing to someone who's not going to be around.' He looked more vulnerable suddenly.

'Do you *want* me to write to you?'

'Yes.'

Their eyes locked.

'But I don't have an address for Marseilles. Papa says we need to be discreet.' His hand went round her waist. His voice was huskier now. 'I wish we could go somewhere else so I could say goodbye to you properly, Rozenn.' Normally Maman would be out of the apartment now, having her hair done or queuing for food. Not today, because of whatever it was Papa was planning. Theo's mother only left the home early in the morning to walk somewhere that would still sell her groceries.

Nowhere to go. But they couldn't leave it like this, a farewell in a public park. For months they'd been playing the part of the respectable young couple, stopping at just the right point, covering up feelings with ironic observations. It had been enough. Not any more.

She stubbed out her cigarette and stood up, holding out a hand to Theo.

'Where're we going?'

'Wait and see.' She took him by the arm and steered him deeper into the park.

Yann had told her about the shed, once perhaps used by the park maintenance people to store tools. Bushes had grown up around it. The roof had partially fallen in. He sometimes sheltered in here if he was caught in a rain shower. He'd told her how the padlock on the door wasn't really locked.

'It's not as bad inside as it looks,' she said, glancing over her shoulder before she removed the padlock and opened the door.

In the corner Yann had stacked a pile of old hessian sacks he must have found at some market.

'I've walked past this place a hundred times without spotting it. It would be a good—' Theo swallowed. *Hiding place?* she wondered.

He was smiling. 'What?'

'You always find a solution, Rozenn. If you want to do something you just find a way.'

'Why wouldn't I?' Rozenn placed her mother's raffia bag carefully on a shelf. If it acquired even a speck of dirt there'd be hell to pay. 'Wilful, my parents say.' She pulled the sacks out along the

15

floor and lay herself down, ensuring her skirt rose above her knees. She wore no stockings, just little ankle socks, which she flicked off with her feet.

'Not wilful as much as determined. More like a little cat who knows what she desires.' He sat down next to her and ran a finger up her naked thigh. She felt her nerves tingle. 'You don't know what you're doing to me, Rozenn.'

Oh but she did. She looked up at him from beneath her lashes. 'So show me?'

He bent over her, weight supported on his elbows. 'Really?' His voice was thick with what must be desire.

'Are you worried I'll lose my bandbox freshness, spoil some future husband's wedding night?' She had herself considered this possibility but had thought up ways of covering up if it ever became necessary. 'Or that I might find myself in a difficult situation?' One heard rumours, of course, of girls who'd made mistakes. It didn't happen often to people like her because their parents kept them so closeted – or tried to. But war and occupation had shaken things up.

'My God, that would be awful. I can't—' He started to sit up. She pulled him down again, her hands brushing casually across the front of his trousers. He very obviously wanted her. The touch and sight of undeniable male desire made a shiver run down her spine.

'I know ways of making it safe.' She whispered her suggestions into his ear, enjoying the smell of him. 'You just need to pull away at the right moment. And I'll . . . take care of myself at home.' The bidet would be her friend here. She drew in a breath of Theo. Lemon and bay: his family could obviously still find scented soap. 'Wouldn't you like a happy memory to take with you?' He looked at Rozenn through eyes that seemed unable to focus.

What she was proposing was so outside the normal behaviour expected of a middle-class girl. Until a few weeks ago she hadn't appreciated just how . . . raw sex could be. She'd found a pornographic magazine a German private had discarded in a metro carriage. She'd been unable to resist picking it up when the carriage was emptying and bringing it home. Flicking through the pages had made Rozenn want to scrub her hands, but also made her wonder whether Theo dreamt of doing things like the man in the photographs. And she hadn't been able to push the images, shocking as they were, out of her mind.

He swallowed. 'But . . . ?'

'You still think of me as good little Rozenn, whose maman keeps a close eye on her?'

She told him about the pornographic magazine. For a moment he looked appalled. And then his features creased up in laughter. 'Suppose your mother found it in your room? Rozenn, she'd lock you up.'

'That magazine was in the stove within twenty minutes, I can tell you. If she'd seen it, I was going to say it was Yann's.'

'You'd let your brother take the rap? You're a devil, you know.'

She shrugged. 'Maman's golden boy can do no wrong. Anyway . . .' She ran a finger over his lips. 'Wouldn't you like me to show you some of the things I saw the girls in the photos doing?'

'You found the illustrations . . . ?' He swallowed.

'Arousing?' She took his hand and placed it on the front of her sateen dress. 'What do you think?' His mouth found hers and any reservations seemed to float away through the cracked glass, into the Parisian afternoon.

'I'll remember this,' he told her, breaking off for a moment to pull at her buttons and sounding almost fierce.

'So will I.' Rozenn placed a hand on his groin and watched his face but it was hard to stay in the moment. She saw Theo in shabby clothes, queuing outside embassies, sitting in third-class railway carriages, his face thin and watchful. She pushed the images away,

17

and removed her hand so she could pull her dress over her head and scoop off her underpants (a peach lace confection that she'd miraculously found in the Samaritaine department store before some German could grab it for his mistress). Her attention turned to Theo's trousers. He was watching her like someone mesmerised, gasping as her hand moved. Hitler himself might have been marching towards the shed but they wouldn't have noticed.

Theo stopped. Moved away from her. 'Rozenn. We can't.'

Her cheeks were burning. She certainly hadn't been expecting this. Humiliation made her eyes water.

'This isn't the way to treat a girl like you. What would your brother say?'

'My brother? Why are you thinking of him now?'

'I have a sister. If someone did . . . what we were about to do, I'd be furious. It's exploiting you, especially when I'm about to run away.' He took her hand.

'But that's exactly why we should do it. Everything's changing—'

'You don't know what it's cost me to pull back.' His voice shook. 'Let's not fight on our last meeting.' He pulled her into his arms, stroking her face, kissing the shoulder that was still exposed, but gently. 'Let's just be still here together, block out the world.'

His embrace became her universe. Minutes passed. Birds flying over the broken roof cast quick shadows over them as they lay entwined. 'I should go,' he said.

When they'd brushed themselves down and closed the door on the shed Rozenn fastened the padlock, making it look as though it was locked. Theo watched. Perhaps he was noting this place as a hideaway if he couldn't escape Paris. 'Rozenn.' He put his hands on her shoulders, face shadowed by the separation to come.

She couldn't bear a lengthy goodbye. '*Bon voyage* and *bonne chance.*' His cheek was smooth under her lips like a boy's. Well, he was a boy, for all his sophisticated manner. 'Perhaps we'll meet here again sometime soon. And there won't be any of *them* here.'

'And there'll be pistachio *and* chocolate ice cream.'

She smiled and raised a hand in farewell as Theo walked away, his clothes still uncreased and elegant despite the rolling around on the hessian sacks. Yet once again Rozenn seemed to glimpse another version of Theo, scurrying through faraway cities, dishevelled, furtive, looking for somewhere to hide himself away. The unfairness of it made her want to scream, but it would just be a waste of energy.

The skirt of her dress was creased. Rozenn's fingers smoothed the pleats out. She'd have to change before Maman noticed. But Maman would be otherwise occupied this evening. Rozenn had forgotten about what was going on at home: Papa's excursion, the mention of packing.

Her eyes felt sore but that was probably just the lime blossom irritating them.

4

I stood with Dad and Gwen outside the oak front door that our grandmother would never again open to welcome us. Probate was concluded. The keys to Vue Claire were in Gwen's hand.

'It's really both of ours.' Gwen squeezed my shoulder. 'I'm sure it was just a mistake that Rozenn left it to me alone.'

But the will was clear enough. Gwen was an accountant in a City bank. She should know that there was no mistake. Gwen was the sole inheritor of Vue Claire. She and her husband owned a spacious flat in Muswell Hill in north London and now they had a whole house on a Cornish creek to themselves, too.

My grandmother had left me just one thing: a silver compass that nobody remembered seeing before her death, which she'd been clutching as she died. She must have hidden it under her pillow. 'That's your grandmother, always full of surprises,' Dad said sorrowfully.

Had Rozenn left me the compass as a message: an indication that I needed to steer a better course through life?

I squared back my shoulders and composed my face into what I hoped was a neutral expression, busying myself by letting the dog off her lead. Pearl, Rozenn's small cross-breed terrier, was revisiting her old home along with Dad. Gwen unlocked the door and we went inside. Pearl dropped her nose towards the wooden floor, sniffing as she ran towards the balcony.

The interior still smelt of Rozenn's scent, woody with a hint of something sharper, though it was fainter now. For a moment the three of us paused in the hallway. Pearl pattered into the sitting room, whining at the French windows. I followed her and unlocked the doors so she could lie in her favourite position on the small balcony. She flopped down with a slight sigh, draping her head under the iron railing to watch the comings and goings on the estuary, her tail occasionally beating on the tiles. High tide. Blue and green waters lapped the jetty at the end of the lawn. Rozenn's small rowing boat lay upside down on the grass, rowlocks and oars locked away. I wanted to stay out here letting the scene swallow me up, but knew I had to go back inside to show I wasn't resenting my sister's fortune.

I told myself for the millionth time that my grandmother was entitled to leave her property as she wished. She'd arrived on this very shore not yet nineteen, with only the clothes she wore and her ID papers. Everything she'd created here had been the result of her own work, my grandfather having built up a business fortune but later losing it all. Rozenn must have watched what had happened to my construction project management company and seen Grand-père Luc's misadventures all over again.

I went back into the room Rozenn had called her *salon*. Everything was arranged with such apparent casualness and yet so perfectly, playing with light and angles. A chaise longue faced the creek. Long mirrors each side of the French windows bounced more light around. She'd reached into the water and sky, pulling them into the shapes and spaces of her interior. At high tide the house seemed to float. From the outside it might have sat by the estuary for a hundred years or more. She'd actually bought the original 1920s bungalow on the site in the seventies and pulled it down, starting from scratch. The house's granite walls and lead roof used the traditional building materials of this part of Cornwall. It was long in design, proportioned like a barn with three sections, the middle containing the living rooms and bedrooms above. A lower-pitched section on one side housed the kitchen with Rozenn's little office above it, and a further single-storey section contained her utility room. Every time I visited, the changes in the light surprised and delighted me. Vue Claire reflected the vital element of Rozenn Caradec: daring yet restrained, knowing when to challenge the limits of a building and when to pull back and let it speak for itself. *People are their surroundings and surroundings are imprinted by the people who live there* had been her mantra. Rozenn had spoken so often about the Paris apartment she'd grown up in, and yet she'd poured so much of herself into Vue Claire: sea and sky, rather than boulevards and apartments, seeming to matter more to her.

And now Vue Claire was all Gwen's. The light from the creek, the shadows the trees cast, the granite walls, the wooden floors belonged to her alone. She would imprint her personality on the house. I clenched the silver compass in my hand and placed it on the coffee table. 'It's not too late for that variation of deed,' Gwen said, watching me. 'I could make the call to the solicitor right now.'

The deed would alter the terms of the will so that I shared Vue Claire with my sister. I couldn't stand the thought of receiving something I wasn't meant to have: a pity offering. When I didn't answer Gwen sighed. 'Stubborn as a mule.'

'Maman can't have been in her right mind.' Dad sat on the sofa, looking every one of his sixty-six years.

Gwen put out a hand and touched the off-white painted wall as though reassuring herself it really belonged to her. 'I'm going to start in the kitchen,' she said. 'Decide what to keep.'

'Your grandmother cleared most of her things out before she took to her bed,' Dad said. 'Anything that's left in there will be good-quality kitchenware.'

Gwen and James were both big earners. They'd probably want new cooking pots, saucepans and knives to fling into the expensive German dishwasher they'd already ordered. I could put in a bid for the discarded casseroles and pans. Crumbs from the rich woman's table . . . But the small kitchen I now shared in Brentford, west London, wouldn't have storage space for them.

Gwen is my sister, I love her, I reminded myself, trying to dispel the sour taste in my mouth.

'I'll go through these papers and photographs.' Dad stood up and went to the dresser, pausing, perhaps remembering it was all Gwen's now. 'If you don't mind, darling?'

'Don't be silly,' Gwen told him.

Dad pulled a large leather album out of the drawer. 'May I?' I took it from him. I'd often looked at the pictures with my grandmother. They started with Luc and Rozenn in Trafalgar Square on Victory in Europe Day: 8 May 1945, the caption told me. They stood arms around one another, Luc clutching a bottle of champagne, a conga snaking around them. The next picture had been taken at their marriage in 1946. The bride wore an austerity-cut satin dress perfectly showing off her slender form.

Shortly after the photo was taken Rozenn returned to Paris to sell her parents' old apartment, shipping back the sleigh-beds and some of the bureaus and console tables still in use in Vue Claire.

A couple of loose photos of Rozenn as a child with her parents were pushed between the last page and the album cover, along with sketches of mice and birds she must have produced as a girl.

I looked at a picture of Rozenn's parents, my great-grandparents, an elegant Parisian couple in their early forties, presumably taken before the German tanks rolled in, judging by their unlined faces.

He'd been a chest specialist before the war, I remembered, with a patient list of wealthy Parisians. My great-grandmother was the epitome of a woman from a smart *arrondissement*, her clothes and hair suggesting the same attention to detail as that possessed by her daughter. Rozenn hadn't talked much about them and Dad knew only that they'd died in an air raid in France in 1944.

I placed the photo on the table and looked at the next one, Rozenn herself aged about four on a beach, a huge smile on her face. 'Look.' I showed the picture to Dad. 'Just beaming, isn't she?'

He took it from me looking thoughtful.

'What?'

'She was obviously such an exuberant child at one stage. I wonder what happened to her more high-spirited side?' I knew what he meant: Rozenn had been a content person, taking pleasure in life and in her family, but never one bursting with joy. He reached over and picked up the sketches. 'Look how she's drawn these birds and mice, such relish, mischief, in them.'

'The war made her more guarded, perhaps,' Gwen said, coming in from the kitchen with an old ironware casserole pot large enough to bath a baby in. 'And that's why she turned to buildings rather than carrying on with her drawing? More financial security too. Would you like this, Morie?'

I wanted to say no. Apart from anything else, the pot was nearly half the size of the room I was currently living in. But how many meals had I eaten that Rozenn had prepared in that pot? The night our mother had died she'd served Gwen and me, nine and eight, a chicken dish prepared in a white-wine and cream sauce, simple, comforting. The world had seemed less hostile as we ate it. 'Shame to let it go,' I said tersely, trying not to notice the look Gwen and Dad exchanged. I could probably store the pot under my bed, or Dad would let me keep it in his box room, along with all the other things I hadn't been able to take with me to Brentford.

Dad handed me back the little pencil drawings of mice, blue tits, and chaffinches, pecking at the earth for worms, peering out from behind a stone wall, balanced on a windowsill. She'd been such a talented artist. I glanced from the drawings to the portrait of Rozenn on the wall. Luc had commissioned it a year or so after Dad's birth. The Rozenn of the 1950s wore a New-Look-style dress with a tight waist and full dark-red skirt. Her face was seemingly make-up free, except for a dash of lipstick in the same red as the skirt. Her dark auburn hair, the same colour as mine, was pulled into a half-chignon, with a wave falling over one shoulder. She could have stepped out of a French film. Her eyes seemed to meet mine, as though asking me what on earth we were doing in her house, riffling through her possessions. *Her* possessions, her house and her furniture, sketches, photos and kitchenware, which she was perfectly entitled to leave to whomever she wanted. I hadn't loved my grandmother for what she might or might not leave me in her will. The will hadn't even crossed my mind until we'd read it after her death.

I looked from the open-faced little girl on the beach to the woman in the picture whose face gave nothing away. I could feel the energy and determination pulsing through her, but Dad was right. Something in life had knocked that sense of fun out of her, that enjoyment of the way a small wild creature darted across a field.

'What made you who you were?' I asked her silently. 'What were you trying to tell me?' I should have asked her more questions. I'd always expected there'd be another conversation. That last stroke had robbed us of the chance of an explanation.

My eyes filled as I remembered the day of her death. By the time we'd arrived from London she could no longer speak, though she pressed our hands in response to questions. I spotted the silver compass in her left hand. 'You never told us about that compass.'

Her mouth opened but her lips couldn't form the words. 'Was it from your family?'

'Y . . .' Her eyes were balls of fury at her inability to speak. 'Y . . .'

'Yes.' I pressed her hand. 'Don't say any more. Rest.' But there was still more she was trying to say. Her hand tensed in mine.

'*Fr* . . .'

'It came from France.' I nodded. But she looked at me as she had when she'd helped me with my homework and I'd written a letter back to front.

'Not France? May I?' I took the compass gently from her. On the back were engraved letters. 'Your *father's* initials?' I replaced the compass in her hand.

'*Fr* . . .' she said again, but nearly in despair. For the first time in her illness I felt Rozenn's vulnerability as a cold slap. Even well into her nineties she'd possessed a vitality, a combativeness at times. We didn't often attempt to argue with her. 'Yours,' she said, clearly.

'You want me to have the compass?'

She blinked.

'How lovely, thank you. I'll treasure it.' I'd blinked hard.

'Leave you . . . Morane. And leave . . . Gwen.' I imagined she'd bequeath Gwen some other personal object in turn to remember her by.

I hadn't imagined she'd leave Gwen the house.

'I can't forgive her for doing this to you and Gwen,' Dad told me.

Gwen. Yes, my sister was perhaps also a victim of the will. Unexpectedly receiving the house placed Gwen in a position she hadn't chosen and which she'd tried to alter by having the will revised. Perhaps I should let her change it, for the sake of our future relationship. Gwen and I had been so close until recently. Although she was only a year and a half older than me she'd looked after me after Mum's death, insisting that I move into her bedroom in our family home in Barnes, south-west London: *Morie might feel sad if she wakes up in the night.* Gwen had wanted to help me again more recently, but I'd kept her at a distance, stunned and ashamed, too proud to let my sister close to me.

I glanced up again at Rozenn in her portrait. She'd never been a cosy, cake-baking type of grandmother. For all her tenderness at the time of our mother's death, her rocking of us in her arms on that day and on the days afterwards when the loss was too much to bear, she'd usually been more of a champion than a comforter, drying tears and sending us back to battle with the impossibly hard homework or the unjust maths teacher.

And when she talked to us about our adult lives she'd pepper pride in our – mostly Gwen's – achievements with criticism of our skincare regimes or sartorial choices. '*I know you're stomping around building sites, Morane, but those boots are for labourers . . . If you don't use that cream I gave you, Gwen, the skin under your brows will shortly resemble orange peel.*'

At times her comments infuriated me. At times they cut deep. But now I felt a physical longing for Rozenn, which curdled as it mixed with the hurt at the bequest. She'd been so tender with me after the accident, reassuring me that it hadn't been my fault, listening to me again and again as I went through what had happened. Nick had listened to me, too, held my hand without saying anything. But there'd come a point when he couldn't hear it all again, not without finding his own prop. My former boyfriend and business partner had turned to his laptop and mobile, discovering his own dopamine boost, a way of bolstering himself up so he could support me.

I picked up the silver compass again. It looked delicate but felt surprisingly heavy in my palm.

5

The clock in the hallway struck eleven just as Papa returned. On her way back from the Bois Rozenn had managed to sneak up to the apartment without the concierge spotting her, crumpled and probably flushed. Even more to her relief, Maman was in the *salon* with a magazine, distracting herself with photographs of clothes, one of many *Parisiennes* trying to persuade themselves that early June in Paris was just as it had always been. Unseen, Rozenn tiptoed into her room to change. Her dress would need sponging and pressing when Maman wasn't around. She pulled on a cotton frock and went into the *salon*. Yann was sitting on the sofa absorbed in one of his many American comic books. As usual Maman was trying to persuade him to read something more improving. As usual he was politely refusing.

Rozenn offered to go out for the evening bread. 'You went to the *boulangerie* this morning,' Maman said, sounding suspicious. They both knew Rozenn wasn't a fan of errands involving queuing and ration cards. Her eyes narrowed. 'What happened to your other dress?'

'I got a grass stain on the back of the skirt when I sat on the grass.'

'I've warned you about that before.' Could Maman see what had, nearly, happened in the shed?

Later on, when Rozenn had returned with the grey-coloured bread for supper, Maman broke off from stirring the soup to glance at her, curious. If she knew the truth, she'd probably lock Rozenn up for the rest of the summer. But fretting about Papa's trip this afternoon was distracting Maman.

At last Papa's key turned in the lock. Maman rushed to meet him. 'How was she?' she asked, before he could even remove his hat.

'Thin but healthy. Apart from bleeding gums. Lack of vitamin C, must be months since she's seen an orange. Possibly a little anaemic. She's had plenty of fresh air, though.' He managed a smile. 'You'll need another place setting, Louise. She's in the taxi downstairs. I just came up to warn you.'

'What?' Maman said. Rozenn felt the room spin, the atoms fall apart. She clutched at the dining-room door handle. 'She can't be. She needs . . .'

Constant supervision. Which she received from the nuns who were so kind to her. Fresh air and exercise. Helping in the vegetable garden. Regular and frequent prayer in the chapel. Singing hymns and psalms in that husky voice of hers.

'The convent farm can't feed all the patients, not when most of the men are still away. The sisters are desperately sorry but they can't look after her any more. They need to grow food for themselves and look after the very sick. And with what I've decided— But I must bring her up, she'll be fretting alone by herself in the taxi. I'm sorry I couldn't warn you, Louise. The convent telephone is down. Perhaps you could make up the bed in her old room, Rozenn?'

Maman looked at her.

Non, Rozenn screamed silently. *Don't make me share a room with her.*

'She won't be used to sleeping alone,' Maman said. 'Make up the other bed in your room, Rozenn. You can be together like you used to be.'

Rozenn could leave this moment, despite the approaching curfew. Run out of the apartment, down on to the boulevard and back to the shed in the Bois de Boulogne, where Theo's scent might still linger on the old sacks. From there she could make for the south, find work. Escape.

'Rozenn.' Maman's tone implied she could read all the thoughts bubbling around in her mind.

'*D'accord.*' The reply snapped out like gunshot. 'I'll make up the other bed.' Ordinarily a rebuke for her tone would have rung out but Maman merely looked relieved. Yann had come out into the hall and he glanced from one to the other.

'I'll help.' In her bedroom he handed her blankets and bolster.

'I don't even know where the wretched rubber sheet is,' she burst out.

'In the bathroom cupboard.' He brought in the object with its sinister smell and jelly-like feel. Without a word she tucked it over the mattress and placed a cotton sheet over it. The maid had carried out all these tasks before but she'd been gone for nearly a year now. If Rozenn had to strip wet sheets in the morning, she would die.

'You haven't seen her for six months,' Yann said. 'She's probably come on a lot.'

Rozenn could hear her father's gentle tones, as the two of them came upstairs. 'There we are, remember your numbers? *Numéro trois*, on our door, see?'

'*Trois*,' the girl repeated.

'And here's Maman waiting for you.'

Maman sounding overjoyed. Claire mumbling something. 'Come on,' Yann said, pulling at her sleeve.

Rozenn was going to be sick. Not because of Claire herself but because of her own selfish, shallow response to the girl. At a time like this you were supposed to be selfless. Especially if you were female. Give your meat ration to a male. Ensure you looked as immaculate as ever. Keep conversation witty and distracting. But she wanted to scream and shout. Bad enough that life had been ruined in so many other ways. Now this.

She followed Yann out. Maman had released Claire, who turned towards the other two as they came into the hallway. Rozenn gazed into the face that was a mirror image of her own.

'Zenn.' Claire's face lit up. She threw her arms around her twin. Rozenn breathed in the convent laundry soap and the faint smell of her sister's sweat underneath her coarse long-sleeved cotton frock. The journey must have been a long one in warm weather. Claire's arms were strong around Rozenn. After a second she disentangled herself.

'Are you hungry?' Maman nodded towards the dining room. 'Come and have some soup.'

'Zenn too?'

Rozenn forced a smile. 'I've already eaten, *chérie*.' She watched Claire as she sat down. The cells of her body screamed at her to run away from this facsimile of herself, slurping her soup, dripping it on to the tablecloth. She couldn't watch this version of Rozenn Guillou as she might have been if she'd been the second twin, the one who'd been damaged at birth.

6

I had a long list of tasks to carry out for my clients this morning. Builders to chase, quotations from kitchen fitters to pin down, interior designers to brief onsite. My flatmates were all out at work so I cleared the small table of their cereal bowls and coffee mugs, placing it all out of my sight in the sink, and switched on my laptop, feeling relief at distracting myself with work. My phone vibrated. Gwen. Asking me to keep her company in Vue Claire.

Not much to do, decor-wise, but I'd like to paint some of the rooms and I need to talk to R's cleaner and gardener. Come and keep me company? Like old days – ice creams and clotted cream, ferry across to the pub?

I started typing a message telling her I was too busy. Something stopped me, an instinct warning me that I shouldn't push my sister any further away, that the fine thread binding us together might snap if I did. As long as she didn't continue to nag me about the deed of variation to the will.

All right, I messaged back. *Monday to Thursday. I can do some site visits on the way down.* I'd been in email conversation with a couple who wanted to convert an old barn in Wiltshire, referred to me by a surveyor I'd worked with on a previous project. Describing a possible preliminary meeting as 'site visits' was stretching the truth.

Hope you don't think I just want to pick your brains about paint! she messaged back. *But in truth I'd love your advice.*

In my head I'd redecorated Vue Claire many, many times. Not that a centimetre of it really needed redoing. Rozenn'd had a good eye and chosen classic neutral colour schemes and quality materials. But someone with my sister's money would want to stamp her own identity on the house. I was surprised she hadn't already brought in an interior designer from Notting Hill.

I looked around my shared kitchen with its stained floor and flimsy cupboards – only a few years old with door hinges already falling out of alignment. If I'd supervised the fitting of this kitchen I'd have been more picky about the quality of what was installed. Like my grandmother I believed that attention to small details mattered. 'Why be happy with the imperfect?' had been another of her mantras.

None of us renting this flat knew one another. The other three were all men, working in technology companies. One was very tidy – leaving barely any evidence he lived in the flat. The other two seemed oblivious to the mess they created. At first I'd loaded their dishes in the dishwasher but now I simply stacked them out of sight in the sink. For London this was a cheap place to rent. Perhaps by next year I'd be more financially secure again and could look for a single occupancy rental or a flat-share with people more on my wavelength. Or I could run back home to Dad in Barnes: he kept offering me my old bedroom. But returning to my childhood home would just underline my complete failure to operate as an adult.

It was only nine in the morning. I felt as burdened as if I'd undertaken a day's tasks. I rested my head on my arm. From this slant the crumbs left on the table looked like boulders. Just today and the weekend to get through and I could escape London for Cornwall.

I forced myself to sit up and find the dishcloth to wipe the table, feeling all the time the yearning to be on the little creek off the Helford. Rozenn had named the house well: it really did offer a clear view, a wide perspective. I could sit on that balcony and watch the tides coming and going and feel that there was some mysterious rhythm governing existence. Whatever happened in love and life, whatever awful things we did or were done to us, the water would rise and fall, obeying the pull of the moon.

'You and Gwen,' James had said last summer, when we were down there for the August bank holiday. 'This place is like your shrine.' He hadn't said it unkindly, but I bristled.

I would find it hard to be with Gwen and James in Vue Claire. The happy couple. And poor old Morane, still not recovered, now partner-less and with an all but ruined business, living like a student, begging space on a cramped and crumb-scattered kitchen table for a desk. Silly Morane, who should return to her father's house but was too proud. *What do you want in life, Morane?* I heard Rozenn's voice ask me. *To build up your business? To find love again? Find what you want and make it yours.*

But the only thing I wanted was something I couldn't have. Was I just feeling resentful? I sat staring at the tabletop, trying to decipher my own emotions. Puzzled. That was the word that still came to mind when I tried to describe myself. I'd missed something about Rozenn. She hadn't volunteered much information about herself: she'd been a loving grandmother but not an expansive one.

Rozenn had talked a little about the years during the war when she'd worked as a secretary for a Free French office in London, telling us droll anecdotes about errands she'd run for General de Gaulle himself. But on the subject of living in France under German occupation, she'd been silent. Once Gwen and I had been visiting when a documentary had come up on television one evening. Swastikas in Paris, Germans laughing as they took photographs of the Eiffel Tower.

'Turn that off,' Rozenn said, sounding weary. 'It was quite enough to live through those times. The English are obsessed with the war. I'm not.' I could see her point of view, although other older people seemed to talk about the war, even the harsh parts. Yet why assume that anything that had happened to Rozenn as a young girl could affect an inheritance decision made so very late in life? I reminded myself that she had only had the one child – Dad. Perhaps she was uncomfortable with the idea of splitting her property between siblings?

※

By the time I drove down the A303 to visit the barn on the Monday the worst of my sense of alienation had left me. As soon as I turned off the Wiltshire lane into what had once been a farmyard and saw the soft lines of the barn, I felt more like the real me. I lapped up the old stone, the generous proportions of the structure built five hundred years ago to store hay and shelter animals. My synapses began to fire as I talked to Jenny and Sam, the couple who'd recently bought it with an inheritance. I sketched rough ideas for them, showing them how they could make the best of the high windows, how planning permission requirements could be adhered to without sacrificing modern comforts.

Jenny's eyes followed my finger as I pointed out the texture of the interior stonework: soft yet eye-catching, the way the light fell on what could be the main living room. The oak beams could be sanded and treated and would frame the high ceiling. Bedrooms could be fitted along a first-floor gallery, all overlooking the living area. 'It would look stunning but welcoming,' I told her. 'And I know some great architects,' I added. 'If we go ahead, I can draw up preliminary ideas to speed up the next stage. I could project-manage the whole conversion, too, or just any aspects you don't want to handle yourselves.'

I'd trained as a surveyor and in an early job had worked alongside Nick, an architect four years older than I. We'd started our company three years ago. Between us we had built up a network of professionals in all areas from architecture to roofing services and kitchen fitting. My forte was pulling a project together: making sure everyone did what they were supposed to do, when they were supposed to do it and at the price agreed. In modern management-speak, I was a completer-finisher. Apparently I was good at knowing how and when to charm, reason or cajole suppliers and designers, builders and fitters into keeping to schedule. Shame I hadn't been able to bring the same skills to bear on my personal life.

I felt the current pulsing between Jenny and me as we joined Sam at the front of the barn. Their tentative ideas were coming alive at the flash of my pencil on paper. More prosaically I checked the position of drains in the farmyard and questioned Sam about the water supply. I'd check all the details myself later on, as well as any local-authority restrictions on barn conversions. As they walked me back to my car we discussed the planting of a row of small trees at the field boundary on the far side to provide shelter from the wind and shade in the summer. 'Not large ones,' I said. 'Possibly willows or rowans. I'll check what's been grown here locally.' Jenny had told me in our first telephone conversation that they were anxious about doing anything too radical with the barn, wanting it to blend in. That suited me, I'd always hated grandstanding, statement builds, oversized for their locations, with large, empty interiors and industrial-looking kitchens. On the other hand, I hated whimsical, mock-rural design, too. I'd inherited Rozenn's belief that nothing in a building, whether factory, office block or house, should appear forced or contrived.

I said goodbye and continued down to Cornwall, the blood still rushing through me. I was alive, thinking, functioning, being. I might have lost things that mattered most to me, but I wasn't going to wilt away. Live to work, that's what I'd always done, just as my grandmother had when she'd come to England. Eventually I turned off the main roads again. The lanes grew progressively narrower, banked with tall hedges, passing over fords, twisting and turning, silvery water flitting into view from time to time between the trees, birds flying overhead, hedgerows blooming pink with foxgloves and white with the last cow parsley. Every year at this time the colours and brightness caused me to draw in a breath of surprise, even though I'd seen it all scores of times before.

I turned down the last narrow, steep lane and into the drive leading down to the creek, an inlet of the Helford estuary, parking up outside Vue Claire. Rozenn had always seemed to know exactly when we'd appear, even though she never owned a mobile phone and we couldn't message her to relay our progress. She'd be standing in the porch to greet us. After that, we'd use the back door to come and go during our stay.

I walked to the front door, pausing a moment to admire the last purple blossoms on a rhododendron, and knocked. Gwen answered, blonde hair pulled casually yet fetchingly off her face in a scarf in her favourite casual style, wearing an old T-shirt, but looking as put-together as ever, if a little shadowed under the eyes. She frowned. 'No need to knock like a stranger, idiot.' She pulled me into a hug. The scent of the Iris perfume she'd worn for years made the awkwardness between us dissolve. Gwen was still my sister.

I was on the verge of finding it too much. I pulled back slightly, examining the T-shirt. 'You've been painting.'

'Gosh, Sherlock.' She raised a hand. 'Now don't start critiquing my colour choices. I'm just trying out samples.'

I walked in behind her. 'Not bad.' I nodded at rectangles of grey-greens on the entrance hall and *salon* walls. 'I always liked Rozenn's whites but a bit of colour makes it more interesting.'

'You don't think these look too grungy?'

'Nope. You're not into mud territory.' A small, bitter part of me wanted to suggest she painted the whole house in a deep greige that would look like the bottom of a swamp on dark winter days when the tide was out. I pushed down the sentiment. Gwen looked at me sharply. Could she read my mind?

'I used the silver compass,' she said, sounding embarrassed. 'I hope you don't mind, but you forgot to take it with you last time and I wanted to check orientation.'

I smirked.

'Yes I know,' she blushed. 'I always thought this room faced north, but it's actually north-north-west, so there's some evening sunlight.'

'I'll have to take you with me on a site visit,' I said. I could picture Gwen in beautifully understated yet costly brown leather boots and a pair of expensive jeans, blonde hair pulled back into a casual-looking but efficient bun. All my clients would fall in love with her. Everyone always did. Gwen was interested in people, had a way of making them feel they were interesting too. And she was clever, not only with figures but with understanding how businesses ticked, how they made money and lost it, how to spot when they were about to do either of these things. I knew she was aching to advise me on my drooping enterprise. Perhaps I'd let her, in due course. Then again, it would just provide Gwen with more evidence that I needed pitying, that I couldn't function like an ordinary adult. *Why can't you just be normal, Morie?* I wasn't sure I could bear that.

The compass would have been useful earlier on this morning at the barn. As usual I'd taken a reading on the convenient mobile phone app, but the compass had a comforting solidity belying its

38

small size. I'd left it here in the sitting room half deliberately last time. Perhaps I'd been rejecting Rozenn's bequest, showing her, as if she was still alive, that I wasn't going to forgive her, acting like a sulky schoolgirl.

'Show me your sample tins and colour charts.' Although I spent so many hours of my working life advising on decor, my spirits always lifted at the sight of paint. As a small child I'd repainted the walls of my doll's house at least twice a year. Even in my poky room in Brentford with its view of cranes and high-rises I lay on my bed, mentally decorating walls, turning the magnolia into a deep ink-blue, making the most of the cramped space instead of trying to make it look larger, using mirrors to throw light around. Paint, if you took the time to prepare your walls first, was such a quick way to transform surroundings and in some cases make you feel different about where you lived or worked. Shame you couldn't whitewash your own life or transform it into jewel colours.

'I'll make you some tea first.' Gwen gave me the tender smile I remembered from our childhood, when she'd tried to do some of the things Mum had done for me. She helped Dad buy my school shoes, gravely advising on laces versus straps. As the years passed and I followed her to the girls' high school she told me to learn the oboe because there was always a shortage of oboists in the first orchestra. She spent hours on the tennis court helping me perfect my serve and aiming balls at my backhand so I could strengthen my game and gain a place in the team. Gwen and I had been so close you could barely see the space between us. In the last year the Helford itself could have flowed between us.

I sat down on Rozenn's recently reupholstered and venerable chaise longue from the Paris apartment. She'd never liked squishy sofas, bad for the posture, she claimed. Gwen placed her paint sample pots on a sheet of newspaper on the coffee table. I examined the labels and eyed the daubs she'd made on the walls. My sister had a fine eye; if she hadn't gone into the City she could have made it in my sphere. She'd probably be more successful than I was, pushing me into second place there too. I tried to repress the shadow-me intent on spoiling this time with Gwen, just the two of us at the most glorious time of the year in the place we'd always loved.

My compass sat beside the paint tins. I picked it up and turned it over to read the initials. *FJG*. Rozenn's father? I seemed to remember his name had been François and his wife was Louise. I didn't know much about my grandfather. I'd once asked her whether Grand-père Luc had returned to his home to see his family after the war too. *Nobody left there so he just came to Paris with me to clear the apartment*, she told me. All we had of Luc was the photos of him with Rozenn and the clippings describing his business triumphs, and Dad's memories of a kind father who hadn't been at home much.

Gwen had left the loose photos and album on top of the dresser. I hopped up and brought them over to the coffee table. What a man my grandfather had been, I reflected, as I turned the album's pages. How handsome he was in his Free French uniform, and on the day of his marriage to Rozenn. He had a full, generous mouth, like Gwen's, and large, twinkling eyes. Rozenn gazed at him with a smile that was unusually shy, clutching his arm tightly, clearly enchanted by her bridegroom. I flicked through the leaves of the album, showing Dad as a child, growing up and then on his wedding day. Mum was a slim, smiling blonde bride. She'd been dead for so long now. I liked seeing pictures of her: it made me feel nostalgic for her with a pang that was still intense but brief, not a tugging pain of loss such as I felt for Rozenn. I turned to a photograph of me as a toddler on Rozenn's lap, smiling at the similarity in the way our chins both jutted out.

I put the album down and turned to the loose photos taken in the golden pre-war years, examining Rozenn as a small girl on the beach, smiling again at her expression, the way she revelled in sun, sand, ice cream . . . the brightness of a childhood summer. I flicked through the photographs of François and Louise in their chic clothes. At the very bottom of the pile there was a second photograph of young Rozenn on the same beach. She wore a different swimming costume this time: striped, rather than polka dotted, and she was more thoughtful – staring at something ahead of her. Her expression was more like that of the woman we'd known: reserved, never confiding much, but quietly determined. I wondered whether it had been taken the following year, but the date on the back was the same, *10 juillet 1926*.

'Small children change moods so quickly, don't they?' I said as Gwen came in bearing a tray of mugs. I laid out the photographs on the coffee table. 'So exuberant one second, just as Dad said, but so self-contained the next.'

Gwen set down the mugs and looked at the pictures, turning them over to examine the dates. Something about the way her hands moved, swiftly but carefully, reminded me of Mum's hands, laying the table. I blinked hard.

'Our grandmother was a woman of mystery, that's for sure.' I tried for a brighter tone. 'There was a lighter side to her. Those sketches of the birds and mice, for instance.'

'She was mysterious all right in the way she chose to leave her property,' Gwen said drily. 'I asked her solicitor if he knew why she'd done it this way. He said she'd sounded quite determined, said it would all become clear.' She handed me a mug, frowning. 'We missed something.'

'She certainly didn't tell us much about her early life, other than growing up in Paris.' I wanted to move on from discussions about Rozenn's will. 'What made the British bring a young French civilian – two French civilians – over to England in the middle of a war, for a start?' I said.

Gwen frowned at her mug and sighed. 'It must have been costly. Dangerous.'

'Perhaps they were working for the Resistance?' I suggested. I'd always harboured romantic ideas about Rozenn helping them destroy railway lines.

Gwen shook her head. 'They didn't really get going until later on in the Occupation. James and I visited some of the Resistance museums last time we were in France. Rozenn left the country in the summer of 1941, before Germany invaded Russia and forced labour was brought in.'

'She never even told us whereabouts in France she sailed from.'

'Did Grand-père Luc and Rozenn actually leave together?' Gwen frowned. 'I always assumed they'd met in London, when they were both working for the Free French.'

I tried to remember what Rozenn had told me and could only recall her describing how she and Luc had slunk off for picnics in St James's Park at lunchtime, before he was posted away from London.

'She never said much at all about the start of their relationship,' I said. 'Where and how they met, those kind of things.'

'Grand-père Luc was a Breton too, wasn't he? And her family came from there originally. Hence our names.'

Gwen'd been christened Gwenaëlle and I of course was Morane, though we'd been called Gwen and Morie from our first days of school. Our names were really the only nod to Rozenn and Luc's roots.

'Perhaps they met in Brittany,' Gwen said. 'Or on the escape boat?'

So much we didn't know. 'And I wonder why they landed here,' I said. 'Though I suppose if it was a fishing boat it made sense to choose somewhere sheltered, on one of the closest parts of the south-west coast. But it all seems so risky.'

Gwen nodded. 'I remember one night James and I were in the pub in Helford Passage. These elderly people were talking about the war years, the boats coming and going to and from France. They said special services were running operations in Brittany.'

'Special services? If Rozenn and Luc weren't even in the Resistance why would they be involved in something like that?'

'It does sound unlikely.' Gwen sipped her tea and shuffled in her chair as though she felt uncomfortable. Perhaps the itch to get on with painting the house was pulling at her. I put the photographs down.

'This one.' I reached for a sample paint tin. 'It's what you've painted on the wall to the right side of the window, isn't it?'

She looked at me as though I were a witch.

I shrugged. 'It's a good colour.'

'How can you tell? It looks just like the others to me.'

'I've recommended it enough times to recognise it. Don't worry,' I hastened to add. 'It's not *common*, Gwen. Tasteful people appreciate it.'

She scowled at my grin. 'You make me out to be such a snob.'

'You're just discerning. But which colour do you like best?'

If it had been me, I would have said any of the other colours than the one Gwen preferred, but she was always nicer than I was. 'I like that one, too. To be honest, I can barely tell the difference between them.'

'What do you like about it?' It was interesting to treat my sister as though she were a client, listening objectively to her.

She gazed at the wall, brow furrowed. 'It's the way it seems blue in some lights and green in others.'

'Can you imagine yourself sitting in here at Christmas, when it's dark and the blinds are down? Do you still feel the same sense of ease?'

She nodded.

'Can you see yourself bringing down some of your things from London and them fitting in as though they belong here?'

'Yes, I think I can.'

'Then you've chosen the right paint.'

She blinked. 'That was really useful.'

'No need to sound so surprised.'

'I'm not.'

She was trying to butter me up. 'If you hate the walls when they're done, we can change the paint, Gwen.'

It wasn't as if she couldn't afford to bring in decorators any time she wanted.

'I'll drive to the shop and buy it tomorrow.'

'You're going to do the decorating yourself?' I couldn't keep surprise out of my voice.

'Of course.' She pointed at her paint-splattered T-shirt. 'You can help if you can spare the time.'

'Why not?'

'Busman's holiday for you?'

'I'm not a painter.' The words came out like little bullets. Gwen flushed.

'I didn't mean to imply you did the hard labour on your projects . . .'

But perhaps that was how she really assumed things were – that I was just a gopher, that Nick had been the brains behind the company. I forced myself to dismiss the thought.

'I just mean people tend to bring in decorators rather than get me to do it.' I took a sip of tea, slightly scented, served in a new bone-china mug. 'Which is a shame, because I'm an ace painter and it's much more fun than advising on planning.'

'How's the business going?' Gwen asked it casually but I could see the concern in her expression.

'I'm hopeful of hooking this barn conversion in Wiltshire. It would be a great project.' I told her about it.

'They'd be lucky to have you, with all your experience.'

I could hold a whole complex building project in my mind and recall what needed doing and when. I barely needed my notebooks and computer programmes, the calendar reminders and workflow diagrams, but found they reassured clients who couldn't quite believe that I could memorise and recall paint numbers and the names of fabric swatches at the same time as the size of kitchen cabinets and diameter of outlet pipes. And I was quick with numbers, not like my sister with her trained accountant's brain, but at sorting them into estimates and quotes in my head. Nick, as an architect, had all the training, the ability to transform an idea into detailed plans drawing on his artistic, scientific and mathematical talent, but I apparently had an eye for finding the potential in a project and pushing it through to completion. Together, we'd been quite a team. Until it had all fallen apart.

'Any sign of Nick?' Gwen asked, reading my mind, but making it sound as though he was some casual acquaintance.

'No.'

'You know James and I—'

'I'm managing.'

'It must be tough.' She pushed aside her half-drunk mug of tea.

At first I'd barely had time to reflect on the fact that I'd lost both my boyfriend and my business partner. There'd been too much to do: talking to clients, to the bank, finding somewhere new to live as I couldn't afford the rent on the Clapham flat by myself. And then Rozenn had become so ill. At least it had all stopped me obsessing about the accident. But I suspected that the black worm was still somewhere inside me, if dormant. At any moment it could start coiling itself around my mind, telling me how I'd failed. Not today, though.

I stood up. 'Why don't you show me upstairs?'

'Morie—'

I knew she was trying to give me space to talk about what had happened. I'd confided in her before but now, with the inheritance between us, I couldn't face showing her just how broken I still felt at times. 'The light's perfect for looking at Rozenn's old room. I'd love to see what you're planning up there.'

Gwen sighed, putting our mugs on the tray. 'I still think she must have had a plan for you,' she said. 'She seemed distracted in the last weeks.'

'I suppose death is quite distracting.'

'Rozenn's still dictating how we go forward.' Gwen stood up abruptly. 'I wish you'd let me put it right.'

If it had been just Gwen perhaps I would have caved in now, agreed to the deed of variation, shared the house with my sister. But she was part of a couple and I couldn't bear the thought of being the spare wheel, the little sister who'd mucked up her relationship, who needed propping up.

'James wouldn't be on the deeds,' she said, with that sorceress's ability to read my mind. 'Just us two.'

Us two. Standing together as we had at Mum's graveside, next to Dad and Rozenn, wearing matching navy velvet coats and black patent shoes, chosen by Rozenn. At her own funeral I'd dressed with care, too, going to Dad's to open suitcases and find a fitted black dress, shoes with a decent heel and a grey jacket too formal for most of my life.

I looked out at the creek and the larger expanse of estuary beyond. The tide was coming in: the water blue and green and so dark grey in spots that it looked black. Where the light caught it, the darkness turned to silver. Birds swooped and called, filled with the energy of the returning sea. A single small white cloud drifted in the sky.

It could be my view too, shared with Gwen. I looked down at the compass as though it would show me the direction I should take. And the dogged, stubborn, resentful part of me still knew I couldn't do what Gwen wanted. I longed for something that was just mine. But although I couldn't admit it to Gwen, I too couldn't throw off that sense of puzzlement. I needed to understand Rozenn's decision, to understand her. I felt an urge to delve into Rozenn's past, find out who'd she'd been before she'd become an architect, a wife, mother and grandmother. Perhaps the mix of emotions inside me was pushing me to ask questions I should have asked years earlier. Perhaps grandchildren are always complacent about loving grandparents, expecting them to have existed purely for the purpose of supporting them, not thinking of them as they once were: young people with hopes and passions of their own.

I looked at my sister, watching me, anxiety painted on her face. This was my opportunity to shore up my relationship with Gwen, put aside my hurt feelings.

'Let's bring the paint charts upstairs with us,' I told her. 'I can't wait to get started.'

7

'We're going to Brittany?' Rozenn heard the astonishment in her own voice. 'But that's for . . .'

For holidays. They'd visited Rennes when their grandparents had still been alive, usually at Easter when the city's streets were full of festivities: processions that were sombre on Good Friday, celebratory on Easter Sunday itself. Sometimes they spent a week or two by the seaside north of Rennes in August, when Paris emptied.

'They need a doctor up near Lannion, between Brest and St Malo, further west from where we used to stay on holiday.' Papa took a final sip of his bowl of coffee. 'The local physician has just retired.'

'The coast's a prohibited zone,' Yann said. 'Nobody's allowed in, are they?'

'Are there even many locals still around?' Rozenn asked.

'Essential workers such as fishermen and farmers. Germans, too, of course, with many more expected.'

'To guard the coast?' Rozenn asked. Papa nodded. 'But if we're moving up there just as they bring in more troops how does it make Yann safer?' Maman pursed her lips, probably disapproving of Rozenn interrogating her father with such scepticism. Girls should do as they were told, or, at most, raise questions in a light, respectful manner.

'I'll explain more another time.' Papa glanced at Claire – God knows why: she was incapable of understanding anything more complicated than the simplest instructions. Her twin's table manners had improved a bit, Rozenn conceded. She could hold the cutlery in a civilised way and no longer left a pile of crumbs on the floor. The nuns had obviously worked some kind of magic on her.

Maman smiled tenderly at Claire. 'You and I are going to do some more lessons, *chérie*. There's more going on in your head than we think.'

Claire set down her slice of bread and moved her hand to her forehead, frowning.

'She doesn't understand anything that's not completely literal.' Rozenn's words sounded harsh but it was true.

'When you go back to the nuns they'll be amazed at your progress,' Maman went on, ignoring Rozenn. Papa looked away briefly. Unconvinced that Claire could make any educational strides forward, or unsure that the return to the convent could ever happen? Or both?

'Nuns.' Claire looked around, lower lip trembling. Yann caught her eye and pulled his mouth into a weird smile. Claire laughed. She was just like a baby: emotions rippled across her and disappeared immediately. Typically she had drawn all the attention to herself, distracting everyone from the more serious matter of their relocation.

It had always been like this. Rozenn remembered visiting a playground with her brother and sister. She and Claire had been about five. Rozenn fell off the swing face first, cutting her lip. The blood gushing from her mouth frightened her and she ran to Maman. But Maman was holding Claire, staring at her face. 'She's very pale. I think she's coming down with something. These public places are full of germs.' She didn't even notice Rozenn's lip until seven-year-old Yann ran up and pointed at it.

'I still don't understand why we have to go to the coast,' Rozenn said.

'The food shortages here will only get worse,' Papa said. 'In Brittany we can grow vegetables. Perhaps keep chickens.'

'*Cot cot codet.*' Claire clucked, flapping her arms. Yann laughed. Rozenn wanted to laugh too but the familiar constraint she felt in Claire's presence engulfed her. Her twin's features were identical to her own, Claire's face was her face, albeit thinner, but her expression was softer, less focused than her own, and she wore her long auburn hair in a single plait. When she'd woken up this morning Rozenn found Claire sitting on the end of her bed holding a brush and a ribbon. 'Zenn do my hair?'

Obviously it was now her responsibility to plait Claire's hair. As her fingers braided it the silken auburn strands felt just like her own. But Claire's mind was definitely not Rozenn's. They'd never be able to communicate at a meaningful level. Perhaps that was another reason why she found her twin so disconcerting.

'We're Bretons by blood,' Maman said. They'd all been born in the large house in Rennes belonging to Maman's father. Rozenn had once heard Maman weeping on Papa's shoulder, saying that if they'd been in Paris at the time of the birth, perhaps the doctors there would have managed it better.

Rennes was tiny by the standards of Paris, but Rozenn had loved Christmas and Easter holidays there. A small coastal village would be a very different proposition. There were still films and plays to see in Paris, occasionally exhibitions too. And Rozenn walked, for hours some afternoons, looking at buildings, observing shapes, shadows, angles, sketching them if there was nobody around to stare at her. All that would be stolen from her if they moved to some tiny windblown settlement without a cinema or library to its name.

'What about Claire?' she said. 'In bad weather she won't have much to do, stuck indoors. I bet there's no electric light, is there? At least here we can take her to museums. She likes going out, even if she hasn't a clue what she's looking at.'

'We will do lessons,' Maman said firmly. 'We will manage with oil lamps, as so many other families do.'

No electricity also meant no wireless. Another deprivation. Rozenn shuddered at the thought of dark nights indoors straining to read books with no music to lighten the atmosphere.

'But it will be so unfamiliar for Claire,' she said. 'She's confused enough as it is.'

'She'll be properly fed. Look at her, those nuns must have been saving the food for themselves.' Maman sounded fierce. It was true: Claire looked scrawny. Her collar bones stood out like two pale ridges.

'You know that's not the case, Louise,' Papa said. 'They just didn't have enough help with the farm to harvest food.'

'Thin.' Claire pulled up her plain cotton chemise to expose her chest. She wore no brassiere as there was nothing needing support. Yann and Papa looked away.

'Pull that down,' Rozenn hissed. 'We don't do that in front of other people.' An image of her own dress coming off in that hut swept into her memory as she said it and the flush on her cheeks grew warmer.

'*Désolée*, Zenn.' Claire blinked and did as she was told.

'No need to be so harsh,' Maman told Rozenn. She muttered an apology. It was always the same when she was with Claire: resentment would build and she'd snap, only to be filled with remorse. All because of that original guilt, that knowledge that by pushing her way into the world first she had avoided Claire's fate. Rozenn had never liked to ask Papa about what had happened and knew Maman would refuse to answer such a personal question, but she'd picked up enough snatches of conversation between her parents to know that the second-born twin's less favourable birthing position cut off the blood flow to her brain for precious minutes. The result had been Claire, with her angelic smile but inability to function in such a dangerous world. Tucked away in the convent she'd lived a happy and quiet life, helping with the garden and the animals, saying her prayers in the chapel. The Germans had stolen that from her just as they'd snatched everything else.

Rozenn pulled at the lock of her own hair falling over her right shoulder. It took her ages in the morning to arrange the style so that the body of hair was pinned at the back with the small wave to the front on each side. Who on earth would she find in a small Breton village to cut and set it as she liked? Her hairdresser here had resorted to cutting hair outdoors in natural light because the power supply regularly shut off during the day, but it was still worth going to her, even on chilly days, because she had such a good eye.

'What would Rozenn and I do in Brittany?' Yann asked. He was supposedly looking for work but spending his free time sketching. Even his hope of finding a draftsman's apprenticeship, a *déclassé* option for a member of the Guillou family, had failed. Sometimes he joined Rozenn and her friends at cafés to drink the strange version of coffee or thin vinegary wine now on offer, or he walked with her, pointing out interesting buildings, seeming not to care that his enthusiastic comments drew sharp looks from pedestrians.

Papa sighed. 'It's going to be a stopgap. Not perfect, but at least we'll be safe for six months or so. Once I see how things are going, I'll make other plans for the two of you.'

'When do we go?' Yann asked.

'Monday.'

'What?' Rozenn sat bolt upright. So little time to see her friends, to have her hair set one last time and buy any art materials and sketch pads she could get her hands on.

'Is that enough time for you to see your patients and hand them over to other physicians, François?' Maman asked.

'I may need to come back for consultations from time to time.'

'You'll come back here?' Rozenn felt a wash of relief. She could return with Papa for visits. The city wasn't lost to her.

'I'll stay in a hotel if I can find somewhere affordable and reasonably central.' The Germans had colonised the pick of the places.

'So this apartment . . . ?' The morning light was flooding in, illuminating the bone-china crockery on the table, turning it into a still life. Rozenn could see and smell the blossom on the lime trees from where she sat. June was her favourite month in Paris: the light was perfect and barely seemed to give way to dusk. 'You're going to let Germans live here?' She could just manage not to let the words come out as a scream. A Nazi, sitting at this table, admiring the lime trees through the elegant windows? Perhaps he'd bring his family here and some German brat would sleep in her sleigh-bed and place its books on her shelves. They'd walk down the boulevard in the evening sun and know they were living in the best place in the world.

'Who else do you think could afford to live here now, Rozenn?' Papa's voice was gentle. 'We need the rent to keep it going so we can come home when the war's over.'

'Whenever that is,' she muttered.

Maman folded her napkin. 'You should be on your way, François. Let's clear the table. Claire, pass me your plate.'

Rozenn waited until she could corner her father alone as he packed his medical bag. 'Why are we really leaving, Papa? Your work seems to be going well enough here. The position in Brittany will be bunions and earaches, won't it? Any doctor could do it.'

'Those complaints may seem minor to you but they aren't insignificant to the people suffering from them.' He glanced back at the kitchen, where Maman was setting up Claire with a basin of warm water to wash the cutlery. There was more to this plan than he'd admitted.

'Tell me, Papa.' Perhaps he'd been struck off or reported to the Gestapo – failed to diagnose some senior man's fatal disease or been indiscreet about still treating Jews.

'I told you, it's Yann,' he said softly. 'We can't have him sent back to Germany for forced labour.'

That factory in Frankfurt. 'They nearly let him die.' Papa's voice had risen. 'And the Germans will become harsher as the war progresses.' He glanced at the kitchen and lowered his voice. 'They won't send young men back if they fall ill.'

'But they're winning? Why would they become harsher?' Yet she thought of Theo's family, getting out of the country now while they still could.

'If the Americans eventually come in to fight alongside the British, and the Russians change their tune, Hitler will be a cornered dog, Rozenn.'

It seemed impossible to imagine both these things happening, the Americans and Russians both fighting Hitler together with the British. 'But how does this relocation help Yann in the meantime? If they don't send him to some German factory they'll simply make him build bunkers and pillboxes up there on the coast.'

He shuffled, looked away, seemed to mull something over briefly. 'We're not going to register him in Brittany.'

Everyone had to be registered at the local *mairie*. Failure to do so was severely punished.

'What do you mean?'

'Once he's in St Martin, your brother is going to drop off the face of the earth, Rozenn.'

8

I left Helford and drove through the twisting lanes to the main roads heading east. As always I felt the dragging sense of loss afflicting me as I started the journey back to London. The emotion was more complicated now: I felt a pang at saying goodbye to Gwen and to the house, for the days spent painting walls and singing unmelodiously along to the radio, taking the ferry across the estuary to the pub and eating too much clotted cream on our scones. We'd skirted the subject of the inheritance and any other topics of conversation that would have clamped me shut again. We were like teenage girls, giggling together and drinking too much cider. Or at least I'd drunk too much of it. Gwen was going through some kind of health kick.

I felt a pang for something else, a knowledge that holidays down here wouldn't feature as much in my future. I'd return, of course, for special occasions, and had promised to come back if Gwen needed my help. She was already talking about a family Christmas down here. But as the miles divided the two of us I couldn't see myself spending much more time at Vue Claire.

Emptiness filled me. Rozenn was gone. I wasn't returning to Clapham, to Nick, to the companionship we'd had before the accident: something fragrant he'd prepared bubbling away on the hob, a bottle of wine open, catching up on what had happened with our clients. Once again I pushed aside memories of him. I passed the riding stables where Gwen and I had gone for our pony trekking as children, keeping my eyes on the road in case there were ponies being saddled up in the yard, children chattering excitedly. Everything I thought I wanted most was gone and I didn't yet know how to replace it, to fill my life up again.

I looked down at my petrol gauge. When I reached the main road I pulled in to fill the car up, trying not to grimace as I swiped my credit card.

As I got back into the car, the phone trilled. A message from Tatiana, a Russian client. She texted me at all hours, expecting immediate responses, but always paid within an hour of receiving my invoices. I could forgive any number of messages about bathroom-tile finishes at two in the morning to know that my battered bank account would be instantly revived with her payments. But the project for Tatiana was nearing completion now – just the kitchen cupboards to be installed, a new underfloor heating system to be covered with the wooden flooring and the bathroom fittings to be finalised.

I'd started working for her after Nick had left me. By then I'd set up my own business bank account, relieved Tatiana's payments wouldn't go the same way as the rest of our money. *Sorry*, his parting text said. *I couldn't seem to stop even though I wanted to and knew what I was doing was wrong. You didn't deserve this, Morie.*

One of my tasks when I reached my rented room would be one I'd been putting off – going through any invoices and receipts I could lay my hands on to check the amounts Nick had actually paid for various fittings against what he'd claimed from our account. My solicitor had warned me he might have bought supplies at wholesale rates but charged the account the retail amount, pocketing the difference. Or he might have arranged for our suppliers to bill clients directly but charged the account. Apparently people like him, as the solicitor put it, were remarkably inventive in the ways they acquired money. I couldn't really believe that Nick would have done this.

On the other hand I wouldn't have believed him capable of using our business account for gambling. Even now, recalling how I'd found out, my stomach lurched. I'd been out on a construction site when I'd logged on to our bank account and found we'd exceeded our overdraft limit, something that had never happened before. I knew several large client payments had gone in that same week. I spotted a large debit that I certainly hadn't made and clicked on the payment to find a vague narrative referring to a company in Malta. Puzzled, convinced the account had been hacked, I rang the bank. They asked me to check with Nick before they took matters further. I returned to our spacious rented two-bedroom flat in Clapham to find his clothes gone from the wardrobe and chest of drawers, and his car keys no longer sitting in the pot on the kitchen table. Feeling dizzy, I logged back on to our business account and saw the near-zero balance. Another large payment had been made to the same Maltese company. Nick's mobile number no longer seemed to be recognised so I couldn't even reply to his final text message.

An internet search told me that the Maltese company was actually a gambling site. I'd trusted Nick, but I had nobody to blame apart from myself. It wasn't his fault; it was mine. Nick had been so patient with me for months, letting me talk about the accident over and over again. Even now I still dreamt of the boy, motionless on the muddy ground, staring up at me. And the horse, breathing gently on my shoulder as I shook, nuzzling me: *Can we get on with our ride now?*

As the M4 ascended on to the Chiswick flyover and the western suburbs of London enfolded me I thought of Rozenn's face when I had told her what had happened with Nick. She was ill then, but was still able to come downstairs for part of the day, refusing to let us fuss over her.

'Nick took all your money?' Her mouth tightened. 'Tell me, Morane, it is not all gone?' I explained that some client invoices hadn't yet been paid and I'd managed to contact them and asked them to hold off until I provided them with new account details. 'And these are client accounts you alone worked on?' I told her how these clients had never met or communicated with Nick and how he had done nothing on their projects. Perhaps he'd been protecting me, trying, in his own mind at least, to ring-fence some of the money so that he couldn't spend it.

Rozenn had seen the hurt in my face. '*Un honteux abus de confiance.*' She looked stricken for me. 'In fact, a double betrayal. Personally and in your work, this man has injured you.' Her face hardened. I half-smiled, picturing the treatment Nick would receive if my grandmother happened upon him.

'He was addicted,' I said. 'I never even noticed. Sometimes he'd be placing bets, huge bets, for hundreds of pounds, right in front of me at night. He'd have alerts on his mobile to tell him when goals had been scored, so he could trade them out.' For the first few months Nick had used free bets from bookies or been careful to match his own money on betting exchanges. He'd sat next to me when he came back in the evenings while I watched endless box sets. Why hadn't I asked him what he was doing instead of assuming it was just some innocuous game? Why didn't I question the way he'd raised his hand to silence me on a few occasions when I initiated a conversation, asking him if he wanted a coffee or a glass of wine, or whether he'd seen a client email? The state of numbness affecting me since the accident had stopped me noticing that something was very wrong. Anyway, he was only behaving in the way I deserved.

Nick must have grown overconfident, taking huge risks, trying to cover losses with even larger bets. He'd started dipping into the business account to fund his bookies – the Maltese company was one of a dozen he used, I discovered when, feeling guilty, I managed to get into his email account just before he changed the password. The big gains he'd needed to cover the losses had never materialised. Even if they had, he probably would have found it hard to stop gambling, hooked on the dopamine rush, the distraction from coping with me.

Rozenn nodded. 'We can be blind, trusting where we should not.' I knew something of the troubles she'd had with Grand-père Luc and his drinking.

'It was my fault,' I said. 'I was in such a state.' Still was. 'It was a strain for him.' He'd sat through all the hours of Netflix with me, asking gently if I remembered a single plot point, knowing that my mind hadn't been on the television screen at all.

'A real man steps up to the challenge at a time like that. But that is all behind you now, Morane. You will fight back. You will make your business even stronger than it was before.' She took my hand and squeezed it in her own, which felt fragile and warm. 'Throw yourself into work.'

Work was always the answer for Rozenn. Work brought you self-respect and security. It was an insurance against life. 'Your grandfather hurt me badly when he drank away the profits of his company,' she told me. Until the contents of his glass became more compelling than anything else Luc had run a successful fish wholesale business, supplying most of the West End's fashionable restaurants and hotels in the post-war years.

'Do you know why he started drinking? Was it business stress?'

She gave a half-laugh. 'Luc could have run the fish company with a hand tied behind his back and he employed excellent people. He loved his work.'

But if not business pressure she didn't say what had driven him to the bottle.

'After it fell apart I was like a crumpled little girl for a few months. We had no money, we owed the bank so much and they were chasing us for repayment. And I had no family other than him and your father. But I fought back.' Her chin jutted out. 'I stopped only working on little house extensions. I wanted more than that. I pushed my way into designing factories and office blocks, small projects at first, then larger plants even though I was a one-woman practice. I went for bigger money, with the big boys, designing places where men worked making things for other men. At first they scoffed at me. But I knew my worth.'

Her eyes, really a hazel colour, took on a steel-blue hue. 'And I know your worth, too, Morane.' She let go of my hand to light a Senior Service. 'Nick cannot blame you for his bad choices.'

'I feel paralysed.'

She blew out a well-formed puff of smoke. I should have hated being with her when she smoked but I never could. 'You are a Guillou woman. You will survive. And you will flourish.'

Interesting she hadn't said I was a Caradec woman.

Below, in the wider waters of the estuary beyond the creek, the sails of a small boat billowed in the breeze. Rozenn stubbed out her cigarette. 'Work out what you want in life and make it happen.'

She'd bolstered me up. And then hurt me after she'd died. Gwen must be right: something had been missed; some explanation had not taken place.

As the roads grew increasingly congested I recalled more of that conversation with Rozenn. She'd been in good spirits, laughing as I forced myself to buck up and told her about the antics of Tatiana in the lighting store when I'd taken her shopping for a drawing-room chandelier. Tatiana spent our hour there snapping the lights with her phone and checking Instagram to see if any of her friends had anything more spectacular.

'But you say Tatiana always pays on time?' Rozenn asked.

'Always. And she's very appreciative, buys me lovely lunches and gives me small presents.'

Rozenn nodded appreciatively. 'Keep her. She's a good client.' I remembered her telling me that in her early years in her own practice she'd fought to have her invoices paid in a timely way. She'd kept one or two of her more modestly paying clients for decades because they'd always settled up promptly and respected her. Loyalty was everything to my grandmother. In another time and place she would have made a good mafia matriarch. Rozenn had seemed so animated as we talked, her eyes bright in her thin face. I thought of how Gwen had said Rozenn had been distracted before her death. Perhaps this was the case and I'd mistaken it for a last relishing of life.

The traffic stopped in front of me. Roadworks. But I wasn't really seeing the cars and buildings. My grandmother filled my mind. I saw the dark-blue jumper, the soft wool trousers. The navy ballerina slippers she wore most of the year. The French windows were just ajar and she'd placed a light cashmere blanket over her knees as she sat reading the morning's post. A breeze blew in from the estuary and a pile of papers to her left on the sofa fluttered to the floor. I leant over to pick them up and she put out a hand to stop me. 'I can reach.' And she had done so, although it had cost her quite a bit in effort: she drew in harsh breaths when she straightened up again. She tucked the letters – most of them looked like junk mail or bills, but one was an unopened handwritten envelope – under the cashmere blanket.

Dad had sorted out the probate as he was her executor. I wondered whether he'd come across the personal letter she hadn't wanted me to see. Perhaps she'd read it and thrown it into the wood-burning stove she lit most evenings.

The traffic started to move again. I braced myself for arrival at the flat. 'Adversity shows us who people really are, *chérie*,' Rozenn had told me when I left her.

Her face had looked suddenly younger as she'd said this, the lines less noticeable. But there was a steeliness to her voice, a renewed strength, that made me blink for a moment as she opened her arms to embrace me.

Perhaps she'd left me out of the inheritance of Vue Claire to force me to become more resilient, to push me out into the world? But that seemed cruel in a way Rozenn had never been. I remembered her in Paris, buying one of us a souvenir or an item of clothing we'd fallen in love with and then meticulously finding something for the other so that it would be fair.

I told myself again that I needed to move on, but the sense of something left unsaid continued to haunt me. Dad had gone through all Rozenn's paperwork but surely there might still be something in the house we'd missed?

I might have been premature in deciding I wouldn't return to Vue Claire.

9

At Rennes Claire's curiosity got the better of her. 'All fall down,' she said, pointing out of the carriage window at the crumpled walls and piles of rubble as the train pulled into the railway station.

'The Germans did that last year,' Rozenn told her. 'Hundreds of people died.'

'Germans did it,' Claire echoed.

'Not that you'd understand a word of that.'

Maman tutted. 'Really, Rozenn, do you have to be so curt with her?'

'It's war. Claire needs to know what happened in the invasion.' But how could someone with a mental age of four or five at best possibly understand? Rozenn turned her attention back to the ruins. Her grandparents' house was only a few blocks away from here. It had been sold after they'd both died, but she could remember Easters spent there: hours in church on Good Friday, the statues covered up, flowers taken out of the church. The explosion of light on Easter morning, the whiteness of women's traditional lace headdresses and the priest's vestments as he stood at the altar, the feast that seemed to last all day: daffodils and hyacinths in vases all over the spacious house. The breads, gateaux and chocolate Easter eggs and chickens. She caught sight of Papa also peering out of the train window, perhaps trying to work out whether his childhood home had survived the bombardment.

The Germans hadn't bombed Paris last year when they'd invaded and there hadn't been fighting on the streets, some kind of pact to preserve the city. The Guillou family had already retreated to the village where Claire's convent was situated once it was clear that the capital would fall. Maman had wanted to be close to Claire. When they'd returned home a week later they'd found their corner of the *arrondissement* quiet but seemingly untouched. The same woman with the white terrier was sitting at her accustomed place in the café just opposite and the same annoying small boy in the apartment across the road was still practising his early-evening shrieking.

The rubble and half-ruined buildings outside the window now made Rozenn's mouth taste as though she was sucking a piece of rusty metal. At times you could forget what was happening, bury yourself in a book or watch a film that distracted you from the Occupation, smell the scent of the lime trees and let it pull you out of reality. But it was still here, the war, the occupiers, the damage. She pulled the water bottle out of Maman's wicker basket and took a sip.

The carriage door opened. The inspector came in. He'd already checked their papers and she wondered why he was back until she saw the German behind him, some kind of policeman in plain clothes.

'You're travelling to the coastal zone?' the German policeman asked Papa. 'What is your business there?'

'I have papers.' Papa opened his medical case, letting the policeman catch a glimpse of the bottles and equipment inside. He pulled out the five sets of papers showing they had permission to travel by rail and enter the zone, and handed them over. Yann was legal for this part of the relocation. The policeman scrutinised the papers.

'You're twenty-one?' he asked, turning to Yann, who nodded. 'And what are your plans, Monsieur?'

'I'd like to train . . .' Yann seemed to remember that it wouldn't be a good idea to say he wanted to become a draftsman. Not when he was entering a coastal zone where the Germans were so paranoid about spies recording their defences. 'I'm not sure yet.'

'Our son has been ill,' Maman interjected. 'He's recovering from surgery and a serious post-operative infection.'

The German nodded. 'I'm sure you'll find something useful to do for your country.' He turned to Claire and Rozenn, raising an eyebrow as he looked from one to the other. 'At least you two do your hair differently. Otherwise you'd be hard to tell apart.' Rozenn felt her jaw clench.

'*Chien.*' Claire's attention had gone to something on the platform. A pair of soldiers were dragging a young man off towards the barrier. A third held the lead of a large Alsatian dog.

'You like animals, Mademoiselle?' The German sounded softer. 'That dog's too fierce for you but there's a station cat here.'

'I like cats too.' Claire gave him that wide smile of hers. He probably hadn't been smiled at like that by anyone else in France. He handed their papers back to Papa and wished them *bon voyage*.

'You can never tell,' Papa said, when the carriage door was closed. 'Some of them are kind.'

'Not sure that fellow would agree.' Yann was still looking at the young man being dragged off the platform. He hadn't spoken much until now, probably brooding on being the cause of this evacuation to Brittany, blaming himself for the disruption, for being old enough not still to be the responsibility of his parents. Rozenn wanted to tell him not to be an idiot. None of this was his fault. They should blame the older generation who'd been so feeble for all those years while Hitler was building up his might, shuddering over the losses in the earlier war against the Germans instead of preparing themselves properly, appointing old men to lead them instead of young, fierce fighters. They might have been traumatised, all very sad and understandable, but they'd still owed something to their children, to their country. Rozenn looked at Papa, replacing their documents in his case and her heart softened. She couldn't blame him. He hadn't been much more than a boy himself at the time of Verdun.

The carriage door opened again and a woman with a boy of about thirteen came in. The woman shuffled her broad backside on to the seat beside Claire, nudging her with the basket she carried and glaring at her as though her thin body was taking up more than its fair share of seat. Claire smiled as the train pulled out of the station. '*Tchou-tchou*,' she chanted.

The boy grinned. 'An imbecile,' he told his mother.

Rozenn leant towards him. 'If you say another word about my sister,' she said quietly, 'I'll call that German policeman back and tell him you have black-market goods in that basket.'

His mouth fell open. Papa was shaking his head. She couldn't bear to look at Maman.

'I wish I had your nerve,' Yann whispered. She smiled at him. If only Claire could have stayed safely in the convent, unexposed to dolts like these two. A small guilty voice inside Rozenn told her that she wished Claire was hidden away for her own benefit, too.

Feeling shame, Rozenn looked down at the carriage floor with its cigarette stubs and discarded tickets. Her left sandal strap caught her attention. It had just been repaired but already hung by a few threads to the body of the shoe. Even if she had it re-stitched, the soles were now so thin she could feel every bump and stone under her foot. Papa had told them that Bretons still wore traditional wooden *sabots*. Perhaps she'd be reduced to dressing like a peasant too while carrying out the myriad chores Maman would require of her. This wasn't how she'd imagined herself seeing out the war.

Last autumn she'd been to see a Chekhov play, immersing herself in scenes from another world. She closed her eyes and tried to imagine herself as an alluring Russian heiress, exiled to the remote countryside, fascinating the local population, planting trees and contemplating the meaning of life.

Yann kicked her. '*Mal du voyage?* You've got the weirdest expression on your face.'

'Zenn ill.' Claire's face looked as though it might crumple. Any moment now she'd start to cry. She'd always hated Rozenn being ill, not that it often happened. Rozenn had always been the most robust of the Guillou children. Papa reached inside his medical bag, muttering something about a sedative for Claire.

'I'm fine,' Rozenn told her. But Claire still looked on the point of tears. Rozenn sighed. 'Where's that book about the farm you like? Shall we read it together?'

Papa fastened the medical bag again.

&

'That's the old doctor's house,' the taxi driver told them. 'Shame you couldn't live there, Monsieur. Those Germans take all the best properties.' They gazed at the fine early-nineteenth-century house with its steps up from the street and the garden full of irises and roses.

The village was tiny. A couple of shops, most of which were boarded up like many of the houses. Most of the residents had been removed from the area and the seasonal visitors wouldn't be staying this year. A hotel on the beachside. A church. 'Look, the sea.' Claire roused herself from the torpor she'd been in since they'd got off the train. A long beach spread out to the west. Rozenn spotted huge spools of barbed wire, waiting to be rolled out along the sand.

Another thing the Germans had stolen from them. And yet her own heart leapt too at the sight of the sea.

They bumped along a lane rising up the steep hill and turned off down a rough track, making for the headland. The taxi juddered as it hit pothole after pothole and the driver swore. 'Hard to see in this damn light.' Rozenn was about to say she wanted to get out and walk when they stopped.

The *longère*, literally a longhouse, spread out in front of them. The name was apt: it seemed unusually wide but was barely two floors tall, with a single-storey outbuilding to the right and another, even lower in height, to the side of it in turn, like father, mother and baby structures. Granite stone walls, slate roof. A smaller detached outbuilding sat at a right angle. The privy, Rozenn guessed. The house's shutters were open, as though it were welcoming them. Rozenn wasn't certain she returned the sentiment.

Papa put his hand under a large pebble lying at the doorstep, unlocked the door and peered inside. 'Thank goodness for the long summer days,' he said. 'We wouldn't see a thing otherwise.'

Maman placed a handkerchief to her nose.

'They've had pigs in here,' Yann said. 'Chickens at least.'

'I hope they cleared up after them.' Rozenn stared into the gloomy interior.

'They promised it would be ready to inhabit,' Papa said, sounding tired.

'Good luck,' the driver told Papa. 'I'll be back to pick you up tomorrow at ten, *monsieur le docteur*. So you can collect that Citroën of yours from the garage.' Papa had organised a car and a ration of petrol for his work. At least she'd be able to go into Lannion with him when he held a surgery there, Rozenn thought. Small consolation: it was a tiny town.

Although there was still daylight outside the interior was dark, illuminated by two small windows at the back. She made out the shape of a primitive kitchen: a stove, sink and dresser. On the table in front of them sat an oil lamp and matches. Rozenn went inside and lit the lamp. To her right she saw a room that looked as though it might be a living room, with a more formal table and chairs in it.

'*Très bien*,' Papa said brightly behind her. 'Let's bring in the bags. Yann, pay the taxi driver.' Coins clinked as Yann took the money. Claire and Maman walked inside.

'Oh, François.' Maman flopped on to one of the chairs around the table. 'There's barely any furniture.'

Claire sniffed loudly. 'Smells like *ca-ca*.' Maman seemed too weary to reprimand her.

'It probably just needs airing,' Papa said.

'I'll go upstairs and open the windows,' Rozenn said. The stench of farm animals grew milder as she ascended but the scent of mould or mildew took its place. She opened the window on the landing and pushed the shutter back. A salty, fresh breeze blew in. The sea. Papa had said the house was on the cliffs but she hadn't expected to be so close to the water. Something loosened inside her as she gazed at its blue expanse. The moon was already rising in the sky. Beside it a single planet burnt bright. Stars glistened around them, their light muted as it was barely dark yet.

'What's it like upstairs, Rozenn?' Maman called up.

'I don't know,' she said. It was dirty and malodorous, but that view, the sea, the sky . . .

'What on earth do you mean?' Maman sounded as though she might snap.

'*Désolée*.' Maman wouldn't want to hear about the moon. 'I'm just looking.' Rozenn wrenched herself away. She went into the first of the rooms, which opened one by one from a narrow corridor. They looked as though they'd been built up here in the last ten years or so, utilising the roof cavity. Sagging mattresses on the beds, stained old bolsters. Threadbare rugs on the floors. The window of one room shuttered, the other windows just covered with black-out blinds. She opened all the windows and shutters. They'd probably be attacked by insects and she was breaking the blackout. But nobody would be able to sleep unless the air was freshened.

Downstairs Claire was crying. Papa was trying to console her. Rozenn felt tears prickling behind her own eyes, but they were manifestations of rage rather than exhaustion or misery.

Yet something was forcing her to go back to that landing window again. In the moonlight the sea was a navy band, its texture and colour changing constantly. Not really just blue, but green and grey, sometimes coal-black in places. The sea was still the sea, just as she'd remembered from childhood. She was no child to be delighted by the waves and yet part of her might have been seven again. Rozenn went downstairs. 'It needs work but I think we can do something with this house.' She took Claire by the hand. 'Come upstairs and look at the sea.'

Claire looked at Maman. 'Go with your sister,' Maman said. 'But don't get her hopes up too much,' she whispered to Rozenn. 'We probably won't be allowed on any of the beaches, they'll have shut them all off.'

The Germans claimed the seashore just as they'd claimed the sights of Paris and any food worth eating, but tonight Rozenn wasn't going to think about that. Claire followed her. 'Look.' Rozenn took her to the window. 'The sea with the moon shining on it.'

Claire's eyes opened wide. She must have seen it before, she'd come on the family excursions to the coast as a small child when they'd stayed with their grandparents in Rennes. But the last of those trips had been several years ago now and for Claire it would be impossible to remember. Or perhaps not. As Claire stared out of the window a flicker of something like recognition seemed to pass over her face. 'Fish,' she said. 'Swimming in the sea.'

'*Oui*.' Rozenn turned to look through the first bedroom door at the two single beds. 'This must be our room.' It looked out over fields towards the lane they had driven up. 'Shall we unpack your bag?'

'Sharing with Zenn?' Claire's delight swept over her face. Rozenn felt something underneath her ribs, like claws clutching at her insides, making her feel vulnerable and irritable. She wanted to shake them all off: Maman, Papa and Claire. Perhaps even Yann. Run away, be by herself.

'Of course.' Her voice was clipped. 'Where else would you sleep? Fetch your *valise*.'

'*Valise*,' Claire said to herself as she went downstairs for her small black suitcase, her feet nimble on the steep wooden staircase – at times it seemed her body worked at a higher level than her mind. Yann came upstairs and joined Rozenn at the window.

'This is all madness.' Reality washed through Rozenn. 'I don't know why Papa thinks you're better off here.'

'He bought me return rail tickets and a travel permit back to Paris the day after tomorrow.'

She looked at him, puzzled.

'As we know, they'd never allow a male of fighting age to live here. Unless it's as some kind of slave labour. So officially I'll go back to Paris . . .' He shrugged. In reality he'd be hiding here.

'Maman registers the four of you at the *mairie* and I stay out of sight. Papa's a respectable doctor, they won't be suspicious of his family.'

'You'll suffocate, go mad with boredom.'

'There are the outbuildings. Papa says I can use one of them, perhaps even sleep out there. But I'll need some fresh air and exercise to stay healthy.' He sounded wistful. Yann had always loved being outdoors. As a small boy Papa had had to beg the concierge to watch the main door on to the street because Yann would creep down the stairs, wait for someone to unlock the door from the outside and dart on to the street after they'd walked through.

'I'll have to rely on you to describe St Martin to me fully, Rozenn,' he said. 'Every building, what it's made of, how tall, which way it faces. How old you think it is.'

She peeped out of the window. It was now too dark to see much and the sea was more of a feeling than a sight. 'If we got you a telescope you'd see it yourself from here. The Germans will probably ruin the view with their pillboxes and bunkers, though.'

'Papa says this little port and bay isn't considered as strategically important as other ports. It was another reason for coming here. Though Rennes might have been better. More for you to do, Rozenn.'

'People in Rennes know our family. They'd recognise you. We're more anonymous here.' She pulled down the blind. 'But it might have been better to go somewhere in the *Zone Libre*. Marseilles, perhaps. You could have got out of the country, joined the fight.'

He blinked. 'The Free French?'

She turned to him. 'That's what you want to do, isn't it?' They hadn't been able to talk together privately for days.

'Yes.' He spoke with a quiet firmness. 'Though I'd rather resist from inside the country.'

'Not much happening here so far.' A few acts of sabotage. Posters on Parisian walls. A couple of Germans shot.

'There'll be more resistance once they start rounding us up for their factories.' He looked at her. 'I can't go back to Germany, Rozenn.' He spoke with a firmness that was unusual.

'*Mes enfants*,' Papa called. 'Luggage needs taking upstairs if you've finished admiring the view.' He sounded unusually testy, probably realising that they were stuck in this dump with no prospect of an easy return to Paris, the apartment having already been rented out to a German officer who'd be moving in the next day.

Yann looked at Rozenn. 'It's not easy for you, sharing with Claire, spending so much time with her.'

It was dark. She hoped he couldn't see her blink hard. 'I must be patient with her,' she muttered. 'I know I'm awful sometimes.'

He touched her shoulder briefly. 'I don't know how I'd feel if it had happened to me.'

Yann the golden boy, lumbered with a shadow-double. Her imagination failed her. She followed him down the narrow steps that groaned and swayed as they ran downstairs.

10

I perched on my bed in the Brentford flat, laptop beside me, ordering kitchen cupboard handles for Tatiana, the previous consignment having been rejected on the grounds that she now wanted something she'd seen on Instagram. Except she couldn't remember exactly on which influencer's stream she'd seen the pewter handles. I'd spent hours on my mobile doing my best to work out what Tatiana might have viewed and ordered something seeming to match her description.

I pushed the 'Send' button. Too much of my time was going on these little projects but I found they distracted me from myself, which I reckoned was a positive. Handles ordered, I could bury myself in drawing up a shortlist of electric blinds for Tatiana to look at. Or a shortlist of architects ready to brief once Jenny and Sam had had a chance to look at my preliminary sketches for the barn. I was sure I'd captured everything we'd talked about. The prospect of taking the project through to the next stage was exciting.

Gwen was still urging me to let her help me write a proper business plan, to budget for some marketing of myself. Dad was still offering me money to rent somewhere more spacious and central, or even as a deposit on a flat purchase. But stubborn pride still kept me from accepting their help. I wanted to do things on my own terms.

Anyway, I didn't mind Brentford. The riverside provided me with interesting walks and I enjoyed trips across the Thames to nearby Richmond and Kew Gardens. The flat itself was on the fourth floor of a new-build block, on a busy road overlooked by west London's emulation of a Far Eastern metropolis and surrounded by building sites.

I stared at the tiny rectangle of light falling on the already worn carpet. Even in midsummer, this room never gained any more sun than this patch. At least it was easy to head west out of London from here: five minutes to the M4. I picked up my mobile. *If you wanted someone to stay in for those deliveries to Vue Claire I'm still available – need to head west anyway for work.* I pushed send, not knowing why. So much for breaking free of Cornwall. The last bit of my message to Gwen wasn't even the truth. Despite their enthusiasm last week, Jenny and Sam had been silent. I could text and tell them I was passing, but I didn't want to seem too eager for the work.

Gwen texted back immediately. *Fantastic! I was finding it hard to get more time off and James has to be in London for meetings this week.*

Busy, successful *normal* people couldn't usually find time to head out of the office on a whim, unlike those without enough work to fill a diary. Gwen sent me a follow-on message, reminding me that she'd fitted a key box and I should remember the code as it was a particularly significant birthdate. Rozenn's, I recalled. 31/07/22. We'd usually been with her on her birthday. As children Gwen and I would insist on baking a misshapen cake for her, which she'd eaten with vocal enthusiasm, unlike her usual restraint when it came to anything sweet. Rozenn had always been the disciplined Parisian woman, consistently weighing the same as she had at the time of her marriage, she told me. Although she must have lost a good stone and a half from her slender frame in her final illness.

Except, I thought, as I threw clothes into a bag, my grand-mother hadn't actually been a born *Parisienne*, had she? Rozenn was a Breton name, like Morane and Gwenaëlle. People had sometimes thought Gwen and I might be Welsh. Explaining that our father's family actually came from Brittany, which was part of France, was a complication too far.

Rozenn had taken Gwen and me on that first trip to Paris after Mum had died and it had become a tradition: either in the summer half-term, when the lime blossom was still out, or just after school broke up at Christmas, so we could admire the lights on the Champs-Élysées. She'd never suggested visiting Brittany. As she'd barely mentioned the region to us, this hadn't seemed remarkable.

Paris had been so exciting that for us it had become synony-mous with France itself. Rozenn herself opened up in the capital, becoming girlish and animated.

Strange perhaps that she'd chosen to retire to coastal Cornwall rather than spending her latter years in either London or Paris. 'This house reminds me of what mattered most to me,' she said, when I asked her why she'd built here. 'As a girl your age I loved the bustle of the city, the shapes of the buildings around me, the way the views opened up. But I couldn't do without the sky and sea now, the way the light changes, the sound of the water and the birds. It reminds me . . .' She gave one of those Gallic shrugs. 'It just suits me. And when I retired it seemed natural to come back here. It was so close to where I arrived.'

It was a rare mention of her arrival in England and she'd clammed up immediately, changing the subject.

I locked the door to my bedroom, forgetting I'd left my silver compass in the chest of drawers. I hesitated, no need to take it really, I knew every inch of the creeks around the house. But I unlocked the door again to retrieve the compass.

Surely Rozenn's point of departure to England must have been Brittany? Had my grandparents known one another before they came to England? I stowed my bag in the boot and pulled out my mobile.

About to leave for Cornwall. But just wondered, do you know where and when Rozenn and Luc met? I texted Dad. *Could it have been Brittany?* I wasn't even sure why this might matter but the urge to know more, to fill in the blanks Rozenn left me with, wouldn't settle.

Your grandmother never said, he replied. *Could well have been.*

Do we know where exactly Grand-père Luc came from?

I could feel Dad's brain straining to remember. *Are you becoming the family genealogist, M? Got your grandfather's birth certificate somewhere. I'll text you when I'm home. Must go now, next patient waiting.*

In my car I turned the radio on to a station promising only music, no talk, and sang along loudly. The traffic gods were looking on me benevolently – I moved swiftly along the M4 and M25, reaching the M3 with the barest of hold-ups. I'd brought no food with me but knew I could stop at a farm shop or top up at a petrol station if necessary. Gwen would probably have left a few things in the freezer from our stay last week, which I could use and replace.

I warned myself as I always did to take care, not to drive too fast, to watch other cars like a hawk. Accidents could happen – in a flash. But if there were shadows chasing me as I joined the A303 and started to look out for Stonehenge, I brushed them off as I headed into the late afternoon sun.

～✿～

Arriving at Vue Claire with a bag of groceries to tide me over, I keyed in Rozenn's birthdate and retrieved the key. Already the scent of my grandmother was fading from the interior. In its place I made out the notes of the fig-scented candles Gwen liked. In the fridge sat a couple of bottles of James's expensive white wine. I placed my bottle of local cider next to them, along with a block of Cornish cheddar, a pint of milk and some salad.

Nick had been lactose intolerant and had joked that Cornwall would kill him with its cream and cheeses. He'd come down with me in October. The mornings on the estuary had started misty and overcast before the sun came out, pretending it was still August. We'd walked right around the point and down to the coastguard's station.

Upstairs I smelt fresh paint above the scented candles. My usual room had been painted a sea-blue, playing on the shade of the water in the estuary just visible from the window. Rozenn had designed the house so that all the rooms had at least a glimpse of the water. I'd chosen the paint with Gwen when I'd been down last week and she'd obviously finished the room after I'd left. Gwen and James had taken over Rozenn's room. They hadn't redecorated it yet and the large sleigh-bed was still covered in her satin quilt, with Gwen's newly purchased linen sheets beneath.

Where did you go? I asked Rozenn silently, looking around the room as though she might be hiding. *Is part of you still here?* We'd buried her ashes in the garden below. I tried to sense her presence, but could only feel the memory of the woman I'd known. I turned to the view. The tide was going out, just as it had when she'd been dying. Perhaps it had taken her with it to that mysterious place far out to sea from where nobody returned.

Back in 1941 Rozenn must have been so relieved to reach the safety of solid ground after a presumably hazardous voyage across the Channel. Again I puzzled over the reasons pushing her to make the journey. Surely there'd have been German boats and planes guarding the Channel? And leaving the French coast must have been risky.

It still seemed strange that Rozenn, a girl of not quite nineteen, might have anything to do with Allied special operations. She'd said nothing about it but that wasn't unusual for people of her generation who didn't feel the need to promote their every deed on social media. As children we'd taken her reticence for granted, not pushing her to answer questions. We'd never really thought about what it must be like to leave your homeland and take refuge in another country. Rozenn had seemed so perfectly adapted to her life in England, speaking the language with just that faintest of accents. It was hard to even imagine her living in another country.

What didn't you tell us? I asked my grandmother silently. Rozenn didn't do anything on impulse so omissions would have been intentional. *Were you going to tell us more about yourself before you died?*

But if any part of Rozenn's spirit was still lurking in the house she'd decided not to answer me.

11

Papa's new car was a black Citroën saloon. 'A Traction Avant, better than I'd expected.'

'What's that mean?' Rozenn asked.

'Good steering and suspension on these country lanes. Let's hope it flourishes in damp winter weather too.'

This morning he wasn't seeing any of his patients. Yann sat in the front seat, Rozenn behind. Even though they were playing a part, Rozenn felt a sense of doom, of endings. Yann would be coming back with them to the *longère*, hidden under the travel rug. He'd carry a suitcase into the station like any other traveller, but the case contained old sheets rather than clothes and would be left in the gentlemen's at Lannion station. On his way out, Yann would put on the cap he was carrying in his pocket, covering the head of hair that was a darker auburn than his sisters' but as eye-catching.

As they came to the outskirts of town a temporary road-block barrier stretched across the lane. Armed Germans waved them down. Papa swore softly. Yann had their papers in his lap. A local policeman checked them carefully. His German counterpart lounged against a wall, watching attentively, but not too interested, not yet. On the way out of town it might be different. 'You work in the zone, Monsieur? How is that?'

'I'm the new doctor at St Martin,' Papa told him.

'And these two?'

'My dependent daughter.'

Rozenn bristled.

'And my son. He helped move us into our new home and now he's returning to Paris.'

The policeman nodded at the guards to pull the pole over so the Citroën could pass.

She could tell by the set of Yann's shoulders that he was nervous. On the way back they'd have to drive through the roadblock and the policeman might want to check that Yann wasn't still sitting in the car.

'Come back down this road and meet us here.' Papa pointed as they passed out of sight of the roadblock. 'See the house with the blue shutters? Walk quickly, don't run.'

'Suppose someone finds out he never arrived in Paris?' Rozenn asked.

'We'd be shocked at this news of our son's disappearance,' Papa said. 'I'd telegram and write to various friends in Paris asking if they'd seen Yann, call in at the local police station to ask if there's news.'

'You could have been a spy, Papa,' Rozenn told him.

'What if I'm stopped on the street?' Yann asked, voice tight.

Rozenn stared at Papa's creased forehead in the rear-view mirror as he answered. 'There's no market on today, it's quiet.'

It would only take one suspicious policeman or German for the plan to fall apart.

'If you're questioned, show your ID,' he went on. 'Say you missed your train and mislaid your suitcase.'

'You've been having terrible stomach trouble,' Rozenn said. 'A bad shellfish. You had to dash into the gentlemen's at the last moment. It cost Papa time and money to sort out your tickets and permission to travel and now you're worried about a clip to the ear.'

'If it doesn't work, we'll try again in a week or two,' Papa said. 'It's risky but it's not as though you're . . .'

Jewish. Or the son of a known socialist. Rozenn's thoughts drifted to Theo. Was he still in Marseilles? Guiltily she realised she hadn't thought of him much in the last few days. They reached the outskirts of Lannion. The approach to the station seemed busy – this was the morning service to Rennes, from where people changed for Paris, if they had permits to travel that far. A few soldiers stood at the entrance. Rozenn tasted bile in her mouth.

'Don't worry about the soldiers,' Papa said. 'Yann has permission to travel to Paris.'

Yann looked in good health now. He might be questioned by an inquisitive *gendarme* or Gestapo officer as to why he wasn't still a POW in a camp or why he didn't have proper demob papers.

The soldiers disappeared into the station, perhaps on leave themselves, judging by the way they joked and bumped one another. Papa pulled up. He got out of the car and threw his arms around Yann, kissing him on both cheeks, wishing him *bon voyage* in a louder than usual voice. Rozenn got out as well and removed the suitcase from the boot for her brother. They exchanged looks. '*À bientôt*,' she said, kissing him.

She wanted to stay close to Yann rather than driving off, make sure nobody was watching him, but knew they had to stick to the plan. As they drove away she craned her neck but couldn't see whether the soldiers had gone straight on to the platform. Suppose they'd gone into the gentlemen's or noticed Yann'd left the suitcase in there? They might think he'd planted a bomb. It seemed unlikely anyone would target Lannion's small station, though.

Papa turned the Citroën back on to the road leading south out of town. They drove in silence. She sat beside him in the front, looking out of the wing mirror.

'Delivery van behind,' she said.

82

Papa swore softly. 'I need him to overtake me.'

'The engine looks hot,' she said. He peered at the dashboard, frowning. 'Shouldn't we pull over and check the water or whatever you do with overheating?'

He nodded and did as she suggested.

But the van driver pulled up behind them and got out. 'Can I help, Monsieur?' Friendly face, local accent.

'Too kind.' Papa smiled that gentle smile that was so like Yann's. 'I'm just going to lift the bonnet and check all's well. Probably over-cautious, but it's hard to get parts these days if something breaks.'

The van driver started to remove his jacket. 'I've got a good eye for engines.'

'It just needs to cool down.' Papa kept his voice level. 'The garage said to pull over for ten minutes if it's overheating. I wouldn't want to keep you from your deliveries.'

'It shouldn't be overheating.' The driver scowled at the car. 'If you've been looking after it?'

'My father nurses the car like a child. I keep telling him he's too anxious.' Rozenn gave the drive a sidelong smile. 'Thank you for stopping, Monsieur.'

Papa shot her a warning look. *Don't do anything to make us stick in his memory.*

The driver gave Rozenn an appreciative stare. She removed her book from her satchel and sat down on the grass. 'Might as well enjoy the sun while we wait.'

'I'll be off then.' The driver sounded disappointed.

'There was a roadblock further on,' Papa said. 'I hope it doesn't slow you down.'

'Not again.' The driver swore. '*Au revoir,* Monsieur, Mademoiselle.'

'*Au revoir,*' she said, without looking up. The small van shook back into motion. They watched him disappear up the lane. Where was Yann? Perhaps they should turn round and drive back to the station, scoop him up as quickly as possible. But Papa still had the Citroën's hood up, was lighting a cigarette.

Rozenn counted to one hundred, almost wishing Claire was with them to act as a distraction. Claire could only count to twenty. Maman was confident that thirty would soon be reached, though. But if Claire were there she'd be prattling on about her brother coming to meet them, pretending to get on a train. It had been hard enough talking through the plans out of her earshot. How could you make someone like her understand that Yann would have to be a secret now?

'There he is.' Papa closed the bonnet. The road was still clear. Rozenn willed her brother on before someone else came along. Yann looked pale, almost breaking into a run as Papa beckoned him on. 'In the back, quick.' Papa lifted up the blanket to cover him. 'That van's still somewhere ahead.' Papa sounded rattled. He'd seemed so relaxed earlier on. The interest of the van driver had perhaps indicated to him how fragile their plan was. And they still had to get through the roadblock again.

'What happened?' she asked Yann.

'I dropped the wretched suitcase inside the station,' Yann said from behind the seats. 'The handle came unscrewed on one side. Thank God it didn't fall open on the ground. Those German soldiers helped me pick it up, told me I needed a screwdriver to tighten the screw. They asked me where I was going and I had to make an excuse to go to the lavatory and just pray they got on to the train without noticing I hadn't made it.'

Rozenn looked over her shoulder. Nobody else on the road. Suppose someone had recognised Yann as he walked in with the suitcase, known him as the doctor's son? Seen him exit without the case? Yann hadn't left the longhouse and its immediate surroundings, she told herself. He hadn't met anyone in the area. They'd only been here for a week.

They approached the roadblock. Papa slowed. The same policeman frowned at the car, before recognising the Citroën and waving them through. '*Dieu merci*,' Papa said quietly.

The rest of the journey was made in silence.

They bumped up the track to the longhouse. Papa looked around. 'All clear, you can get out, Yann.'

Maman welcomed Yann as though he had actually been to Paris and back, embracing him and closing her eyes briefly. 'I worried there'd be Gestapo at the station.'

Papa and Rozenn exchanged glances: no need to fill her in on all the details, the roadblock, Yann's incident with the suitcase, the interest from the German soldiers, the van stopping to offer help.

Routine checks. Friendly curiosity. People trying to help. Perhaps the customary indifference of Parisians would have been safer after all.

Yann seemed weary after the morning's pretence, happy to stay quietly indoors after lunch. Maman was clearing the smaller outhouse for him to use. He'd be safe in the grassed rectangle in front of the house as it was invisible from the track, and he could enjoy the sunshine. 'I have to get fit,' he said. 'Since the appendix I've been so weak. How can I do that if I can't leave for a walk?'

'We'll find a way,' Papa said.

※

Rozenn drove back to Lannion with Papa the following morning, trying not to notice Maman's pursed lips, feeling the need to escape from the house. No roadblock today. While Papa saw his patients Rozenn strolled by the river, watching a man cast a line for fish. In a shop claiming to sell antiques but in reality old and unremarkable bits of furniture, she found a much-used but apparently still-intact grinder for roasted barley and bought it in excitement. The bag of coffee brought with them from Paris was all but empty. Maman claimed that roasted barley coffee wasn't so bad, really. She'd be pleased to see the grinder and might excuse Rozenn some Claire-watching.

Rozenn wandered through winding, cobbled side streets heading uphill from the river and found a second-hand bookshop where she spent the rest of her money on a book on the buildings of Paris. A bit of an indulgence really, but it was up to date and included photographs of the property that fascinated her the most: not an Empire-apartment-block-lined boulevard or an ancient church but the modernist Maison la Roche their side of Paris, near the Bois de Boulogne. It wasn't actually the building or interior she loved the most: that was probably the gold, many-balconied cupola of the Galeries Lafayette department store for its sheer exuberance. Recreating the cupola on paper from memory would certainly be a challenge. Rozenn found a café and ordered an infusion of camomile, rather than risking the coffee. She studied the photographs of the Maison la Roche and then tested herself by closing the book and trying to picture it in her mind's eye, concentrating hard on its clean lines, curved upper section, black window frames, feeling her mind calming and focusing . . .

A young German lieutenant in field grey smiled at her. Instinctively she started to smile back at the handsome boy with his tanned, friendly face, before remembering who he was. A curt nod ensured he wouldn't repeat the familiarity. He flushed and looked away. What world was this where two young people couldn't exchange a few words because one of them was on the side of the occupiers and one the vanquished? This boy wasn't old enough to have voted in Hitler. But he was still an enemy. Her heart hardened.

Why should a German be free to sit in a café in Lannion while Yann hid in an outbuilding?

Papa's morning surgery ended at twelve-thirty. They met in the street where the Citroën was parked. He would spend the afternoon driving around the neighbourhood to the housebound. Rozenn would have asked to go with him, but Maman would surely explode if she escaped twice in one day.

Papa talked brightly about his morning: the little boy whose septic finger was healing well, the pregnant woman whose blood pressure was stabilising.

'But you still have to see *them*?' Rozenn folded her arms.

'Yes. But when it's young German conscripts of about Yann's age it doesn't feel as compromising as it does when it's middle-aged Nazi industrialists.'

She nodded, thinking of the young German officer in the café. 'I suppose I can see that.' She looked sidelong at him. 'Nobody said anything about Yann, did they?'

'The receptionist knows he went back to Paris yesterday. She asked if the train had left on time. I said we'd dropped him off outside the station and joked that he was never very good at writing to us so we wouldn't be holding our breath for a letter.'

'Boys always have excuses,' she said.

He looked at her. 'You were helpful yesterday, *chérie*. Calm. I couldn't have managed without you.'

'I wouldn't have been as calm if the Germans had searched us at the roadblock, with Yann under that blanket on the floor.'

He was silent. They drove on another kilometre and he spoke again. 'The situation with Yann can't go on indefinitely. I'm looking at ways to get him out of France.'

The road made a left-hand loop. The long blue-green band of sea stretched out ahead of them. Rozenn felt what was becoming a familiar rush of joy at the sight of it. It might be patrolled by

German boats and submarines but its waves crashed unperturbed on the shore and it linked France to the free world. People had been evacuated off the coast at the time of the invasion. In Paris word had reached them of fishing boats taking men of fighting age and people with a particular need to escape the Germans to England. Did that still happen now?

The car passed the sign to St Martin. Maman would want her to watch over Claire after lunch. Well, she'd had her morning of freedom. Perhaps some distraction for Claire could be found that would allow Rozenn some snatched moments with the architecture book she'd bought in Lannion or her sketch pad.

⚜

After they'd eaten lunch Rozenn took Claire into the garden and threw an old tennis ball to her, trying to encourage better hand-eye coordination, which Papa said might help her develop in all kinds of ways. Like a toddler, Claire grabbed at the ball moving towards her with both hands, squealing with rage when it evaded her. The tennis ball was too small. In past summers there'd probably been a shop or kiosk in St Martin selling large rubber balls for tourists. Claire wearied of the ball game and squatted down, picking up stones from the soil Maman hadn't yet had time to rake out, and piling them up carefully into a small heap. Perhaps there was a section of sand not yet wired off by the Germans where she could collect shells and make a sandcastle. It was cruel that Claire was so close to the beach but unable to play there.

Claire was mumbling something to herself as she sorted the stones. Rozenn made out fragments of prayer. *Ave María, gratia plena, Dominus tecum.* If Claire could memorise Latin prayers, numbers and a wider vocabulary must be possible too. Rozenn looked at her sister. The sunshine had brought a glow to Claire's

88

cheeks. Absorbed in the counting of the stones she looked more focused, less of an infant in a woman's body. Despite the fact that they had to use a strange-smelling soap made from rendered animal fat and ash to wash their hair, Claire's auburn mane shone. She was wearing it loose today because Rozenn had left in a hurry with Papa after breakfast and hadn't had time to plait it. The bronze tints sparkled in the sunshine. It could be her own hair Rozenn was looking at. She was so like Claire but so very different.

Rozenn spotted a small round stone and picked it up. 'Here.' Claire took it from her with a smile. 'Let's count,' Rozenn said. 'See how far you can get.'

Claire shook her head. 'Don't want to.' Rozenn took her up the track towards the lane. Claire stopped every metre or so to scrutinise blades of grass or pick up stones from the track. Rozenn looked at her watch and wanted to shake it. But it hadn't stopped. They turned back towards the house.

'*Merci, chérie.*' Maman came outside. 'Go and see if there's anything left in the market. Claire, I need your help with my garden.' She seemed unusually mellow this afternoon. 'Let's find some rakes and hoes and attack the weeds.'

Maman was planning a major assault on the overgrown vegetable garden. Probably a little late for this year, Papa said. But there were carrots, radishes and spinach ready to harvest, planted by the previous tenants. Last night they'd even had new potatoes. 'Take the ration books, Rozenn,' Maman called. 'I forgot the market was on this morning. It's probably packed up by now, but you never know.' She sounded cheerfully resigned to the probability that there wouldn't be anything left. Why hadn't Maman thought to walk down with Claire in the morning? Probably too distracted with housework.

Rozenn took the four cards. Four sets of rations, five people to feed. Yann and the twins received more calories in rations than their parents because of their age. Without his share the family was even more stretched for food. Surely in this village there must be supplies off-ration, if you knew where to look? She checked she had her ID papers and residence permit. Too warm for a jacket and her dress didn't have pockets so she put the papers into her satchel and took Maman's string bag as well, in case there was anything to buy. Her hair was misbehaving today. She should have brought a summer hat. Her blue beret would have to hold it in place, even though it was hot.

In peacetime she'd have borrowed Papa's camera and taken photographs of the little port and rocky cliffs behind it. These days, photographing along the coast could have you shot for espionage. Rozenn could sketch the clusters of rose-pink granite, but even that would mean keeping an eye out for surveyors or German patrols on the cliffs. She'd have to develop her eye, studying the rocks and buildings until she knew them by heart and could go back to the *longère* and reproduce them from memory. Her supplies of paper were running low.

She'd only walked the cliff path down to the village once since they'd arrived a week ago – so much time had been needed to make the house inhabitable and she'd jumped at the chance to explore the larger Lannion when Papa went in to hold his surgery. But now Yann had safely returned from the railway station Rozenn wanted to assess any possible threats to him.

She could never take this view for granted. Rozenn paused at the top of the headland and looked out to sea. This afternoon it was still, apparently uniformly azure unless you studied it intently and made out the flashes of emerald and navy, sometimes grey where waves passed over rocks. Look even more closely and you'd even see brief gleams of gold as the sun's rays bounced off a patch of water.

Somewhere across the sea was England, where the Germans had no hold. Thousands of men and boys had gone there to fight for General de Gaulle and the Free French. She thought again of the fishing boats that had helped them escape, screwing up her eyes to look for the vessels. The Germans allowed the fleet to sail out under guard because they wanted the fish supplies to continue. A quantity of the catch was now packed in ice and sent to Paris or further east if it could be managed so that the Germans could gorge themselves on it. Papa'd told them that Breton sardines were a renowned delicacy, canned in local factories in attractive little tins and sent around the world, or probably just to Germany now. Yet people on the coast must still be able to benefit from their own fish, mustn't they? It was surely worth hanging around the quay when the boats came in.

Rozenn looked down and spotted a small cove, horseshoe shaped, tucked away under the cliffs curving up to the headland. The cove looked like a good place to hunt for crabs and the Germans hadn't wired it off. Claire would like it, but the narrow, curving track down would make it treacherous for her. Tempting for Rozenn to climb down there and spread herself out on the sand to catch the sun or seek out cockles on the rocks. But in these sandals with their worn soles she'd be risking a broken ankle. She should have worn her old gym shoes.

She continued across the neck of the headland, catching the scent of wild flowers and fresh grass, undercut by tangy, salty air. The wide sandy bay stretched out in front of her now. Out to sea white surf broke on what must have been a sandbar. The path dropped towards the village. Rozenn hadn't really looked at the place properly when they'd driven through on the way from the station. Now she marvelled at how the church was built into the sea wall, its small cemetery housing the local dead, who must almost find themselves in the sea when the tide was very high. The Guillous hadn't been to Mass here since their arrival. In Paris they hadn't been as regular as they ought to have been. Rozenn hadn't gone to confession since

91

before Easter. She'd not been truthful on that occasion either, not admitting to kissing Theo in an undoubtedly impure way. None of her friends would have admitted to something like that in a confessional, though. Especially not when the boy you were kissing wasn't a Catholic.

Papa said attendance at Mass and confession would be important here. Friday evening Benediction would also be a good idea. She'd groaned at the prospect. Maman thought Claire would like the familiar Latin and hymns of the services. At least the nuns would have taught her to behave in church.

Let her parents worry about religion. It had bored Rozenn in Paris and would probably be even more tedious here. She'd go to Mass as usual but find excuses to avoid Benediction.

She looked down at the beach. The Germans had rolled out more barbed wire. Once holidaymakers had played volleyball on the sand, or dashed into the water. On a day like this children should be shouting with excitement as they ran around.

The path descended to the quay. No boats. They must still be out to sea. A pair of cats stretched out in the sun. Just above the quay perched a small house with a curious curved eave, almost like a raised, friendly eyebrow. Rozenn wanted to smile back at it. She memorised the outline of the house to draw for Yann.

She walked towards the white hotel overlooking the beach she'd spotted from the taxi. Once this must have been the place to go for a mid-morning coffee or for a *citron* on a hot afternoon on the beach. Today the clientele was limited to a group of German officers on the balcony, legs stretched out, sunglasses on, enjoying what looked like beers, as though they were on holiday. Perhaps this was in fact almost a vacation for them – posted to a peaceful seaside village at the start of summer. Better than actually fighting somewhere. Papa said most of them were artillery corps though, rather than regular *Wehrmacht*, so perhaps not the fittest or brightest. One of them spotted her, and pointed her out to his companion, who picked up his binoculars from the table and focused them on her. She flushed and walked to the gate leading up to the street.

A few discarded cabbage leaves on the cobbled street and a single stall was all that remained of the market. Rozenn watched a woman approach and hand over a basket and coins in return for something passed to her from a hessian sack below the table. The recipient turned quickly as she took the basket back, perhaps to ensure no policeman was watching. No ration card was proffered. Rozenn walked closer. An elderly man shuffled to the stall, holding out a bag and receiving a rabbit from the sack, handing over coins in return. Rozenn approached and pointed at the sack and opened her string bag. The woman pointed at the satchel instead. Rozenn opened it, hoping the rabbit wouldn't leave blood in the interior. The stallholder woman had parsnips too. Nothing else. Parsnips in June? Was that all? She caught a glimpse of long green spears under the stall. Asparagus, new season, in another hessian sack. Rozenn pointed at it and asked for half a kilo.

'Not for sale,' the woman said.

'Why's it here then?'

The woman shifted her weight from leg to leg.

'Why won't you sell me asparagus?' Something of the strain of the last few days must have caught up with Rozenn; her voice sounded sharp.

'This isn't Paris.' She turned to see a girl who must have come up silently behind her. 'You won't get what you want by raising your voice and drawing attention.' She nodded at the woman and handed over a basket, which the woman loaded with asparagus spears.

The girl muttered something in return in a strange language that must be Breton. 'She needs to know you. Then she'll sell you the best stuff.' She cast an amused look at Rozenn. 'In the meantime you could make a little *pâté* with your rabbit, I suppose.'

With a nod the girl walked on, her fair hair uncovered by a hat and catching the sun. Rozenn paid for the rabbit. That girl was right: it was barely enough for two of them. She ought to have taken the ration books into Lannion, but the shopkeepers probably wouldn't have let her purchase anything. Perhaps Papa could register them there instead for food. The empty string bag flapped against her legs.

'Martine.' A boy of about Rozenn's age came out of an alleyway, greeting the girl with the fair hair with a kiss to each cheek. He whispered something to her and they made for a steep alleyway. Rozenn heard boots coming towards her. A German. Of course – you were always being watched around here.

'Papers, Mademoiselle.' She was a new face in a place where civilians were not welcome at the moment. Her hand was on the satchel buckle when she remembered that the black-market rabbit was in there. The German's eyes were cold but appraising.

She inserted one hand gingerly and managed to pull the papers out without the rabbit appearing. Illicit food purchasing was probably just a French police matter, anyway, she told herself.

'*Voilà.*' She handed him her ID card and permit.

'Why are you in residence in the zone?' He looked her up and down. 'It is forbidden. No civilians. How did you get in?'

'My father's the new doctor.'

'Where do you live?'

'Up in the *longère* on the cliffs.'

'With your *famille*? You are registered?'

'That's right.' Any moment now he'd ask for details about who the family comprised.

'And you are . . .' He looked at her ID again. 'Eighteen years old, nearly nineteen?' His tone was on the verge of menacing, as though he wanted to find something to accuse her of doing. Could he tell by looking at her that there was a fugitive up in the house?

'*Oui.*'

He handed back the papers, nodded and walked away.

'It's because you're a stranger,' a voice said behind her.

The same boy who'd strolled up the alleyway with the girl. He must have parted company with her and circled back.

'*Mat ar jeu,*' he added. Papa had taught them a few Breton words and she returned the greeting.

'Are there many of them around?' she added in French, not wanting to draw any more attention to herself but feeling a longing to talk to someone her own age. Something about that last encounter had shaken her in a way she hadn't felt back in Paris. The boy was local, certainly no picture of metropolitan smartness, but he was well-dressed and his expression quizzical and bright. He was looking her up and down, noting her clothes. Her sandals. Her bare legs, which she was shaving as stockings were becoming rare. She shuffled under his gaze.

'They've been patrolling the fleet for months, but as they get going on their fortifications, more artillerymen are appearing. The new ones are more aggressive to civilians and they'll be watching you, even when you can't see them, unless you know how to keep yourself out of their sight.' He finished his examination of her, and turned his attention to a loose thread on his jacket sleeve. 'Paris girl, aren't you? Might be hard for you to go unnoticed. What's your name?'

'Rozenn Guillou.'

He nodded. 'A good Breton name.' His accent had a slight Breton sing-song to it and he rolled his Rs.

'My parents were both from Rennes. I was born there, too.' How easy it was to make it sound as though there had just been the one of them born.

'But you've always lived in the city?'

She nodded. A longing for Paris swept her, for the lime trees, the clatter and scrape of coffee cups and glasses on zinc café table-tops, to be there at this strange part of the afternoon when the city seemed to hold its breath between the rush of the business day and the whirl of the early evening. She'd have given anything to hear the whoosh as a metro train drew in to a station, to feel the breath of warm, metallic air on her face that had once irritated her because it disturbed her hair.

'Must be a bit lonely for you here?'

She looked down, unwilling to show weakness, her desire to see her friends.

'What's it like in Paris?' His eyes were curious. How could she explain the city to someone like him? He'd probably never even left the province.

'Grim. They move the curfew around to punish us. They take most of the food. In the winter it was freezing but there was barely any coal.' She shivered, remembering how they'd huddled around the stove in the kitchen as Maman struggled to keep it going on the paltry fuel allowance.

'Same here. They push us around as if it's their country, not ours.' His shoulders stiffened. She looked at him more closely. Despite the accent he was obviously educated and from a fairly prosperous family. His jacket was good-quality cotton, although not cut in a way Theo would have chosen. He wasn't distinguished-looking but he wasn't bad for a local boy.

'I hate them.' She was taking a risk speaking like this to a stranger.

'Of course you do. Why should you be trying to make that skinny rabbit you bought into a meal while they dine on the pick of the catch?'

'That woman won't even sell me asparagus.'

'I'll have a word with her.' He said it so casually, as though he were mayor of the place instead of just a kid her age.

'What's your name?' He seemed to know an awful lot and she felt a need to redress the balance.

'Luc. Luc Caradec.' His eyes twinkled at her briefly. 'Must go.' He sounded brisk, like a man twice his age. What did he do? she wondered.

'Luc? *Tu viens?*' That same girl as before – was she everywhere in St Martin?

'You again.' Her cool blue eyes appraised Rozenn, taking in the dress that was still smart, if on the short side, the sandals that no longer looked as they had done when they'd been bought on the Boulevard Haussmann last summer. The girl wore wooden-soled shoes. On the lapel of her dress was a small pin with a Breton flag on it. A nationalist. Some of them supported the Germans, Papa said.

'You've already met our newcomer, Rozenn?' Luc asked. At least he had some manners. Rozenn extended a hand.

'Martine.' She was pretty enough, this Martine. Round, even-faced with full pink lips. Her fair hair was carefully combed into an almost-fashionable long bob. She was as slim as Rozenn herself, but with a more developed chest. More access to butter and cream, perhaps.

'You're living up in the *longère*, aren't you?' Martine smiled. 'How are you getting on in the dear old place?'

'You know it?'

'We lived there once. Before we moved on to somewhere more convenient. We live in the harbour master's house now.'

'With your pigs?' Rozenn opened her eyes wide. Martine flushed slightly. Rozenn cursed herself: that sharp tongue of hers. She'd make an enemy of this girl and in a small village you couldn't do that. '*Pardon,*' she added. 'I didn't mean to sound rude.'

'Want to go down to the quay?' Martine shuffled so that the question was directed solely at Luc.

He shrugged. 'Why not?'

'*À bientôt*,' Martine told Rozenn brightly. Was she Luc's girl-friend? What a couple they made in this little place, he in his smart summer jacket, she in her frock that fitted her so well and that wave of blonde hair. Well, good for them. In the *seizième* the two of them would be passable, nothing more. Rozenn heard Theo's laugh in her ear. *That sharp tongue of yours again, Mademoiselle Guillou . . .*

Sharp or feeling sorry for herself because she had nobody to smoke with in the afternoon sun? Nobody to share a joke or a piece of gossip with? Rozenn turned to trudge back up the footpath to the cliffs. She caught a glimpse of Luc and Martine as they upended barrels to sit on and lit one another's cigarettes. A couple of cats lay in the sunshine on the worn stones, probably waiting for the discarded bits of the catch. Rozenn turned away, hit by a pang of homesickness. Only weeks ago she and a group had taken what passed for a picnic into the Bois de Boulogne. They'd smirked at the sight of a plump German sergeant trying to catch their eye and smile at them. *Not even if I were dying . . . Not even if he offered me an enormous* filet de boeuf.

It had all been taken from her: the apartment, the cafés, the friends. Blasted, blasted war. *Sales Boches*. If she'd had a rock to throw through the window of the hotel bar she would have done it.

Coming down the footpath came the clop of hooves. A donkey, piled high with baskets of what looked like potatoes. A woman, toothless, old, led him. She nodded at Rozenn, her wrinkled face suspicious, as Rozenn stood back to let them pass. Claire would like the donkey even if that old woman scowled at her. Thinking of her sister brought the familiar ache of guilt. Not so much whining from Claire now. She seemed to have accepted her new home, enjoying the gardening, tolerating lessons, singing to herself.

She could perhaps bring Claire down at this time of the afternoon to see the cats on the quay before the boats came in. It seemed quiet, nobody around to hear her prattle about Yann.

As she approached the house Maman and Claire were outside the larger outbuilding, winding sheets through a mangle though it was surely too late in the afternoon for them to dry on the line? The coastal breeze always seemed to hold a little moisture. Despite her best intentions Rozenn felt her feet grow heavy in their worn sandals. Just as she hadn't had time to go to the market, Maman probably hadn't had time to wring out the washing this morning. Claire was fascinated with the mangle. Maman had to keep stopping to prevent her from trying to poke her fingers into it. Rozenn should offer to take Claire off again, but the walk had made her thirsty and she wanted to sit down in the shade. She groaned silently to herself. She was being selfish, always had been, knowing what she wanted and prepared to do what was needed to achieve it. It was the peril of being the middle child, the one left to her own devices.

If she stayed in St Martin little by little she'd be pulled into doing more of these endless chores: laundry, minding Claire, trying to buy food. Feeling guilty every time she escaped from the grind. She needed to return to the city. Find a job. Papa might know a doctor who needed a receptionist. Even better, she could research universities, extend her education. Some friends from *lycée* planned to do this, now the Occupation seemed to be going on and on and the universities still operated.

Rozenn winced as her worn sole trod on a sharp stone. Let the rest of the family hide out here. She couldn't stand the place a week longer.

12

Jenny and Sam, the owners of the barn, had gone quiet on me. I texted them from Vue Claire, saying that I was driving back to London in three days' time and could pop in if they wanted to talk further. Gwen's new washing machine and dishwasher had arrived. I hosed down the jetty, watered and weeded the garden and mowed the lawn. *Would you like me to do some more painting for you?* I messaged her, keen not to be seen as the family sad case, the one spoken about in soft tones. I wanted talk of changing wills to be dropped. I wanted the feeling of tightness in my chest whenever I thought about Rozenn to lift. I tried wrestling openly with my negative feelings, telling myself I was acting like a kid who'd been given a smaller Christmas present than her sibling. It was pathetic to be almost into your thirties and still feel like this. The accident and my failure to come to terms with it were influencing my emotions. None of that was Gwen's fault. Nor was it Rozenn's.

'I still want to buy my own place one day,' I told Dad when he called to find out how I was getting on. 'Some old wreck I can do up using my tradesmen's contacts.' I sounded defiant, but knew I was deluding myself to believe I'd ever afford to do this on my own. All the same I felt a little rush of pleasure at actually wanting to do something again.

'Nobody's better placed than you to do it, Morie,' Dad said. 'You've got the skills and determination. I remember how you and . . . how you built up your business when you started out. You wouldn't take no for an answer.' A pause. 'In that respect you remind me of your grandmother.'

'Do I?' I softened a little.

'There weren't that many practising female architects in the post-war years. Those owning their own practice were even less common. Especially in the areas she chose.'

Those factories. How unfeminine, people must have thought before they met her. I smiled, picturing her in one of her beautifully cut but verging on the austere trouser-suits, a pair of low-heeled but elegant boots and a dab of lipstick, walking on to a building site to inspect progress, workmen staring at her. None of them would have dared whistle at her.

'I hate this wretched will coming between you and Gwen.'

I blinked. Every time I moved on from the bequest, one of them reminded me what had happened. 'It isn't. What does annoy me is people feeling sorry for me. I really don't deserve it.' I sounded like a whiny teenager.

Dad laughed. 'That's Rozenn in you again. She hated pity too. I remember a friend of hers coming to dinner and telling her how sorry she felt for her. Papa had recently died and Maman had no family apart from me. She nearly spat ball bearings at her friend. "I have everything I desire," she told the woman.'

Rozenn had certainly made the most of her small family. While Mum had still been alive we'd seen her regularly. As well as Vue Claire Rozenn had owned a small maisonette in Twickenham, not so far from Barnes. When Mum died she'd come over to stay with us if Dad was away on business or needed her to attend sports days or school concerts. I remembered her cooking us wonderful dinners, tutting at Dad's poor choice of cooking pots and kitchen knives, pressing the school uniforms she so despised into immaculate creases. At the weekend she'd driven us down to Cornwall.

I'd only just finished the call with Dad when a text message came through from my landlord. I saw I'd missed a call from him while I'd been talking to Dad.

I've already let the others know, but I've just got a permanent contract in South Africa and so I'll be selling the flat. Please take this as a month's notice.

So, about to lose my accommodation too. I let out a hollow laugh. Though it was almost a relief to know that my time in that cluttered flat was coming to an end. I'd find something else.

I listened to my own soothing internal voice but still felt an urge to carry on burying myself in Vue Claire, pretending none of this was happening. Before I could stop myself I texted Gwen again. *If you don't need decorating is there anything else I can do for you down here? No urgency for me to get back to London.*

How long were you thinking of staying? she replied. She was probably worried she'd never get me out of the place, that I'd set myself up as some kind of sitting tenant she'd never be able to evict. If she found out about the Brentford tenancy ending she'd be even more concerned. This was my sister, I told myself. Why should she see dark motives in my actions? I needed to stop second-guessing the response of my family to everything I said and did. All the same, I'd wait to tell her about the flat until I'd left Cornwall. My phone pinged with another message from Gwen.

Could arrange delivery and installation of new oven hob tomorrow, if you could stay on a night thx. Could you air Rozenn's quilt on the line and pack away – beautiful but too warm for summer.

I texted back that I'd stay in for the hob and sort out the quilt. A slight breeze had picked up. Through the open French windows I could hear the pinging of the ropes on the little sailing boats beached on the shingle. I went upstairs. Rozenn's quilt was indeed beautiful: embroidered in oyster-coloured silk thread on a satin background. Rozenn had found it in a market in Paris on one of the trips she'd taken us on and spent a small fortune having it professionally restored. I held the quilt up to my face briefly, its smooth texture comforting. Perhaps I'd been too proud when Gwen had offered me anything I wanted from the house and I'd accepted the cooking pot and nothing else.

As I folded the quilt my mobile fell out of my back pocket, sliding under the bed. I put the quilt down and knelt on the carpet, lowering my head to look for it. The phone lay close to the wall. I'd have to move the bed and squeeze my hand down to pull it out. The sleigh-bed was heavy and it took me some time to heave it away from the wall. As my fingers reached down towards the carpet for the phone, they touched something else. Paper: caught between the base of the bed and the wall. I pulled it up. A sheet of thick writing paper, handwritten in black ink. I put it down while I extracted my mobile.

A letter to Rozenn. Should I read it? What did one do with opened private letters found after someone died? Tear them up, unread? I stood up, intending to text Dad and ask if he wanted to see it. It was in French. I spoke and read the language fluently, not merely because Rozenn often talked to us in French, but because I'd spent a year after I'd left school working on a dig in the Cevennes. I caught sight of my own name. After that it was impossible to stop reading.

> . . . *in touch with Morane myself, perhaps by email if you could give me her address. In the meantime, I really wanted to write to you again the old-fashioned way even though I love our telephone calls. I'm so pleased, ma très chère Rozenn, that we've found our way back to one another, to the closeness we shared in St Martin,*

even though it's so very late for both of us. I'm producing
something . . .

That was all. The first and subsequent pages must have been thrown out. I couldn't believe that Rozenn would have done this deliberately but it might have been accidentally caught up in a newspaper and placed in the recycling bin, which would long since have been emptied.

The writer of the letter said they'd be . . . *in touch with Morane myself.* Who were they? I'd received no email or letter. I'd been careful to fill in a change-of-address form when I'd moved to Brentford. I texted one of my flatmates there and asked if any private mail had come for me.

Just a few catalogues and what looks like a bank statement, the answer came back. I thought of mentioning the sale of the flat, but was too impatient to find out about the mysterious communication from Rozenn's correspondent. I texted the landlord of the flat I'd shared with Nick before the split. He replied immediately, saying he'd been over just the previous day and nothing had arrived for me.

I put down the letter and took the quilt outside to hang on the line, thinking. When I came inside again I photographed the page and forwarded the image on to Dad and Gwen. *Any idea who this friend of Rozenn's might be and why they're going to be in touch with me?!*

How intriguing! Not a clue, sorry, Gwen texted. Dad rang up and we spent twenty minutes trying to think of any of Rozenn's friends who would have been writing to her in French.

'I don't remember her mentioning anyone at all from France,' he said. 'Let alone from this St Martin place specifically. Anyone she knew as a child would probably be dead by now.'

'Did we check her emails?' I asked. Rozenn had kept an old and stately desktop PC. She'd used email and shopped online occasionally, preferring to make trips to London to buy her – usually very expensive – clothes.

'Maman gave me her password some time ago and I went through her messages when we were planning the funeral,' Dad said. 'There were a few emails from friends, but they were all English.' He was quiet for a few moments. 'I'm afraid I'm no graphologist and can't even work out if the writer of that bit of letter is male or female.'

'What about her phone bills? Could we look at them?'

'I checked the latest statements briefly after she died, but didn't go through them number by number as they seemed to be in order. They're all shredded now and I closed the account with BT.'

Dad couldn't tell me any more. I texted Gwen again, asking if she'd mind me stripping the bed to see if the rest of the letter might have become caught up between the mattress topper and wall.

As long as it's made up so J and I can crash when we're down late on Friday – busy week for both of us.

James was travelling, I remembered. Was Gwen giving me a gentle hint that she'd want Vue Claire for their exclusive use and I was to be gone by the end of the week? I removed the duvet and peeled off its cover. Nothing there. Or under the fitted bottom sheet or in the high-cotton-count pillowcases and protectors. I shone my mobile's torch between mattress and wall. No sheets of writing paper. My phone alerted me to another message. Dad.

I've made a discovery, he messaged back. *See attachment!*

It was a scanned image that I had to squint to read. A birth certificate. *Luc Caradec*. He'd been born somewhere that looked like St M . . ., near Lannion. St Martin, I saw when I enlarged the image. The same place referred to in the letter I'd found. Luc had been born there and it seemed that my grandmother had a connection with it too. I opened my maps app and found the village on the coast in central northern Brittany. Gwen'd related that conversation she'd heard in the pub about people sailing back and forth between this estuary and Brittany during the war, carrying out all kinds of clandestine activity. We had no idea how Rozenn might have been involved in this but our grandfather had been born in an area of Brittany that looked as though it might have been a striking point for Cornwall. Coincidence? Although we'd assumed their relationship had started once they'd reached England, she'd never actually told us this.

I texted Dad again, asking if he knew more about how his parents had met.

She really only talked about their life in London. But come to think of it, I do vaguely remember my father talking about disembarking in Helford. Not sure whether it was with Maman or not. Do you think it's significant, Morie?

His last sentence probably meant, *why are you obsessing about this and not getting on with building up your business?*

Not sure, I answered. *Just wondered whether they'd known one another in Brittany before they arrived in England, if they'd planned to leave together.*

Amid the stress of leaving wartime Paris, and then France itself, for England, Rozenn might not have considered a short stay in Brittany as very meaningful.

But if she had met her future husband over there, Brittany would have meant something to her, surely? It was strange that she hadn't talked about it. Even if they hadn't met there, she and Luc both had roots in the region.

I wondered how she'd felt when Dad and Mum had given us those Breton names? Thrilled at the continued connection?

Our names, I texted Dad. *Was R pleased G and I had Breton names?*

106

R said your mother was obsessed with all things Celtic and that nobody in England would be able to spell them, but they were pretty names. And talking of obsession, Morie . . .

He was right. I ought to be thinking about my own future, not Rozenn's past. I'd allowed myself to become distracted.

Back upstairs I remade Gwen's bed, carefully fitting the sheets crisply around the mattress. I shoved the bed back against the wall, my mind somewhere else, across the Channel and beyond.

13

Papa brought back a battered copy of *Marie Claire* the following day when he returned for lunch. 'The wife of one of the surveyors working on the cliffs has it mailed to her,' he told Rozenn as she all but snatched it from him. 'Part-payment for treating his ingrowing toenail. Never let it be said that this new job doesn't have its rewards.'

Rozenn hugged him, surprised at how cheered she felt by this connection with the old world after a morning spent in the vegetable garden. Maman laughed. 'A tatty old magazine and you might have won a thousand francs, Rozenn.' She put out a hand for the magazine. 'No reading until you've set the table.'

'*Moi.*' Claire walked in, hand out for the magazine. Before publications had become so sparse and paper so rationed she'd liked cutting out pictures from old magazines and newspapers and sticking them into her scrapbook. Maman put the magazine on the top shelf of the dresser.

'Only when we've finished reading it.'

'*Non, non.*' Claire tried to jump up and pull it down. Her sleeve swept against the handle of a jug. Rozenn caught it in mid-air.

'*Arrête.* Stop.' Maman took Claire's wrists. Claire's lip trembled. She'd been fractious all morning.

'Claire.' Yann came in, a small wooden object in his hand. 'Look what I've made for you.' It was a carved horse, with a mane made from what looked like frayed rope. Claire's eyes opened with wonder. She squatted on the floor, making clicking noises as she cantered the horse across the rug.

Rozenn eyed Yann with fresh appreciation. 'I didn't know you could carve wood.'

He shrugged. 'Passes the time. And it's interesting working in three dimensions.'

After lunch, which seemed to comprise mainly root vegetables boiled with lentils in a stew followed by a tin of peaches shared between the five of them, Maman told Rozenn she could sit outside and read the magazine. 'Once the washing up is done, I'll take Claire for a walk. She needs some exercise, don't you, *chérie?*' Claire was humming to herself as she scraped her spoon around the empty bowl. Maman never looked at Rozenn with the gentle expression she used for Claire.

But, she reminded herself, Maman was giving her time off to read the magazine without being pestered by Claire. Perhaps this was her way of caring for the tougher twin, the middle child who didn't need as much attention as the others.

When Maman had placed Claire's straw hat on her and led her down the lane, Rozenn sat on one of the two old deckchairs they'd found in the outhouse. Papa took the other chair. 'Just ten minutes.' He stretched out his legs with a sigh. 'Before I head out around the farms. Tomorrow morning I'm down in the village and it will be good to stay in one place. The Germans have roadblocks everywhere.'

The surgery in St Martin was tiny, barely space for Papa, the desk and examination table and one patient. No receptionist. No running water in the room – he relied on a jug and basin of water to wash his hands between patients. 'So different from Paris,' she said.

'Different isn't necessarily worse.' He glanced at her. 'Oh, I miss the lunches in my favourite restaurants and the income, the nights at the opera, but this lifestyle has compensations.'

He was letting himself sink into the place, she thought. Slowing down, blinkering himself to the Occupation.

'I'm aware this place isn't ideal for you, though. We'll make a plan for you, Rozenn, once Yann is away.'

She wondered what exactly he was doing about getting Yann out. Making inquiries in Lannion? Writing to friends back in Paris? He'd closed his eyes. She didn't want to disturb him by asking more questions. Rozenn turned to her magazine. The mannequin wore a small straw hat, though even giving it the same name as the object worn by Claire seemed wrong. This hat was small and neat, angled on the mannequin's head. Rozenn could imagine herself wearing something like that to the races. Maman's raffia bag would go well with it: close enough in shade to match but different enough in texture to look interesting. The raffia bag had been left in Paris, locked away in the wardrobe, so at least some German Frau couldn't get her porky fingers on it.

She turned the pages, trying to be disciplined and not gobble it all up at once. Before the war *Marie Claire* had been a Paris publication. Now it was published in the *Zone Libre*. Judging by the variety of lipstick colours displayed in one of the advertisements, life down there was more indulgent than it was up in the north. Or perhaps it was just propaganda. Rozenn had a single lipstick in the top drawer of the chest she shared with Claire, hidden in a sock so that Claire couldn't smear it round her lips like a clown. Rozenn flicked through the pages, pausing at a photograph of a platter of fish, artichokes, lettuces and radishes with an exhortation for readers to eat nutritious food.

Despite Rozenn's vow to save some of the articles for later she found her attention caught by a piece on the '12 Things Most

Likely to Get You Fired from Your Job'. The women in the accompanying photographs seemed unlikely to fall into these traps. Their manicured hands juggled telephone receivers and diaries. They opened filing cabinets as they smiled at their male bosses. Could life still be like this? They didn't have German soldiers on the streets in the south, that was true, but could there still be a life preoccupied with getting on in the office, buying clothes and make-up and preparing nutritious food? If so, what on earth was the Guillou family doing up here on a windblown northern headland that would soon resemble a fortress? She wanted the life of the girls in the magazine.

Rozenn muttered something to Papa and stood up. Reading the magazine was supposed to have been a treat but it had flung up something that felt very close to jealousy. She was being silly; life in the south was probably no picnic.

She knocked on the half-open outbuilding door. Yann had cleared the floor of the old agricultural implements and swept it. On an improvised desk made from old pallets sat a few pieces of wood and a knife, along with his sketchbook. A muttered greeting reached her. Yann was face down on the floor, propped up on his hands, sweat beading on his brow. 'Should have left more time after lunch before doing press-ups,' he gasped.

'How many are you doing?'

'Building up to a hundred a day. In batches of ten.' He sat up. 'And there's that.' He nodded at a keg in the corner.

'What's that for?'

'Try to pick it up.'

She squeezed her fingers through the handle and lifted it, blinking at the unexpected weight. 'It's got sand in it,' Yann said. 'Try bending your legs, push up through your back.' This time she managed to lift it above her shoulders.

'Not bad,' he said, standing up.

'It's killing my fingers.' She winced and put the keg down.

'If we can find another one I'm going to make a bar out of a broom handle.'

'You'll be very fit.'

'I have to do something while I'm waiting for, well, whatever it is I *am* waiting for.'

'Are you very bored?'

'Sometimes I feel like volunteering to help the surveyors out on the cliffs.' He smiled at her face. 'Just joking, but I can't stay in here all the time. I've been going down to the cove that hasn't been wired off.'

'What?' So that was where the sand in the keg had come from.

'I think I can get away with it.'

'It's light until so late this time of year.'

'Once I'm clear of the footpath it's not likely a patrol would see me.'

She turned away.

'What is it?'

'We came here because it was safer for you. But already we're chipping away at all the things that make it safe.'

He got up, eyes lowered. 'You've given up a lot for me.'

She could never be angry with him for long. 'I'm not the only one. Have you seen Maman's hands from doing the laundry?'

'She's happier, though.'

Rozenn was going to dispute that, but then thought of Maman singing to herself as she worked in the garden.

'And Claire seems content.'

'Until it's winter and dark and rainy.' Rozenn remembered a school trip to the natural history museum in Paris and staring at tiny creatures preserved in amber. That's what would become of her: an insect, imprisoned here, paralysed while the war lasted, her brain slowing down, her complexion growing weathered, countrified.

Yann stood up. 'Keep working on your drawing skills,' he said. 'I am, too. I know what I want to do now, when this is all over.'

'Oh?'

He picked up a pile of the American comics he'd brought with him from Paris. Their ends were curling up and the paper yellowing – there hadn't been any new editions for almost a year now. 'These.'

'You're serious? They're just for kids, surely?'

'Adults like them too. But it's not just cartoons in print form. It's film, too. Moving pictures out of cartoons. We've only seen a few over here. But I think it's the future.'

She looked over to Yann's own sketchbook. 'May I?'

He handed it to her. He'd drawn people dressed as cats, scaling walls, walking upside down on the ceiling with suckers on their feet. One of the cats wore a Breton beret. In another scene Yann had made the cat roll himself into a ball and launch himself like a bowl at a line of square-jawed skittles dressed in German uniform, sending them flying.

She laughed and handed it back to him. 'I just hope you've got a safe place to hide it in case the Germans ever search this barn.' Mocking the invaders was the kind of thing that could land you in prison. If only they really did have a superhero like Yann's cat to throw them out of the country. In London there was General de Gaulle and the Free French, but what could they do from across the sea?

'Don't worry, I'll hide them.'

If you have time when they hammer on the door in the middle of the night. She tried to repress a shudder, remembering the woman in their building in Paris who'd been arrested.

'One day I'll go to America,' Yann said. 'I'll work in one of the new studios where they make films out of cartoon images.' The boy who'd been the despair of Maman and Papa for his lack of focus sounded so determined.

'Like *Snow White*?' They'd seen the film in Paris, three years ago, when it first came out in French. It was like nothing else Rozenn had seen: the moving figures, the music.

'Yes.' With so many frames, so many characters to draw and colour in, surely those studios must need talent like Yann's?

'You'd be brilliant at that.'

He nodded, modest but accepting the praise. Yann was always honest about his own abilities. If he thought he could do something well, he could.

'And you, Rozenn, you will design beautiful buildings.'

'I will?' She felt a flush of confidence in her own ability.

He nodded. 'I've seen you as you walk around this place. How you look at every centimetre of wall and assess it. You've got an eye for it. You're thinking about what you'd do if you owned the house, aren't you?'

She sat down on the old mattress he was using as a sofa. 'I'd enlarge the windows in the kitchen,' she said. 'So it has a sea view. And I'd definitely put in an indoor lavatory and a bathroom, extending into the outbuildings possibly.'

'What?' He feigned indignation.

'You must admit the current arrangements are primitive.'

Yann screwed up his nose in agreement. Despite Maman's efforts, the smell in the outdoor privy was still pungent. 'Even the POW camp had better facilities than that.'

She looked at him for a second, not wanting to say anything that would remind him of that place. 'You could extend the size of the bedrooms upstairs,' she continued. 'Perhaps put in a fourth. This place was designed for people living with animals but it could be so much more.'

Yann had his eyes half-closed, listening.

'They must have oriented it away from the coast so they were protected from the wind,' she said. 'They probably didn't have time for sitting around admiring the view like us idle Parisians. It could be so special. I wouldn't do anything that spoils it, though. The house has its own beauty, the long line of it, the way the outbuildings nestle up beside it. The granite stone.' She could hear the enthusiasm in her own voice and it surprised her.

'Not such a city girl after all, eh?'

'I miss Paris,' she said. 'Having the world at our front door: libraries, parks, shops. Even in the Occupation. If I knew we'd be going home in a few weeks' time I'd be happy here.' It was the crushing sensation of knowing the stay could go on for months: Yann keeping himself hidden – but for how long? Rozenn herself deprived of books and stimulation. The weather turning to autumn and then winter.

'One day you'll have your clear view of the sea and your place in the city. If that's what you want, that's what you'll have, Rozenn.'

She barely knew what to say. 'I'll let you get on.' She stood up. 'Just be very careful if you go out swimming at night.'

Rozenn blinked as she walked into the bright sunshine. As her eyes grew used to the light she spotted Maman and Claire returning from their walk. Well, Maman was walking. Still clutching her wooden horse Claire sprang along, stopping and squatting every few metres to examine an insect or flower. Maman stopped patiently each time. Something about the scene simultaneously irritated and pulled at Rozenn. Claire could be living with them for years. Perhaps she'd never return to the convent. Maman's life would be completely taken up with caring for her: cutting up her food at mealtimes, trying to teach her as much as possible. The fashionable woman who'd read all the latest novels, visited all the new exhibitions and seen all the latest plays would lose all the things she'd once relished.

Claire spotted Rozenn and waved. '*Cheval*, Claire.'

'Yann's so clever.'

'No, a real horse.'

Rozenn looked at Maman. 'A real horse indeed,' she said. 'Ridden by a real and unusual woman.'

Claire clutched at imaginary reins, clicking her tongue at her mount.

'We met her on the track,' Maman said. 'She talked to us, said Claire could come and look at the *chiots* her spaniel has had.'

'*Chiots.*' Claire gave a series of high-pitched yaps.

'She's Irish,' Maman went on.

'What's an Irish woman doing here?'

'Perhaps she's a neutral subject. Your father mentioned something about a woman living in a manor house near here with German officers billeted on her. One of them has an eye infection and he paid a house call.'

'What happens,' Rozenn asked, 'when the Germans come up to fetch Papa because someone's had an accident and Claire's babbling on about Yann? Do we just say he's a make-believe friend? If they take her seriously and search the place, they'll find him.'

Maman seemed to slump. 'I know,' she muttered. 'We can't go on like this. It's dangerous – for everyone. For now they're not treating us too badly.'

Rozenn made a scoffing noise.

'They take our food but it's not like it is for civilians in Poland,' Maman said defensively.

'Sooner or later someone's going to blow up a barracks,' Rozenn said. 'Or pull out a gun and shoot high-ranking German officers. The Germans will retaliate harshly. They've already started mistreating the Jews.'

Maman's gaze switched to Claire, who was twirling around on one foot, singing to herself. 'If something happened to your father and me I dread to think what would become of her.'

'I'd look after her.' Rozenn heard the words emerge from her mouth with surprise. Claire had always been a nuisance, an embarrassment. The day, years ago, she'd left with Papa for the convent, Rozenn felt a boulder lift from her shoulders. She could invite friends back to the apartment without worrying about Claire doing something inappropriate. But when that boy on the train had called Claire an imbecile, laughed at her, it had unleashed some protective instinct in Rozenn.

Maman's hand, wrinkled and red nowadays, was gentle on her arm. 'You are a good sister to her, *chérie*. But what if the Germans arrested you too?'

Rozenn wanted to laugh. Here they stood, in June sunshine, a middle-class family, professional, respected, with resources, talking about being arrested as though they were criminals in their own country. Would the Germans take Claire as well? Would it be better for her to be in some squalid camp with her family or sent by herself to some institution?

'Yann has to leave as soon as possible.' She looked at Maman, expecting opposition. But something passed between them, some understanding. It wasn't just about Yann, it was about Claire, too.

'*Oui.*' For the first time she could remember Rozenn had the feeling that Maman and she wanted the same thing.

Wanting something wasn't enough. Someone had to act. And it seemed Rozenn was the only one who would.

14

Stay as long as you want, Morie, Gwen texted me. *Delay until the weekend and spend some time with us? I'm sure we can find plenty of work to do on the house!*

I imagined her talking to James, discussing ways of making me feel useful. I knew I should leave. Vue Claire would start to embrace me too closely. The new induction hob was now in place in the kitchen. I'd finally worked out how to turn on a plate to prepare scrambled eggs for my dinner. I took a mug of coffee into the room I still thought of as Rozenn's *salon.* The evening sun poured in. Gwen had chosen the right paint: it didn't distract from the view of the estuary through the windows, but was an inviting colour, encouraging you to sit and relax. I ought to take some photographs on my phone and send them to her so she could see how well it worked, but something stopped me. Gwen and I were both trying so hard. Too hard.

The pile of loose photographs was still stacked on the table. I flicked through them slowly, taking out the pictures of the very young Rozenn: the first where she beamed into the camera and the second showing her more guarded and wearing a different swimming costume. I laid the two pictures side by side on the sofa next to me and examined them closely, checking the background. In each photo a volleyball net was placed at the same position behind

Rozenn, its shadow falling at the same angle. The clouds drifting in from the sea were identical. The same dachshund sniffed at the sand.

So the photographs were taken at the same time or a minute or so apart on the same day. The guileless, beaming version of Rozenn had a small mark under her left cheekbone. A drip from an ice cream wiped away before the next picture was taken? But why change her swimming costume when the original still looked pristine?

A riddle. A spot-the-difference puzzle. Perhaps Rozenn's mother had liked dressing her small daughter up in different outfits and photographing them. Plenty of mothers on Instagram did the same thing nowadays. Thinking of Instagram made me think of Tatiana and her relentless trawling of home-decor influencers. One of these days she'd see something on her stream that would provoke her into wanting a completely different house in a new neighbourhood – by tomorrow.

I glanced at the closed laptop I had brought downstairs with me so that I could catch up on work. But my grandmother and her past were still tugging at me. Once this visit was over I would probably never be alone in Vue Claire again, free to potter around Rozenn's possessions without feeling awkward. Dad planned on taking most of the photos back to his house next time he visited. If I wanted to search for more information about Rozenn now was probably the last and best chance. I went to the dresser to pick up the photo album.

I turned the pages, seeing Luc dressed in the well-cut wedding suit that reappeared frequently in subsequent photographs. Rozenn wore a series of simple dresses that must have outshone other women's clothes in austerity post-war Britain. On her finger was a small diamond ring. Luc had been doing well by now. Dad had told me that the fish wholesale business had flourished in the fifties and sixties. 'They called my father the Frogmonger,' he said. 'Probably not kindly at first. But Papa had charm, charisma. He turned the Frogmonger moniker to his own advantage, even made a logo for his van.' I'd seen a photograph of the vehicle with its beret-wearing frog carrying a lobster over a shoulder and a basket of sardines in the other hand.

Grand-père Luc had a long obituary in *The Grocer* when he died. Rozenn had pasted this into the album, along with a few snippets from society diaries in the *Daily Mail*. Luc had 'Gallic flair', an eye for the 'juiciest' catches. I wondered if this was a suggestion that he'd been a ladies' man, as it would have been called back then. He certainly had the looks, with that wide mouth and those expressive eyes.

There was a photograph of the two of them in a nightclub, Rozenn wearing her hair shoulder length and swept behind a band, Jackie Kennedy style, Luc in a dinner jacket and black tie, his eyes creased up as he smiled at someone off-camera. At this time Rozenn had also been bringing up Dad, studying for her architecture degree and slowly starting to find work for herself. I couldn't imagine how hard it must have been at a time when working and studying mothers weren't supported with nurseries and efficient household gadgets.

And then there'd been Luc's drinking.

'In the beginning, he was what they called a social drinker,' Dad had told me, soon after Nick had left. 'But eventually he couldn't function without the brandy with his breakfast at some fish-market café, the midday gin and tonic and the one-for-the-road whisky before he came home.'

I knew the point he was making. It had been online gambling for Nick, not drink. For fun at first, using free bets dangled by bookies, distracting himself from the work of supporting me. He'd done well, without risking his own money, and used some of the early profits to take me out for meals in restaurants, trying to bolster me. He'd even managed to get hold of tickets for *Hamilton*. The hours in the theatre had made me feel lighter, even if only temporarily. And he'd bought me the most beautiful handbag, one I'd lusted after for months, unable to justify the expense. 'Thought it might help cheer you up,' he said. 'Before . . . Well, a while back I saw you gawping at it online.'

'I never dreamt I could own something like this.' I was stroking the oxblood leather, examining the clasps and buckles, planning where I could take the bag to, what I'd wear, what Gwen would say when she saw it.

I wondered if Luc had bought presents for Rozenn to apologise for the times he'd been too drunk to make the drives between London and Cornwall or the times she'd had to write him a cheque to cover a bill. Eventually he'd suffered a series of strokes that incapacitated him so seriously he'd given up his business.

The photographs of Rozenn in the seventies, after Luc's death, showed a woman in middle age with a guarded yet amused expression on her face. Gone was the openness of that little girl in the photograph on the beach or the older girl who'd drawn the birds and mice with such relish.

Something about those photographs of her on the beach was nagging at me. I couldn't work out what it was. I needed fresh air. Work could wait. I pulled on the light walking shoes I'd brought down with me and, taking only my phone, went out through the back door, hearing it close behind me, putting the key in my pocket.

The tide in the creek was out. I jumped down on to the exposed shingle, my feet beating out a pleasant rhythm as I walked. A white bird with long black legs and beak waded through a shallow pool of water. An egret? Dad would know. I snapped the bird on my phone to send it to him later. A good artist, like Rozenn, would have been able to catch the bird's movement with a few dashes of a pencil. I remembered her drawings of birds and mice and smiled, walking on, heading up to the estuary, turning to follow it downstream and climbing up on to the footpath. What a shame she hadn't returned to drawing when she'd obviously been so talented and the area she lived in during retirement was so rich with wildlife.

My sluggishness had vanished. I wanted to walk on and on, my legs, my whole body falling into a hypnotic rhythm. I could cross Gillan Creek at the stepping stones at low tide and walk south around the headland to the start of the Lizard Peninsula with its rocky cliffs and coves, carry on and on along the coast. I checked the tide times on my mobile: not today – the stepping stones would be covered. I forced myself to turn around, noting that the water was higher now.

As I approached Vue Claire I saw the tide had actually risen enough for a small motorboat to pull up and moor at the end of the jetty. A friend of Rozenn's who didn't know she'd died? The rising tide forced me to jump up on to the footpath and approach from the front of the house. 'Hello?' I called as I opened the side gate. Footsteps rang out along the wooden jetty. I ran into the garden. One man was casting off, the other was at the wheel. I sprinted up the jetty, reaching the boat as it pulled away, spotting my laptop and Gwen's Bluetooth speaker in it, along with the wine from the fridge and some other objects I didn't have time to identify. 'Stop!' I yelled at them. The man who'd cast off waved something metallic at me – the blade of a knife. I gasped and stepped back. Pulling myself together, I took out my mobile and snapped the boat and its occupants as it roared away. A van was probably waiting for the stolen goods somewhere quiet upstream.

The back door was unlocked. I put a hand to my pocket and felt the key in it. Had I actually turned it in the lock as I left? Coldness washed through me. I tried to remember.

No sound of anyone else inside. I went into the kitchen and grabbed one of Rozenn's old carving knives from a drawer. The initial shock left me, replaced by nausea as I walked through the rooms. As well as the speaker and my laptop, Gwen's new coffee machine had gone. I backed up everything on to the Cloud, so none of my work was lost for good, but other than my mobile I had no way of accessing my projects for now. The silver compass – I couldn't see it. I threw the cushions off the chaise longue. There it was. I let out a sigh of relief. Something else was now exposed, protruding from the bottom of Rozenn's cashmere throw. The edge of a sheet of writing paper, matching the ivory sheet I'd found under Rozenn's bed. Our house-clearing obviously hadn't been thorough enough. I didn't have time to read it now – I had to call Gwen, but I could see it was the last page of a letter, written in French. I was reading the first sentence before I could stop myself.

I have set the St Martin plan in motion, so please tell the family what we've agreed, chère Rozenn . . .

St Martin, my grandfather's birthplace, mentioned again in connection with Rozenn herself. If the place was simply her long-deceased husband's former home, why would someone write to her about it three-quarters of a century later?

I ran upstairs to Rozenn's desk. The burglars obviously hadn't thought her cumbersome desktop computer worth stealing. I switched it on and waited, tapping my fingers, for it to load. I went into Rozenn's email, searching the inbox, the junk box, the deleted messages, for anything that might have come through since Dad last checked her account. Nothing.

This, I reminded myself, was not the priority. I had to ring the police and report the burglary and then tell Gwen what had happened. I dialled the non-emergency number. The operator was sympathetic and gave me a crime number but couldn't promise that anyone would be out to the house any time soon.

I called Gwen. We usually messaged one another, video calling sometimes.

'I'm fine and so's Dad, as far as I know,' I said hurriedly before she could worry about accidents or sudden illness. When I'd finished telling her about the burglary, she sighed. 'The French windows? Do we need to get a locksmith in?'

'They're fine.'

A pause. 'How did they break in?'

'The back door.'

'The lock was forced?'

'It was unlocked. I thought I'd locked it, though.' Another pause. I knew what she was thinking.

'I had the key in my pocket,' I added. Did I sound defensive?

'Insurance will cover it,' she said, sounding unconvinced. If the door was unlocked we both knew it wouldn't. 'When did it happen?'

I looked at the time on my phone. 'About forty minutes ago.'

'Oh.' She'd be thinking that I'd taken my time letting her know. I shuffled in the chair.

'Anyway,' I said. 'I'm really sorry. Of course I'll replace the coffee machine and speaker. And the wine.'

'You can't afford to do that.'

It was the truth. This month's credit-card bill was going to be hard enough and it only really comprised petrol and groceries: nothing non-essential. And without my laptop it was going to be hard to work. Recover from one blow and suffer another. But Gwen thought I was a loser, incapable even of locking up a house. I had to replace her stolen goods.

'I'm ordering them now. I'll stay on another day or so until they've been delivered.'

'You don't need to.'

She didn't want me in the house. I couldn't blame her. 'Or I can have them delivered when you and James come down?'

She sighed. 'We planned on hiring a boat if the weather's good, or popping over to the north coast to surf so I'm not sure when we'll be in. Hang on.' I heard her say something to someone in the office. 'They need me in a meeting.'

'I'll send the replacements to Sue. She can bring them over next time she's due here.' Sue was Rozenn's cleaning lady, now retained by Gwen.

'I've got to go, Morane.'

Morane, not Morie. No time to tell her about the latest extract of the letter I'd found, about the reference to St Martin. I stared at the mobile in my hand, feeling lost and alone, like a child.

I sat at Rozenn's desk, the silver compass beside me. Trying not to think about the damage to my credit card I tracked down a replacement speaker and coffee machine online and ordered them. I couldn't find the wine online anywhere. I remembered that James and Gwen had toured vineyards in France last year and groaned.

My laptop could wait until I had time to search eBay and find a reconditioned second-hand model. From now on, I'd be relying on my smartphone and, once I was back home, the very old tablet I'd left there. I'd have to hope that the software I'd downloaded on to the laptop could be made to function on the tablet. At least I had my memory, I told myself, my ability to recall measurements and quotations. And the small notepad I scribbled notes and figures on was upstairs beside my bed. Fortunately I'd sold the bag Nick had given me and that hadn't gone in the burglary. I'd wrapped up the soft leather in tissue paper, pausing for a moment, recalling how unwrapping the bag had stirred me out of my depressed torpor, breathing in the scent one last time.

I finally allowed myself to glance down at the newly discovered page of the letter and read the rest of it.

> *I have set the St Martin plan in motion, so please tell the family what we've agreed,* chère *Rozenn. I wish we could meet again, but perhaps those granddaughters of yours could help organise an 'online' face to face? Our telephone calls delight me. How fortunate that we both still have sharp ears, or perhaps good hearing aids. All the same, I love writing to you too. Electronic communication sometimes seems impersonal, or perhaps that's just me being nearly ninety-six now. Do you remember how precious paper was in the war – how we would do anything to get our hands on it, reusing it, rationing ourselves? So much for us to talk about. I wish we could have reunited in person, sitting outside the house in St Martin. I know you disliked the village at first, but by the end the girl from the* seizième *was happy living there, until those very last minutes when it all went so horrifically wrong . . .*

It ended there – a page still missing. A third reference to St Martin – implying that Rozenn had been there for at least a period of time. And then something had happened to her? Surely something relating to the war – to her decision to come here? I stared at the handwriting, as though hoping it would tell me more. As Dad said, it wasn't possible to determine whether a man or a woman had written it. The letters were well-formed, classically French, but with something particularly expressive about them.

An impulse was flooding me. I sat back, trying to resist it. I should ring Dad first. If I did, he'd rightly caution me that a trip to France was something I couldn't afford at the moment. If I told Gwen, she'd take it as more proof of my feckless approach to life, running off instead of concentrating on work. Or finding a new place to live. Lucky she didn't yet know about my landlord selling up.

I looked at the compass again.

Had Rozenn retrieved it from the Paris apartment or could the compass actually have come with her on the voyage over from Brittany? If so, leaving it to me was perhaps a message, guiding me to a place that meant something to her.

Places mattered to my grandmother. *People are their surroundings and surroundings become imprinted by the people who live there.* I could hear her saying the words. St Martin had been important to Rozenn, had imprinted itself on her somehow. It was a leap to conclude that any of this might have had any bearing on how, decades later, she'd written her will, but there'd been no other explanation. It was more than just Vue Claire now too, I admitted. My curiosity about Rozenn had become almost obsessive. I needed to know what had become of the girl who'd drawn those birds and mice with such verve, such a sense of fun. I needed to see the house referred to in the letter.

I gave up resisting and searched for Channel crossings and accommodation in Brittany. I was lucky: there was still overnight availability on the Plymouth to Roscoff crossing. I couldn't justify a cabin so I booked a seat for myself. My car insurance covered France and I could use my battered credit card to pay for most of what I would need during my five-day stay in northern Brittany.

I paused, dazed from the rush of online activity, the realisation of what I was doing making me blink. I was running away from it all with the few clothes I had brought down here, the silver compass, two pages of a letter and a vague idea that a coastal village west of Lannion might hold the answers to my questions about my grandmother. What took her to St Martin? Did she meet Luc there? Why did they leave for England? And why hadn't she talked about it?

I called the cleaner, Sue. She was happy for me to redirect the deliveries to her house a few miles away and said she'd bring them over when she came in to Vue Claire on Friday morning. She commiserated about the burglary and told me to give the police her number in case they needed her key to follow up.

It was going to be a push to make the 10 p.m. ferry from Plymouth. I gathered up my clothes and possessions and stuffed them into the bag and raced around, cleaning the kitchen and bathroom, plumping up cushions and vacuuming floors. I double-checked every door and window lock in the place. I wasn't going to give Gwen any more reason to think that my stay here had been a big mistake.

I drove down the banked lanes from Helford, filled with a heady mixture of guilt and excitement, but more upbeat than I had felt for a long time. My own problems seemed to dissolve into the more absorbing world that was my grandmother's past.

15

The afternoon was dragging on into infinity. Rozenn sat in a deck-chair outside the house, watching Claire as she picked daisies while Maman cleaned. If this were a Chekhov play surely someone ought to have turned up by now to challenge the monotony? She'd already thrown the tennis ball to Claire for fifteen minutes and walked around the outbuildings with her, discouraging her from going inside to disturb Yann while he was drawing. Looking after Claire was surprisingly wearying. You couldn't take your eye off her for a second because she would wander off. Maman worried about the clifftop. If Claire spotted a flower or butterfly on the edge and chased it, she could fall to her death. She might have the brain capacity of a young child but Claire's legs were strong and she could run as fast as Rozenn, perhaps faster, as she had so little concern for looking dignified.

The inside of the house smelt fresher now that the door was left open all through the day. Maman was even talking about Yann painting the downstairs walls if the landlord didn't mind and if paint could be found. Refreshing the off-white would make the interior brighter. Rozenn had to admit it was becoming more bear-able here. In the evenings, after dinner, if the breeze wasn't too insistent, they sat outside with a good view of the track leading up the lane, but sheltered by a row of shrubs. Yann sat in the doorway, the oil lamps turned off indoors so he was invisible if anyone came past the house. With the curfew, it seemed unlikely. Each night the same planet shone in the sky, even when the moon was invisible and before the stars appeared. Papa said it was Venus. When they shared these meals, meagre though they often were, it felt possible for Rozenn to shake off some of her anxiety and impatience. The old house seemed to embrace them, reassure them. Even Claire seemed to behave more calmly. Perhaps because they weren't always nagging at her to hold her cutlery properly.

Maman came outside at last, shaking dusters, her hair covered in a scarf. 'You go for your walk now, Rozenn. Claire can help me feed the chickens.' The chickens were new, given to Papa in exchange for him treating a farmer's chest infection.

She stood up quickly before guilt at leaving Maman could overcome her. Her satchel was hanging on the peg by the door and she grabbed it, checking that her dark glasses and papers were inside it. No point taking the string bag as the small grocery would be closed for the afternoon. The wind would blow her hair around so once again she took her beret, although it was really too warm for it.

She set off briskly up the track, heading inland. A stretch of grass in the sunshine beckoned to her, sheltered by the stone wall. Nobody around. Rozenn lay down and rolled up her skirt so that her knees were exposed. She wore ankle socks, no stockings. Keeping her legs free of hair was becoming harder as her razor blunted. Shaving them had seemed such a modern, Hollywood thing to do when she'd first started last year. She didn't like to ask Papa or Yann if she could use their razors. Another trip to Lannion would be needed. If she could find some decent stockings to cover up her lower legs, it would be easier, if hotter, but the chances of that were remote. As for her sandals, the soles were now so thin she might as well go barefoot. Papa was trying to find *sabots* for her and

Claire. Wooden clogs would make her feel like a janitor. She'd wear them to do housework but never in public.

Thankfully she'd remembered to pack her dark glasses when they'd left Paris in such a hurry. Theo'd said she resembled a film star in them. If only her skin wouldn't freckle. Really she oughtn't to expose it to the sun like this, but the feeling of the rays on her face was so relaxing. If only Theo could be lying beside her too, his hands about to explore her body, his lips about to push her mouth open . . .

'Whatever you're thinking about is obviously good.'

That boy. She sprang up, glaring at Luc. The nerve of him, coming up suddenly on her like that. Her blood pounded inside her.

'A man?'

'What?' The accuracy of the guess made her blush. 'I don't know what you mean.'

'I take it back, *désolé*.' His wide mouth broadened even more.

She didn't want to continue the conversation here, so dangerously close to the house where Claire might be overheard blurting something out about Yann, or her brother himself might amble outside and say something Luc would hear.

'Fancy a stroll?' she said, tugging down her skirt.

'Those sandals have seen better days.' He was frowning at them. What a nerve.

'I don't like wearing good shoes on these rough tracks.'

He nodded. 'Want to go on the cliff path?'

'I'd rather go down the lane.' Walking to the headland would mean skirting the garden of the *longère*. Yann's ears were sharp, he'd get out of sight, but Claire might prattle on about him in earshot of the path.

The two of them set off. Her foot landed on a sharp stone. She winced. Perhaps she could line the sandals with layers of newspaper to cushion the soles.

'That shoe of yours is about to die,' Luc said. 'You'd be better off with something with a thicker sole.'

'There's not much in the shops in Lannion.'

His lip curled. 'Wouldn't bother looking there. I can find you a pair of decent summer shoes.'

Something cheap with paper soles, probably.

'Tell me your size?' He stopped, pulling a notebook and pencil out of his pocket and scribbling something.

'I have *tickets*.'

'Don't worry about those.'

'But . . . ?'

'You have to make things work for you.' He grinned at her. 'Not everything needs to be done on the ration.'

'But isn't that—?'

'Black market? Yes, but we didn't choose the Occupation, did we?'

She gave a harsh laugh. 'It's completely ruined my life.' She probably sounded like a spoilt girl. Well, that's what she was, in fact. Admitting this felt shameful.

'Buying a pair of shoes is nothing. Not sure why you're so worried?'

She could have told him what Papa had told them last year: that it wouldn't be the Germans who suffered if the rationing system fell apart; they wouldn't reduce their demands for French food and clothing. Those who'd suffer would be old or sick civilians who didn't have anything to barter with or couldn't walk and cycle around the country in search of something to eat or wear. She could have told Luc this, but she didn't. Apart from anything else, hadn't Papa himself brought home those chickens, the meat, in return for his services? That was all outside the ration system.

'What keeps you here?' she asked Luc, to change the subject. 'You're about my age, eighteen or so, aren't you? Do you have family in the village?'

'My father owns a canning business in Brest. But I'm staying in our house in the village for a few weeks to keep an eye on another of his businesses.'

She wondered what other business the Germans would regard as so important that Luc's family could live in the zone.

'Another business?'

He kicked a loose stone. 'This used to be just a place for fishing. Now there'll be other things to trade. When the Germans start building their fortifications they'll need gravel, sand, wood. All the other sidelines: cooking pots so they can cater for the workers. Accommodation.'

'And your family will help them with these things?' It sounded even more like collaboration.

'If we don't, someone else will. At least the money stays in the community this way, with the people who need it.'

'Don't you mind working for the Germans?' she burst out.

He shrugged. 'I'm Breton. What's Paris ever done for me apart from telling me which language to speak?'

'You really don't feel French?'

He frowned. 'I hate seeing those field-grey uniforms everywhere. But round here we put family first, before country if necessary.' He sounded younger as he said the last bit.

'Yes,' she said. 'Family first.' They walked closer to one another, saying nothing further, reaching the outskirts of the village. She spotted flowering azaleas in gardens and slowed to look at them. Lawns needed mowing, window boxes and pots were filled with weeds, but there were still peonies and irises to look at.

'So many people have been forced out. And the holiday visitors won't be coming this year. Nobody is looking after their gardens for them,' Luc said, putting out a hand to touch a blossom in a way that was delicate for a man.

'It's still beautiful, this village,' she said, surprising herself with this rush of pleasure at the place.

'We've delighted the *Parisienne*.' Luc swept low into a bow. 'People like these old stone houses, say they're picturesque or something.' He shrugged. 'Me, I'd like to live in a new apartment in a city. Or in a completely new house with an indoor bathroom.'

'I'm with you on that particular aspect.' The words came out with feeling.

'Facilities at the *longère* not to your liking?' He laughed at her expression. 'We're used to it. Most people here don't have indoor bathrooms and lavatories. If you'd moved into the proper doctor's house, that's what you'd have now.'

'Don't remind me.' In the villa there'd have been more space, perhaps a room she could claim as her own. Yann had been granted the outbuilding to use during the day, but her personal space was limited to the bedroom she shared with Claire.

His face grew more serious. 'Why don't you bring your sister down here? I've seen her at church.'

'She . . .' She paused, about to say that Claire was shy, which wasn't true. 'I find it hard being with her in public.' Her cheeks burnt. She'd only ever admitted this to Yann. Luc would think she was a dreadful human being, ashamed of her own sister. Did she even care what he thought? He was just a local boy with a nose for making money from the Germans – irrelevant.

He nodded. 'You must feel protective of your sister. But it must be hard to hear the cruel things some people say about her – as if they're judging you, in a way?' Even Yann hadn't quite put in words what she felt about Claire.

She remembered the sneering boy on the train. 'Sometimes I want to slap them round the face when they make comments.'

'Painful for your mother, I expect.' She looked at him, quizzical. 'She sees you, the perfect Parisian girl: clever, pretty, well turned out. Then she looks at your twin.'

She'd never thought of it from Maman's point of view before.

'Nature can be cruel. Especially for females.' Perhaps he was thinking of the cows blamed for malformed calves or the married couples who couldn't have children, which was, of course, always assumed to be the woman's fault. 'Round here there are all kinds of old wives' tales about twins. Some people say they bring good fortune and some that they are a sign of bad luck.'

'Let's hope it's the former.'

'I never rely on luck.' He looked at her intently. 'I take what I want. When I can.'

She looked at him and felt a connection. Their philosophy on life was similar, which was strange when he was a local boy and she was a girl from the *seizième*. But perhaps that old snobbishness was no longer relevant.

He raised an eyebrow at her. 'Take what you want today while you can, Rozenn Guillou.'

Sandals today, what else tomorrow?

They'd reached a stone bench on the seafront. Luc stopped and took out a packet of cigarettes. He offered one and lit it for her. They sat watching the Germans rolling out more of the barbed wire. On this sunny afternoon they didn't seem enthusiastic about their work. It would take them days to cover the whole length of the bay. Rozenn imagined they'd rather kick a football around. She told herself to stop seeing them as normal human beings, boys like Yann. They weren't normal. Arguably they weren't even human, either. Luc seemed unmoved by the sight of them. But this was a village he'd grown up in, surely he was angered by the appropriation of the beach?

'They'll go,' he said, reading her mind. 'One day. Either because they've been killed or because they've lost the war.' The sudden coolness in his tone made her blink.

'A patriot after all?' she said, wondering why she found this young man so interesting. He was good-looking, but that wasn't usually enough for her.

He considered the question. 'Of France? Or of Brittany?' A shrug. 'As I said, family matters most.' It might have been her imagination but when he talked about his family his accent became more sing-song, those Rs rolled more. It wasn't the kind of French Maman would regard as correct, but Rozenn liked the way it sounded.

A door closed above them. Rozenn glanced up to see Martine approaching from the house above the quay. From the set of the girl's shoulders it was clear she wasn't happy to see Luc smoking with Rozenn. 'What's that badge Martine wears?' Rozenn asked quietly, remembering it from the previous encounter.

'A Breton independence group. They're still hoping they'll get some kind of special political deal, separation from France.'

'Is that what you want too?' Rozenn was going to continue the conversation to spite Martine.

He shrugged. 'We need things that we can't produce ourselves. France needs our fish and vegetables. Doesn't make sense to me to go it alone.'

'It's all down to getting what you want,' she said, as much to herself as to him.

'At a price you can afford. You're a fast learner, Rozenn.' He looked at her with approval. Martine was almost upon them now. Emboldened by what he'd just said there was something she wanted to ask Luc before the girl came down the steps and reached them.

'Fishermen took refugees off just before the Fall of France, didn't they?' The words came out quickly. He blinked. 'Do they still do that?'

Every sinew of Luc's body seemed to stiffen.

'I just want to know who I can speak to.'

Rozenn could hear Martine's wooden soles clattering over the stones now. 'There must be someone. It's urgent.'

'We don't talk about it,' he said, looking away. 'It's too dangerous.'

'You said I should take what I wanted.'

'I didn't say you should get yourself shot.' He stopped, seeming to relax his body by force of will as Martine approached. 'Martine. *Mat ar jeu.*' He sounded as relaxed as ever as he kissed her cheeks. Martine extended a hand to Rozenn politely.

'I should be getting back.' Rozenn stood up to shake it. 'My mother will need me.'

'To help with your sister?' Martine asked.

'I didn't know you'd met her?'

'My mother works for Madame O'Donnell up at the *manoir*. Madame O'Donnell said that there was a family with identical twins living in our old *longère*.' She looked at Rozenn. 'I was hoping you'd be sweet little girls.'

'Sorry to disappoint you.'

Martine laughed. Rozenn couldn't tell if the laughter was benevolent or not. As she walked away she wondered whether Martine and Luc were more than friends. There was no sign of anything closer between them, but Bretons were supposedly religious people, not keen on public demonstrations of affection between men and women. She felt irritated at herself for hoping that the two of them weren't romantically attached.

Rozenn walked back along the cliff path to the *longère*. The water flowing in over the sandbar was a strip of yellow in this light.

The tide was coming back in again. She watched it ripple over the rocks fringing the small cove, bubbling and hissing.

This was the cove where Yann swam at night. Because the cliffs overhung the shore here, he'd be invisible getting in and out of the sea. Only moonlight or a flashlight shining on his auburn head would expose him in the water. He swam like a seal, a natural, almost soundlessly, arms curving through the water without a splash, always had done since he'd been very small and Papa had taught him in a hotel swimming pool near Nice. She supposed Germans came down to the cove themselves to swim in the moonlight. Rozenn shivered. What would Yann do then? Surely he'd have the nous to hide his towel and clothes in the rocks before he went into the water? Perhaps he'd swim far out to sea and wait for them to go. She pictured him growing cold, cramp seizing his muscles, while German artillerymen splashed and shouted metres away.

As if to underline the dangers she heard German voices. Coming towards her on the cliff path were a small group of artillerymen, laughing, chatting. She glanced to the side, hoping there might be a way of leaving the path before they reached her. On her right, it banked steeply upwards. Rozenn carried on. The young men stood politely to the side, wishing her *Bonjour.* She nodded a thanks and walked quickly on, feeling their eyes on her back.

One night Yann would make a mistake, bump into a patrol on this footpath. Or someone would unexpectedly call at the house and spot him, ask questions about the young man who wasn't registered in St Martin.

Despite his reaction this afternoon, she would have to ask Luc again about those fishing boats.

16

I locked my car and ran up the steps to the viewing deck, like a child, so that I could relish every inch of Plymouth Sound as we sailed out of the ferry port, even though it was dark now. The city lights twinkled at me. I felt a rush of excitement as they grew smaller and fainter and the darkness of the sea engulfed us.

'Off on your holiday?' a woman beside me asked. 'You should have lovely weather, dear.'

I smiled. It wasn't really a holiday I was embarking on, more an escape. Or perhaps a pilgrimage. But I felt the thrill of being on the move at last, seeing England drop away. I hadn't been anywhere since the accident. There'd been so much to do in the months since Nick had gone, the business to resuscitate, finding a flat. Standing here on the deck I realised I no longer felt the bolt to my heart when I thought of what he'd done. When I'd packed up the bag he'd given me to post it, I'd felt a wave of emotion for lost hopes breaking through the numb guilt and depression. The last I'd heard of him had been weeks ago via a friend of a friend, who said he'd stopped betting and was working in the planning department of a local authority.

If I thought of Nick now it was with regret tinged with annoyance. Parcelling up the handbag had been a way of packaging up some of the negative feelings I'd felt for him. My solicitor still hoped that some of the money he'd taken might be recoverable, if not through the process of law then through appealing to Nick's conscience. He wasn't a bad person, though he had done a bad thing. I knew he must feel terrible guilt for what he'd done. It had only been months since he'd left me; the chances were I'd still occasionally be filled with feelings of loss and betrayal. But in the meantime, this was what I needed: a complete change of scene, a puzzle to work out.

I turned my back on the last of England as it vanished into darkness and went inside to the self-service restaurant to buy myself a plate of pasta and a glass of wine. When I'd finished my meal and checked messages on my mobile, I decided to enjoy a digital detox. I found the on-board shop and bought a guidebook to Brittany and a novel set in wartime France. I was spending the night in a reclining chair and feared sleep would be hard to find, but I nodded off as I read my guidebook, waking about an hour after dawn. I went back on to the viewing deck on the bow, scanning the horizon for signs of Brittany.

'It'll be a while yet till you see land, ma'am,' an American voice said beside me. I turned to see a friendly elderly man. He wore a peaked cap with a Second World War veterans' logo on it.

'I'm returning for the first time since the summer of forty-four,' he told me. 'Battled my way west from Normandy in the war.'

'I'm researching my family's wartime history,' I told him, surprised at how I was opening up. I didn't often chat to strangers. He asked me where I was heading and when I told him that it was a small coastal village called St Martin, he became very animated.

'I was there, I tell you. We came into the bay in three huge landing craft in August forty-four and drove off on to the beach in our jeeps. Great people, quaint village.' He told me how he'd unloaded supplies and rounded up some German prisoners. 'And this local family had a bottle of their cider and they insisted on giving it to me. I sat on the beach and they couldn't speak English and I couldn't speak French or Breton or whatever, and we all got along just fine.' He laughed, shaking his head.

'I wonder if my great-grandparents were in the village then,' I said. 'We don't know much about what happened to them by that stage in the war. My grandmother told us nothing before she died.' They might not have come to St Martin with Rozenn, I reminded myself.

'I bet she had her reasons.' He nodded to himself. 'Some locals we met really didn't want to talk about the Occupation. They buried things rather than give them life by describing them again.'

'My grandmother didn't even like seeing TV documentaries about the war.'

His expression grew more sombre. 'I know servicemen like that, too. Didn't want to be reminded. Those therapists say talk it out, but for some folk it's best for them and their loved ones just to forget.'

I wondered what had hurt Rozenn so much that she'd never told her closest family anything about the war years.

I wished my companion a good trip and went inside to buy some breakfast. Perhaps Rozenn really had wanted to protect us. I still had no evidence that anything that had happened to her in Brittany was connected with her decisions about Vue Claire. I'd read fragments of a longer letter and allowed myself to obsess about the place they referred to. Probably to distract myself away from my own predicament. And the burglary. I groaned to myself, thinking of Gwen. I took out my mobile and started to type a message to her. No coverage. Were we still too far out to sea to pick up the French mobile network?

I ate my croissant watching out for land on the horizon. I made out the spire of a church protruding into the sky. From my reading of the guidebook, I guessed this was the double-rowed bell-tower of

Roscoff parish church. Excitement pulsed through me again. Had Rozenn herself ever visited Roscoff and wondered at the church tower's curious shape? The guidebook told me how the coastal zone had been restricted, forbidden even, to civilians. I wondered how Rozenn had even managed to enter St Martin.

From the guidebook map I calculated it would take me just over an hour to drive east from Roscoff to St Martin itself. I was staying in Lannion as I hadn't found anywhere to rent in St Martin at short notice.

The morning sun shone into my face as I drove off the ferry. Eventually the road took me away from the coast and I lost sight of the sea. After I'd driven through Morlaix, blinking at its impressive viaduct, the route took me north-east and eventually a huge bay opened to the left. St Martin itself sat on the far eastern side. I remembered my American friend's descriptions of how the huge landing craft had sailed in to discharge trucks and jeeps on to the sand, and imagined how excited the local people still living there must have been after four years of German occupation. But Rozenn herself was long gone by then. Had she watched the news films as the Allies spanned out from Normandy, wondering what had happened to her parents? And the writer of the letter fragment I'd found? Was he or she a friend or neighbour? Or perhaps a cousin, fighting the Germans at that stage – part of the Resistance?

I stopped to buy groceries at an out-of-town supermarket. Listening to the French spoken in the store reminded me of my last conversation with Rozenn. She could hardly talk by then but had uttered those fragments of French as she clutched the compass. In front of me two little boys whined for biscuits on a shelf. Their mother scolded them: French mothers didn't seem to tolerate as much as their English counterparts. When she looked away the smaller one hit the bigger one. He thumped his little brother back.

The mother turned just in time to catch him and shouted at him not to be horrible to his *frère*. His brother.

I felt a tingling down my back. In that last conversation I'd thought Rozenn was trying to tell me that the silver compass had come from France. It dawned on me now that she might have been trying to tell me it had come from a *frère*. Her father's brother – her uncle? Had there been an uncle? I thought I remembered Rozenn telling me that they'd been lost in the First World War.

The silver compass itself was safe in my rucksack. I patted the bag, feeling the compass's solidity through the canvas. When I was back in my car, I took it out and set it so that it showed me my route: east along the bay, through the village where Rozenn had spent at least some time during the war. *I'll find out what you were trying to tell me*, I promised my grandmother silently. *I'm going to track down the place where you lived and see if anyone remembers you.*

As I drove along the edge of the bay, a group of horses cantered across the sand, slowing to a trot as they reached the end of the beach, passing close to a man kicking a ball to his toddler. The riders' faces were relaxed – why wouldn't they be on a morning like this?

I clenched the steering wheel until I passed all of them, forcing myself to look ahead at the little village opening up. Just a quiet summer day, nothing to feel anxious about. But it had also been quiet that day months ago when I'd been riding up on the Ridgeway, in south Oxfordshire.

I needed coffee. I needed distraction away from myself. A white hotel on the beachside with an Edwardian, *belle-époque* feel to it caught my eye. It would be good to stop and sit out on the balcony on the first floor to enjoy the sun and the view across the bay, imagine how things would have looked back in those carefree summers right at the beginning of the twentieth century. I found a parking space in the small square, noting only a few shops. Perhaps the arrival of the school holidays brought more trade to the village and pop-up stores opened.

The hotel had obviously been recently refurbished. I walked through to the bar and after I'd ordered a cappuccino to drink on the terrace, I asked the barman if there were any museums I could visit in the village. With an apologetic smile he told me in accented French that he'd only arrived weeks ago from Croatia and was still finding his feet.

I sat outside with my cappuccino, imagining women promenading on the beach over a century ago, wearing white frocks and wide summer hats, children in striped swimsuits playing on the sand. I couldn't see much about this village in my guidebook, other than the mention of the landing in 1944 my American on the ferry had told me about. The view distracted me from reading. To the east the bay was cut by a steep headland. A couple of houses dotted the cliffs. I swung my gaze back down to the beach, admiring the way the church cemetery bordered the sea wall. If fishermen were buried in there, they certainly hadn't gone far from their workplace.

My mobile vibrated. *Are you still in Cornwall?* Dad.

I'm in St Martin, where Luc was born, I texted back. *I found another page of the letter – see attached.* On the ferry I'd photographed the page on my mobile. *Sorry, all happened in a rush.*

Silence. I imagined the messages pulsing between him and Gwen and couldn't help smiling. They must be thinking I'd finally flipped. Sure enough, Gwen's message came through two minutes later.

Sounds a bit random. G.

No Xs.

It's what I need, I messaged back.

I'm sure, the reply came back. *But weren't you talking about throwing yourself into work?*

144

I wanted to tell her to mind her own business, but forced myself to put the phone away. It had been Gwen herself who'd first said we'd missed something about Rozenn. Gwen was probably still angry about the break-in at Vue Claire. I mused on the meaning of the name of Rozenn's house: Clear View. Of the creek and trees and sky, perhaps. And yet so much about her life wasn't clear at all. Even those photographs of her on the beach showed two versions of the same small child: an open-faced little girl and that more guarded version. Was this the same beach as that one? I had scanned the photographs and looked at them now. No, the beach here was wider, less built up.

I stood up with reluctance. I could spend all morning here, ordering cappuccinos, pretending I had time and leisure to do nothing. I worked out what I was paying in pounds for a cup and grimaced.

I walked along the beach to the west for a bit, so that I could turn and look back at the settlement with its soaring church steeple and sea walls. The view didn't seem as if it would have changed much since the war. Although the centre of the village was compact, houses and farm buildings peppered the hill behind it and the headland to the east. It would take me days to explore the whole area and unless I could find someone old enough to know the details of the inhabitants in 1941, that time would probably yield nothing. I'd rushed into this trip without planning how I'd go about researching Rozenn. She wouldn't have approved of my lack of preparation.

I took out my mobile and tried tapping in phrases including St Martin and the *Seconde Guerre mondiale* to see if this would direct me to useful local archives. When this failed, I tried searching for *Guillou St Martin*. Nothing came up. If Rozenn had come here with her parents, her father practising as a physician, might someone in the village still remember the family? If St Martin was anything like Helford in Cornwall, everyone quickly found out everything about families moving in, especially if they had some kind of public profile, such as a doctor would have. But it was so long ago now, three-quarters of a century.

I retraced my steps to the hotel, peering up lanes and reading municipal information boards in the hope of spotting something helpful.

As I neared the hotel the Croatian barman was on the street, cigarette in hand, chatting to a woman in late middle age, dressed in navy trousers and grey-checked blazer, scarf immaculately tied around her neck, tan leather tote bag over a shoulder. He pointed to me. 'That's the lady I was telling you about.'

She smiled at me. 'I heard you were interested in St Martin's wartime history, Madame?'

'I am.'

'You know about the big landings of 1944 in the bay?' she said, in French. 'Excuse me, but I do not speak much English.'

My year in the Cevennes had made me fluent and the language was coming back to me quickly now. I told her about the American and his description of the landing. 'But it was more civilian life that interests me.'

'Ah yes. You are in a rush now, Madame?'

I shook my head. 'May I buy you a coffee?' I pushed fears about expenses to the back of my mind: no point trying to research Rozenn's history if I didn't invest in useful sources.

She nodded. We sat inside this time and the barman brought us two more coffees. 'My name is Joséphine. I live here in St Martin. My mother was a young girl here during the Occupation. She lived in a little stone house just above the quay, you can still see it there today: the one with the curved eave.'

I'd already noted the quaint cottage.

'Her father was the harbour master. That makes it sound like more of a job than it was, but he kept an eye on the fishing boats coming in and out, acted as a kind of lifeguard, too, when people came here for the holidays before the war.'

'He must have known a lot about the village.'

She smiled. 'They didn't miss much. My mother told me about the Germans coming to St Martin in 1940. How at first they didn't quite know how to control the place. People were still getting out of the country on fishing boats. My grandfather turned a blind eye while he could.'

I sat up.

'But then the Germans increased their presence. They ran barbed wire over the beach so the villagers couldn't use it. They guarded the fishing fleet in case they tried to make a dash for it or aid the English.'

'So by 1941 the fishermen couldn't help with escapes?'

'The fishermen knew there'd be reprisals if they helped. And at certain times of the year the nights weren't long enough to get clear of the German patrols in darkness. As the war went on, the German presence in La Manche increased, so the boats were even more vulnerable. It takes a long time to sail to England.'

So Rozenn probably hadn't come to Cornwall on one of the picturesque boats photographed in my Brittany guidebook, with their graceful sails.

'It must have been a very difficult time for your grandmother and her family?' I asked.

'Rationing was tight. Of course, they were a fishing community. The Germans tried to take a lot of what they caught but they couldn't control it, not completely. With the fish and the local produce, they probably did better than people in the cities. Food was severely rationed: only fourteen hundred calories a day for most people.'

'Like being on a diet every day of your life?'

She smiled. 'Some groups had more rations – youngsters, for instance. But it was very harsh. My mother told me she gathered shellfish on the rocks where the Germans hadn't barbed-wired them. They kept rabbits as well, so they didn't do as badly as some. The French police watched the black market but they couldn't be everywhere.'

Joséphine sipped her cappuccino.

'The Germans must have worried this was a good place for the Allies to land,' I said.

'Hitler was particularly worried about them attacking the submarine base at Brest further west, but this wide bay was a concern, too. He started building fortifications from 1942. The Atlantic Wall, he called it. Lots of locals, those who were still allowed to live here, were pressed into working on it. And more Germans arrived to build it.'

'A wall?'

'More a line of pillboxes and gun emplacements at intervals.' She looked at me shrewdly. 'You have a particular reason for wanting to know about St Martin, Madame?'

'I believe my grandmother might have lived here, possibly with her family for a period in 1941,' I said.

'What was her name?'

'Rozenn Guillou.'

She lowered her coffee cup slowly. 'Rozenn?'

'You know her name?'

'I've heard it . . . My mother never knew what had become of her. She thought . . .'

'What?'

Joséphine seemed to be struggling for words. 'My mother's been dead for some years now. But she told me about Rozenn disappearing on the beach one night and never reappearing.'

'She landed in Cornwall, possibly at the same time as my grandfather, who was from this village.'

She took a sip of coffee, eyes on me. 'What was his name?'

'Luc Caradec.'

Joséphine nodded. 'Luc.' She didn't seem surprised.

'You know of him?'

She seemed to hesitate. 'It's not a large village. Children growing up together become close. Luc went to school here as a small child, and returned during the early part of the war. Then he vanished the same night as Rozenn.'

So they had left together.

'The villagers never heard another thing from them.'

'Nobody ever tried to find him after the war?'

'Apparently not. His father died. The house he grew up in was demolished twenty-odd years ago to build something more modern.'

Nobody had missed my grandfather, had wanted to find out what had happened to him. I felt a pang of sorrow for Luc. At least before the drinking undid him he'd had those years of prosperity with Rozenn, business thriving, a son he doted upon. Dad had told me his father had been a warm presence in his early childhood, kicking a football around with him, taking him to matches.

'Rumour had it that British special operations took Luc and Rozenn to England,' she went on. 'And he'd died working for them.'

It seemed so unlikely. 'What would they be doing with special operations agents? They were surely too young?'

She gave a Gallic shrug. 'So it would seem.'

'And your mother was a friend of my grandmother?'

'She knew her, yes.' Joséphine sounded a little wary now. My instinct that Rozenn had been in this village was correct, but I told myself not to push things.

'When Rozenn died I found a letter,' I told Joséphine.

'Rozenn is dead?' She nodded to herself. 'I am not surprised, really. She must have been well into her nineties.'

'Ninety-six,' I said.

'What did the letter tell you?' she asked.

'Nothing terribly clear,' I admitted. 'But it referred to this village.'

'And you came here to find out more about Rozenn and Luc?'

'That's right.'

She pushed an invisible hair off her forehead, looking at her watch. 'I have to collect my granddaughter from school for lunch.' She picked her tote bag off the spare chair.

'Could we meet again?' I asked. 'I'm only here for a few days.'

As she rose she paused, seeming to weigh something up. 'I could meet you here at eleven the day after tomorrow.'

'*Merci.*' I stood up too. 'Can you tell me where Rozenn lived? I'm assuming her parents were here too?'

'*Oui.*' She pointed up towards the headland. 'Up on the cliffs. In the old *longère.*'

'A longhouse?'

She smiled. 'Like its name, built this way.' She extended her hands. 'Outwards rather than upwards. It was actually where my mother's family lived before my grandfather got the harbour master's job.'

'Is the house still standing?'

She nodded. 'Someone bought the place last autumn and started renovating it. They've still got a lot of work to do to clear the surroundings. There's a row of granite boulders just before you turn off the footpath to the right. It's a bit hard to find with all the shrubs and undergrowth.' With a quick nod and *bonne journée* she left me.

I paid for the coffees. 'She told you anything interesting?' the barman asked.

'Very interesting, *merci*.' I looked at my watch. No real reason to carry on to Lannion: nobody was expecting me before I checked into the apartment by six. The realisation made me feel simultaneously liberated and adrift. Pathetic, I told myself. If Rozenn could escape to England at barely nineteen, her granddaughter could surely manage a short solo trip at twenty-nine. I hadn't asked Joséphine why Rozenn's family had come here, I realised. Why would she know, though? She wouldn't even have been born in 1941.

I was wearing trainers with a good grip on the soles and the footpath looked steep but not difficult. I was well used to walking on clifftops around the Lizard. I decided to start by looking at the quay and the cottage where Joséphine's mother had lived.

The barman told me the easiest way to get to the quay was to walk along the street and over the footbridge crossing the stream. 'On the other side there are steps down to the beach and at low tide you can walk across the sand to the harbour.'

I thanked him and followed his instructions. The quay itself was small. I couldn't imagine how many fishing boats must have used it in the forties. Had Rozenn come down here regularly in search of fish? The harbour master's house made me smile. It was made of what looked like the local stone, with a slate-tiled roof and a gable dormer curved like an eyebrow. Below the dormer a small alcove housed a stone statue of a bishop. The St Martin of the village's name? The little house seemed to be part of the cliffside, growing out of it. I could have spent a lot of time examining it. Picturesque on a day like this, but I wondered how it would be to live there on a stormy winter night during the war. But this wasn't Rozenn's old home. I needed to move on.

I started the steep ascent up the footpath. Pink campion skirted the path, and clumps of foxgloves broke through the grassy banks on the right. As I turned a bend in the headland, a small cove came into sight below me, a carpet of dark-pink wild flowers dripping down the cliffside into it. From above I could hear the faint fizz of the waves as they met the sand. I felt the same singing happiness I'd always felt on the first day of the school summer holidays, the sense that everything here had just been waiting for me.

The village and bay fell behind me. I stepped out at an even pace, feeling myself relaxing just as I did when I walked in Cornwall. I took out my mobile and sent photos to Gwen and Dad. *Look where I am! St Martin. Isn't it beautiful? On the hunt for Rozenn's old house.* After I'd pushed send I realised I'd almost forgotten about the burglary and wondered whether this was also the case for my sister. The ozone was going to my head but she was still in her office in London.

The grey-pink granite boulders to the side of the path looked as though a giant had played marbles with rocks. I couldn't see any signs of a track to the *longère* and some of the euphoria left me. I wished I'd asked Joséphine more detailed questions about the house's location. To my right, over a low bank, I saw a large clump of scrubby-looking bushes and more of the foxgloves.

I looked behind me guiltily. Nobody there. I clambered up the bank towards the bushes. Buddleia, I thought, about to flower. I'd come across it on sites I'd helped develop: it flourished in derelict, previously built-on areas. Rosebay willowherb, too, I noted, also fond of abandoned locations. The house was here – I just needed to cut through the overgrowth to find it.

Beneath my feet I felt a change in texture. I was walking over the boundary of an old garden. And there was the house to my left. Long, as its name suggested: one main section with two connected lower outbuildings on its right and a third at right angles to it. I'd never been here before but immediately felt as if I'd already seen this house.

Someone was shouting at me from a well-maintained track leading, I guessed, to the lane. A man, elderly, indignant, telling me I was on private property. I shouted an apology, trying to explain that I was looking for the home of my great-grandparents. I couldn't understand everything he was bellowing at me and my explanation became more of a grovelling *désolée*. He walked on. I moved round the granite walls to the front of the house, which faced away from the cliffs, presumably to shield the inhabitants from the worst of the onshore winds. From this side the house looked less abandoned: vehicles had left tyre marks on the track.

A single word was painted in faded red on the door.

Traître.

Traitor.

17

The postgirl brought the letter with the address written carefully in spiky ink on the envelope. Rozenn recognised the concierge's handwriting, often seen on missives scolding residents. *Please carry out the correct procedure for rubbish bins . . . Residents with children are reminded that slamming doors and shouting is anti-social. Gramophones and radios should* not *disturb other residents . . .* The woman was perfectly suited for operating under the Nazis. Papa paid her a small retainer for forwarding mail to St Martin, careful to drop into his last conversation with her the information that Yann was only accompanying them temporarily, to help settle them in, before returning to the city.

When he returned at lunchtime Papa opened the brown envelope without even taking off his hat. Inside was a single sheet of writing paper and a folded official-looking envelope addressed to Yann. When he'd read the concierge's letter, Papa let out a sigh.

'What is it?' Rozenn asked.

'"People" have been asking about Yann.'

'The police?'

'Hopefully just ours, not the Germans.'

Yann came downstairs. Papa handed over the envelope. Yann opened it.

'They want to know why I haven't registered with the Ministry of Labour and provided my new address at the relevant *mairie*.'

'What if she tells them?' Rozenn asked. 'And they telephone their counterparts here and send them out to search the house for Yann?'

Papa removed his hat. 'We knew this would happen. It was just a matter of when.'

'We need to get him away.' Maman spoke from the kitchen, a stack of plates in her hands.

Papa gazed at his hat as if it might provide a solution. 'I've made enquiries in Lannion. I thought asking outside the village might be safer. But they haven't come to anything.' He sounded surprised. Rozenn wasn't. He'd be asking in his vague, kind way, so polite that people didn't even realise what he wanted.

'I've made enquiries, too,' Rozenn said.

'What?' Maman looked at her as though suspecting sunstroke.

'I didn't mention Yann.'

The plates in Maman's hands rattled. Rozenn hoped she wasn't going to drop them. 'You don't know who we can trust.'

'Trust.' Claire looked up from the table where she sat playing with her horse. 'Who can you trust?' Sometimes it sounded as though she knew what she was talking about.

Rozenn felt a wave of impatience at them all. They sat here so passively, hoping an opportunity would fall into their laps. She needed to find Luc again. 'I have a contact,' she said. 'He's reliable and he knows what goes on in the village.'

'I forbid you to continue these conversations,' Papa said. He had rarely looked so furious with her. 'You're just a girl, Rozenn, you have no idea.' He kicked out at the medical bag at his feet. The glass bottles inside rattled.

'Sometimes I think I'm the only one who wants to do anything.' She said it quietly but with conviction. 'The rest of you are just waiting for something to turn up for Yann. It won't.'

For a moment she thought he might actually strike her. Maman looked too shocked to reprimand her, but there was something else in Maman's expression that Rozenn didn't remember seeing before: grudging acceptance?

'We have fish for lunch,' Maman said brightly. 'Thanks to Yann. It's ready, let's enjoy it.'

Last night Yann had returned five or ten minutes after curfew, carrying two *dorades* and a handful of mussels and looking proud. He'd found an old rod in the outbuilding and dug up some worms in the vegetable garden and had managed to catch the fish off the rocks. He'd have scraped off more mussels but had forgotten to bring anything to carry them in. They were going to eat Yann's haul for lunch, Maman said. A real treat.

'The seals were out on the rocks last night,' Yann said, pouring them glasses of water from the carafe as they sat down. 'Competing for the fish. I'm sure they were scowling at me as I walked off.'

'I wonder if the fishermen shoot the seals?' Papa said, appearing to make a big effort to show he'd recovered from his previous loss of temper. 'Poor creatures, they're just hungry like we are.' So they were all to make conversation as though there hadn't been an argument minutes before? Everything unpleasant must be swept aside?

'I envied the seals in their group,' Yann said. 'They seemed so companionable. They can just dive under the waves and escape, whenever they want to.' His eyes met hers and she understood that he was silently approving of what she'd done.

'I wish you had company now,' Maman said. Yann was living such a strange, covert existence: creeping into the house when the postgirl was due each morning, not daring to go beyond the confines of the garden except at night when he went to the cove, seeing nobody apart from his family.

'Sometimes I even wonder whether I should take a chance, go back to Paris, make myself official again, find any useful job I can, even if it's portering in a hospital or working in a restaurant kitchen.'

'You couldn't do that.' Maman looked appalled. Her golden son was a Guillou, not someone who did that kind of work. 'You'd be better off finding farm work somewhere remote, getting fresh air,' she said.

'If I register in a new place they'll be suspicious, wanting to know where I've been in the meantime.'

Rozenn ate her fish and mussels, almost feeling the cells of her body quivering with delight at the protein despite her irritation with her parents. Her skin felt dryer these days, probably lacking some kind of essential oils or minerals. Claire was puzzled by the mussels, poking the black shells with her fork and peering at the golden flesh inside with suspicion. 'Take your fork like this.' Maman showed her. 'Pull out the juicy yellow bit. It tastes very good.'

Eyes narrowed, Claire stuck the prongs of her fork into the shell, extracting the mussel, and eating it cautiously. '*C'est bon.*'

Yann laughed. 'We'll make a *gourmande* of you yet, Claire.'

After lunch Yann offered to read the farm book to Claire, and was greeted with a squeal of delight. Papa drank a cup of roasted-barley coffee and Maman sat with him outside the front door. Maman, despite her ruined nails, appeared to have taken to vegetable growing and was issuing him with a list of seeds he was to buy or barter for if he saw them for sale. 'Scratch any French person and you'll find a peasant who knows how to work the land,' Papa said. 'You're no exception, Louise.'

It sounded as if he believed that acting the peasant at times like this was a good idea. Keep your head down, grow food and wait for it all to pass, just as peasants in France had done over the centuries at times of war.

But Rozenn wasn't going to be a peasant, waiting patiently, mulishly, for things to improve; crossing her fingers that the police would never make their way to the house to ask if Yann was there. She'd seen both the French and German police pull people out of apartments in Paris. On each occasion a particular expression passed over the faces of those witnessing the arrests: horror, usually, quickly followed by a freezing of features, heads lowering towards the pavement as though looking for a dropped coin, pace quickening as though they were going to miss a train.

She was going to take action. Murmuring a farewell, she grabbed her satchel and dark glasses and wandered outside. She wasn't concentrating on where she was going and found herself on the track, heading towards the lane. Something grey moved towards the edge of the field. She froze. A German? No, a donkey – one of a pair, its companion grazing on the far side of the field. The first donkey ambled over to meet Rozenn at the gate. She plucked a handful of grass for him and patted his soft neck. Claire would love the donkeys. Footsteps made her jump. An old man stood behind her, looking accusing. 'These are your donkeys, Monsieur?' She smiled. 'I hope you don't mind me feeding them the grass?'

He observed her silently. 'I live up there,' she added, pointing towards the house.

'The doctor's daughter?' She nodded. 'My Marie went to see him with her cough.'

Rozenn raised a concerned-looking eyebrow.

'He gave her something for her chest.'

'I hope she feels better now?' Papa said that just the act of handing over a bottle of something inactive and innocuous could make patients feel better.

He nodded. 'Seen you with young Martine and Luc.' It was said almost as an accusation.

'I met them down in the village.'

His features almost softened into a smile. 'He's a good boy, Luc.'

'It's good to get to know people who know the area,' she said. 'It's all so new to us.'

'People from Paris come here in July and August with fancy bathing suits and smart motor cars,' he told her.

'It must be very different in winter. And now, with the Germans?' She wondered how he'd managed to stay on here when so many people had been deported from the coastal zone. Perhaps he still managed to produce enough from his land to count as essential labour.

He nodded. Rozenn felt she'd passed a test, acknowledging her own lack of local intelligence. He lifted the scythe he carried. 'Grass won't wait.'

The scent of the meadows floated towards them on the breeze: sweet, somehow youthful and promising. Whatever happened, the grass would always need cutting in early summer. The elderly man walked away.

The donkey batted Rozenn's arm gently. She stroked him under the nose.

'At least I don't have to worry what I say to you,' she told him. 'Or about what you see.' Clearly, in these parts everyone knew what you were up to, who you were spending time with. Another reason for acting sooner rather than later to extract Yann from here.

She walked on, her mind going back to Paris, striding along boulevards or through parks or museums where nobody knew who you were. Longing for home filled her. If she stayed in St Martin every cell of hers would become lethargic, stupefied. Perhaps the Germans would throw her out of the zone. It would almost be a relief to be sent back to Paris, food shortages or not. If it wasn't for Yann. And Claire.

The clip-clop of a horse's hooves roused her. A woman on horseback was approaching the crossing where the track met the lane. The rider sat very straight, handling a lively chestnut with ease. The Irishwoman, Rozenn guessed. The track was narrow. Rozenn stopped, but the rider held the horse back, waving her on.

Rozenn nodded a thanks as she passed. 'You must be Claire's sister,' the rider said, with a slight accent.

'I'm Rozenn, yes.'

'Do remind Claire to come and see the puppies. Your mother knows where I live.'

'I will. *Merci.*' Adults weren't always hospitable towards Claire. A brief outing like this could do wonders for Maman's morale. And give Claire something to talk about for days. She'd probably want a puppy herself, though. How would they feed it?

Rozenn walked on. Luc seemed to spring from a bank of campion. 'It's like the Café de la Paix here this afternoon,' she said. He looked at her enquiringly and then grinned. That smile of his was annoyingly disarming.

'That's a café in Paris, *non*? You were talking to Madame O'Donnell?'

'Does everyone in St Martin know absolutely everything about everyone?'

'If they don't, they'll be sure to ask their neighbours.'

'It seems strange, someone like her still living in the zone.'

'She protested so much when the Boche tried to throw her out they gave up and billeted two officers in the house instead.'

'You know her well?'

'There aren't many of us left. Everyone knows everything about everyone.'

Rozenn tried not to shiver. She distracted herself with the view of the bay. The fishing boats were still out at sea, sails just visible today on the horizon. A single boat was moored in the quay, a man

160

throwing buckets of water over the deck and sweeping it down. 'Does each fishing port have its own colour?' she asked, pointing at its blue and green hull.

'*Oui.* We identify with our local fleet.' There was a note of pride in his voice that made her want to push on, ask again about the boats taking people off the coast. Before she could say any more he reached inside the rucksack he was carrying and took a brown paper bag out. 'Your sandals, Mademoiselle.'

She'd forgotten about them, preoccupied with Yann. 'Oh.' Rozenn blushed at the enthusiasm in her voice. Unwrapping the paper she saw a pair of pale-chestnut sandals, the leather soft and pliable, the soles thick and rubberised. Smart enough to wear with her best frock, but sturdy enough to walk on the path. For clambering over rocks she'd still need her rubber-soled gym shoes. Sitting down on the grass verge she threw off the old pair and put on the new ones. He watched her intently. When she stood up and walked along the lane a little, they felt comfortable. 'They fit perfectly.'

He nodded, unsurprised, and handed her a small piece of paper. 'That's the price.' She winced at the sight of it, but fair enough, this was good leather. He was looking at her as though challenging her to say she couldn't afford the sandals. Well, she never turned down a challenge.

'No rush. You can always find me.' He pulled the string tight on the rucksack top. 'And I can find you too, Rozenn.'

She swallowed hard, picturing him turning up at the house, seeing Yann in the outbuilding. 'I can give you the money now if you wait here while I go back home quickly.' Her savings were hidden away from Claire's curious eyes in a tin in the chest of drawers in their bedroom.

'It can wait.'

He trusted her to pay. In a community so small a word about a dishonest *Parisienne*, even if the daughter of the doctor, would

161

be enough to condemn her and her family. Everything worked on trust. Everything *started* with trust. Luc trusted her. She felt a flush of pleasure.

'Please let me know if I can help with anything else.' He sounded suddenly formal as he extended a hand. It felt warm and firm as he took hers, the skin brown, slightly calloused on the palm. This was a boy who spent time out of doors carrying out physical labour. She wanted to cling to the hand.

'There is something else.' The words came out in a rush.

'*Oui?*' He looked quizzical.

'What we were talking about before, the fishing boats—'

'Fishing boats catch fish.' His face was set. 'That's all.'

'But before—'

'Before was different.'

'I want to get someone out,' she said again.

He tensed, like an alert animal, glancing from side to side.

'Please.' Rozenn had never begged anyone before. Friends, boys, Yann – they tended to do what she wanted them to do. Even Claire, unruly as she could be, would try to please her. Pleading made her feel shaky inside, as though she was using weak muscles. 'We're worried they'll try to send him back to Germany.'

'Was he a POW? Why's he back?'

She nodded. 'He needed an emergency operation. He's twenty-one. If they bring in the new forced labour, the Germans will want him back.'

For a moment it looked as though he was going to say something. Then he gave a half-shrug and turned. 'Glad you like the sandals.'

Tears of shame and frustration pricked at her eyes. She'd told him everything and he'd rejected her plea. He'd rejected *her*. Rozenn watched him walk away.

She picked up the old pair of sandals and stuffed them into the satchel. She took a side track vaguely thinking it would bring her out on the parallel cliff path. The campion and foxgloves would ordinarily lift her spirits, but now she trudged along in her new sandals, finding herself turning left as she joined the cliff path, heading down towards the village. Was she trying to follow Luc, plead with him again? Rozenn flushed. As she dropped down towards the houses, their gardens filled with the last irises and peonies and the early summer roses – pinky-white and gold, honey scented – it seemed as though the flowers were mocking her. She felt an urge to pull all the petals off, trample them into the dirt, spoil the beauty of the village for the Germans. Why should the occupiers enjoy the scent, the dazzling blooms? Her hand went to a creamy-pink rosebud. The petals were waxy in her fingers, like human skin, and as warm in the sun. She let go of the bud.

'Take the flower, Mademoiselle.' Rozenn jumped. In the garden, an elderly black-clad woman straightened herself from a row of young beans. 'It's pretty like you.' The woman smiled at her. Was she a fisherman's mother, perhaps, allowed to stay on in the zone?

'*Merci*, Madame.' Rozenn forced a smile and plucked the rosebud, pulling the stem through the buttonhole on her blouse collar.

'Your *tadig* is the doctor, isn't he? I saw him for my arthritis. He is a kind man.'

'Yes, he's my *tadig*.' She nodded a farewell and walked on. She wasn't an anonymous girl in a still-bustling city. The doctor was her *tadig*, the Breton for father. People would be watching her, judging her for any breach of propriety.

Rozenn stopped above the quay. On an afternoon like this, the beach beyond should have been ringing with the sounds of children playing. Claire ought to be building sandcastles, playing in the sea. The world was topsy-turvy. She wanted to scream at the heedless waves still flowing in one after the other while soldiers built up defences and people were killed and tortured all across Europe from France to Poland. Yann needed to escape, put things right. Every blow he struck for the Free French would be retribution for Theo and his family having to run from their home, for Maman's ruined hands, for Papa having to examine German bunions and boils. And for Claire, forced from the quiet rhythm of life with the nuns.

I'm going to get you out, she promised Yann silently. I will make that boy help me.

18

I stared at the red letters on the front door of the house my grand-mother had lived in until they blurred in front of me. *Traitor.* I touched the paint: it was almost worn away in places, probably hastily slapped-on cheap stuff that would come off with white spirits and a bit of patience.

'*Vous empiétez,*' a female voice said.

I turned around, feeling a mixture of guilt and irritation as I faced a woman on horseback, calling out to me from the footpath. I started to apologise for trespassing. She cut me off with a wave of the hand. 'You were talking to Joséphine in the bar earlier on?'

I blinked. Word had travelled very fast. I'd only left the bar forty minutes ago. The rider's lips twitched. 'Gossip travels fast here. She said you were interested in the house?'

I took a step towards her, eyeing the horse with caution. 'My grandmother lived here.'

'Your grandmother being Rozenn Guillou?'

I nodded. The horse, a bay gelding, shifted his weight around.

'He won't hurt you,' she said.

'I think he's lost a shoe?'

'*Merde.*' She dismounted to look. 'You're right.' She patted the horse's glossy side. 'The farrier for you.' She turned to me. '*Merci.* Nobody's paid this place much attention until recently.'

'They carried out basic repairs at least.' I pointed up at the new tiles and guttering on the roof. The window frames and shutters looked new too and I could see some repointing on the granite stone walls.

'It was sold last year.'

'What does the graffiti mean?' I asked.

She straightened out a strand of the bay's mane. 'Long memories in this part of the world.'

'Long enough to remember Rozenn Guillou?'

She looked down at her horse's mane for a moment and nodded.

What is the problem? I wanted to ask. *Why do you and Joséphine stall when I ask you questions?* I thought back to the American veteran on the ferry. He'd been right when he told me people didn't want to rake up the past. I changed tack.

'Who is the owner? Does he know about this graffiti?'

'He's an American. We haven't seen him. But he's started a refurbishment inside – he's rewired, improved the plumbing, plastered the walls, put in a new kitchen and bathroom.' She sounded annoyed. Perhaps this part of Brittany was like Cornwall, where properties were bought and sold for a fortune, pricing out locals. I felt a slight, professional, pang. What fun to buy a place like this and choose your own bathroom and kitchen fittings.

'I'm Morane Caradec,' I said, watching her closely as I gave my name. I thought I saw a flicker of something.

'Lise O'Donnell.' She extended a hand. I didn't want to go any closer to the bay, but forced myself to dart forward and take the hand quickly, keeping an eye on his rear hooves. I noted the Irish surname.

'Your family have never been back since your grandmother left, Morane?'

I shook my head. 'My grandmother didn't talk about her time here.' We were still speaking French; it felt so natural to use the language.

Lise nodded.

'Do you have longstanding family connections here?' I asked.

She looked amused. 'Not by local standards: we've only been here for ninety-five years. Our house is a kilometre or so along there.' She nodded back up the track towards the fields. I saw that she was older than I'd first thought, early fifties, perhaps, her skin well looked-after, only the faintest of lines around her eyes. A well-maintained Frenchwoman in Rozenn's mould. 'My father was just ten when the war ended.'

The horse dropped his head and Lise let him nibble at the grass. She seemed to be considering something.

'He remembers the German officers billeted in the house. And the arrival of the Americans. And snatches of conversation, though I think his mother kept a lot from him.'

'That seems to have been a common response – keeping things from the children,' I said drily. 'We didn't even know that my grandmother had lived here.'

She laughed and the last of her reserve seemed to drop away. 'You must come up and meet my papa. He's pretty well house-bound now, much to his irritation. But on sunny days he likes to sit out on the terrace with his coffee and he loves talking about local history.'

I couldn't resist beaming at her. 'I'd like that.'

She gave me her number and the address of the house, which I entered into my mobile's contacts.

Lise clicked at the horse and he lifted his head. She led him off, probably not wanting to risk his unshod hoof on the rough track. I stood back, shaking slightly. Irritation at myself made me turn away from the *longère* and return to the cliff path, Gwen's voice echoing in my head. 'You could have cognitive behavioural therapy or something, push those intrusive thoughts away? You can't let them haunt you like this.'

I couldn't explain that part of me didn't want to push the thoughts away because I deserved them. The punishment I felt every time I was near a horse was appropriate. 'But it's becoming worse, isn't it?' Gwen had said gently. 'You seem frightened of even seeing horses.'

'I am. But so what?' I'd said. 'I spend a lot of time in London, so it doesn't matter that I'm not keen on them. As long as I stay out of the parks, I'm fine.'

'But you loved them so much—'

I silenced her with a glare before she could remind me that as a child and teenager I'd spent hours at a stables near our home, hacking out in Richmond Park. During our Cornish holidays there'd always been pony trekking, Gwen sometimes accompanying me but less enthusiastic. I'd ridden at weekends as an adult, too, enjoyed a bit of jumping, but mainly I hacked out. As the business had started to prosper I'd even thought about buying my own horse. Nick had supported this desire, *as long as you don't move the nag in with us.* The days when I'd had enough disposable income even to contemplate an expense like this were long gone now.

A friend on the Oxfordshire–Berkshire border had a gelding I'd ride for her when she was busy. I'd take him on to the Ridgeway, an ancient trail across the Downs. He was steady and they'd banned motor vehicles on the trail.

I'd fallen into a relaxed, almost meditative state, lulled by the rhythm of the horse's movements, the fresh smell of the winter morning and the leathery scent of the tack. It was early enough on a Sunday to mean I had the stretch of Ridgeway almost to myself. I'd pushed my horse into a canter.

Spotting a father and two boys ahead, I slowed to a trot, and then a walk. As I passed I exchanged greetings with them and the younger boy said he liked my horse. I smiled at him and trotted on.

Ahead of me I saw the road descending steeply from my left, intersecting the trail at right angles. I started checking for cars. I could still hear the children behind me, chatting.

The cyclist shot down the road from the left, turning on to the trail in front of us so fast he and his bicycle must have felt like some ancestral predator to my horse, who squealed with terror. He reversed fast, tossing his head, bucking. I managed to soothe him, holding him with my legs, pushing him onwards towards the road.

'Poor horse is scared,' the little boy said behind me. The group had caught me up while I'd been settling the horse.

A second cyclist shot down the road from the left and turned on to the trail in front of us. I felt the horse jerk beneath me, a rush of air on my face.

I was on the ground, winded, dazed, uninjured. The horse was standing behind me, nuzzling me, a rein broken, otherwise unhurt. I stood up, thankful that the ground was still soft from rain earlier in the week. My ears were ringing, I didn't make out the screams behind me for a second.

I turned. The boy who'd admired my horse lay motionless on the ground.

~✤~

When Lise had ridden off I stayed in front of the house and the longer I remained there the more familiar it felt. I forced myself to return to the village and my parked car. As I reached it my mobile trilled. I blinked and stared at it. A message from Tatiana, with a photograph attached of her sitting room. *Looks awful, walls all yellow now?! You said they would be off-white.* Had someone delivered the wrong paint to the decorator? I opened the email order to the paint supplier and checked what I'd asked for. No mistake. I studied Tatiana's picture again, screwing up my eyes, and smiled.

You changed the light bulbs in the sitting room, Tatiana?

I could almost feel the static in the atmosphere between Brittany and Notting Hill as she investigated. *Oleg do light bulbs when they ran out, but he bought wrong ones! That man. He will change them. Or I shall change him.*

I'm glad it's nothing more serious, I texted back. *Don't change Oleg!* How straightforward life was when it was simply a matter of swapping bulbs over, changing the light in a room, transforming the way it looked. Perhaps I needed to change my own light bulbs. I certainly needed to do something to transform my relationship with my sister. I checked my email and saw that the Bluetooth speaker and coffee machine had arrived at Sue's house. I texted Gwen, telling her this. Her reply came almost instantly. *Sue texted me: the boxes were damaged and I asked her to open them. The speaker looked battered and needs to go back. G.*

Will contact the store and sort this out, sorry, I replied.

Already sorted. Replacements on the way.

Gwen didn't even trust me to resolve a delivery, although so much of my work life was spent ordering supplies and checking them. She hadn't even referred to my trip here or to the photos I'd sent her. Distracted at work or still thinking I was reckless? I couldn't think of a good way to respond to the message.

I drove towards Lannion, through green fields and rushes of blossom and flowers in hedgerows and gardens, a heaviness in my heart despite the colour and light.

19

The second half of June decided it wasn't really summer after all. Rain blew in from the west, slapping you in the face and insinuating its way beneath layers of clothing. When it wasn't raining, a fine mist hung over the coast. Maman set up washing lines and clothes horses in the larger outbuilding with a lighted brazier, but the clothes and sheets didn't seem to dry, retaining a salty dampness for several days. Papa reported a surge in chesty coughs among his patients.

Laundry had never been such a performance in Paris. Before the Occupation the maid bundled it up, taking it down to the concierge. A man came to pick it up from her each week, driving off in a laundry van. Smaller items, as Maman put it, were washed by hand by the same maid and hung in the bathroom when the heater was on overnight. The laundry van returned the shirts, blouses, towels and sheets, parcelled up and neatly labelled and the maid placed it all in the correct wardrobes and drawers. After the maid went they continued to send laundry to the *blanchisserie*.

'There must still be a *blanchisserie* running in the village,' Rozenn said.

'If there is, we haven't found it.' Maman shook out a towel and replaced it on the clothes horse. 'Your father thinks there was one during the summer season, for the visitors before the war.'

'We should ask him to make enquiries in Lannion.'

'Perhaps I should put this through the mangle again.' Maman was still eyeing the damp towel. 'I can't imagine how we'll manage in the winter.'

The women were now wearing cotton pads safety-pinned underneath the armpits of their dresses and blouses: easier to wash and dry. Claire kept pulling hers out at first, but was getting used to them. In the convent clothes hadn't been changed more than once or twice a week anyway. Papa needed to look professional for his surgery and home visits and more attention was given to his shirts. Yann spent much of his time in a singlet and old trousers, though Maman made him put on a shirt at mealtimes. Maman was less anxious now about cooking. She even laughed as they sat over the meals. Something about this old house seemed to suit her. It was certainly better than it had first seemed, Rozenn conceded, though she would still have given an arm to be back in Paris.

'Maybe I could go into Lannion with your father tomorrow, take the laundry in myself, have a look around the town.' Maman looked wistful, perhaps picturing herself having coffee in a café, reading a novel or what passed for a newspaper. Being somewhere alone, somewhere without Claire to watch, imagining herself as her old self for a brief period.

'I'll watch Claire. You and Papa have lunch out together,' Rozenn offered, before she could stop herself. What was she doing, giving away even more of her freedom? Her mother's face lit up. For a moment Rozenn could see Maman as a girl her age, enjoying the Paris of the twenties, full of vitality, desperately trying to put aside its memories of war. The insight unsettled Rozenn. She mumbled an excuse and went outside.

Maman and Papa couldn't have dreamt there'd be another war, that their own son would be dragged into it, that they'd be living in exile to prevent him from being snatched up into its talons. The trenches mightn't claim Yann, but those German factories, those work camps, would swallow him up. He'd made such progress, even on a restricted diet, with his fitness training and swimming. But a few months in harsh conditions could undo all the progress. Papa said that some infections could linger, almost undetectable, waiting to reinvade a weakened constitution.

Yann was in his outbuilding, performing his daily exercise routine. She watched him from the doorway as he performed a set of press-ups. He and Rozenn had been strong as children, unlike Claire, who picked up every illness. Perhaps that was why Maman never spent much time with Rozenn when she'd been small: she hadn't needed her as desperately as Claire did and she wasn't as appealing as her handsome, sunny-natured older brother. She recalled the times she'd asked Maman to take her to the park. Maman had always needed to listen to Yann's violin practice or play therapeutic games with Claire. The nurse had taken Rozenn out to play instead. Papa, when he wasn't working, had spent time with her, taking her to art galleries and zoos and to run around in the Bois.

Perhaps that was why Maman still seemed to love Yann and Claire more than Rozenn: she could do more for them. Hide Yann, build up his strength with whatever food they could acquire. Nurture Claire.

Rozenn was prickly with Maman, she admitted to herself now. When her mother paid her attention, offering advice on her clothes or hair, she'd often snub her. It was too late. She'd needed her mother when she was younger.

Rozenn gave herself a mental shake. She was becoming someone rather different from the witty, light-hearted girl she'd once been. Too much introspection, too much earnestness, was unappealing, like being a German. Men liked a bit of intellectual spark – an interest in philosophy or literature, or in Rozenn's case architecture: serious but not heavy. She'd prided herself on being self-contained but thoughtful, ready with a quick riposte. Perhaps she wasn't so very unlike Maman in that respect: before the war Maman and Papa had entertained at home and Rozenn had observed her mother making conversation with the guests. A few well-chosen questions of the person you were talking to; then listen attentively to them. Respond to enquiries about your own self or your family with graceful but not over-lengthy replies, careful not to bore but without being facile. A *Parisienne* was like a willow constructed from steel. But they chopped willows down, didn't they?

Claire was sitting on the front doorstep, staring at her, head slightly cocked. 'Zenn sad?' Her lower lip wobbled.

Sometimes the girl was more perceptive than she could possibly know.

'Sad? *Mais non.*' She forced a smile. 'Of course not. The rain's eased off a little. Where's your ball, Claire?'

They played catch for fifteen minutes, hair falling damp over their faces, skirts becoming heavy. Claire dropped the slippery ball, clutching her lower abdomen.

'I'm wet. It hurts.'

Rozenn felt the cramps too. She and her sister seemed fated to go through the monthly cycle simultaneously. Rozenn loathed the whole business, the humiliation of dealing with the bloodied pads and underclothes – not just hers, but Claire's too. In Paris they'd been placed discreetly in a lidded enamel bucket for the maid to manage.

'I'll make us some peppermint tea. Come inside.' Rozenn boiled water on the stove. Maman had picked mint leaves and hung them, stalks up, from a nail on the dresser. Rozenn bruised them in her fingers to release the oil and pulled out a bottle of aspirin. Only one tablet left. Papa said he'd bring more back this evening. Another cramp made her double over. Claire wouldn't know there

174

was only one aspirin. She wouldn't even understand that the little white pills could stop the clenching pains. Rozenn could crumble the tablet into her own mint tea and feel better within minutes.

She looked at her sister. Claire's eyes were ringed with shadows and she was pale. Muttering a curse to herself she broke the tablet into Claire's cup. They drank the tea together.

'Play with my horse?' Claire asked, seeming brighter.

'*Désolée.*' Rozenn shook her head. She was going to go for a walk, regardless of whether the rain had stopped. Claire'd had the aspirin, that was enough. She wasn't going to bore herself further this afternoon with her sister. Walking would stop her cramps from becoming too severe. In wet weather in Paris, she'd sometimes walked round and round an art gallery or department store to ease the pain. Sometimes she'd run herself a long hot bath. Here they only had an old tin bath that had to be used in the kitchen when Yann and Papa were banished. Heating the water took at least an hour. Maman had told her just months before they'd come here that pregnancy would help with the pains and that hopefully, within a year or two, Rozenn herself would be married and expecting a baby. The prospect seemed a worse fate, however.

Claire's face crumpled. 'Ask Yann to play with you,' Rozenn told her. If they stayed in Yann's outbuilding, they'd be safe.

If Yann escaped to England and Rozenn herself ever managed to return to Paris, how would Maman cope on days like this? She pictured her mother waving Papa off to work and spending the dark winter days alone with Claire, who could barely conduct even the most basic conversation. Going over and over letters with Claire, playing infantile games with her. Couldn't they find a local woman to watch Claire out of this house for Maman a few mornings a week? Rozenn made a note to ask Papa. He'd probably say it was too much of a risk: Claire might blab about her brother. Everything came back to the fact that while Yann was here, everyone was in limbo. There'd been no word from Luc and she hadn't even seen him for well over a week. Perhaps he was avoiding her. Why bother herself about some local boy? He'd made it clear he wasn't going to do what she wanted and help find a boat for Yann. Some of the disappointment she felt about this seemed to come from a more personal sense of rejection. Perhaps he wasn't interested in her in the way she'd suspected he was. He wasn't her type, she reminded herself. She liked intellectual men. Like Theo. Guiltily she realised she hadn't been thinking as much about Theo recently.

Before she left for the village Rozenn went to find Yann in the outbuilding. He was exercising. Papa had found a second keg for him, which he'd filled with sand. '*Regarde*,' he said, picking up both kegs and raising them above his shoulders in a single easy movement. 'I couldn't have done that a few weeks ago.'

She looked out of the open door at the drizzle. 'Do you think we could all get into the *Zone Libre*?' she asked. She pictured them sitting in the sunshine.

'Perhaps.' But he didn't sound convinced. 'We wouldn't have German soldiers everywhere but the regime's pretty similar. And I don't think there's much more food. Quite a lot of their wheat came from the northern zone.'

'I remember the wheat plains we saw from the train on the way here.' A lifetime ago.

'Wheat. Dairy produce from Normandy. Pork and fish. Mostly going to Germany now instead of the south. I bet a lot of their own produce goes to the Reich as well.'

'Tomatoes, oranges, sunflower seeds.'

'Cooking oils. Maize. Grapes.'

Rozenn was frowning.

'What is it?'

'If you went to England the food would be diabolical but perhaps nobody goes hungry over there?'

'Papa told me their rationing is severe but fair. But they eat dried eggs and margarine.'

'I heard it was all cabbage, boiled up for hours until it's soggy. Or that soup made from oats they eat for breakfast.'

He grimaced. 'What I'm prepared to do to serve my country.' He picked up his sketch pad and flicked through the pages. Rozenn made out the images of his characters flexing their muscles, jumping, punching, flying.

'Be careful what you draw.' She tried to say it casually.

'I am. Couldn't resist doing this, though.' He passed her the pad. She saw a group of slave labourers rising up to kick a uniformed German overseer over a cliff while a female figure resembling Marianne, the personification of French womanhood, blew them a kiss. She smiled, despite herself.

'And this.' He took back the pad and turned the page. The same female character was raising a leg to aim a high-heeled shoe at Hitler's backside.

She laughed out loud. 'The sooner you're out of here the better. That could have you shot.' The drizzle was barely perceptible now. Rozenn stood up.

'You're going out?' He sounded wistful.

'I thought I smelt wild garlic along the footpaths. Papa says it's good for the blood. Maman said it would liven up the soup.'

'Beetroot and potato soup is becoming a little predictable.' He let out a long breath. 'I know we're better off than most people in France now but I dream of the meals we used to eat. Do you remember those feasts of oysters and lobster when we stayed in Rennes? The fillet of beef at Christmas? That mushroom sauce? And, *mon Dieu*, those gateaux we used to buy on the way home from Mass on Sundays?'

'You used to insist on chocolate when I always wanted the chestnut meringue. And Claire always had to have anything with

177

strawberries in it.' And of course Yann and Claire's choices had come before hers.

Yann moaned. 'Don't remind me. It's unbearable.'

'One day, I'm going to eat in the best restaurants. Whatever I want, whatever it costs. And so will you.'

He nodded slowly. 'I plan on making something of myself too.' She blinked at the determination in his voice. He'd always been such an easy-going young man, letting others make decisions, never so vehement about his demands as she was. No wonder Maman loved him so much. He was looking at her.

'What?'

'I'm not like you. If you'd been a boy you'd already have formed your own private militia to push the Germans off the cliffs.' He was still looking at her, puzzled. 'Rozenn?'

'What?'

He shrugged. 'I have a feeling there's something on your mind?'

She was going to deny it but this was Yann. 'You know I was making enquiries? It's this boy I met.'

'Ah.'

'No, not like that, he's not . . . Well, not a romantic prospect.' She scowled at him. 'He's good at finding things.'

'Your new sandals?'

'Those. But as I told Papa, I'm sure he knows people who could help get you out. I have to tread very carefully, of course.'

He looked down at the sketch pad. 'It's not just me you have to be careful about, Rozenn.'

'Maman, Papa and Claire. I know.' It felt vital that Yann trusted her.

'Of course you do.' He gave her his radiant smile, reminding her of Claire.

'In the meantime, foraging in the hedgerows and fields is today's mission.' She lifted a hand in farewell.

It really had stopped raining. Her satchel was in the kitchen and she'd need it for collecting the wild garlic. Her sandals were upstairs. Claire and Maman had come inside and sat at the kitchen table, the barley grinder in front of them. 'The handle goes around like this, see?' Maman said.

'Do you want to see the donkeys, Claire?' Why on earth had she said this? Sitting with Yann for a few minutes had worked some kind of spell on her.

Claire leapt up. An expression of relief passed over her mother's face. 'Would you do that?' Maman asked. 'I could get on quietly, at my own pace.'

'Where're your papers, Claire?' Claire now understood that she had to have her papers every time she went out. She ran upstairs to fetch them from the top of the chest of drawers. 'Bring down my new shoes,' Rozenn called. Claire returned almost immediately, her feet light and rapid on the staircase, and handed papers and sandals to Rozenn.

'She couldn't manage more than one thing at a time before we came here,' Maman said. 'I know you think I'm deluding myself, but I think she's coming on.'

Both her parents were deluding themselves in different ways. Papa that coming here would delay hard decisions about Yann. Maman that Claire was capable of doing more. Rozenn felt a stab of pity for them both: for Yann, trapped, bored, and for Claire, imprisoned in her own damaged head.

'The sun's coming out,' Rozenn told Maman. 'Take your chair out and read my magazine. Fantasise about all the wonderful, exciting things they do in the south.'

Maman laughed. 'Fantasise is probably the right word.' She frowned. 'I don't think I have noticed those rather lovely objects before?' She was looking down at Rozenn's sandals. Around the house Rozenn wore the *sabots*.

'I bought them a few days ago.' She still had the money in the satchel to give Luc.

'In Lannion?' When Rozenn said nothing her mother narrowed her eyes. 'I won't ask. Obviously your *contacts* are useful to you but I hope you remember what your father and I told you about keeping your mouth closed?'

Rozenn nodded.

'Don't get the sandals muddy.' She said it like the amused, cynical woman Rozenn remembered from Paris, but for a moment there was a softness in her expression as she smiled at Rozenn.

'Look out for rabbits,' Rozenn told Claire as they walked along the track towards the lane. 'You might see babies.' Papa was talking about buying a shotgun, though it was hard to see how this could be done in the prohibited zone. Perhaps a doctor would be exempt, though. Shooting rabbits would increase their protein levels very nicely but it would be more efficient to breed their own, Rozenn thought. Yann would be good at hutch construction.

'Donkeys!' Claire had spotted something more exciting than the rabbits and ran ahead. Rozenn plucked a few handfuls of grass. The donkeys stood at the far end of the field, refusing to turn around in response to the girls' clicks and encouragements.

Claire's lip trembled. 'They don't like us.'

'Let's find some wild flowers for Maman.' Rozenn waited for the outburst, but Claire trotted beside Rozenn, pointing out a ladybird on her arm, a butterfly in the hedge and a small mouse scuttling through the grass. In the distance a man was scything hay – not the elderly man, someone younger. As they came closer Rozenn saw it was a boy, muscles firm under the singlet top which was all he wore with his light trousers. Each of his movements was rhythmic, easy. It was Luc. Rozenn swallowed hard. The sun came out and struck the metal blade of his scythe. Rozenn blinked and walked on. Damn him, why did he have to look the way he did?

The lane curled down towards the village. As they rounded a bend they saw a couple ahead of them, leaning against a gate. The man, really a boy, she saw as they approached, wore a corporal's artillery uniform. 'Yann could draw the mouse,' Claire said her mind still on the creature.

'Shh, don't talk about Yann out of the house,' Rozenn told her. 'Remember?'

Martine nodded at Rozenn, seemingly unbothered that she'd been spotted standing so close to the German that their heads were almost touching. Currying favour with the occupiers in return for extra rations? Rozenn thought of the pin in Martine's lapel: perhaps she didn't feel too strongly about the Occupation, believing it might gain Brittany freedom from France.

Martine looked at Claire, who was hopping, singing to herself. Amusement filled her eyes. 'Easily pleased, bless her.'

'No bad thing these days.' Rozenn took her sister's hand and tried to hurry her on, but Claire had spotted something.

'Money.' She pulled herself free and stooped down to pick up a coin. A twenty-centime piece made from zinc, with a hole in the middle.

'You can put it on a chain and wear it round your neck like a necklace,' Rozenn told her. 'A lucky charm.'

'Lucky charm,' Claire repeated.

'Better than trying to find anything to buy with it,' Martine said. The German shuffled and blushed. Rozenn noticed a small nick on his cheek. Had he cut himself shaving like Yann had done when first mastering the art?

'Come on.' Rozenn put a hand on Claire's arm. 'Let's go and see the cats.'

'Cats!' Claire ran down the lane like a small child, arms pumping, head slightly lowered. Martine's laughter rang out. Anger burnt in Rozenn's cheeks. She wanted to walk back and slap Martine round the face, tell her she was a jumped-up little nobody who flirted with the enemy.

She forced herself to keep her attention on Claire. '*Attends.*' Rozenn ran after her. If Claire reached the quay by herself she might topple into the water. The tide was high now. They shot down the steps, Rozenn praying Claire wouldn't slip. A single cat observed them, licking its paws.

A wolf whistle startled them. Rozenn spun around to see a young German being pulled away by two of his fellow artillerymen. She couldn't understand what he was saying but from his hand gestures he seemed to be impressed by her hair. Her cheeks burnt.

'No fish for her.' Claire sounded worried. 'The cat's hungry.' She patted her stomach. 'So am I.'

Normally at this time of the afternoon Maman would give her a piece of bread, with a tiny scraping of conserve or butter on it. All the bread had gone at lunchtime today. Rozenn tried not to think of Yann's missing ration, about how much difference it would have made.

'Hungry.' Claire said it more loudly. A middle-aged woman walking on the path above them tutted loudly. Rozenn wasn't sure it was disapproval of Claire or of her. 'And I hurt again.' She put her hands on her lower abdomen.

'Have this.' Luc appeared seemingly from thin air, leaping down from the footpath above. He'd put a shirt on over his singlet. Her insides gave a little lurch at the sight of him, which annoyed her. He reached inside his trouser pocket, opened a sheet of greased paper and handed Claire a biscuit, what looked like a traditional Breton *sablé* made with sugar and real butter. Her own mouth watered. Why did this local boy have such grace? Not just in the way he carried himself but in the way he was with people?

'Remember your manners,' she reminded Claire. Claire said *merci* with her most radiant smile and took a large bite out of the biscuit.

'It must be so hard for her, not understanding where all the food's gone, why she feels hungry.' Luc was watching Claire eat, his eyes gentle, his voice low.

'It's hard to explain. She hasn't had a biscuit for months now.' Rozenn was speaking quietly too. 'She's in heaven.'

'A friend made them for me.'

Everything here seemed to be based on friendships and who you knew. And trusted.

'Her husband's a dairy farmer, just outside the zone. All their butter's supposed to go to the Germans, but some of it gets lost in the dairy, it seems.'

He was still observing Claire. 'Was she born like that or was it an accident?' Asked by anyone else the question would have had Rozenn's palms itching, but Luc sounded sympathetic rather than judgmental.

'Damage at birth. Apparently the second twin is more at risk.'

He nodded. '*La pauvre*. But your sister lives in the present and perhaps that's no bad way to live these days.'

She remembered the money for the sandals and took the envelope out of the satchel and passed it to him, checking nobody was in sight.

He placed it in his pocket with a quick thanks. They stood watching Claire. The biscuit must have done the trick because she smiled at the cat, who let her stroke it. With the animal to distract her she was less likely to prattle on about Yann in front of Luc.

'Stay away from the edge,' Rozenn warned her. 'It's slippery.' Luc removed his cigarettes from an inside pocket and offered her one, lighting it for her. He turned over a bucket and beckoned to her to sit down, before finding a barrel and turning it over for himself.

'As the season comes on she'll have a bit more to eat,' he said, looking at Claire. 'Your mother's growing vegetables, isn't she?' He grinned at her surprise. 'Your father bought seeds in Lannion for her – a friend of a friend told me.'

Her heartbeat slowed. Luc hadn't been watching the house.

'My mother's optimistic she can grow a lot of food for us. I suppose it will help.'

'Your father's well thought of. I expect people are making their gratitude known.'

'They've been very kind. Someone gave us hens and they're actually producing eggs.'

'One day this will be no more than a bad dream.' He seemed so confident, and yet so able to understand what she was thinking, fearing. He reached out and took her hand, squeezing it briefly. The skin on her palm tingled. Fleetingly she wondered what the hand would feel like elsewhere on her body.

'I saw you scything the hay,' she said, the words coming out huskily. He must have spotted them walking into the village and taken the shortcut over the cliff path to meet them here. The thought was like a taste of honey.

'I put in a few hours for the farmer. It's too much work for him to do the whole of the field and his son's still in Germany.'

A prisoner of war like Yann had been.

He gave a rueful grin. 'All right, I took leave of my work to come and talk to you.'

'What about the hay?' She made her voice sound playful.

'It'll stay fine for the rest of the day.'

He could predict the weather. He knew how things worked around here. He was kind. And he liked her. And she, well, she'd been telling herself it was just his looks that appealed.

She decided to take the chance. 'The fishermen,' she started. 'I know it's sensitive—'

He dropped her hand. 'I told you before, they can't do it any more. Too dangerous.' He wasn't looking at her and the words sounded rehearsed.

'The person who needs to get out of the country is my brother.' There, the words were out. She'd taken the plunge and God only knew what the consequences would be.

'Your brother?' He sounded puzzled. Good. Yann hadn't been seen. 'Where's he? In Paris?' She looked him directly in the eye and said nothing. He whistled. 'He's up there in the house, isn't he? You're hiding him in the prohibited zone? What's he done? Put up anti-German posters? Dropped leaflets in the metro? Actually, don't tell me.'

'He's done nothing.' Until he'd failed to return to Paris on the train. 'He just can't be sent back to Germany.'

Luc let out a long, slow breath.

'Will you help me?' She found herself stepping towards him.

He looked down at Claire, now sitting cross-legged on the quay, talking to the cat.

'Do you really not understand how dangerous it is to even have these conversations?' He spoke kindly, as though Rozenn was like Claire, slow-witted.

'He's my brother,' she repeated. 'I want to do this for him.'

They stared at one another. Something seemed to shift behind his gaze. 'Of course you want to help your brother.' He put a hand out to stop her saying more. 'I'll come and see you. Later on.' She didn't bother asking where and when, she knew he'd find her. For a moment they maintained eye contact. 'Why?' he asked. 'Why did you ask me again after I said no?' His hand went to the back of his neck. The sun had tanned it.

She shrugged. 'I don't know. Some kind of instinct.'

'Nothing more?' He rubbed his neck, looking at her.

Rozenn shook her head. 'I don't know what you mean.' She'd seen how generous he was. Was that all he meant? She barely knew herself.

His face relaxed.

'We should go home now,' she said. 'My mother will need me.' She thought of something else. 'We saw Martine on our way down. With a German.' She watched him closely to see if this would worry him.

He gave a sniff. 'Martine's convinced the Germans have great plans for her family. But so far it's just one artillery corporal who's showing interest in Breton nationalism. Or so he tells her.'

'I thought she was your . . . you know?'

'Martine?' He smiled. 'Lovely girl. But she wouldn't be interested in me. My father owns a canning business with a sideline in cement. Martine has ambitions.'

'Would you be interested in her?' She felt like a jealous schoolgirl asking him and blushed.

'There's only one person in St Martin who interests me.' He looked at her full on. She felt almost naked. 'And she probably has no interest in fish and cement.'

Rozenn laughed too, curiously relieved. 'Fish and cement sound good. Not at the same time perhaps.' He moved closer to her and put his hands on her shoulders, brushing each of her cheeks with his, pausing each time for a second longer than was normal for a parting kiss. His breath felt like a summer's breeze on her skin.

Luc must have taken her slight movement towards him as assent. His hands went around her waist. His lips found hers. Claire was still distracted by the cat. Nobody else was around. Rozenn closed her eyes, let herself surrender to the sensation of his lips on hers. It was a brief kiss, his tongue only pushing between her lips for a moment, but a kiss all the same. Little nerves along her spine and down her flanks awoke, made themselves known, told her that she'd missed this, that she wanted more from Luc. She placed a hand on his chest, felt his heart beating under the cotton shirt.

'It's hot work, labouring in the fields,' he said. 'I'm not at my smartest.'

'I like what you wear.'

Claire would see. Rozenn stood back, disentangling herself. He smiled at her. 'Someone told me Parisian girls were cold.'

'They told you wrong.' There was a shake in her voice.

'That's what I thought,' he said, probably trying to sound like a man of the world. She wanted to wind her arms around his neck and rub herself against him like a cat.

❧

'Luc, Luc, Luc,' Claire chanted as they walked home. 'I like Luc.'

'So do I.' The words fell out naturally. She more than liked Luc. And it was no longer just because of his physical grace and easy manner. Or because he could get her what she wanted.

Claire was pointing at something. 'Yann.'

About to tell her she was wrong, Rozenn looked at the clump of pink granite. Yann sat with his back against one of the rocks, almost invisible, out of the breeze, sketching. Rage boiled through her. What the hell did he think he was doing?

'And a soldier.' Claire was looking at the track that intersected with the cliff path ahead of Yann.

Feeling helpless, Rozenn watched the same German who'd been with Martine earlier on as he strolled towards Yann.

20

I deposited my few pieces of luggage and a bag of basic groceries in the apartment I'd rented in Lannion. The owner had left me a plate of *sablé* biscuits, similar to shortbread, and a bottle of local cider. As I sat at the kitchen table to enjoy these, my mobile trilled. Lise.

My father suggests tomorrow morning, if you would like to join us for coffee at 10.45?

I gratefully accepted the invitation then checked my emails. A message from a builder in England querying the depth of the engineered wooden floorboards I'd ordered for Tatiana.

It would have been easier to have found the details on my stolen laptop, with its projects filed in folders I could access at a click of the mouse rather than peering at a tiny screen. But I managed to retrieve the emailed order and forward it to the builder. Relying on a mobile phone for work wasn't going to be sustainable: I'd have to get on to eBay shortly. My credit card was going to ignite.

I wasn't going to think about that now. Feeling hungry I set out to find a brasserie for an early evening dinner. The walk on the cliff path earlier on had given me an appetite, just as the sea air around Rozenn's house did. Lannion was compact enough to cross in all directions. I admired its steep cobbled streets. The town lay some miles inland, the river leading to its own small port on the coast, but the light and atmosphere was similar to that of the seaside towns I knew in Cornwall. The use of granite as a building stone made me feel at home too. I peered into shop windows, admiring the pastries and cheeses and sniffing the scent of pancakes wafting out of doorways. I'd always felt shy eating by myself but decided this was foolish when I could be feasting. A modestly priced menu lured me into a *crêperie*. I ordered a buckwheat pancake filled with ham and cheese and a jug of cider: comfort food. The cider came with a little bowl instead of a glass. I wondered whether this was how Rozenn would have drunk it in the forties. But perhaps cider had been hard to find in the war?

So much I didn't know, questions I hadn't asked. A pang of loss for Rozenn hit me. But perhaps she wouldn't have told me much more than she'd already described: her childhood in Paris, growing up in a Haussmann boulevard in an apartment on the second floor, a prosperous childhood, she'd said, because her father had progressed well in his medical profession, building a fashionable list of patients. She'd shown us the outside of the apartment. 'The iron railings are the same,' she said. 'I used to sit on the dining-room floor and trace the patterns their shadow cast on the parquet. Strange the things you remember.'

Rozenn had lived in the *seizième*: a respectable but very fashionable area. Her mother's parents had left their only surviving child a sizeable inheritance and her father had received money from his side, too. 'We did better than many other professionals,' Rozenn told us. 'My father worked long hours when he started out. He was a young and handsome doctor with a good bedside manner. His area of expertise was chest problems. Plenty of weak lungs around, after all the gassing in the First World War and the terrible influenza afterwards. The apartment up there,' she pointed to the second floor, 'was so light and airy and the rooms were spacious. I loved living there. I could still describe every centimetre of the entire building to you.'

She could certainly draw out memories of physical objects. When we were about ten and twelve, she'd taken Gwen and me to the modernist Maison la Roche. 'Look at the lines and curves,' she'd said. 'So different from that apartment building, but just as beautiful, *n'est-ce pas?*'

'I want to live there,' I said.

Gwen rolled her eyes. 'You always want things you can't have, Morie.'

Rozenn stroked the top of my head. 'It's no bad thing to have ambition.'

Gwen probably suspected me of still wanting what I couldn't have: namely her house.

Instead of prowling around the Breton coast asking questions about things that had happened so long ago, I should probably concentrate on proving to Gwen and to myself that I could make my own way.

Just a few seconds and your life can spin into another path altogether. If the bikes hadn't turned off the road into the track I was riding along, startling my horse. If I'd stayed on his back . . . If, if, if . . . *You can't keep re-running your life on a series of ifs,* Rozenn had told me gently several times.

For a moment the tastes of the pancake and cider curdled in my stomach. I thought I might actually vomit – a frequent response when I replayed the scene. I'd run those few seconds through my mind obsessively and could not escape from the same conclusion: if I hadn't been riding on that part of the Ridgeway at that particular time, the boy, Max, his name was, would still be alive now. And Nick and I would still be together. Or would some other future stress have awakened an addiction to online gambling in him?

The proprietor came over to ask me if I'd enjoyed my meal. I pushed the thoughts away and chatted to her about the food and about Lannion and Brexit deals and no-deals and what would happen in Europe. Rozenn would have been proud of how I managed to use my French. I wondered how much Breton was actually spoken here instead these days.

'I only have a few words of the language myself,' she admitted. 'Further west it's more commonly spoken. They wouldn't let us use Breton officially at all until my mother was born, around 1960.'

I told her about Cornwall, and how some of the names here reminded me of Cornish place names. She looked pleased. 'I've heard we are alike,' she said. 'That doesn't change, Brexit or not.'

'Did your grandparents live here during the war?' I asked.

'It was a restricted zone but my mother's father was permitted to stay: he was seventeen, but they made him work on the Atlantic Wall, as they called the bunkers and gun emplacements. It was very hard labour. He hated working for the Germans, but at least he was fed a bit better than most people. Rations were very meagre for the French during the Occupation.'

I recalled Rozenn's expression when Gwen and I had been children and left too much uneaten on our plates. She'd loved food and cooking but had always been careful not to waste anything, buying only what she needed, eating moderately all her life, knowing how to make leftovers into something delicious the next day.

'So what do you hope to find out about your grandmother?' the proprietor asked me.

'I'd really like to know why she came here and what her life would have been like.'

'What a shame you could not ask her before she died.' She cleared my plate.

I paid my bill and returned to the apartment. I'd left the compass on the sofa. Picking it up I flipped it over and looked at the inscription. *FJG.* François Guillou was Rozenn's father but she'd talked about a *frère* that last time. Her father's brother, her uncle, my great-great uncle, I wondered again? Or perhaps I'd simply misinterpreted the word she'd been trying to utter.

❧

The next morning was a repeat of the previous day: clear skies, the sea once again a swathe of blue when I glimpsed it on the drive over to the *manoir*. Lise's father had just been a child during the war, I reflected. Perhaps that would make him more willing to talk openly. On the other hand, he might have been protected from the worst of the Occupation. The satnav directed me along quiet lanes past more of the granite *longères*, their walls shining gold in the sunshine. Roses wound around their doors and I made out the flash of blue delphiniums and creamy lupins in their gardens, a gentle coastal wind blowing bushes and trees.

I spotted the sign to the *manoir* where Lise and her father lived and turned off.

The *manoir* itself was not dissimilar in design to a *longère*: a taller central structure dropping down on each side to a series of lower levels, the one on the left boasting a gable dormer that I admired. How lovely for a child to have a bedroom with a window seat to curl up in and keep guard over the front door. I made a mental note for future client projects. On the right side, an extension connected to the main building at a right angle. A white rose bush fanned across the granite frontage. A square of formal garden was laid out with topiary hedges, skirted by relaxed herbaceous borders blooming with stocks, hollyhocks and banks of azure geraniums spilling on to the grass.

Enchanted by what I saw, I almost didn't want to ring the bell and go inside. My fingers itched to take photographs on my phone. I thought of Sam and Jenny and the barn. They might be interested in how the formal area contrasted with the softer lines of the herbaceous borders further back.

Clopping hooves made me turn. This morning Lise was on a grey mare. 'I'll be with you in a moment,' she called.

'Did you get a farrier for your other horse?'

'This afternoon.' She hopped off. 'Just let me untack this one and rub her down quickly.' I followed her around the side of the house at a wary distance. There were a couple of stalls, a tack room and a paddock, where the bay was grazing. He whinnied as he saw his stablemate.

Lise untacked the horse and put on a headcollar and lead rope. She took her to drink from the trough and then tied the rope around a post. I saw her looking towards a bucket and sponge beside me and passed them to her. The smell of warm horse made me feel almost dizzy. 'You know a bit about horses, even if you don't like them,' she said, sponging the grey.

'I don't dislike them.' I swallowed. 'I just . . .'

'An accident? You were hurt?'

'Someone else was.' I told her what had happened on the Ridgeway. She scowled and shook her head.

'How very sad. Poor little boy. Those cyclists can be a menace. The times I've told them off for their behaviour on local tracks and footpaths. Luckily Canna here is steady and puts up with a lot.'

She led the horse into the paddock. 'I'll take you round through the main door,' she called over her shoulder. 'You'll see more of the house that way.'

On the front of the house I noticed an inscription on the granite lintel. '*Labore et honore*,' Lise said with a smile. 'Though I think a lot of the people here were probably smugglers or receivers. This was a wild coast.'

She ushered me in. 'We'll have coffee at the back of the house. There's a sheltered little terrace my father likes when he's having a good morning.'

I wasn't sure whether to ask what was wrong with him.

'He has a motor-neurone disorder,' she said, seeming to read my mind. 'Fortunately slow moving. He'll probably die of something else, he says, before total paralysis gets him. That's his plan, anyway.' She gave a little shrug.

We walked through rooms furnished traditionally but with some modern pieces added along with colourful Persian rugs, giving an air of informal elegance. I had the impression that this had been a place where people had worked outside and come in for meals, not standing on more ceremony than was necessary. 'My father and his parents weren't pretentious types,' Lise said. 'In the winter, they liked roaring fires and dogs dozing on the hearthrugs. They came from Ireland originally, hence our surname.'

'It's wonderful. It feels homely, despite its size.' I was admiring the old wooden beams. 'And I love the way the new pieces of furniture blend in. Old stone and wood work well with almost anything. The way the mirrors are positioned must mean it's light in here, even in the dead of winter.' She looked at me quizzically. 'Sorry,' I said. 'I have a professional interest in buildings.' I told her briefly about my work. 'When my clients restore old houses I'm always begging them to work with what's already there, not fight it and turn the interiors into bland factory lookalikes.' I thought of the prospective clients who'd bought a Victorian terraced house and rather than working in sympathy with it, planned to gut the whole interior and replace it with a single white-and-grey cube, extending into a glass box over most of the garden. While I admired the clean lines and light, it wasn't a project I could throw my heart into, although Nick had been keener.

'We don't use most of the house unless a lot of family is staying,' Lise told me. 'We used to rent out the outbuildings for holidays before Papa grew weaker.' We walked past a grand piano with a cluster of photographs in silver frames on top of it. I glanced at them, blinking as something about one of them caught my attention: a young woman standing outside this house in a small group including some American servicemen, waving flags – American, British and French – and beaming at the camera. A victory party. So taken some time after the Normandy landings in June 1944?

'Would you mind if I took a moment to wash my hands?' Lise asked. 'You know how grimy you can get doing anything with horses.'

She walked to a door off the passageway ahead of us. I stayed looking at the photo. Something about it puzzled me. I felt as I had looking at the pictures of young Rozenn on the beach. The young woman was familiar but I was missing something, waiting for something to click into place. I wanted to pick up the photo and examine it more closely but didn't like to. I must be mistaken, that was all.

Lise returned, smelling of sandalwood soap. 'I should have turned for home a little earlier and been ready for you. I lost track of time.'

I'd had that happen to me, too. Ridden on a little further, just to the start of a copse, then found myself still riding on half an hour later. Lise beckoned me through a door on to a small paved area outside. 'Morane Caradec is here, Papa. Morane, my father, Louis O'Donnell.'

'The coffee will be getting cold. So, Madame, you are the granddaughter of Rozenn Guillou who lived for a short period in St Martin?' The man in the wheelchair must have been in his mid-eighties, but his face was open and inquisitive, making him look younger. 'Forgive me for not getting up.' He extended a hand. 'This wretched condition makes me discourteous.' His English was only slightly accented.

I shook his hand. 'I know so little about Rozenn's time here. I'm grateful to you for seeing me, Monsieur O'Donnell.'

'Louis, please. Too much Gallic formality wearies me.' He waved me to my seat and Lise poured me coffee. Presumably there was help in the house to prepare refreshments and assist Louis. 'To talk about the past is a joy for me – as my daughter may have

195

warned you.' He darted her a mischievous look and she pretended to make a face at him. 'I promise not to bore on for hours.'

'To be honest, it's good to find someone who will actually tell me what I'd like to know about Rozenn's time here.' I blushed at my own words. 'I'm sorry, that sounds a bit entitled.'

He was watching me from beneath his sharp-angled eyebrows. 'Your grandmother told you nothing about her short time on this coast?'

I shook my head, though the length of Rozenn's stay here was puzzling me, given what I'd seen in the photograph on the piano. 'She never brought you here?' He shook his head. 'I suppose I would have heard.'

'We only ever went to Paris with her.'

'We?'

I told him about Gwen.

'Sisters.' He nodded. 'And you understand what was meant by this area being restricted, forbidden, at one stage, in fact? How the Germans tightened their grip on the coast as the war progressed? They couldn't literally build a wall down every part of it, but around the big ports they were very twitchy? Is that the right English word? Paranoid.'

He sipped his coffee. 'They evicted a lot of the locals in case they were a security risk, but they let my mother stay in this house. My father was away fighting in North Africa by then. He'd escaped to England by fishing boat when it was clear the Germans were going to occupy the country.'

'To Helford, too?'

'Indeed.'

'Your mother must have missed him.'

'She was very resourceful and determined that the Germans wouldn't take the house from us. The fact they were a kind of naturalised Irish-French couple seemed to baffle the Nazis. They

196

couldn't really work out whether or not they were dealing with neutral citizens.'

'And my grandmother would certainly have exploited their caution,' Lise said.

Louis laughed. 'To the nth degree.' He sipped his coffee, managing to control the tremor in his hand. 'But Morane Caradec, you want to know about your grandmother, not Lise's.'

'I actually find it all fascinating.' The wartime past was seeping into me. I felt hungry to consume more and more of it. 'I could listen to your stories all day. But I suppose I should limit my curiosity to my own grandmother. Why did she come here? It doesn't sound like a place that would welcome Parisians.'

'I can only tell you what my mother told me about Rozenn and her family. Living up there on the cliffs.' He shook his head. 'Elegant Parisians transplanted to a somewhat ramshackle and ill-appointed dwelling.'

'So she came with her parents?' I didn't mention the brother, waiting to see if Louis would refer to him.

'Indeed. Your grandfather was said to be a kind and conscientious doctor, and people were grateful to him. I remember him visiting once, when one of our German "guests" had an infected eye. I was playing football out the front as he came out and your grandfather kicked the ball back to me.'

I smiled.

'But he wasn't here for very long.' His face grew shadowed. 'None of them were.'

I remembered the graffiti. 'Someone wrote "traitor" on the house. Does that relate to something that happened during the war?'

He paused. 'She really didn't tell you anything?' I knew he meant my grandmother.

'Joséphine in St Martin started to tell me something but became slightly flustered.'

'Ah, Joséphine.' He gave a smile. 'Another member of a local family with long memories.' He picked up the teaspoon on his saucer and beat it against the fingers of his other hand. I smiled a thanks as Lise refilled my coffee.

'Joséphine's mother Martine thought the invaders might bring about a Free Brittany.'

'Obviously they didn't?'

He laughed. 'The Germans issued vague promises of independence that came to nothing.' He looked more thoughtful. 'Then there was your grandfather Luc Caradec: a local boy, handsome, well liked, with a family who trod a fine line between resistance and, well, something rather different.'

'What do you mean?' I asked.

'Helping the Germans obtain the supplies they needed.'

'Collaborating?' I felt quite shocked.

Louis raised an eyebrow. 'Some called it that. Others thought it was simply being realistic, staying afloat when times were so hard. And there was another side to Luc's family. Some of them had a costly interest in Bolshevism.'

'They were communist sympathisers?' I'd never heard Rozenn talk about anything like that in connection with Luc, the entrepreneur. 'The Nazis wouldn't have liked that?'

'Definitely not. Very dangerous interest to have. But, to be cynical, during the war having a foot in each camp was no bad thing. My own mother may or may not have occasionally lent the Resistance a hand. But she also rented out two bedrooms to German officers.'

'A smokescreen?'

He nodded. 'Did Luc prosper in England?' he asked. 'I imagine a young man with his famed charm would do well.'

'For many years. Sadly he developed a problem with drink. But until then he ran a very successful wholesale fish business.'

'You can take a St Martin boy away from the fishing boats but he will never be free of the fish.'

'I wondered how they met,' I said. 'I suppose they were both young people living in an isolated community.'

Louis looked at me shrewdly. 'Luc had something your grandmother needed very much.'

'The passage to Helford, if he was involved with the fishing fleet?'

'She was desperate.'

'Desperate? Why? What had she done?'

He contemplated the coffee spoon again. 'Rozenn was a Breton by birth. Family is everything for Bretons.' He'd switched to French.

The answer puzzled me. Then I thought of the photo on top of the piano. And of the photos I'd seen back in Helford.

'Family is everything,' I repeated slowly, also in French. I met his gaze, quizzical, humorous. 'There was something she tried to tell me when she was dying. I didn't understand. But now I think she meant she had a brother, a *frère* she didn't want to talk about until it was too late.'

He nodded, still looking at the spoon. 'She had a brother, yes. Yann.'

Yann. Another traditional name.

'And just a day or so ago that would have been a huge discovery in its own right. But I saw that photograph on your piano and now . . .'

Louis put down the teaspoon and looked at me sharply. 'You've pulled one thread and more has come out than you expected, *non*?'

'I feel as if everything I thought I knew about my grandmother is unravelling,' I said.

21

The artilleryman came down the cliff path towards Yann, who was still sitting with his back to the granite boulders, seemingly incapable of moving. Rozenn's stomach threatened to turn itself inside out. She grabbed Claire's hand. Impossible for them to pass the German, rush on to the *longère* and warn Maman. If he insisted on knowing where Yann lived and marched him to the house, could Maman show him the original travel permit, stave off questions about Yann's registration papers, say there'd been a most regrettable oversight, and she'd register him the very next day? Could they get Yann on a train this evening or first thing tomorrow, send him back to Paris? Or would the police – either the *gendarmes* or the Germans – arrest him and throw him on a train back to Germany? Or into a holding camp somewhere? Images of her brother, confined, hungry, filthy, flashed through her imagination.

Rozenn waited for the artilleryman to pull out a gun. He was asking Yann to give him something – his identity card? Yann handed him the sketch pad. She felt cold. If the German flicked through those pages and saw the cartoon Nazis . . . The two males stood so close their heads were almost touching. Yann turned a page, and then another one.

Rozenn heard a sound that made her blink. Laughter. Her brother and this German were laughing at something on the page. It brought her back to Paris, to the sound of boys joking and jostling as they came out of school on to the street. Yann was saying something. She took a few steps closer to the pair, pulling Claire with her.

'If that's what you want, corporal, I'll draw it for you right now.'

The artilleryman raised a hand in farewell. He was the young man who'd been with Martine earlier on. As they walked towards him, he stood back to let them pass on the narrow path, giving a polite nod.

'*Espèce d'idiot*,' Rozenn all but spat at Yann when they were out of earshot. 'What were you thinking? Why are you out here?'

'He saw me sketching.' Yann's eyes were wide. 'He asked to see what I was doing. I wanted to tell him to mind his own business.' He caught sight of her expression. 'But of course I didn't. He might have thought I was a spy.'

'Oh why ever would he think that? A stranger on a cliff in the prohibited zone, drawing, who won't say what he's doing?'

Claire looked from one to the other, lip trembling.

'When he saw it was cartoons, not drawings of the coast, he became very relaxed,' Yann said. 'Asked me if I still read comics, whether I'd seen any recent editions. Said he'd bought some in Paris, months ago, passed them round the mess.'

'Please tell me he didn't see some of those cartoons you showed me? The woman kicking Hitler's backside?'

'I cut those pages out of the book before I left my room. The ones in here,' he patted the sketch pad, 'are perfectly innocent. Well, almost. There are mermaids.' He looked away.

'Mermaids? Why on earth would a soldier want to look at mermaids?'

'They . . . aren't wearing anything. On their . . . tops.'

'Smutty drawings of girls with fishtails?' Rozenn nodded. 'Naked women have universal appeal to men, don't they?'

'Naked,' Claire said thoughtfully.

Yann hung his head.

'Does he know where you live?'

'He wants me to draw some cartoons. For his younger brother. In exchange for some of his rations. A can of ham. Chocolate.'

'Chocolate.' Claire clapped her hands.

'And how do you deliver the cartoons to him?' He still hadn't answered the question about the house.

Yann was silent.

'My God, he's coming to the house, isn't he?' Her voice was rising. 'He knows where you live?'

'I suggested meeting here, but he said it would be better to meet somewhere private. I couldn't really tell him not to, it would have made him suspicious.'

The words inside her were going to burst out. She clenched her hands, felt the nails bite into her palms.

'He's going to give me tins of meat, Rozenn. Think about Maman eating something good like that.'

'You think tins of meat make up for what you've done? The risk you've placed us all in?' The tension in her head was pressing itself into a headache. She wanted to run away from both of them, find somewhere out of the wind where she could hide herself away. Let them all look after themselves.

Yann kicked out at a boulder. 'You don't know what it's like, stuck indoors.' He sounded rattled in a way she'd never heard before but she wanted to shake every tooth out of his mouth. The three of them walked slowly back to the outhouse. 'Don't tell her,' Yann said, looking at Maman, hoeing her vegetable garden. 'Nothing bad will come of it, honestly, Rozenn.'

No words came to her lips. She shook her head and went inside with Claire. Claire picked her little wooden horse off the table and squatted down on the earth floor to play with it. The sound of tyres outside made Rozenn spin towards the door. Papa was getting out of the Citroën, holding a newspaper in his hand. On his face was an expression she couldn't interpret. He came inside. 'What's happened?' she asked him.

'The Germans have invaded the Soviet Union,' he said, sitting down.

'But they had a non-aggression pact?' It had always seemed strange: German fascists in bed with Russian communists. 'Does it mean fewer military here because they'll move troops east?'

'Perhaps. Though they might be even more paranoid about an attack here while they're fighting on another front.' Papa shrugged and shook his head. 'It's a rash move on the part of the Germans, could bite them hard.'

'And in turn they'll become even more vicious?'

He nodded. 'Indeed. More paranoid. Communists are open enemies now, whether they're in Brest Litovsk or Brest in Brittany. They'll see Bolshevik plots in every corner.'

Maman came inside, carrying a trug filled with newly dug carrots. 'Aren't they lovely? And I have this.' In her other hand she held a bunch of parsley. 'Carrots with parsley. There might even be a tiny bit of butter left.'

Even now Rozenn's mouth watered at the thought of tender, new carrots with butter melted over them. Yann had not come inside, probably going straight to the outbuilding to start work on his cartoons. 'I'll wash them for you,' she told Maman, picking up the trug and going out to the pump.

It was chance only that made her look up and see Luc coming along the track. Instinctively she checked that Yann was out of sight. But of course Luc knew about him now anyway. And so did the artilleryman. She set the carrots on the ground and darted up the lane.

'*T'inquiètes pas*,' Luc told her. He kissed her on the cheeks. 'I don't see what I'm not supposed to.'

203

'You've heard the news?' She wanted to cling to him.

'The invasion of the Soviet Union?' He nodded. She noticed how pale he seemed this evening, despite the afternoon's work scything the hay. 'Bad news for Communists here.'

'Are there many in Brittany?'

He started to say something and gave a half-shrug as though the subject wasn't worth pursuing, looking at her intensely. 'Can you come with me now?'

'Where to?'

'You'll see.'

'Is this—?'

'Just come.' He took her at a pace that was almost a run, down the track to the lane, turning from there through a field gate and across a rough track she hadn't noticed before, heading inland and dipping through a clump of small trees. When they emerged from the trees she saw a hut, perhaps once used for livestock, now almost camouflaged, its wood and stone structure so weathered it was hard to make it out.

'What's going on?' she asked. He put a hand on her arm, his expression suddenly cold.

'You're going to meet some dangerous people, Rozenn Guillou. If you're tempted to tell anyone who you see here this evening, I can't guarantee your safety.'

She shook his arm off.

His face softened. 'I know I can trust you. Come on.' The hut door, what was left of it, opened to Luc's three rapid knocks. Her nostrils twitched at the smell of closely confined human beings. Her eyes adjusted to the dark and she made out two figures – men. Something about the shape of their faces told her they weren't French. They didn't look German, either. British. She felt herself clutch the decaying door.

'*Bonsoir,*' one of them said. She had the feeling it might be the only words of the language he spoke.

'This is the girl?' the other said in accented but fluent French. She noticed the bandage on his left arm. Some of the smell in the hut seemed to emanate from it.

'The doctor's daughter, yes,' Luc answered. 'I told you, no names.'

The wounded man extended his right hand. 'We need your help, Mademoiselle.'

'You mean you want my father to look at that arm.' She couldn't resist glancing over her shoulder as though there might already be uniformed men running towards the hut to arrest her. 'What are you doing here?'

'No details,' the man said.

'It's a boat, *non*?' She looked towards Luc, his expression hard to make out in the gloom. 'They're waiting to be taken off the coast, aren't they?'

He said nothing, switching on his torch so they could see more. The wounded man sat down, beads of perspiration gleaming on his brow. If he had blood poisoning there wouldn't be much anyone could do for him. Luc pulled a stone bottle out of his rucksack. 'Have some water.' The man drank in gulps, holding the bottle in his uninjured hand.

'You were supposed to escape earlier on, weren't you?' she said. 'Before the evenings grew so long and light. Things went badly wrong and you were held up?'

There was silence. They were watching her, weighing her up.

'Oh well, sorry about your arm.' She started to go.

'Wait,' Luc said. 'This man needs a doctor.'

'You want my father to risk his life, all our lives, to help a stranger?'

'He swore an oath when he became a doctor, didn't he? To help the sick?'

'We're on the same side,' the wounded man said.

'My father can't do much for an infection. Clean the wound and bandage it up, that's all.'

'That would be a help,' the wounded man said.

'I can bring you some supplies, I suppose. For you to patch the arm up.'

How many times had she listened to Papa lament the fact that a septic finger could kill an otherwise healthy patient? Yann had been dangerously ill after his appendectomy.

'We need someone who knows what they're doing.' Luc folded his arms, a nerve twitching in his face. 'Your father could set the arm if it's broken.'

'How could he do that up here without plaster and water?' She looked at him again. 'Don't even suggest that this man comes to the house. My sister, remember?'

Claire would burble on to anyone she might meet about strange men coming to the house at night.

'Anyway, how are you involved in this?' she asked him.

He looked down at the earthen floor of the hut.

'But you want me to risk my father, my family?' She let the silence hang.

'We need your father, Mademoiselle,' the second English man said in halting, broken French.

She waited a beat, letting the silence grow unbearable. 'I'll bring my father to you if you take my brother with you.'

'What brother?' Broken-arm Man said. 'What do you mean?'

'He's a prisoner of war with combat experience and he wants to fight with the Free French. At the moment he's stuck here, doing nothing.'

'It's not our show,' Broken-arm Man told her. 'We're reliant on a team operating from . . . the other side of the Channel. It's taken months to organise our pickup, the boat to row us out and all the rest of it.'

A boat from the port itself: one of the dories the fishing boats used to transfer crews and catches to shore? Or a dinghy launched from a larger vessel out to sea?

'The pickup crew won't accept a third man,' he said.

She studied him carefully, as well as she could in the gloom. 'How did you hurt your arm?' she asked. When he didn't answer, she nodded. 'Shame the bullet didn't exit cleanly. Let's hope the Germans don't follow you to this hut. *Bonne chance.*' She spun around and walked out.

'So much for patriotism,' Broken-arm Man shouted at her. Luc shushed him.

'My brother's a patriot,' she hissed back. 'Nobody gives him a chance to prove it.'

She'd walked through the clump of trees before she heard Luc running towards her. 'Rozenn, wait.'

She continued. He grabbed her arm. 'They'll do it. Yann can go with them to England. Bring your father to the hut later on.' The expression of concentration on his face made her stare at him. He pulled her towards him, stronger than she might have thought, and held her by both shoulders.

He looked at her straight on. 'You said you'd do anything for your brother – anything, didn't you?'

She nodded. His muscles seemed to relax. He moved towards her, holding her round her waist and pulling her in. This time the kiss was long and deep. He tasted of tobacco and salt and something else, something sweet and vital. The tension fell from her as she lost herself in the embrace – the men in the hut, Yann, Claire, all forgotten. When she pulled away, every nerve in her body protested, her lips swollen from his. Was he kissing her like this just to seal the deal? It didn't feel like it. But she needed to be careful, not let her churned-up emotions control her. For everyone's sake.

22

'You've seen that photograph, you must have worked it out, *non?*'
Louis was still watching me closely over his white bone-china coffee cup. I wondered if he'd once been an academic or some kind
of lecturer. He seemed keen for me to draw my own conclusion.

'At first I thought it was just because my grandmother died. I
miss her and perhaps I see her in places she couldn't be,' I said, almost
to myself. 'That happens sometimes in bereavement, doesn't it?'

Louis nodded.

'But it's not the first time I've been confused by photographs
of Rozenn,' I said. 'Last time I just wondered whether I was seeing
something that wasn't there.'

He raised an eyebrow. I told him briefly about the photos on
the beach showing her as a small child wearing different swimsuits,
contrasting emotions rippling over her face.

'But those flags in the photograph on the piano, that young
woman in the group celebrating the end of the war . . . She's with
a boy who I think must be you,' I glanced at Louis, who nodded,
'and possibly your mother?'

'Mary O'Donnell, my mother indeed. Go on, Morane.'

'Rozenn couldn't possibly have been here then. The dates . . .' I
clenched my hands together. 'Remind me exactly when that photo
was taken?'

'*Le Jour de la Victoire en Europe*,' Lise said quietly. Victory in Europe Day. 'Eighth of May 1945.'

Louis's eyes when he fixed them on me were like those of a kindly confessor.

'I know Rozenn was in Trafalgar Square on that day. There's a photo of her and Luc. She couldn't have been in two places at the same time.' I was looking down at my clenched hands.

Lise and Louis exchanged another glance.

'So who's that girl in your photograph?' I asked him.

'Who do you think she might be?' Lise asked gently.

'The expression on her face is different even though she looks the same . . . So I think my grandmother had a sister.' I released my hands. 'A twin sister. Identical. But my grandmother . . .'

Rozenn had never mentioned her – why not?

'How did Rozenn's twin come to be living here?' I asked Louis. 'After Rozenn had gone, I assume?'

He looked down at his long, tapered fingers, only lightly spotted with age. 'Claire was a sweet young woman. She'd been damaged at birth and had a mental handicap.'

'A learning disability,' Lise corrected him.

'Intellectual impairment.' Louis waved a hand. 'She could wash herself, dress, manage most everyday tasks but she was like a six-year-old, vulnerable, trusting. And yet sometimes very astute too.'

Why had Rozenn not come to find her sister after the war? Or ever mentioned her to us?

'Claire lived with us until July 1945.' He smiled at me. 'I remember her as happy, once she'd . . . Once she'd settled in. I have fond memories of her playing with the animals here: cats and dogs, in particular. Donkeys, too. My father came back from the war and we were briefly a family again.'

'What happened to her?'

'My mother needed hospital treatment for cancer. I was sent to boarding school. Claire went to a convent just outside Rennes. The plan was that she'd return once Maman was recovered. The operation seemed to have been successful. Meanwhile diphtheria swept the convent.' He looked at me with more softness in his expression. 'I'm afraid Claire succumbed.'

I'd never met this great-aunt, had no suspicion that she'd even existed until weeks ago, but I felt a pang for the young woman who'd died when she was, what, barely twenty-three?

'Nobody contacted Rozenn in England to tell her Claire had died?'

'Sadly my mother's operation hadn't succeeded as well as we thought. She herself died a month or so after Claire.' He gazed down at his hands again. 'None of Luc's own family were left in the area. I went back to school. My father had never met Luc and Rozenn and sank into a depression which lasted a few years.'

'It's frightening how people can vanish from memory,' Lise said.

'Indeed. Martine, who worked up here occasionally, and possibly her mother were the only ones left who knew that Claire had been here, living in plain sight of the Germans.'

'What did Martine do here?'

'Helped with the estate paperwork. When I was home from school the two of us talked about Claire and what had happened to her family.' He stopped abruptly.

'What did happen to them?' I asked.

'The parents were arrested.' He was speaking more slowly, looking visibly older. 'Rozenn didn't tell you much at all, did she? Perhaps she never knew about all of it.'

'She talked about Paris quite a bit, about her schooldays, the Germans arriving in 1940. But she didn't like conversations about the war and made it sound as though it was just her and her parents. I think she was building herself up to tell us more, but her last stroke came suddenly.' That hand of hers clasping mine, those eyes, frustrated as she realised she couldn't make me understand.

'The advantage of a lengthy and ultimately fatal illness is that you have time to prepare yourself,' Louis said quietly.

Lise started to say something, probably that she thought we should leave the rest of the conversation for now as he was obviously failing.

I stood up, nodding, still looking at Louis.

'Yann was the one Rozenn did it all for.' He sank back in his chair, pale with the effort of telling me this.

'Yann?'

'Claire could never tell us much but it was clear that both she and her sister worshipped their brother. Claire said Rozenn wanted Yann to go on a boat.'

'So why . . . ?'

Why had Rozenn herself and Luc ended up on that boat to Cornwall? Had they met, fallen in love and then decided to run away together? Perhaps theirs was some kind of forbidden love affair.

'They weren't supposed to be on the boat at all,' Louis said. 'From what we could piece together from Claire's and Martine's accounts, and from what the locals working in the hotel saw from the bar, things went badly wrong that night.'

23

'Nine o'clock,' Luc told Rozenn. 'I will see you and your father here then.'

She nodded, still drunk from the kiss, surprised that her feet remembered the way back home. Arriving outside the house she blinked, trying to return herself to normal. Her wristwatch told her she'd been gone fifty minutes. She stared at it, convinced it must have stopped. If only she could go somewhere quiet, somewhere where she could think only of Luc, of how she felt. But first she had to carry out her side of the agreement struck with the Englishmen.

Papa was drinking a small bowl of cider at the kitchen table, the newspaper folded beside him. As he lifted the bowl to his lips, Rozenn noticed the frayed cuffs of his shirt. She should offer to turn them for Maman. But there was no time to think about this now. 'Papa?'

He looked at her, face softening. Unlike Maman, Papa had always made Rozenn feel that she mattered to him. He'd helped her with her studies, shown such pride in her last year when she received her results in the final examinations.

'What is it, *chérie*?'

'It's Yann.' She came straight to the point. 'He was up on the cliff this afternoon and a German artilleryman saw him.'

Papa replaced the bowl on the table very slowly. He started to stand up. 'Wait.' She held up a hand. 'There's something else you need to know. I've organised a place in a boat for him. To England.'

'What are you talking about?' He peered at her as though worried she had a fever.

'There are two Englishmen up in the fields in a hut.' He flinched. 'One of them has a badly injured arm. If you help him they'll take Yann with them on the boat to England.'

Papa's laughter hadn't been heard for so long it caught her by surprise. 'For a moment you took me in,' he said.

'*C'est vrai.*'

His laughter stopped. His face seemed to hollow out, develop lines, his mouth opening and closing.

'The local boy I know took me to meet them.'

He did stand up this time. 'Pack a bag, Rozenn.'

'What?'

'We've missed the trains this evening, but you and Yann can spend the night in the surgery in Lannion and catch the first service out tomorrow morning. If they come looking for the two of you, it might give you time.' His face was the colour of the ashes in the stove. 'This was my fault, bringing you here.'

'There's no need. It's Yann who's the risk – to himself and the rest of us. If we do what these Englishmen ask—'

'Have you lost your mind?' He hadn't shouted at her for years. 'Liaising with English spies?'

'They've got a vessel taking them to England.'

He seemed to be struggling to control himself, swallowing hard, clenching his hands in front of him. 'Rozenn, *chérie*, you've lived a sheltered life. You've no idea how to judge whether these people are trustworthy. That's why I told you not to talk to anyone about Yann.'

'I trust this person.' How could she not trust him now? 'Those Englishmen will take Yann somewhere much safer than this place.'

'Haven't you seen the German naval patrols out there?' His voice had risen again. 'And the Luftwaffe, patrolling the Channel?'

'That German Yann's talked to will go back to the mess to tell them about the boy up in the longhouse who does these wonderful cartoons. A boy with a drawing pad and pencils who doesn't appear on the register of approved people in a restricted zone? They'll shoot him for spying.'

Papa's arms flopped out in a gesture of despair, but she wouldn't drop the subject. 'A disaster is waiting to happen,' she said. 'For the whole family. All you have to do to make it safer for everyone is look at a wounded arm. Those men are our allies, they're still fighting the Germans. We should help them.' She remembered her own words to the Englishmen back in the hut and blushed.

Papa was very pale, seemingly beyond speech. 'This friend of yours?' The words seemed to come with effort.

'Luc's his name. Luc Caradec.' She hoped she'd said it in a normal tone.

'What makes you think he's trustworthy?'

'He's been kind to Claire. And he knows how things work around here.'

'What's he doing with British fugitives?'

'I didn't ask him.'

He gave an ironic smile. 'At least you showed some sense. You know that helping the enemy could mean execution or deportation to some awful camp?'

'The same penalty as hiding an unregistered French combatant in the coastal zone?'

He blinked.

Yann came inside, looking from one of them to the other. 'What's happening?'

She was calmer now. 'There's a boat leaving for England,' she said in a lower tone. 'I've got you a place on it, if Papa helps some . . . people.'

The words had just been uttered when someone knocked on the half-open door. Rozenn's heart thumped like someone banging a drum. Luc? No. She made out field-grey uniform and felt sick. Please God, don't let the corporal have heard what she'd just said. Yann stepped silently back into the recess under the stairs.

'*Bonsoir*, corporal,' Papa said, his professional carapace snapped into place. 'How may I help you?'

'I search for the young Monsieur?' The German's eyes were pale blue, guileless.

'There's no . . . He isn't . . .' But how could Papa deny Yann was here when he was standing just metres away? 'May I ask why you want him?'

'He draw something for me. It's ready now, *oui*?' The corporal was peering into the kitchen, his expression sharper now.

'One moment, please.' Papa turned back to Yann, still standing in the shadows. 'Sort this out,' he hissed.

Yann stepped forward. 'I've finished the cartoons, corporal. Please come this way.' He led the German away from the door. Papa and Rozenn watched as the two young men went into the outbuilding. Silence. Suppose Yann had left something compromising in plain view: the cartoon Nazis, perhaps? Maman had placed a vase of cornflowers on the table. Their deep-blue petals filled Rozenn's vision. She made herself mentally trace the outline of each of the petals to calm herself.

A roar of laughter hit them. Papa sat up, face turned towards the kitchen door. The corporal came out of the outbuilding holding rolled sheets of paper. Yann followed.

'*Merci*, he'll love these.' The corporal handed over a small sack in which something heavy clinked. Yann thanked him and wished him *bonne soirée*.

He came inside, opening the sack. 'Two large tins of ham. A bar of chocolate and all this paper, Rozenn, look.' Papa's slap caught him off balance. He nearly fell, dropping the sack and touching his cheek, stunned. Rozenn could not remember seeing her father strike one of them before, not even on the back of the legs when they'd been infants. Maman had been the disciplinarian.

'How could you, Yann?' His voice was very quiet. 'Risking your family like this? We worked so hard to keep you safe. Your mother gave up everything she had in Paris to come here. Your sisters, too, uprooted, bored, hungry because they share their rations with you.'

'I didn't mean—'

'All we asked you to do was to stay indoors during the day.'

'It was just a matter of time, Papa,' Rozenn said. 'Sooner or later someone would have seen him, especially as more Germans flood in to build the defences. They'll probably billet someone on us. How will we hide Yann then?' Papa was staring at her, seemingly mesmerised. 'You were right to bring us here, to give Yann a chance.' She put a hand on his arm. 'But it's not working any more. You have to do what I've explained. Let Yann take his chance.'

'What chance? What's all the shouting about?' Maman stood in the door, a basket of beetroot and spinach in her arms. Leaning over the garden, her back to the house, she wouldn't have seen or heard the corporal coming to the door to look for Yann. 'You left the carrots by the pump, Rozenn.' She didn't sound annoyed. Out in that vegetable patch she grew calm, almost peasant-like in her ability to let everything float over her. That calm was about to be broken.

Rozenn closed her eyes and said it quickly. 'Yann has a passage in a boat to England.'

'He's got what?' she asked. 'How?'

Rozenn told her.

Maman dropped the vegetable basket. A beetroot rolled out. Rozenn caught it and put it carefully back on top of the new carrots. It seemed important to do everything very precisely.

'But this local friend of mine, Luc, introduced me to them.'

'This Luc,' Maman asked, 'he's reliable?'

The adjective was inadequate. Rozenn nodded. She couldn't really think of how to describe Luc.

'Those air raids in London,' Maman said. 'Tens of thousands of civilians killed.' Her mind seemed to be leapfrogging, incapable of focusing. Perhaps that was what it was like if it was your child's life at stake. Yann was a grown man, but he was still her firstborn.

'Yann nearly died in Germany when they didn't get him prompt treatment for his appendix,' she told her mother. 'And many, many others die in German camps. Nowhere is completely safe for anyone. If Yann's joining the Free French, he probably won't be in the city anyway.'

'For God's sake, don't talk about me as though I'm not here. I'm not nine,' Yann said, but his voice was soft. 'I can take my chances, Maman. Hundreds of thousands of men are fighting. It's my duty.'

Papa let out a sigh. 'I shouldn't have struck you, my boy. I'm so sorry.'

Maman's face filled with horror.

'It's all right, I understand.' Yann looked paternally at Papa.

'I do not understand myself.' Papa sounded like a much older man. 'Our family shouldn't be fighting among ourselves.'

'That's the French,' Maman said. 'Some of us occupied, some not, some fighting with the Allies, some fighting the ones who are fighting the Allies.'

'We should eat,' Rozenn said. 'It will calm us.'

Maman gave a slow nod. 'And then you must go with Rozenn, François.' Papa looked at her, a question on his face. 'It's for the best.' The clink of stones outside made Rozenn look out of the door. Claire was walking towards the kitchen. Rozenn took her by the hand as she came inside.

'It's a secret, what we talk about in this house.'

Claire put a finger to her lips. '*T'inquiète pas*, Zenn. Don't worry.'

'Let's open one of the tins of ham,' Yann said. 'Safer to eat the evidence and bury the tin, *non*?'

Papa sighed. For a moment Rozenn thought he'd explode again, but he went to the dresser drawer and removed the can opener, handing it to Yann. 'We're all complicit now,' he said. 'Collaborators and resisters, at the same time.'

Maman prepared and cooked the vegetables. They ate the meal in silence. The ham was sweet, with the consistency of something that had been pounded into shape, but better than anything Rozenn had eaten since Yann's fish. Perhaps it had originated from Breton pigs, the meat transported to Germany for processing and returned to the province in German tins. Claire seemed quieter than normal, not prattling about puppies and horses but watching her siblings. Rozenn studied her brother too. He was definitely in better form than he had been in Paris. His improvised gymnasium had built up his muscles and the late-night swims must have improved his fitness. A recruiting officer in England would surely snap him up. She looked at her watch. Eight-twenty now. She helped Maman clear and wash the dishes.

'Shall we go?' Papa said, when this was done.

'What about me?' Yann asked.

'Stay here for now,' Papa told him.

'It's me you're going to be discussing with those Englishmen.' He thumped the table.

You should have thought about that when you sat up on the cliff path in full view of that German. Rozenn managed not to utter the words.

'Please stay here.' Maman put a hand on his sleeve. Tears were brimming. It was always the same: the beloved boy needed protecting. 'If you're seen out after curfew it's an additional risk just when we need to be at our most careful.' Yann nodded sullenly, but some of the aggression seemed to leave him.

'I want to go with Zenn,' Claire said.

'*Non, chérie,*' Maman told her. 'You need to stay here with Yann.' She looked intently at him.

Yann seemed to give himself a shake. 'Stay here with me, Claire,' he said.

Papa left the table and returned with his medical bag, opening it on the table. 'I've got iodine,' he said. 'And an anaesthetic spray. Basic surgical tools. I'm short of bandages.'

'I cut up an old linen sheet for you,' Maman said. 'And I'll boil a pan of water and pour it into a flask.' They exchanged glances, both looking briefly less anxious. Maman had acted as Papa's receptionist when he'd first started out and they were newly-weds. He couldn't afford a full-time assistant and receptionist, so she'd helped tidy the surgery, booked appointments and ordered drugs. Maman and Papa must have been happy back then, young, in love, just starting out. *Les années folles,* people called the 1920s. Years of fun, after the war and the terrible flu that followed. Years of forgetting, of embracing the new to cover up the fact that they were all so scarred by war, so scared of another conflict.

Rozenn changed her sandals for the old gym shoes and put the bandages Maman gave her in her satchel. 'Take this, too.' Maman picked up the bread.

Rozenn shook her head. 'They'll have food.' Luc would have seen to that. The Englishmen weren't going to receive anything more from the Guillou family until she was certain of Yann's passage.

'You never take me with you, Zenn,' Claire told her as she left. Rozenn paused, but there wasn't time to talk about it.

Darkness wouldn't fall for at least another hour. Rozenn looked around for the German corporal, in case he'd shown his messmates Yann's cartoons and they'd insisted on coming up to the *longère* to request commissions for themselves. Her ears had grown sharper since they'd come to St Martin: the rustle of a fox through the hedge or a bird in a tree made her turn sharply but silently to look. In the tatty gym shoes she could walk almost like a fox herself, making only the slightest sound.

They arrived at the track leading to the hut, hurrying now, feeling more exposed until they reached the clump of trees. Rozenn thought she could almost see the young medic her father must once have been in the last war, moving purposefully, listening out for danger. But if anyone was watching them, they'd know they were up to something covert. She forced herself to relax her shoulders and unclench her fists.

When they reached the trees, Rozenn stopped, raising a hand to warn Papa to remain silent. Luc took form in front of them, as though he were an apparition. She felt a flush rise on her cheeks at the sight of him and hoped Papa couldn't see. 'Here's my father,' she told him.

Luc extended a hand, '*Monsieur le docteur*, thank you for coming out here.' Papa shook it without replying. They walked through the trees. Casting a long shadow, the hut stood in front of them. Luc rapped on the door. Rozenn half-expected a German gun to appear as it opened.

She realised she was shaking. This wouldn't do; she took control. Let them see she was no pushover. 'It's too dark in here for my father to examine his patient,' she said as the door opened and the dark outlines of the two men appeared in front of them. 'You'll need to shine your torches on that arm.' The smell inside seemed even worse now.

'Leave the door open,' she told Luc. They'd have to risk showing a light. 'Wait outside and keep watch.' She listened to herself: behaving in such an unfeminine manner, issuing instructions to men. They did as she told them without comment. Papa rolled up the sleeve of the man with the broken arm. He swallowed.

'You needed medical attention days ago.'

The man started to say something. Papa cut him off. 'No need to tell me more.'

'Can you set it? Or at least strap it so I can move more easily?'

Papa motioned Rozenn to crouch beside him. 'Pour some boiled water into the enamel bowl and give me a piece of linen.' The water in the dish clouded rapidly as Papa dipped the linen into it.

'We tried to pull the bullet out,' the injured man said, his face white. Rozenn felt her stomach turn. 'Couldn't get a grip on it.'

'I can extract it.' Papa beckoned at Rozenn to pour boiled water over his hands. Only then did he open his bag. 'I'll spray the site with amyl nitrate to numb it a bit, but you'll still feel pain, I'm afraid.' Papa bent over the pouch of surgical tools, pouring alcohol on a pair of tweezers and a long pointy tool.

'Drink this.' Luc came inside and passed the man a bottle of Calvados which he must have had in his rucksack. Rozenn looked away as Papa bent over the wound. How could he even know where to dig for the bullet when all the tissues were so puffy? The Englishman shouted briefly and bit his lip, face gleaming with perspiration. Papa removed the tweezers; something metallic and black was pinched inside them. He dropped both objects on to a linen bandage and wrapped them carefully. The Germans would recognise the bullet as theirs if they found it up here, Rozenn realised, and their attention might move to the *longère*.

Papa wiped the wound with iodine. 'I'll bandage and strap it now. You need to go to a surgery or hospital to have it set once the infection is gone.'

'When does the boat leave?' Rozenn asked the injured man.

He looked at the others. 'Tomorrow night,' he said.

'Where from?'

The men exchanged a silent look.

'Don't ask more, Rozenn.' Papa gave her a frown as he wound the bandage round the man's neck.

'You still want your son to make the voyage?' Luc said, from outside the door. 'You know it's very dangerous, *non*?'

'Of course we do,' Rozenn answered him.

'You've helped me, Monsieur, and I'm more grateful than I can say.' The man with the broken arm sounded as though the pain was easing. 'But now we need your daughter to help us too.'

'Me?' She scowled at them.

'Our young friend here said you'd do anything for your brother.'

'You don't have to do it, Rozenn,' Luc said quickly. 'Forget about the boat and go home, wait for something else to turn up for your brother.'

'No.' She glared at him. 'What do you want? Tell me why you've changed the terms of our deal.'

'We need our wireless transmitter,' the injured man said. 'We want you to retrieve it for us, Mademoiselle. From the rocks.'

24

Louis extended his hand and wished me *bonne journée* in a cracked voice. The strain of talking about what had happened on this coast three-quarters of a century ago had seemingly leached all the strength from him. 'Speak to Martine's daughter again,' he said. 'Her mother might have told her more than I remember.'

'Papa will be fine,' Lise said, accompanying me past the piano with its framed photographs. I paused briefly to look again at the picture of Claire with the Americans, Lise standing beside me. 'He has these spates of sudden exhaustion. An afternoon in bed, a quiet evening watching television or reading, and he'll be back to, well, back to being his new normal.' She touched my arm. 'I will scan that photo and send it to you.'

With a promise to text me when Louis was up to seeing me again and a hope that I hadn't been too *choquée* by what I'd heard this morning, she waved me off from the front door. I walked slowly past the flowers in the front garden to my car and found myself driving back to St Martin. Shocked, *choquée*, was the right word. I wasn't really sure what to do next. I'd come to Brittany imagining that Rozenn had been a single child and had escaped from here for her own sake. In fact she'd had a brother and sister and it had been the brother, Yann, who'd been the sun everyone revolved around. Though how much of the Guillou family's story relied on Claire's witness? How reliable could she have been with her intellectual impediment?

I found I was driving back to St Martin on autopilot. As I reached the outskirts my mobile vibrated in my pocket. I pulled over to read the text, blinking to reground myself in the present.

I'm so sorry, Morane, but I'm going to have to pull the plug on the barn. Things have come to a head with Sam and me. I think we were using the project as a sop, hoping it would bring us closer, but we have decided to separate and sell up. Obviously we'll pay you for your work to date. With apologies and best wishes, Jenny.

I looked at the mobile in my hand and felt a strong urge to throw it out of the window. I'd let this trip to Brittany distract me from my increasingly difficult work situation but reality was still knocking on my door, even here. I closed my eyes, replaying the visit to the barn in Wiltshire. Jenny had addressed her questions to me, not making eye contact with her husband. Sam had wandered off for a short time while Jenny and I talked with enthusiasm about how the interior beams could feature in the design. They hadn't been as together as I'd assumed.

I wanted to ignore the message, ignore everything to do with my business, but a small internal voice screamed at me that I couldn't afford to do that. Still sitting in the car I made a mental note of the projects I had on the go. Tatiana's house refurbishment, with the promise that she'd recommended me to her friend Natalia, who was about to buy a country house in Oxfordshire in need of restoration. A house conversion in Hampstead, working alongside an architect to turn the flats back into one dwelling. I'd been paid for my initial work, but it had gone quiet. I should email the architect, see what was happening, show him I was still enthusiastic. I opened the notes app on my phone and wrote bullets to myself.

I needed to go home. Asking questions about things that had happened so long ago in a country I didn't live in, things that had happened to my dead grandmother, was a distraction from real life. I could make my excuses to Lise and Joséphine and book myself on a ferry tonight.

I felt shaky. Hungry. I hadn't bothered with breakfast. Now my stomach was telling me I had to eat. I picked up my bag and got out of the car. A large coach had parked up in the small car park beside the supermarket. Elderly men in baseball caps were climbing into it. Veterans. I stopped and watched. Was the kindly American I'd met on the ferry one of them? I spotted him in the queue and wondered whether I should say hello. He was distracted by one of his companions, I saw, a man who looked older, frailer. My American was talking gently to him, patting his shoulder. Painful memories? Lost friends? They'd only have been boys, really, when they'd landed in France, unlike me – well into adulthood.

No wonder Rozenn hadn't wanted to talk about whatever had happened to her here. Unlike these elderly men, she hadn't had support from a whole group who'd been through the same experience.

Rozenn's brother had been the one intended for exfiltration by boat. So why hadn't he made the voyage? Or had he? What had happened to him when he'd arrived in England? The only person who might be able to enlighten me was Martine's daughter Joséphine, whom I was meeting again tomorrow but, I reminded myself, hadn't even been alive at the time. This was a fool's errand.

I found a *boulangerie* selling filled *pains* and bought one along with a bottle of fizzy water. With my picnic in my bag I strode past the white hotel and quay and on to the track leading to the cliffs. It was quicker to find this time.

The old house felt like home and I didn't care if I was trespassing or not. I'd tell anyone questioning me that I had been talking to Louis – his name might give me a licence to snoop around. I looked at this house that was almost a mirror image of the one in Cornwall I knew so well. But that was the wrong way round. This was the original house and Vue Claire its replica. Vue Claire. What a subtle clue my grandmother had given us. The other hints had come in that fragment of letter and from what she'd tried to tell me herself, just hours before she died.

I couldn't run back home without finding out what else she'd wanted to tell me. But before I went further I really had to tell Dad what I'd uncovered about Rozenn's family. But how do you tell someone that what they believed about their mother was at best a fragment of the truth? Rozenn had never actually lied to us, unless by omission, but she'd allowed her own son to believe she was an only child.

I sat down, back to the crumbling old stone garden wall, trying to work it all out in my head. Rozenn's brother and twin. Luc, my grandfather. Rozenn had told us very little about Luc, other than showing us the photos in the album and describing his business success. He'd been a loving father. Dad had once described how he'd stand at the window, waiting for Luc to come home from his trips down to the West Country.

'He made me feel like the most important and special person in the world,' Dad said. 'If I had bad marks in a maths test, he'd ruffle my hair and tell me I'd do better next time. And I would. Maman expected so much of me, I always worried about letting her down. But Papa made me feel anything I did was just fine. I'd score a goal in a match and he'd be there on the sidelines, beaming at me.'

Charming, charismatic Luc.

Louis'd told me I'd pulled out an apparently single loose thread and extracted another but it actually felt as though a whole piece of lace was unravelling.

What happened here? I asked my grandmother silently. Did she feel guilty at having escaped? Guilt would account for her silence about the war years. Guilt could wind its fingers around you and refuse to let you go. The image of that boy could flash before my eyes at any moment and I'd feel the acid in my stomach. People could tell me it hadn't been my fault and intellectually I might believe them but emotionally I didn't. Something inside me still insisted that if I hadn't been riding up on the Ridgeway that Sunday morning the boy would still be alive. That fact was incontrovertible.

I stared at a butterfly as it fluttered past me, counted to ten. Let the thoughts float away before taking my mobile out of my pocket to ring Dad.

25

Rozenn came closer to the man whose arm her father had treated. 'You're increasing the price after we made our agreement? Is this how business is done in England?'

His lips twitched very slightly.

'It's not funny.'

'The wireless is hidden in a cache on the rocks in the little cove. We left it there when we landed a few—'

Papa raised a hand. 'No details.' The wounded man gave him a grudging nod.

'I planned on retrieving it myself but it's impossible now.' He lifted his bandaged arm.

'What about your friend here?' Papa nodded at the second Englishman.

'He didn't land on this part of the coast and he's never been down to the cove.'

'No.' Papa snapped his bag shut. 'My daughter's done enough.'

The injured man propped himself up, wincing. 'We can't tell the landing party what time to pick us up if we can't send a signal. It's in your son's interest to help us.'

'Why can't he do it?' Papa gestured at Luc. 'He's your facilitator, after all. Why are you asking a girl? Have you no pride?'

'The Germans are watching me,' Luc said, not meeting Papa's eyes, sounding almost sullen with shame. 'I can move around across the fields without them tracking me, but if they catch me on the cliff path, we're in trouble.'

'What if they catch Rozenn on the cliff path?'

Luc swallowed. 'She could say . . .'

'What?' Papa barked.

'That she was sneaking out to meet someone.' Luc met Papa's furious stare.

'My daughter is not going to risk herself like this.' Papa's voice had risen. He lowered it. 'It's curfew shortly. The rocks will be slippery when it's dark. And if she's caught with a wireless—'

'I'll do it,' she said. 'Where exactly in the cove will I find it?'

'The western edge, bordering the bay,' the wounded Englishman said. 'About halfway down the rocks on the left side. You'll see a boulder with seaweed on it, it looks like a man wearing a toupee. If you put your hand underneath the seaweed, there's a hollow. The wireless case is in there.'

Luc examined his watch. 'The tide will still be low enough to reach the rocks in half an hour. And it will be completely dark then.'

The other Englishman said something that sounded like a warning they'd all be in trouble if the wireless was damaged.

'Treat it like a newborn,' the first one said. 'It's in a waterproof case but we don't want to risk it.' He gave a small laugh as he looked at her face. 'No need to glare at us, Mademoiselle.'

'Of course I'll be careful with your precious wireless.'

'If something happens to my daughter I assure you I'll do more than glare.' Papa said the words very calmly. A chill ran up Rozenn's spine. Did he mean he'd go straight to the Gestapo if she was caught and tell them where to find the Englishmen in exchange for her release? What about Luc?

'Rozenn will not take unnecessary risks,' Luc said. In the gloom their hands touched and he squeezed her fingers briefly. He was so much younger than the men, but they looked at him and nodded. 'Come outside and I'll give you more exact directions, Rozenn. There's no moon – you won't see much, even with a torch.'

Her mouth opened to tell him she already knew how to find the path down to the cove, but she felt a particular charge from him, his hand catching at hers. They left Papa to repack his medical bag. Luc pulled her round the side of the hut, into the shadows. They melted into one another, mouths joining silently. The kiss was long and deep. She wanted to stay like this all night. 'I know where the path is,' she said when their mouths separated.

'I know you do. I needed an excuse to get you by yourself.' They laughed. Their mouths met again. She forgot everything: the boat, the wireless, Yann. It was just her and Luc, holding one another so tightly it was hard to tell where she ended and he began.

'You're not angry with me?' He stroked the back of her head.

'For knowing they'd want more from me?' His silence confirmed her suspicion. 'For a moment you tried to warn me off in there, didn't you, Luc?'

He held her tighter. 'Part of me still doesn't want you to be involved.'

'We all need this to be over.' She sank her head on to his shoulder.

'Over,' he repeated.

'There's something else. A German artilleryman saw Yann this afternoon. All very friendly but later on he came up to the house to speak to him.'

She felt him stiffen. 'Which artilleryman?'

'That corporal who's friends with Martine.'

Luc rested his cheek on the top of her head and she felt his out breath.

'Does it make it more dangerous?' she asked.

'I don't know.' He released her. His face was shadowed with thoughts she couldn't read. She re-pinned the front of her hair and they walked back to Papa. 'You're doing this for your brother,' he said, almost fiercely. 'Any of us would do the same.'

It was as though he really understood how much she'd do for Yann.

'I'll meet you at the gate of the donkey field,' Luc said. 'I can hide behind the wall and they won't see me.'

With muttered farewells to the group, Papa and Rozenn walked back up the track. She felt her father looking at her as though he hadn't seen her properly before. But she hadn't really changed: she had always secretly been this fierce, unfettered person. It simply hadn't been possible to reveal herself until now. She was always playing the part of Rozenn Guillou, middle-class girl destined for marriage with someone from the professional Parisian classes.

Now she was this *person* who kissed local boys behind huts and bartered like a market woman, who told strange men what she would and wouldn't do for them. Her new self terrified and thrilled her.

'Don't tell your mother about the wireless,' Papa said. 'She'll be so worried.'

It was on her lips to tell him that Maman would worry much less about her than she would had it been Yann or Claire putting themselves in jeopardy. But she said nothing. Maman had, after all, been a little more attentive to her since they'd arrived here: letting her read the magazine in peace, thanking her for taking Claire for walks.

'You'll have to tell her Yann's leaving tomorrow night, Papa.'

He groaned.

'She wants the best for him.'

'She always has. When Yann was born we had a nurse, just as we did later for you girls. But your mother insisted on doing

231

everything herself for the baby. Her friends thought it strange. But for her having a boy was magical. So many of the young men she'd grown up with had died. Including her brother.'

Yann was named after that fallen uncle.

'Yann's arrival felt like a fresh start,' Papa said. 'Paris was full of wonderful things, everyone wanted to be happy.'

They reached the clump of trees. As her eyes adjusted to the shade, Rozenn wondered how Maman would handle the probably long separation from Yann. It might be years before he could return. If he fought somewhere dangerous, he might never come back, just like his namesake in the first war. A chink of doubt sounded inside Rozenn. But Yann was a strong young man who wanted to fight. And he was frustrated with his life here.

A boot clinked against a stone. Papa didn't seem to have heard. Rozenn stopped and turned. A middle-aged German. *Merde*. He was about fifteen or twenty metres away, lighting a cigarette, face turned away from them. Rozenn thought she made out a sound behind her. She crept forward praying the German wouldn't hear them.

'What is it?' Papa asked.

'Just a fox or deer jumping into the hedge.' No point in causing panic or Papa might try again to prevent her from going down to the cove.

A cold wave of doubt flowed through her. The mist was settling again, the path down to the rocks would be slippery and almost invisible. One misstep and she'd fall to the rocks below. In the dark it would be hard to identify the boulder under which the wireless was hidden. And suppose she brought them back the wireless and they wanted her to do something else? So many reasons why agreeing to do this was a bad idea.

Rozenn thought of Yann and knew there was no alternative. They walked on into the gloom.

26

Dad sounded stunned when I told him about Claire. 'Let me get this straight: Maman had an identical twin, this Claire. Who stayed in France after Rozenn left. Why, I wonder? And why wouldn't Maman tell us about Claire?'

'Louis said Claire had some kind of mental disability. She wasn't able to do much.' Had Rozenn been ashamed of her sister? I couldn't imagine her feeling like this.

'But did Louis say why your grandparents left in such a hurry? Were they involved in something dangerous?'

'She and Luc weren't supposed to get on to the boat. Yann was.' I paused.

'Yann?'

'That's Rozenn's older brother. She had one of those, too.'

I felt shock radiating across the Channel from south-west London. Dad must have felt hurt – stunned – that his mother had kept all this to herself, going to her death without telling us. Rozenn had been self-contained, cool at times, but it wasn't like her to be unkind. People changed, sometimes, in very old age, I reminded myself. 'She tried to tell me something about Yann, right at the end,' I said. 'But she could barely speak by then and I misunderstood her. I think she was expecting something to happen before she died but whatever it was, it didn't.'

'What do you mean, Morane?' He sounded older suddenly. Perhaps I should have gone home to tell him all this in person. But I couldn't return until I'd found out everything.

'Those fragments of letter to Rozenn I showed you? I think they were from Yann himself. He could still be alive.'

'Why hasn't he made contact with us?'

'I don't know.'

'Do you have any idea where he is now?'

'I'm still asking questions.' I told him about Joséphine. 'I'm actually here at the house now.'

'Are you?' He sounded less distressed now. I pictured him sitting back, perhaps lowering a hand to pat Pearl, lying at his feet. It wasn't one of his days for going into the surgery.

I thought of something else that might cheer him up and told him how I'd been able to approach Lise's horse. 'Without any palpitations.'

'That's good,' he said warmly. After a pause he went on. 'I worried, when you said you'd run away to Brittany.'

'You thought I was running away from life? Perhaps I was. But now,' I gazed at the old house in front of me, 'now I'm realising there are still things I can throw myself into, things that interest me. There's a point to it all.'

'Having a point to it all is the fount of all happiness,' he told me. 'Keep asking questions, Morie.' We finished the call, with promises to keep in touch. A notification flashed up on my phone screen: Lise, sending me the scanned photograph of Claire. I forwarded it on to Dad, assuring him that I was determined to find out all I could about Rozenn's family.

I felt a new resolve inside myself. Rozenn had wanted me to know the truth she'd been trying to tell me herself. It was up to me to uncover it now. I stared at the *longère*. I'd been preoccupied with asking questions of people: Lise, Louis and Joséphine. But perhaps the house itself might tell me something about the past. Who'd bought it? Who'd owned it? Were they or their families still alive? Uncovering more about its ownership would be a start, and if the property had been fairly recently sold, it wouldn't be too hard to find someone who knew a bit of its history.

27

Outside the *longère* Rozenn parted from Papa. He took her by her shoulders. 'Take care on those rocks, *ma chère*.' He released her but stayed where he was.

'If a patrol sees you outside after curfew they'll be suspicious, Papa.' Grimacing, he went inside. She heard Maman question him and his low, reassuring doctor's voice in response.

Rozenn crept on to the cliff path. All was quiet, but she already knew how the mist on the coast could muffle sound. She rehearsed the excuses she would give if a patrol came across her. *A boy, please don't tell* mes parents, *they'll kill me.* She walked with caution, the edge of the path, usually so defined, hard to make out.

The path began the descent towards the village. Rozenn stepped carefully on to the track down to the cove, relief sweeping her as she passed under the overhanging cliff. She was out of sight of the path now.

At the bottom she stepped on to the shingle, heart thumping, listening. No waft of cigarette smoke, no rifle loading. Just the hiss of surf out to sea. The tide would be turning but she could just make out the exposed rocks. The mist lifted for a moment and she spotted the rock like a man wearing a seaweed toupee. Rozenn jogged lightly towards it.

So light was she on her feet that the couple curled around one another mightn't even have noticed her if she hadn't let out a gasp.

'Mademoiselle.' The young German artillery corporal disentangled himself from Martine. He looked at his watch.

'I know,' she said. 'Curfew. I'll go straight home. *Désolée.*' She backed away.

'Were you meeting Luc?' Martine asked. 'He brings girls down here, I've heard.'

'Go straight home, Mademoiselle,' the corporal said, sounding more adult than usual. 'You too, Martine.'

'But Frederick—'

He pulled her up gently. 'See you tomorrow, Martine.' The girls picked their way across to the track.

'Thanks for spoiling my night,' Martine said with feeling.

'Sorry for breaking up your fraternisation.'

The pull at her sleeve nearly made her lose her balance. 'What are you up to, Rozenn Guillou? I've seen a strange boy swimming here at night. He walks up the cliff path towards your house. Who is he?'

Rozenn shrugged. 'Why should I know?'

'My aunt works at the *mairie*. She says there are four of you registered at the *longère*.'

'Does she often blab about her work?'

Martine laughed softly. 'Oh you're so high and mighty with your smart clothes and your manners and that hair of yours. Everyone's noticed you. That's what you like, isn't it? But you know nothing about how things work here, Rozenn Guillou. Or about Luc.'

I know enough, she wanted to reply. Just thinking about him now, about how he'd held her, was enough to make Martine no more than a minor nuisance. Being downgraded like this would probably irritate Martine. This thought made Rozenn smile, even now.

They'd reached the clifftop. Martine turned silently for the village. Rozenn approached the boulders to hide until the corporal was out of the way. Someone stepped out in front of her. She bit down her scream. 'Yann?'

'It's well past curfew. What's going on, Rozenn?'

She put a finger to her lips, pushing him back behind the boulders. The corporal appeared at the top of the track. He paused, looking around, before heading towards the village.

'I have to go back down to the cove,' Rozenn told Yann.

He grabbed her sleeve. 'What's down there that's worth the risk?'

She looked away.

'Let *me* go. I'm used to that path in the dark.'

'No, stay here. If you see the corporal coming back, throw a pebble down to the rocks.'

Yann let her go, reluctance painted over his face.

She picked her way back down the track, stopping to test it with the toes of her gym shoes, making sure it snaked and turned in the way she remembered. Visibility was worse now; her breath was forming a faint mist in front of her.

Scree fell and clattered on the rocks below her. The shingle at the bottom felt solid beneath her feet. For a moment she paused, drew a breath. Hissing in front of her was the returning tide. The mist shifted, revealing the rocks to the left, seaweed marking the top of the wireless's hiding place. Rozenn told herself she'd been good at this kind of thing as a child, always the boldest in the playground, sure on her feet. The rocks nearest the shingle were smooth, their surface hard to grip, even in rubber soles. She lurched. Bile rose to her mouth as her feet slipped. Her shoulder took the brunt of her fall but she didn't slide any further. She crawled to her knees and continued to pick her way out to the toupee-rock.

The water had risen, soaking her arms as she felt underneath the seaweed for the cache. Her numb fingers grabbed at something solid. She tugged a canvas case out of its hiding place and pulled the long strap over her shoulder so the case sat on her hip. The strap was adjusted for a taller person, but there was no time to fiddle with it.

As she clambered back over the rocks towards the beach the wireless shifted on her back, threatening to tilt her into the inky water. Once again nausea swept her. Her breath was coming in gasps. The waves lapped the rocks, soaking her skirt. She could discard the wireless, tell them the strap had slipped off her shoulder. But they had to make the radio transmission.

Surely it must be less than ten metres to the beach now? She could manage that, couldn't she? Assure Yann of his place in that boat? She moved a few centimetres to the next rock and lifted a shaking, grazed leg over it, pulling herself up, feeling the cold shock of a wave douse her, the salt water stinging the blood on the cuts. She repeated the movement again and again, gasping as each wave struck her.

And then she was lying, face-down on the shingle, numb, heart thumping. Rozenn pulled herself up. The mist lifted. She made out the start of the path up to the cliffs and hobbled towards it, dragging her right leg, which seemed to hurt more than other parts of her.

Pausing for a few seconds, she managed to pull the strap of the transmitter case tighter so it didn't sway from side to side. Climbing the track was easier than going down.

A few metres before the top, a sound made her stop. Boots. Not Yann's. The corporal – he'd returned, perhaps checking she'd obeyed his order and gone home. Rozenn swore under her breath. The cliff's overhang and the darkness would shield her from sight, but as soon as she moved, he'd see her. Her teeth chattered: could he hear them? She thought she heard the corporal say something, but it might just have been a muttered curse to himself at being out this late in the mist. The boots moved on. Her legs were solid, bloodless chunks of stone. It took seconds to persuade them to move her to the top of the path.

'Rozenn.' Yann stepped out from behind the boulders. 'You were such a long time. And you're soaked.'

'I'm all right.' The words jerked out between shudders. She bent over, thinking she was going to vomit, but coughing up salt water instead.

'You need to keep moving, get your circulation going before you freeze. I'll boil water for you to have a hot bath.'

'I need to take this to Luc.'

'Let me do it.' His hands were reaching for the canvas strap.

'No.' She stepped back. He sighed loudly. They walked together to the house. 'Wait here,' she said, trudging on down the lane.

A breeze had picked up now, the mist was gone. Venus burnt overhead like a lantern. In a film or book it would have been a symbol of hope. Rozenn shivered and prayed this would be the case tonight. The shifting grey shadows in the field were donkeys. Someone was murmuring to them at the gate. 'Luc.' She fell into his arms.

'I've been waiting ages, what happened?' She told him about coming across Martine and the corporal. Luc swore. 'Do you think he was suspicious?'

'I was out after curfew, of course he was suspicious.'

Luc nodded slowly to himself. 'And he saw your brother up there?'

'I don't think so.'

She disentangled herself, swung the canvas case over her shoulder and gave it to him. She'd gone beyond feeling cold now, just wanted to find somewhere to lie down for a moment and—

Luc caught her just as her legs gave way. He felt warm against her.

'Where should Yann go tomorrow?' she asked sleepily.

'I'll bring word,' Luc told her. 'Meet me at the donkey field at twelve.'

The blood was moving again in Rozenn's limbs; it felt almost painful.

'Tell them to heat soup for you,' Luc said, as gentle as a mother with a baby, steering her towards the house. 'And put a hot brick on your feet. You shouldn't go to bed until you're warmer. When the fishermen here are soaked and frozen, their women won't let them go to sleep.'

'Why not?' She must be feeling warmer now, she felt curious again.

'Because the spirits will take them.'

'You don't believe stories like that, do you?'

'I don't know.' He sounded weary, too. She remembered what he'd said about twins: how the people here believed they brought either good or ill fortune. She laughed to herself: it would be useful to know which one it was.

Luc bent his face to hers and kissed her on the lips, almost chastely. 'See you tomorrow.' She wanted to cling to him, tell him not to leave her, but reluctantly she let him go.

28

Lise texted me the following morning. *Papa hopes to be out of bed tomorrow and would love to see you again before you leave, if convenient.* I expressed my relief at hearing this, said I'd love to see them and would be in touch to confirm a time. I asked if she knew anything about the new owner of the *longère*.

Nobody knows much other than he comes from California. Joséphine might know a bit more? Failing that, the agents immobiliers *in Lannion who sold the house?* She gave me directions.

I could have waited until I met Joséphine again later on, but impatience drove me into town. I found the agency without difficulty as it was across the road from the *crêperie* I'd been in the previous day. In the window, posters advertised half a dozen properties for rent or sale that looked similar to the *longère*, or how it would look if completely restored. I studied the photographs carefully, thinking of work I'd carried out on old properties in England. The two women inside seemed pleased to see me: I appeared to be the only client. I apologetically explained that I wasn't interested in buying or renting properties but wondered if they could help with an inquiry. I was left with the younger woman, who put a polite face on her initial disappointment. She asked me for details of the *longère* and I showed her where it was on my mobile's map app.

She shook her head. 'I remember that property but didn't have any contact with the client. It was my colleague. He's away on holiday. We have to be very careful about client confidentiality anyway, Madame.'

'Is there anyone else who might know?'

She looked doubtful. 'You could try across the road, at the *Office Notarial.*' French notaries, I remembered, handled property transactions in a way similar to English solicitors. 'They might feel more able to tell you what you need to know.' She frowned. 'I know the British are fond of renovating our old properties but that one would be a challenge, even with some of the work inside already done. You'd have all the ground to clear around it. You wouldn't like to look at something already fully modernised, with a landscaped garden?' Across the desk she slid property details for renovated longhouses, complete with painted shutters and intact roofs.

I thanked her for her time but explained that I had a particular interest in the longhouse on the clifftop.

The notary's office was only minutes away across the street. Everything in this town seemed handily positioned. I wondered how much it had changed from the war years. Everyone must have known everything about their neighbours and their business. Surely people must have been curious about the disappearance of Luc and Rozenn?

There were two notaries in the office, an assistant told me when I went inside to the small reception area. Father and son, Henri and Jean Tanguy. Monsieur Jean could perhaps spare me ten minutes. The assistant ushered me into a small meeting room. Five minutes passed and a tall, slim man came in. I admired his crisp white shirt and light-wool summer suit. He was almost a cliché French professional male. I showed him the map on my mobile and the photographs I'd taken.

'I'm trying to find out who bought it.'

'You want to know why?' he asked in English. 'To make a higher offer? To knock it down and build something bigger on the site?' His tone was cooler. 'You would be better buying a fully restored and developed property. Besides, the person who bought the house last autumn has now died and left it to someone else.' He looked towards the door, making it clear his interest in my inquiry was at an end.

'I have a family connection with the house, I'm not looking to buy it.' I couldn't help smiling at the idea that I would be in a position to buy a property.

'Family?' His eyes narrowed. 'How so?'

I told him about Rozenn's escape in a boat in 1941 and how we hadn't known until recently where exactly she had been living at the time.

'What was her name?'

I told him. He stared at me. 'Please could you repeat that?'

'Is something wrong?' I asked after I'd said it for a second time.

He looked at his stylish but discreet watch. 'I have a meeting.' He seemed flustered. 'I will ask my father if . . . He has a long memory and handled the sale of the house to the owner who died recently. If you would like to come back just before lunch, say at twelve thirty, we can perhaps tell you more. Could you just tell me your name?'

I did, thanking him for his time. He looked at me closely. Obviously the name of Caradec was still well known here. 'Until later, then, Madame.' He opened the door for me. I felt his eyes on my back as I walked out. Small-town provincial France: not entirely sure about people from outside, perhaps.

I drove back to St Martin.

Joséphine was waiting for me at the hotel on the beach, sitting at a table out on the balcony, a *café au lait* in front of her. She greeted me with kisses to each cheek, looking at me in a way that was more resolute, somehow. 'I gather you've met Louis. So you must know more about your grandmother's family,' she said, getting straight to the point. 'I didn't want to be the one to tell you about the betrayal.'

'The betrayal?' I remembered the graffiti. 'Has this got something to do with what I saw painted on the door?'

'What was that?'

I told her.

Joséphine sighed. 'The person who did that was probably not even born in the war.'

'What has Rozenn got to do with a betrayal? Are you saying she was some kind of collaborator, Joséphine?' My voice had risen; I looked around. Nobody seemed to be paying us much attention. 'Sorry. It just all seems so bizarre.' I still felt rattled after the meeting with Jean Tanguy.

'My mother's been dead for ten years now.' Joséphine stared out to sea. 'She didn't say much about that night until she was very close to dying. I think it was only me she talked to about it. Things were hard for her after the Germans were driven out. She'd grown . . . close to one of them. After the war, men blamed women, perhaps to avoid feeling bad about what they themselves had done or failed to do,' she said, almost in a whisper.

'What did Martine tell you?' The resolute look on Joséphine's face had gone. She seemed uncertain. I leant closer to her. 'Tell me?'

29

'Zenn.' The petals were falling off the rose Luc was handing her and a thorn scratched Rozenn's skin. Claire was calling out to her, but Rozenn couldn't look away from the disintegrating flower. Luc smiled and plucked another rose for her, but he gave it to Claire, to the wrong twin—

Rozenn's eyes opened. Claire was shaking her shoulder. 'Late. Wake up.' Her twin was sitting on the bed, fully dressed, with only one button on the front of her frock mismatched. Claire frowned at her.

Rozenn looked down at her arms, still clad in her jumper from last night. A sleeve had rolled up to reveal a scratch from the rocks. Her skirt was rucked up around her waist. Claire laughed and Rozenn found herself laughing too. 'I'd better have a wash and get changed, hadn't I?'

Claire ran downstairs. 'She's been bad,' Rozenn heard her tell Maman. 'But don't be cross.'

Rozenn got out of bed, stretching her legs gingerly, expecting aches from the fall on the rocks. The muscles felt tight, but the cuts already seemed to be healing. Rozenn stripped and poured water from the jug into the basin. It was still warm. Maman must have heated it and brought it up. That had never happened before: she'd been responsible for filling the jug from the pan on the range and bringing it upstairs for herself and Claire. Washing with a linen cloth removed the fine grit from the creases behind her knees and around her hairline. She dabbed at the scratch on her leg. Maman would have iodine downstairs. If only she could have filled a bathtub or stood under a shower.

Changed into fresh clothes, she went downstairs. Papa must have gone into the Lannion surgery and Yann to his outbuilding. Maman and Claire sat at the table. 'I wish we had chocolate for you to drink,' Maman said, pouring her the ersatz coffee. 'It sounds as though your night was . . . gruelling.'

Maman glanced at Claire, clearly wishing, for once, that the girl wasn't there, picking up information she couldn't possibly understand but might blab about. When she looked back at Rozenn there was something warm in her expression.

'If it were you crossing the sea, Rozenn, I wouldn't be as worried as I am at the thought of your brother making the voyage.' The words came out in a quick, quiet stream. She couldn't reassure her mother, tell her Yann would be safe.

'You were always so bright as a child,' Maman went on. 'And pretty, too. My friends told me I should be showing you off in the park, enjoying my little girl. That's what I did with Yann. But I always felt I should be with Claire.'

Claire looked up from her wooden horse and gave her mother that beaming smile of hers.

'I worried if I left her for a single hour she might take ill. I *trusted* you to stay well, Rozenn. You were strong. And then years passed and Claire went away to the convent and I realised I'd let you drift away. I barely know you, your friends.'

Rozenn tried to eat the piece of bread in her hand but it stuck in her throat. She ought to say something in response but didn't know what. All the years she and Maman had wasted. Perhaps when Yann had gone there would be time for them to repair the relationship.

❧

Rozenn spent the hours until it was time to meet Luc at the donkey field washing the clothes that had been soaked the previous night and hanging them on the line. Her gym shoes went on the warm stone windowsill to dry. She would have liked to have washed her hair, which felt stiff from the sea salt. Remembering what Martine had said last night she tried defiantly to pin it into something resembling her usual style, but it wouldn't stay in place. Finally she arranged it in a single plait.

'Like me,' Claire said in delight, waving her own plait. 'You and Yann leave me behind,' she went on. 'It makes me sad.'

Rozenn put a hand on her sister's shoulder. As soon as Yann was safely away, she'd spend more time with Claire.

When they went out together into the garden Maman blinked at them. 'I haven't seen you look so alike since you were both about five.'

A day or so ago Rozenn would have hated hearing those words but now she smiled. 'Where's your tennis ball, Claire?' She threw it to her sister in the sunny patch outside the outbuildings before Claire lost concentration and ran away to Maman.

She went to find Yann, to enjoy his company while she still could. But when she peered through the slightly open door to his outbuilding he was sitting at his makeshift desk, staring intently at a page of his drawing pad, pencil in hand. Perhaps this would be his last opportunity for quiet work. For it was his work, she realised now: a passion he would make his profession.

She walked quietly away; the lump in her throat becoming intolerable. But it was time to meet Luc. Images from last night's dream ran through her mind: the perfect rose he was about to give her when Claire had woken her . . .

He was waiting at the donkey-field gate. Luc kissed her on both cheeks, almost formally, as though they were good acquaintances, not . . . whatever it was they were. He was pale, as though he hadn't slept much. She felt almost shy in front of him; could he see what she felt? It was too much. She needed to pull down her old carapace, protect herself from her emotions.

'Tell Yann to wait at the boulders above the cove on the cliff path at half past ten tonight. There's no moon but he should still take care. Just one bag – the boat is small.'

'That German corporal,' she said. 'What happens if he's suspicious after last night and patrols along the cliff path?'

'We'll have to pray he stays out of the way.' He looked down at the stony track.

Rozenn's stomach churned. The reality of Yann's danger became larger. It wouldn't end if he got away from the shore on the small boat. There'd be hours, possibly days, at sea with air and naval patrols to evade.

He looked at his wristwatch. 'I must go.' He came closer, placed a hand on her arm.

'Do they row out of the cove?' she asked. 'Where do they meet the other boat?' He said nothing. 'Out to the sandbar?' Still he was silent. 'Yes, probably safer I don't know the details.'

'The man with the infected arm's doing better this morning,' he said. 'Your father did a good job, Rozenn.' He pulled her into his arms. The kiss was so deep, almost aggressive, that when it ended she was gasping, every hair on her body standing up, her skin tingling, wanting him.

'When this is over,' she said. 'You and I, we—' She stopped, not even sure what she was asking him. Perhaps whether he planned on continuing this . . . whatever it was between them. But she was still Rozenn Guillou and she reminded herself not to sound too anxious about a man.

'Don't think of afterwards,' he said, suddenly looking younger, less sure. 'Just think of what needs to be done an hour at a time. If you try to look ahead, it . . .' He swallowed.

'An hour at a time,' she repeated.

'Don't go down to the meeting place with your brother tonight,' he said, all in a rush. He held her tighter. 'Stay indoors with your parents, Rozenn.'

'I have to see him safe on to the boat.'

'It'll be dangerous.'

'I know.' *I'll be with you*, she wanted to say.

He sighed, kissed her once on the brow and let her go.

As he walked away from her he raised a hand in parting.

Rozenn trudged back home. Maman and Claire were still in the garden. She waited for Claire to wander off towards the chickens pecking in a bush. 'Ten-thirty tonight in the cove.'

Maman brushed away a stray lock of hair under the turban she sometimes wore for gardening and housework and blinked hard. 'I suppose I thought something might happen to prevent him going. I want him to go and I want him to stay.' She sounded wistful. 'So illogical.'

'There's nothing logical about this war.'

Maman was staring at the soil she'd been weeding. 'I need to make sure his clothes are ready . . .'

'He won't need much, he can only take his duffel bag.'

'How will that be enough to fit in everything?' Maman's head dropped. 'I'm being ridiculous. They'll give him a ration card for clothes.' Her face brightened. 'And he'll be in uniform again. I wonder if he'll be able to send—' She grimaced at Rozenn's expression. 'I know, impossible.'

'It's all right,' Rozenn said. 'I understand.' She felt as though the roles had been reversed between the two of them. She went to the half-open door of Yann's outbuilding and knocked. He lifted his head from the page.

'Come in.' He looked at her intently. 'It's really happening tonight?'

She bent down to look at what he was drawing: a cartoon, this time an army of mice in French uniforms gnawing at the cables underneath a production line guarded by rats in German uniforms.

'Yes.'

'I'd better pack.'

She wanted to cling to every last second with him but he'd want to finish the drawing.

When Yann left, their family would lack its keystone. Who could distract Claire, cheer up Maman? One thing was certain, Rozenn was not letting him go to the rendezvous alone. She'd be his eyes and ears until the very last moment.

⁂

The time between lunch and Papa's return from the Lannion surgery that evening seemed to move simultaneously more slowly and more rapidly than normal. Maman and Yann bickered half-heartedly about the clothes he should pack in his duffel bag. She wanted him to leave the sketch pad and take more socks. 'But I need the pad,' he told her.

'We should have a special dinner tonight,' Rozenn said. 'Open some of the tins we brought from Paris, the foie gras, perhaps.'

'Good idea. Claire can collect eggs for us. I may even be able to produce a soufflé. There's butter saved from last week's ration. And I have some cheese.'

'I'll have to go away more often,' Yann said. Maman returned his smile but when she turned away she was biting her lip.

'Yann's going. Claire wants to go too.' Claire looked as though she was about to burst into tears.

'When I come back you'll be able to count to one hundred,' he told her. 'No, one thousand.'

'*Non.* I want to go too.'

'Who'd look after the chickens?' Maman said.

'I want to go on the boat. I like boats.'

Rozenn felt cold. Suppose the German corporal made his way up here again and heard Claire chatting about boats? This evening they should ask Papa to dose her with some of the sedative he'd packed for the train journey from Paris. But perhaps a softer method would work.

'You can't leave me, Claire.' Rozenn put a hand on her twin's shoulder. Claire turned to stare at her. For a second something in her hazel eyes flickered, suggesting more awareness than was usually there.

Claire smiled and it pulled at something inside Rozenn. 'Won't leave you, Zenn,' she said.

Maman was taking a linen tablecloth out of the dresser. 'I didn't know you'd packed that when we left Paris,' Yann said.

'I hoped we might celebrate the *Quatorze Juillet*. But Yann won't be with us then, so . . .' She shrugged.

To distract herself, Rozenn went upstairs. She sat on her bed, undoing her plait, brushing out the hair. Holding her mirror in one hand she pinned the hair back into something resembling its former style. The layers were too long now; she should replait it, but she couldn't face the effort.

The sound of Papa's Citroën arriving made her look out of the window. He carried a small keg of cider along with his bag into the house. She went downstairs to meet him. 'It's happening?' he asked.

'Yes. You've brought cider to toast him?'

He looked at the keg as though he hadn't noticed he was carrying it.

'Are we doing the right thing?' he asked. Just as she had earlier with Maman, she felt the reversal of roles.

'We have to let him go. There's no other way.'

Her father closed his eyes momentarily. When he opened them he was the calm, competent doctor once again.

⚜

The foie gras was served on thin slices of toasted bread, along with smoked oysters. Salad. Yann's ham. New potatoes with parsley. Crêpes made with eggs from Claire's hens, wastefully fried in butter topped with sugar and lemon juice. Rozenn hadn't even known that Maman had a lemon. 'I'd been keeping it in case anyone had a sore throat,' she said guiltily. Rozenn hadn't eaten anything as sweet for months and could almost feel the sugar coursing through her veins. Claire scraped her plate clean and looked up hopefully. Everyone laughed.

'There aren't any more,' Maman told her.

'It feels like Christmas Eve,' Yann said. 'Or one of our feast days.'

'It's better,' Rozenn said. 'I feel . . .' She felt the weight of sorrow at Yann's departure, but something else: a sense of peace with her family, that for once they were all sitting together, relaxed, accepting. Maman wasn't fretting about food. Claire was eating quietly and calmly. She herself wasn't tense, not expecting Claire to make a mistake or waiting for Maman to scold her.

Papa pushed his chair back. 'I remember feast days when I was a child,' he said. 'The endless courses. We sat at the table for hours.'

253

'My family had meals like that, too,' Maman said. 'And some-times we sang.'

'What did you sing?' Rozenn asked. To her surprise Maman sang a few verses of a folk song in Breton. Rozenn couldn't under-stand all of the words but enough to know it was about a bride mar-rying the wrong man, a funeral, a grave, a wraith in black dancing, haunting . . . Maman's voice was warm and deep. Had she sung to them as children? Rozenn couldn't remember.

Claire clapped when her mother finished.

'You should sing more,' Papa said. 'But for something more cheerful . . .' He launched into the famous song about Queen Anne of Brittany in her *sabots* walking to Rennes. They all joined in, even Claire, whose surprisingly assured voice reminded Rozenn that she would have sung most days in the convent chapel.

'I wish . . .' Rozenn started to say when they'd finished singing. They looked at her. She found herself blinking. 'We're so happy tonight, even though . . . I thought I'd hate living here, but this house . . .'

'It has something about it,' Maman said, reaching across to squeeze her hand. 'A warmth.'

'Now it doesn't smell of pigs.' Rozenn forced herself to smile. 'Perhaps after the war we can buy it and use it for holidays.'

'The beach,' Claire said eagerly.

'Yes, the beach will be open again one day,' Yann told her. 'You can have ice creams on the sand again.'

'I remember taking photographs of you two on a beach not so very far from here at St Brieuc,' Papa said. 'You were tiny girls. We could barely tell you apart when we had them developed.'

'I'm going to train as an architect,' Rozenn said. 'I'll modernise this place for you, Maman. You'll have an indoor bathroom and no privy.' She gazed around the interior, lit softly by a single gas lamp in the middle of the table and by the light pouring in from the open front door. 'But I won't change too much.'

They finished the meal with a small tot of brandy, even Claire. She gasped. 'Hot.' Everyone laughed. Rozenn hoped it would ensure Claire felt drowsy. Usually she went to bed by ten, but the lighter nights made it hard for her to sleep. They drank slowly, none of them wanting to be seen to look at wristwatches. 'I almost forgot.' Papa stood up and went upstairs. When he returned he was holding a silver compass in his hand. 'My father gave it to me,' he said, giving it to Yann. 'When I went away to war.'

'It will bring me good luck.' Yann got up and embraced Papa. 'I'll take good care of it.'

Claire leant back, watching her brother. 'You look tired,' Maman told her. 'Time for bed.'

'Not tired,' Claire said, folding her arms.

'Let her stay,' Yann said. 'Please. I can't say goodbye to her,' he whispered to Rozenn. 'I don't want to upset her.'

'You must or she'll ask where you are every hour of every day,' Rozenn warned him.

'Shall I take you up and read you your farm book?' Maman asked Claire, who looked at her as though she hadn't understood.

Yann stood up. 'It's only ten,' Rozenn said.

'I need to check my things.' They heard him tramp across the yard towards his outbuilding. Nobody spoke. Claire was murmuring something under her breath: prayers, nursery rhymes? Even Maman didn't pay her any attention. When Yann returned he had his duffel bag slung over his shoulder. He took his jacket and cap off the peg. It was still warm but the night out at sea would be cold. He went slowly around the table, kissing in turn Papa, Claire and Maman. Maman clung to him for a second. 'I'll find a way of letting you know I'm safe,' he told her. Rozenn could see how Maman was already missing him, even though he was just leaving.

With a wave of his hand Yann walked out of the door. He hadn't kissed her, so it was obvious he was expecting her to accompany him to the meeting place. Rozenn grabbed her own jacket and the blue beret.

'I want to come,' Claire said.

'Not tonight,' Papa said. 'Early nights for us.'

'I'll see you later,' Rozenn called to them, unable to bear her parents' faces.

Yann was waiting by the side of the house, his shoulders set rigid. Without a word they made for the cliffs. Rozenn wore her gym shoes. Yann's boots were almost as silent. At every bend of the path she raised a hand and they paused, listening for a displaced stone, the bark of a dog, a German voice. Tonight it felt as though myriad eyes watched them, and the fairies the Bretons claimed wandered around at night were following them. The wind had picked up. Spray hissed against shingle below. 'The sea's going to be rough down on the bay,' Yann whispered. 'Just as well I don't get seasick.'

Luc emerged from behind the boulders at the top of the path to the cove. 'What are you doing here?' he asked Rozenn, without a greeting.

'I couldn't stay at home,' she said. Behind him the two Englishmen crouched, nodding at Rozenn.

Yann extended a hand. 'Good evening, how do you do?' he said softly, in English. 'I am Yann Guillou.' Even now his easy charm seemed to work on the pair, who returned the greeting.

'The boat's rowing in from the west of the sandbar, as close to the rocks as it can get safely so it's hidden in the shadows of the cliff. But there're more Germans around tonight,' Luc said. 'It's more dangerous than I thought it would be.' He looked at Yann. 'You still have time to go home.'

Rozenn's hand moved instinctively to her brother. *Pull him away now, go back to Maman and Papa, wait for another opportunity to show itself.* Yann looked at her. 'I can't put them through it again, it will destroy Maman.'

'If we meet a patrol we're in trouble.' Luc's voice was taut. 'Rozenn should go back.'

'If the corporal's with them let me distract him while the rest of you get away,' Yann said. 'He likes me, I drew some cartoons for him.'

'I heard you'd been talking to the artillerymen.' Luc made a sound that was half grunt, half laugh. 'Not what I'd expect from a runaway prisoner of war.' Rozenn opened her mouth to start excusing Yann but Luc was already walking on. The two Englishmen followed, Yann and Rozenn bringing up the rear. She watched the duffel bag swinging gently on Yann's back. It had been with him when he'd first gone off to fight the Germans last year and then when he returned from the prisoner-of-war camp. Now the bag was accompanying him to England. She felt an illogical pang of jealousy at the inanimate object. Luc paused, turning to check they were following.

'You should go home, Rozenn,' he said again.

Yann raised a hand. 'I thought I heard something.' He retraced his steps a few paces. 'Can't see anyone.'

'There's nobody there.' Luc sounded impatient. 'Let's go.'

The sand on the beach was a pale wash of gold below, even without moonlight. They'd have to run along the edge to get to the shelter of the rocks. Once the boat came in they'd be exposed again on the open stretch of sand. From the hotel ahead came the sound of swing jazz. Forbidden, supposedly, to the Germans because of its origins among black Americans. But not here.

Luc led them down to the beach. He removed wire cutters and made a hole in the fence and they slipped through. Silently he pointed at the rocks. It had to be close to half-ten now. The sea was a dark band ahead. She screwed up her eyes and made out the outline of a small boat, rowing towards them. 'Get ready,' Luc told the other men. Yann pulled the duffel bag off his shoulder, ready to throw it in to the boat. The injured Englishman fiddled with the bandage around his arm, readying himself for climbing aboard. It was all happening quickly now. The rowers' faces were blacked out, they called out instructions Rozenn couldn't understand and the Englishmen waded into the sea towards the boat. Something made her turn towards the cliffs. She thought she saw a figure. A single German? A local returning to the village, risking curfew? She jerked at Luc's sleeve. 'Someone's coming.'

'*Merde.*' She hadn't heard him swear before. 'It's Claire.'

Claire was running silently down the path.

30

CLAIRE

Yesterday Rozenn had plaited her hair so she looked just like Claire. Claire liked it when they looked the same, her and Zenn. But then this evening Zenn went upstairs, pulled out the plait and pinned her hair into the usual soft and pretty style. Claire would have liked Zenn to do her hair like that, too, but Zenn was too busy to ask.

They were all busy today. And worried. Maman kept trying to smile but the smile didn't reach her eyes. It looked more as though she was going to cry.

Yann retreated to his outbuilding. Yann was kind. He never shouted at her like Zenn did. He made her toys from pieces of wood. Yann was excited about going away on holiday. But he smelt of fear as well. All four of them did.

That evening when they sat around the table everyone spoke in jerky sentences, laughing even though they were sad. Papa gave Yann a beautiful circle-thing made from shiny metal and glass, hanging from a chain. When Yann turned it in his fingers a pointy bit inside the glass went round and round. Claire liked these meals with the family. There was never enough to eat but it felt easy. Papa seemed to lose some of the lines on his face and Maman smiled more. Even tonight, with this strange undercurrent, the house felt right to Claire.

Maman told her she needed to go to bed, she must feel sleepy. Well, she did and she didn't. The brown drink Papa poured each of them when the meal was finished burnt her throat and made her think curling up on her bed might be good. But she had to stay awake. Zenn and Yann were going off together. She was going to be left out. Again. It wasn't fair. She was Zenn's twin. If Zenn was seeing off Yann, she should be allowed to go as well.

Yann kissed them all and said *au revoir* and it made her insides feel like they did when Papa took her back to the convent after the holidays.

Maman buried her head in her hands and Papa swallowed hard. She didn't want to upset them even more so she kissed them goodnight. Maman filled the jug with warm water and Claire went upstairs. It pleased Maman if Claire undressed herself and washed her face and cleaned her teeth, using the water jug and the two basins: one for clean water to wash in and the other for tipping the used water into. Tonight she managed this without spilling a single drop.

Claire pulled her nightdress over her other clothes. On her knees she said her prayers as normal. She knew Maman would come up to kiss her goodnight. Sure enough, she heard the light tread on the stairs. She got into bed and closed her eyes, pretending to be asleep. Papa came upstairs too. She listened to their voices, Maman saying she couldn't sleep until Zenn was home again. Papa saying they should rest for a while, he'd go downstairs again shortly and sit up for Zenn.

Claire rose, pulling off her nightdress. She had her own torch with the tape on it, but she never had a chance to use it because Zenn shouted at her if she waved it around in the dark. Something happened if lights showed at night. Germans came and put you in prison.

On the cliff path it would be dark. She'd need to be careful. How many times had Rozenn and Maman told her it was dangerous and she could slip? But she knew which way her brother and sister were going: to the beach where she wasn't allowed to play.

Claire had shoes with rubber soles a bit like Rozenn's but the laces were difficult. She tried to remember the way Sister Marguerite had shown her to fasten them.

Papa hadn't pulled the metal bolt over the door because he was expecting Zenn back. Yann wouldn't be coming home tonight because of his holiday, Claire reminded herself. The thought made her feel heavy.

Being outside was like having a black blanket thrown over your head. For a second Claire wanted to go back indoors and wait with her parents. The wind ruffled a loose bit of hair that had come out of her plait.

She knew the way to the sea and found the path easily. You turned *à gauche*. Claire patted her left hand. In the convent they'd made a little bracelet out of threads for her right hand so she'd know which one it was. The bracelet had fallen off a long time ago but it didn't matter because she knew one hand from the other now. Claire walked quickly. Ahead of her she made out the shape of the rocks that looked like a lady with a big bosom on top and a fat bottom. '*Bonsoir*, Madame,' she called very softly.

Voices cut the darkness just ahead of her, speaking quietly, but she could hear what they were saying. Luc was telling Rozenn she shouldn't be there, Rozenn was telling him in her strict way that she was staying. Luc's voice had an edge to it that wasn't there last time, when he'd given Claire the biscuit. Luc was scared. And something else: he sounded tight like Papa did when he told Claire it wouldn't hurt as he stuck the needle-thing into her arm. Papa had been telling her *un mensonge*, a lie. There were two other men with them who looked as if they didn't know where they were, staring intently at Luc.

Luc was Zenn's friend. Luc was kind. And when Zenn looked at him her face became less sharp. Those two liked each other in a way they didn't like other people. But Luc was holding himself stiffly tonight, as though he didn't want to be with the others. Something was wrong.

Claire wanted to run towards her brother and sister. But they would be very cross with her. She ought to go home. But she waited, hiding behind the boulders as the others disappeared around a bend.

She was good at *cache-cache*, never got caught when she played at the convent because she could run fast and hide herself like a mouse curled up in a hole. She made up the ground between herself and the group ahead of her as they descended towards the village and the beach. They were only a little in front when they stopped, cutting the wire fence with what looked like scissors, squeezing themselves through the gap they'd made. Maman had explained to her in a stern voice when Claire had wanted to go and play in the sand that the beach was not allowed. The Germans would punish you.

A boat was coming in, two men rowing it, the sea hissing and crashing around it. The two strangers were clambering in, one of them wincing – perhaps he was hurt? Yann threw his duffel bag into the boat as Zenn and Luc held it steady, difficult because the sea was batting it around. The engine of a truck rumbled on the road beyond the big white building. Men's voices rang out, tight and angry. Dogs barked. Claire liked dogs but these sounded angry too.

Zenn turned and stared up at the cliff, as though sensing Claire was there. Her body stiffened. She said something to Luc. Claire ran down towards the beach. As she approached Rozenn she saw her twin's face was tight like it was when Claire did something bad in public. She stopped, feeling as if she'd been slapped.

Luc said something Claire couldn't hear. She stood there blinking at them. Yann had his back to them, scrabbling into the boat, and couldn't say anything to help her.

Zenn stopped looking angry and smiled at her, beckoning her forward on to the beach through the hole in the wire fence. 'Do you want to help us, Claire?' she called, coming to meet her.

Of course she did! She always wanted to help Yann and Zenn.

'Come here. Let's make you look like me.' Zenn was pulling out Claire's plait, loosening her hair, taking her beret and putting it on her head. She must look just like Zenn now.

'Swap torches with me, mine hasn't been taped.' Claire held out her hand for Rozenn's. 'Good. Switch it on and run past the hotel.' Zenn pointed at the white building. 'It's very important that you wave the torch at those Germans so they see you on the beach.' Zenn took her by the shoulders and steered her round. 'Run as fast as you can, see if you can get them to follow you all the way to the other side.'

That was a long way.

'Zenn too?'

'I'll come and find you when I've finished here. Count to a hundred, Claire. Do it for Yann.' Rozenn had that note in her voice that meant Claire had to do what she said. But Rozenn wasn't cross. She was scared. It made Claire even keener to help her. 'Don't turn round, Claire, whatever you hear, not until you've reached a hundred. And keep waving the torch.'

Claire had never counted that high but she could try. It was her chance. Zenn was scared and for once Claire could help her. She threw herself along the beach, arms pumping.

Yann was shouting something, there were splashes behind her. But she'd promised she would run and wave the torch. She reached *trente.* Maman would be so proud of her: she'd never got past the twenties before. Someone was running along the sand behind her now but she wasn't going to turn around, not when she'd promised . . . *Cinquante.* Claire was counting even higher than fifty and she was still running very fast, waving Rozenn's torch. In a moment she'd be at the large white building where the dogs were barking.

A figure jumped out from the shadow of the sea wall and grabbed her, almost sending her flying, putting a hand over her mouth so she couldn't scream. 'Claire. Come with me now.' The person was dragging her up steps. It was Martine who'd laughed when Claire had found the treasure in the lane. She resisted, trying to twist herself free.

'Hurry, Claire.' Martine pulled her up the first few steps before she could make her stop.

'I'm Rozenn.' She said it fiercely it like Zenn would, waving her head so her hair flew around. 'Look.'

Martine's mouth opened. For an instant she didn't seem certain. She looked Claire up and down. 'You're not Rozenn, come up here.'

'I am.' She pointed down the beach towards the white building. The German voices were closer now. 'They have to chase me.'

'Turn the torch off.' Claire blinked and did what she was told. Martine smiled at her. It wasn't a smile like the one she'd given Claire in the lane, it was a kind smile. 'We have to play *cache-cache.*'

'Zenn said—'

Martine put a finger to her lips. 'We need to hide. Up here.' She sounded scared. 'Come on,' she said. 'Please, Claire, before the Germans hear us?'

'*D'accord.*'

She let Martine pull her up the steps into the cemetery. The gate squeaked a little as Martine opened it and she flinched. Dead people were buried in this place. Claire didn't like it. She heard something down on the beach.

'Who's that?' she asked.

'Your brother,' Martine breathed. 'We need to be quiet.'

'Yann's running after me?' Yann was supposed to be on that boat. He'd thrown his bag into it.

Martine didn't answer. This wasn't like a game any more. She wanted to go home. Her eyes watered. Martine held her tight. 'I want to go down to Yann.' She turned her torch on.

Martine grabbed it and switched it off. 'Don't be scared. We're going in a moment.'

'Going home?' Maman and Papa would insist that this game ended and send them all to bed, safe from the Germans.

Martine put a finger to her lips, listening like the cat back in the convent when the gardener's dog came into the garden. 'We have to run now,' she said, releasing Claire.

Her legs felt shaky from the running before but she let Martine lead her. They ran out of the village, past the quay where the cat liked to lie in the sun and on up the lane. Claire recognised the spot where she'd found the lucky coin on the ground. Martine stopped, holding her side. 'Bad stitch.' After a few gasps she straightened herself. 'I'm all right now.' They ran again. Claire made out the dark shapes of the donkeys on one side of the lane. This was where you turned for home.

'Here?' she asked Martine, but Martine shook her head.

'We're going to Madame O'Donnell.'

Claire knew the name: she was the lady on the horse. 'With the *chiots*?'

'*Chiots*? Oh, yes, her spaniel had puppies.' Martine led Claire off the lane and on to a track. 'Listen, Claire, when we get to the house we have to go very quietly round to the back door. There are Germans.'

If there were Germans, why were they going there? But Martine was very certain, like Zenn could be. And when Zenn was like that, even Maman and Papa did what she said.

'Are Yann and Zenn coming too?'

Martine waited a moment before answering. 'Yann and Zenn want you to be safe, Claire.'

The path led them to the top of a hill. At the bottom sat a large house. The shadows in the fields were cows and horses. Claire would have liked to look at them but Martine wouldn't stop.

'Very quietly now,' Martine said. She opened a gate and took her through the gardens. It was like the convent: large beds of vegetables and a glasshouse, wheelbarrows and pots.

Steps led down to somewhere shadowy on the side of the house. 'I'm putting you in the cellar for now,' Martine said. 'Wait down there while I fetch Madame. Here.' Martine switched on the torch she'd taken from Claire and passed it to her. It was really Zenn's torch and the sight of it made Claire feel better and worse at the same time.

The door creaked as Martine pulled it open. At the convent there was a place like this they put you if you did something very naughty. It had spiders in it. Claire started to tell Martine she was sorry for disobeying her parents and going outside tonight, but the girl wouldn't listen, pushing her inside. 'You won't be here long,' she called as she drew the bolt.

Claire sat on the ground, which was damp. She wanted to cry but the spiders would hear her. When you were scared you were supposed to say your prayers. *Ave Maria, gratia plena* . . . But she couldn't find the rest of the words. Counting might work. On the beach she'd gone past *cinquante*. Even now, pride filled her. A door creaked above and to the front of her. She blinked as a rectangle of light opened.

'Claire?' Madame O'Donnell stood there, smiling. 'You must be cold and hungry. Come this way.'

'May I see the *chiots*, Madame?'

'The puppies are sleeping. Martine's heating you up some soup.' Claire stepped up into a kitchen, stone-floored, with a huge stove throwing off warmth. The woman showed her where to sit and Martine brought her a bowl of soup and a glass of milk.

'We're going to play a game, Claire,' Madame told her. 'We've made you a little hidey-hole.' She pointed to a door. 'You're going to sleep in there at nights and when the men aren't in the house you can play in the kitchen and the garden.'

'Like Yann,' Claire said, remembering how he'd had to hide.

'Your brother? Martine told me about him.'

'Is he coming here too? And Zenn?'

Madame and Martine looked at one another. 'I don't know,' Madame said. She put one of her hands, very warm, on Claire's head. 'But your mother and father will be pleased you're safe with us. Now, have that soup before it gets cold. In the morning I need you to help me with the puppies.'

When she'd eaten they showed her out to the privy and Madame lent her a toothbrush and face flannel to use at the kitchen sink. The cupboard was a pantry like the one they'd had in Paris. Martine had put a small mattress and sheets and blankets on the floor to make a bed. 'I have another idea,' Madame said, leaving the room.

She returned with a small black puppy wrapped up in a flannel blanket. 'I'm going to give you a bottle of milk. If he wakes you up, you need to feed him.'

Madame took him out of the box and passed him to Claire. A pink tongue flickered out briefly. He felt warm and soft in her arms.

Claire thought she would stay up all night with the puppy, but when she heard him squealing softly, it was already daylight. Where was she? She listened for Zenn's regular breathing. She was in the cupboard at the convent. A cry broke from her.

The black puppy squealed again and its head turned from side to side. She picked him up and reached for the bottle, placing the teat in his mouth. He knew what to do. When he'd had enough milk, she and the puppy curled back up together under the blanket and slept again.

31

'Maman didn't tell me everything,' Joséphine said. 'She kept some of her secrets. I suspect she may have been jealous of your grandmother, thinking she and Luc were starting a romance. She all but admitted to spying on them that night.'

'And your mother saw Claire running towards the Germans – pretending to be Rozenn?'

'Claire's hair was pulled out of the plait she normally wore so it fell over her shoulders and she had Rozenn's beret on her head.'

I must have looked unconvinced. 'Rozenn was a striking girl and the Germans would certainly have noticed her before,' she continued. 'My mother worked shifts in the hotel bar and said Rozenn's looks had been discussed several times by Germans sitting on the balcony for hours at a time on sunny days. You can see people walking down the cliff path. A girl with beautifully cut auburn hair and a good figure . . .' Joséphine shrugged. 'There were a lot of young men here and not many young women. And Rozenn had already been caught breaking curfew in one of the coves, a troublemaker. But my mother spotted that the girl on the beach was actually Claire. An innocent, sweet girl. Heading towards a German patrol that had obviously been tipped off and meant business.'

'And Rozenn let Claire do this?' It shocked me.

'Perhaps she thought there'd be time for her to run after Claire and pull her to safety after Yann got away. Or that if they caught her, the Germans would realise Claire was really a simple child. Not all of them were barbarians.'

I imagined myself panicking as a plan to save a much-loved sibling started to go wrong. What would I have done? 'So Martine grabbed Claire and took her to the *manoir*? Wasn't that risky seeing as there were Germans billeted there?'

Joséphine smiled. 'The *manoir* is a rambling place.'

'I've only been there once.' I pushed my cup away, too distracted to finish the coffee. 'All the same, it seems remarkable the Germans didn't see her in the house.'

'Claire was no security risk. The German officers might have looked right through her. And Madame O'Donnell was an Irish citizen, neutral. She'd been a good hostess to the Germans.'

My mind went back to the beach. 'Did Martine know what happened to Yann? To their parents?'

'Next morning she walked up to the *longère* to see whether any of the family were still there. It was already boarded up. Later she heard they'd been taken to a jail in Rennes.'

'Even though the Germans hadn't actually caught anyone escaping on a boat? Why punish the doctor?'

'He'd been harbouring an unregistered French POW – Yann. And compromising material was found on the property, apparently.'

'Compromising material?'

She shrugged. 'That could mean anything from pro-Resistance posters to books written by communists.'

'What happened to my great-grandparents then?'

'Rumour had it they went to a prison in Paris, then on to a camp somewhere in the east of France.' She sighed. 'I don't think they died in the camp. But they were Parisians, only here for weeks before this. People liked the doctor but . . .' She shuffled in her seat. 'Word was Yann'd been the one to betray the group to the Germans.'

'Why on earth would Yann do that? Surely he'd keep himself out of the Germans' way?'

'He'd been seen talking to the artillerymen, laughing with them, handing over a paper of some kind.'

'People seem to have had eyes everywhere,' I said.

She gave a wry smile. 'Around here, you think you're walking alone through empty countryside but often there's someone attending to livestock or mending a wall who'll spot you.'

I recalled how the elderly man and then Lise had caught me trespassing at the *longère*.

'A German corporal had been seen bringing a sack of food up to the *longère*. Villagers were already talking about the Guillou household and the young man they were harbouring. But it was only later that suspicion focused on Yann.'

'Later?'

'Luc's brother came back here in the early summer of 1945, asking after his brother. He'd been arrested in the early spring of 1941. He was a communist, you see. He asked questions about your grandmother's family, said Yann must have been discovered hiding in the house and made a deal with the Germans so they wouldn't send the whole family to a camp. Yann told them about the planned pickup.'

Absent-mindedly she rubbed her temples.

'Just as happened with my mother, blaming Yann shifted some of the bad attention away from other people in the village who'd . . . compromised themselves with the Germans.' She paused, looking distressed.

Long memories meant that someone still felt it worth painting the accusation on the front door. But why just now, after so many decades and changes of owners and residents? 'Every time the house changes hands, it seems to reignite the old rumours and gossip,' Joséphine said. 'The old men in the bars start talking about Yann Guillou. I—'

I looked at her. She shook her head. 'Didn't you say you had to be in Lannion?'

I had so much more to ask her but I looked at my watch. 'I'm running late for an appointment to see the lawyer who handled the sale of the house.'

'Henri Tanguy?'

'His son, Jean. You know him?'

'*Bien sûr.*' Of course she did. 'He was in the same sailing club as my daughter when they were children.' Her expression lightened. 'You must hurry. Jean has always been punctual.' She gave me her mobile number and told me to text her for another meeting, if I wanted.

I'd been distracted by what she had told me and had to sprint to the car and then back into Lannion, cursing the speed-limit signs, scrabbling to find a parking place by the river as there wasn't time to park back at the apartment, and running over the bridge, to the mirth of some old men fishing on the bank.

The same assistant greeted me with something more attentive in her expression this afternoon. 'You're just in time. They're through here.' She took me back into the meeting room. A silver-haired man had joined Jean.

'Henri Tanguy, Madame,' he said, extending a hand.

'Thank you for seeing me again,' I said. They looked sidelong at one another. I sensed the same reservation present when I'd talked to Jean that morning. On the table in front of them sat a buff-coloured cardboard file.

'My son told me you were trying to find out who owns the *longère* on the cliffs at St Martin?' Henri said.

'That's right.'

271

'May I ask, Madame, if you have any form of identification on you? Driving licence, passport?'

I stared at him. 'Why?'

'The reason will shortly become clear. If you wouldn't mind?'

I did mind and I wasn't sure why. In my purse I had my driving licence. I took it out and handed it to Jean. He nodded at his father.

'You have additional proof of your address in England?'

I must have looked puzzled. 'Like a utility bill? Not with me. Why?'

Jean shook his head at his father before he could say anything and opened the file, peering at a sheet of paper inside it. Was I on some dossier of suspicious English visitors? They exchanged looks. 'You have moved recently?' Jean asked.

'Three months ago.'

'Where did you live until then?' his father asked. The atmosphere in the room was full of a charge I couldn't interpret. I'd hurried away from Joséphine just as she was telling me what the graffiti on the house meant, and now I was being questioned by these men.

I stood up. 'If I've overstepped the mark asking about the house in St Martin, please excuse me, but I think our meeting is over.'

'Humour us,' Jean said. 'Please, Madame.' Something about his eyes, serious, but less guarded now, made me sit down again.

I gave them the Clapham address. 'But now I want to know why you need my personal information.'

Henri leant towards me. His eyes were twinkling. 'Just one last question and then I promise we will tell you everything. Do you *really* not know who the current owner of the *longère* is?'

I felt my jaw clench. 'I've spent days driving up and down the coast talking to people, trying to find out why someone painted "traitor" on the door. My family think I'm mad. I've emptied my bank account to come here and find out the strangest things about my grandmother and her family. I should be back at home working.' I sighed and looked directly at Jean. 'I haven't a clue who owns the house. Just tell me and I'll leave you to your day.'

Jean and Henri were smiling now. 'Madame, the owner of the house on the cliffs is a woman of twenty-nine residing in London,' Henri said.

'How weird,' I said. 'I was told it was an American man who'd recently died and left it to someone in his will?'

'The new owner is the great-niece of a Mr John Gardiner of California.' Henri studied me as he told me the name. A bell rang very faintly in my memory but it couldn't be . . .

'Known for his animated films, most notably *Treasure*,' Jean said slowly.

'*Treasure?*' I sat up straight. 'That John Gardiner?' I knew the film. Everyone knew the animated film about the two girls growing up on a rubbish heap and turning bits of trash into, well, treasure. Gwen and I could probably still sing every song. The artwork, all hand-drawn, even as computer animation had become the norm, was still regarded as some of the finest since Disney's best, perhaps even finer. It was said to be the prime example of why the human hand, the artist's pen, could still outperform technology.

Even now, if *Treasure* appeared on television I'd stop and marvel at the use of colour, the fine outlines, the humour, the lyrics. A memory of my mother floated through my mind, storing egg trays, cardboard tubes and cereal boxes so that Gwen and I could construct houses like the girls in the film. 'What on earth's John Gardiner's connection with St Martin?' I thought of my American veteran on the ferry. 'Did he land there in 1944?'

'John Gardiner is, or was, a famous American, but like so many, he was originally an immigrant. He was born Yann Guillou.'

Every nerve in my spine was tingling. 'Yann? That Yann? Rozenn's brother?'

'*Excusez-moi.* I must go and telephone the lawyers in Paris.' Henri stood up. 'They need to know this . . . development.'

Jean nodded. 'The new owner of the *longère* is John Gardiner's great-niece, the younger granddaughter of his sister, Rozenn.'

My mouth was trying to make sounds come out of it but unsuccessfully.

'It's you, Morane,' Jean said, his voice now full of delight. 'You own the house on the cliffs.'

32

The letter from California has been read and reread but Rozenn still can't take it in. She holds the silver compass accompanying it, staring at her father's initials on the back.

She has never suspected, never, that Yann was still alive. She asked about him, when she returned to Paris after the war, but the old concierge had died and none of the new people living in the neighbouring apartments knew anything. None of their old friends had seen him. All she had discovered about her family was that her parents had died in the bombardment of St Malo and Claire in a diphtheria outbreak in a convent. Of course Yann would have died too. Why should she be spared that additional guilt?

She's heard the name of John Gardiner, famous animator. If she'd ever seen him talking about his work on television she'd have recognised him. But he was always a reclusive figure, shunning publicity, rarely even giving radio interviews. Yann had been such an adventurous, extrovert boy, but his later life must have made him retreat into his own company. All that time, he'd been living and creating, creating *Treasure* and all the other work. He hadn't come to find her. But had *she* ever really tried hard enough to find *him*?

She'd placed his sketches of birds and mice in the back of her photograph album and looked at them from time to time, but if any of the family questioned her about the drawings, asked why she no longer drew, she'd been vague, said she'd enjoyed sketching as a girl but had never found time to carry on, not even in retirement down here. Lies. Omissions.

So many decades of shame and grief. She's an old woman in a warm bed, with pale winter sunshine streaming in, oystercatchers squealing outside, her family downstairs. But somehow, at this moment, Rozenn's also an eighteen-year-old girl making a single terrible decision.

> *I couldn't forgive you, Rozenn. Not then. And I couldn't forgive myself, either. So I left for America: a US officer I got to know helped me with the paperwork. And years passed . . .*

She reads his words again. Rozenn has controlled herself, her emotions, her memories, for so long, but now tears fall on to the linen sheet. If her sobs aren't heard downstairs it's only because her lungs are no longer capable of broadcasting them past the ears of Pearl, who lifts her head and whines gently at her mistress, dark eyes wide with concern. *Claire. Yann. Maman and Papa.* Rozenn calls the names silently across the years.

> *It's all in the book, a graphic novel: my first and last, I will send it either to you, or to Morane herself, if time runs out, my dearest Rozenn, my sister who did all she could to help me, whom I have neglected so heartlessly. Everything happened so suddenly on the beach.*

So fast, too fast. Rozenn had thought she had it all under control.

It all unravelled. Claire was coming towards them. Her twin was smiling, tentatively, as though she knew she shouldn't be there.

An engine rumbled above them behind the hotel. Dogs barked and doors slammed. German voices shouted. They had a minute at most to get the boat safely away into the shadows of the cliffs. Claire had always wanted to help. Perhaps there was a way she could. But the risk . . .

Images and memories flashed through her mind: Yann's talent, Claire's handicap. Yann was young, fit, a trained soldier, a combatant the Allies could use against the Germans. Claire was obviously harmless. Surely if the Germans caught her they'd just think she was a simple soul who didn't understand about curfews and blackouts? Even that Gestapo officer on the train had been kind to Claire. And it probably wouldn't come to that. As soon as Yann was safely away, Rozenn would run after Claire, pull her up into the cemetery to hide. It was just a question of a minute – less, seconds.

Rozenn tugged the plait out of Claire's hair. 'Do you want to help us, Claire?' She put her own beret on Claire and handed her the torch, which had no blackout tape on it, and directed her across the sand. 'Switch it on and run past the hotel. It's very important that you wave the torch at those Germans so they see you on the beach.' Doubt covered Claire's face but Rozenn could always make her do what she wanted. She forced herself to smile reassuringly at her twin. 'Do it for Yann, Claire. Run!'

And Claire ran. Rozenn raced back to the shore.

A splash as something, someone, fell out of the boat. Yann waded out of the sea and passed her, pursuing Claire, turning briefly to look at Rozenn, his face hard with shock – or contempt. What had she done? Rozenn opened her mouth to call out a warning, an apology.

A wave struck her from behind, dazing her, filling her mouth with water. She was in the sea. Something heavy hit her on the head. *The oar.* Water passed over her face. Quiet. Dark. Cold. She might stay in this peaceful place where the sin she'd just committed would fade from her mind. Someone was pulling her out. Rozenn spat salt water from her mouth. Luc had her. He pleaded with the men in the boat, words coming out in gasps.

'They'll arrest us, you've got to take us too. If they see us they'll know where to search for you.' Hands were grabbing at her.

'Yann,' she said, as they pulled her up. 'Claire.'

'They've gone,' Luc told her roughly. 'Keep down, we're not safe yet.'

Rozenn shook so much she could hardly keep her throbbing head steady enough to look back at the beach. She could still see the Germans' searchlights but whatever was happening on the beach was distracting them. Claire and Yann had vanished. Both arrested?

A question hung in her mind for a fleeting moment, but she didn't have time to ask it.

'The Germans knew.' She leant over the boat's side. 'I've got to go back and help the others.'

Luc grabbed her. 'They'll shoot you. Or you'll drown. You can't help them now.' His voice compelled her attention. 'You need to trust me. Claire did just as you asked her – she distracted them from us.'

The spray on her face, the men struggling with the oars, cursing at the swell. Then a period of confusion as she was pulled out of the boat on the sandbar then rowed out again to what she vaguely made out as a small grey motor gunboat with black numbers on it. Voices hissed at them in English, saying angry things she couldn't completely understand. Her head throbbed; when she moved her stomach tried to turn itself inside out. Luc was telling them she was the one who'd retrieved their wireless for them. 'And they haven't seen us, Rozenn's diversion worked. You've got safely away.'

More angry voices.

They were below deck, in a cramped cabin, moving at speed. She closed her eyes, letting herself slip into darkness. The smell of oil and wet wool dragged her back into consciousness. Her head was resting on Yann's duffel bag, which someone must have transferred on to this motor gunboat. She sat up. Her head ached, pain radiating from a bump on the side. Something had hit her. The oar, she remembered. She looked for Luc, panicking when she couldn't see him. He was curled up on the cabin floor.

The Englishman with the broken arm came down the steps, swaying as the boat cut through the water. It was light enough for her to see the accusation in his eyes. 'So your brother told the Germans about us?'

She fought the nausea and the pain in her head to concentrate. 'Yann would never betray us.'

He scoffed. 'You're sure of that? Perhaps the Germans made it worth his while? A sack of food? A blind eye turned to an unregistered prisoner of war in a prohibited zone?'

Luc was stirring, wincing as he sat up.

'Once we arrive in England you'll be interrogated,' the man told her.

'Rozenn risked her life to get you the wireless,' Luc said. 'Her father did the same when he treated your arm. Do you know what happens to French civilians caught helping the British?'

She sat up straight. 'My sister, my innocent sister, risked her life to get the rowing boat safely away.' A wave of angry fury warmed her briefly, only to be replaced with a cold sense of horror. What had she done to Claire?

The Englishman stomped back up to the deck.

Luc moved to sit beside her, pulling her to him. 'You're still freezing.'

'I wish you'd left me in the water.'

'You'd have drowned. Or the Germans would have found you and arrested you.'

'It's what I deserve for what I did to Claire.'

'You did it for the best.' He held her tight. 'Listen, Rozenn, we're in a difficult situation here.'

'She'd do anything for me, for Yann. She loved us. And I sent her into danger. I thought I could run after her once the boat had left the beach, tell the Germans it was me, not her.' The moan emitting from her was like something an animal would make. What had passed through her mind in those seconds? She must have been possessed by some kind of demon insisting that nothing else mattered apart from getting Yann away safely.

'Claire may have saved this whole operation. But now we need to think about what we're going to say when we land in England.'

She stared at him. 'What do you mean, what we're going to say? We helped those men and because we did, Yann and Claire . . .' Bile rose in her mouth. 'Because of what I did. It's my fault.'

The door at the top of the steps to the deck opened again. Both the Englishmen from St Martin came down to the cabin. The sight of them lit a spark inside her that pushed warm blood back through her veins. 'If it hadn't been for my sister, the Germans would have stopped you getting away. You'd have been tortured and shot.'

'Your brother jumped out of the boat and ran towards the Germans.'

'He went to help Claire. So don't you dare question my family's loyalty.'

The man started to say something; she cut in before he could. 'They may already be dead.' She forced aggression back into her voice. 'Don't talk to me about betrayal.'

Luc nodded beside her.

'When we land we expect you to help us with the authorities,' she went on. 'Or we'll tell them how you mismanaged everything: got yourself shot, couldn't retrieve your own wireless, or were too frightened to try. How you relied on two French kids. How you endangered a local doctor who helped you.'

The Englishmen looked at one another.

'Where exactly are we going, anyway?' Luc asked.

'Helford,' the injured man mumbled. 'Small village on a creek in Cornwall.'

'When we get to this Helford you will talk to your associates and find out about my family.'

'Transmitting to that wireless was the only means of communication with St Martin.' He nodded at the case, stacked under the steps.

'You could broadcast a message over the BBC French service?' Rozenn said.

The Englishman shook his head. 'BBC messages are sent for operational reasons only.'

The fight left Rozenn. Her head slumped. Claire, Yann, Maman, Papa – all swept away in some horror she could not imagine. Were they all imprisoned together? Had Yann told them what she'd done? She pictured her mother's face as Yann told her that Rozenn had effectively handed over Claire to the Germans. She was vaguely aware that the Englishmen had left the cabin.

'It's Yann, not you, who's to blame for this,' Luc said softly. She lifted her head. 'He must have told the Germans. Nobody else knew.' Luc took her hands. 'You're still freezing.'

She shook her hands free. 'Why would Yann risk his chance to get to England?'

'Perhaps they threatened all your family for not registering him in the restricted zone? People have been shot for coming to the coast without permission.'

'But Yann got into the boat as though he was expecting to leave.' Zone, coast, boat: the words sounded like vocabulary from an unknown language.

'Perhaps part of him hoped he could still escape, that the Germans wouldn't reach the beach in time.' Luc sounded as though he was far away now. 'Nobody wants to be the traitor.' It was as if he could see into Yann's mind. Rozenn remembered how Yann had loitered up on the cliff path the previous night while she'd retrieved the wireless. Had Yann spoken to the corporal while she was down on the rocks? But Yann wouldn't have said anything, he just wouldn't.

'Rest now.' Luc's voice was tender. She looked up at him. He was the one constant, the only one left to her. He'd saved her from drowning, had always helped her. Fleetingly her interrupted dream about the rose came back to her. Claire had been in that dream.

She abandoned herself to sleep.

❧

He woke her. 'We're only a few miles off the Cornish coast. You slept through some terrible weather. And a bit of trouble with a German plane that followed us until an RAF fighter chased it away.'

She sat up, blinking.

'Do you have your papers?'

She'd stuffed them into her jacket. 'They're soaked.'

The ID card was soggy but the ink was still legible and the photograph probably still looked something like she did now.

'*Bon.*' He pushed a white enamel mug across the table towards her. 'They heated up some soup. You should drink it.' Unbelievably she was ravenous, as though her body, shocked, full of grief, was reminding her that it was alive, still needed nourishment. She drank the orange liquid greedily, unsure what flavour it was supposed to be. Luc pushed a single thin slice of grey bread on a plate to her. 'And this.' He looked at her admiringly. 'You've frightened them. They think you're going to get them into trouble.'

'Good.'

'I don't think we'll have problems when we land.'

She finished eating and undid Yann's duffel bag. Shirts, socks and underpants. A clean handkerchief. Pad and pencils. He'd torn some of the pages out of the pad. Sketches of mice and birds, carefully observed and reproduced with his zest for everything that lived. Had he planned to create more cartoons based on them? A small flannel bag contained his comb, razor, toothbrush and a sliver of soap. No silver compass – it must have been in his pocket.

If the Germans hadn't seen him on the beach, if they hadn't actually spotted the boat, if there was no proof that it had even landed, had the whole matter already been dropped? Perhaps Yann and Claire were back in the house with Maman and Papa?

Yann would be telling them that she'd sent Claire running off as a lure, deliberately risking her sister's life. The orange soup rose from Rozenn's stomach into her mouth. She swallowed hard.

She could never go home again. She'd seen herself as the family's redeemer. From this moment on, she would be a stranger to them, the person never mentioned, whose photograph was no longer displayed.

She needed to push thoughts of her family out of her head now or she'd sink. Rozenn opened Yann's sponge bag and removed the comb, doing her best to tidy her hair. She wiped her face with the handkerchief Maman had ironed for Yann only yesterday.

The mouth of an estuary opened up through the smeared porthole. This was England. The hills visible were as greeny-blue as the ones they'd left behind. Chugging towards them was some kind of military craft. Uniformed men looked purposefully towards them.

They'd be landing soon, perhaps in just minutes. She knew not a soul in this country, had never imagined herself living here.

She looked at Luc. His face had already regained some colour. 'Rozenn.' His voice was thick with something: regret? Desire? 'Come here.' She felt herself flush as her body responded.

Feeling like this was all wrong. It must be delayed shock or something. She moved into his arms. All the emotions and sensations she'd ever felt for Luc Caradec seemed to boil up to the surface. She desperately wanted his body against hers, in hers. She reached under his shirt and undid the belt of his trousers. When his mouth came down hard on hers, Rozenn's lips were already swollen and the touch of his made her desperate.

Luc stopped. She thought he was going to push her away. 'Just a moment,' he whispered, picking up the duffel bag and the wireless case. He stacked the bag on the case, against the door, along with a cardboard box that contained cans of food and a bottle of water.

She pulled her skirt and pants off and undid the buttons of her shirt, leaning back on the bench. It was as though the part of her brain controlling rational thought had been overtaken by something older and more primitive. She needed Luc to make her forget or distract herself away from what was happening, what a voice inside her was whispering about him. She needed to quash that suspicion. It couldn't be right, he was Luc. He was all she had. 'Quickly,' she said.

For better or worse the two of them were bound together now. She saw it in his eyes as he moved on top of her. The mixture of lust, urgency and tenderness was a reflection of her own emotions.

33

I stood at the door of my inheritance, holding the keys. The Paris lawyers had couriered them down to Lannion overnight after Henri had telephoned to tell them that the beneficiary of John Gardiner's will had finally been found.

The graffiti had gone. I ran my hand over the door's oak surface and could feel rougher patches where the wood had been rubbed.

'I can't believe this,' Dad had said when I called to tell him. He sounded concerned, perhaps thinking I'd had a breakdown. 'Yann, my long-lost uncle, has left you a house, *the* house that Maman lived in? It's not a bureaucratic or legal misunderstanding?'

I had a copy of Yann's will in my hand and read him the paragraphs relating to the *longère*. Yann Guillou, or John Gardiner, had been a wealthy man. Other than the house and a sum of money for paying any taxes and completing the basic renovations he hadn't had time to complete before his death, the rest of his wealth was bequeathed to arts charities and foundations for disadvantaged young people.

Henri told me that I would also find a letter addressed to me inside the house. 'I do not know why Yann Guillou did not post it to you, but perhaps he wanted you to read it in situ.' I liked the way he referred to John by his Breton name.

Just going inside the house now, I texted Dad and Gwen. Dad had been concerned about the graffiti on the front door and told me not to stay in the house overnight, in case it was targeted by *some Breton nationalist nutter*.

I hadn't said I would spend the night in the house. On the other hand, I hadn't said I wouldn't.

Jean had told me it had been repaired, renovated, all walls plastered but not all of them had yet been painted. It had been furnished with the basics, all the services connected. 'You will have work to do, though. And you'll want to put your own mark on it,' he added. 'I looked at your website, Morane, you have a talent.' I blushed like a stereotypical female under his warm gaze and kicked myself for my response.

He looked at me more shrewdly. 'You know, you might find there are British expats here who would be interested in your work.'

'Oh?'

'It always surprises me how little French some of them speak. Someone who understands building projects and could liaise with builders and other contractors in the language could find themselves very popular. You may even find some of the locals are interested too. I'd be happy to put any enquiries I receive your way.'

'Thank you.'

Could it be that I might actually gain some fresh business as well as a house?

'I'm not too tainted by association with old grudges?' I asked.

'I don't think anyone could consider you or your work tainted.' My cheeks still glowed.

'I'm still not sure how the locals found out who John Gardiner was.'

'A man from the water company was curious when he came up to the house to reconnect the supply. He dug around into the American owner on the internet. Somewhere online John Gardiner

286

must have mentioned his childhood in France. Then the old gossip started up again.'

'Memories are long.'

'And sometimes inaccurate.' He twinkled at me. 'I suspect you will drive all those old rumours out of the village now, Morane.'

I wasn't sure I yet knew enough about what had happened on the beach in June 1941.

The front door opened easily – the lock was new, I noted, and highly secure, with four bolts. I stepped into an open-plan space with a kitchen to the front. Like Rozenn's house in Helford, I thought. Of course. This house had lived on in her imagination for all the years of her exile and when she'd been able to, she'd recreated it. John – Yann – had had walls re-plastered and painted in a pale-stone colour that was warm yet light enough to brighten the interior. The floor was covered in engineered wooden floorboards that looked both beautiful and tough, and would match any other decoration. Sofas from Ikea were arranged around a black stove. To the right, in what had once been an outbuilding, a small dining area had been set up, with a row of spotlights above it. I could add a floor lamp, or perhaps a pendant ceiling light in copper, hanging over the table. I reached automatically for my notepad and laughed at myself.

The house wasn't as dusty or damp as I'd feared – Jean had told me that John Gardiner had paid for a deep clean after he'd had the repairs and renovations carried out and the Tanguys' office assistant came over regularly to air it.

The windows at the rear behind the kitchen sink and worktops were the high, shallow ones I'd noted from the exterior, set too high to provide much of a view. Would planning permission to enlarge them be possible? I shook my head at myself, falling into professional mode again, assessing, noting, when all I had to do, for now, was enjoy.

The staircase and bannisters were wooden: treated but not painted. Yann had left me a blank canvas to work on. It was as if he'd known me. Upstairs I found two bedrooms and a small bathroom, which looked as though it had been installed within the last decade and must formerly have been the third bedroom. The walls up here had been plastered and whitewashed. A pile of white towels sat wrapped in cellophane, along with a bar of new soap. I imagined I could knock through to the space above the dining room and create another bedroom.

Rozenn had lived here for such a short period of time before she'd come to England. I wondered which room had been hers – and perhaps Claire's? There was a double bed in one of the rooms, duvet, cover, pillowcases and sheets all in their original packaging, ready to make up the bed.

I went back down to the kitchen. The units were probably another Ikea purchase: simple, sturdy, doors painted off-white. I pictured Rozenn's old ironware pots and pans in here: their worn, rich colours looking good against the simple paintwork and the warm wooden floors.

I opened a drawer and found a basic set of cutlery. An upper cupboard housed a plain white dinner service, the lower a set of simple but high-quality saucepans. The refrigerator door was open. I closed it and plugged the refrigerator in. It started humming. A simple control by a small storage heater must operate the hot water and heating. A pile of instruction booklets sat on the table.

'I'm Goldilocks.' I said it out loud, smiling at myself. Except I was allowed to be here; it was all mine. My views from the upstairs windows. My new, sweet-wooden-smelling staircase and floors. My kitchen. My bedrooms. My garden. I swallowed hard, reminding myself that it was really more of a jungle at the front. I wasn't sure how easy it would be for me to live here with Brexit on the way. Perhaps I could rent the house out in high season and spend lengthy periods the rest of the time working from here myself? There was wifi: my phone showed a signal and Jean had already texted me the password.

In all the excitement I'd missed the A4 white envelope, sitting on the table.

'Morane', it said.

I sat down on one of my chairs and opened the envelope. Inside there was a sheet of writing paper and what looked like an A4 magazine.

Ma chère Morane

It has taken me some months to complete the enclosed. I hope it helps you understand why you have inherited this house. I regret very much that I never met you, your father and your sister.

Your loving great-uncle

Yann

I opened the book: actually a graphic novel, I saw. Pages of apparently hand-drawn images and text, finely done yet powerful. *I'm producing something...* Those words in Yann's letter I found under Rozenn's bed: this was it. John Gardiner had turned to his art to explain the past to me.

The first panel showed me a family arriving here at this house, carrying suitcases, faces full of doubt. A young man and his twin sisters, identical but for their hairstyles. The girl with the smart waves was clearly Rozenn. I smiled, recognising her familiar expression. *I don't like the look of this place*, the caption said.

The next panel showed the family settling in. My great-grandfather waved as he opened the door of a smart black car, a doctor's bag in his other hand. Rozenn was strolling off towards the cliffs, a satchel swung around her shoulders. Her mother and Claire were feeding chickens. Yann was visible through the half-open door of one of the outbuildings, head over a sketch pad. The colours were bright, it might have been a summer holiday, but for the distant grey-green figures of armed Germans on the cliffs.

I turned a page and read about how Rozenn became friendly with a local boy, Luc, how she secured a passage for Yann. I gasped when I saw the images of my young grandmother scrabbling over slippery boulders to retrieve a wireless.

The illustrations of Rozenn's family, sitting at a sending-off dinner for Yann, brought a smile to my face. Yann had chosen soft, warm colours to depict the vase of wild flowers on the table and the glow from the oil lamp. The interior of the *longère* where I sat myself, seventy-five years later, was inviting and the people around the table looked tenderly at one another, as though they were storing up memories. I could see why Rozenn had tried to recreate this house on the Cornish side of the Channel, to preserve some kind of connection with her lost family.

As I turned the pages I saw Yann with a duffel bag swung over his shoulder saying goodbye to his family. Rozenn put on a navy beret. Claire, upset at being left behind yet again, slipped out of the house to follow her siblings. And as the pages showed the sky turning heavy and the waves growing treacherous, I found myself lost in Yann's story, transported to that night that changed everything for my family . . .

34

The weather had turned. The men rowing the boat into the cove had to work hard. Surf drenched the group on the beach as Yann threw his duffel bag into the boat.

As she spotted Claire above them on the cliffs, Rozenn's face was a white, shocked oval against the dark sky.

An engine rumbled beyond the hotel. Shouts and slamming doors. A group of Germans came out on to the hotel balcony, shining lights along the sand, unlocking the metal gate to the beach. Dogs barked. The Germans hadn't seen them yet but they were so close.

Rozenn tugged the plait out of Claire's hair. 'You do want to help us, don't you?' She put her own beret on Claire and handed her the torch, which had no blackout tape on it, and directed her across the sand. 'Run across the beach. Wave the light around, make sure they see you!'

Claire ran. A whistle blew. Footsteps hammered down from the hotel to the sand, the metal gate screeching as it was unlocked.

Yann's mouth was an O of shock. 'Claire!' He jumped out of the boat, waded through the surf on to the shore and tore across the wide beach after her. A searchlight dazzled him, forcing him to stop while it swung across the sand. He blinked, waiting for guns to fire. Nothing. They hadn't seen him. But while he was temporarily blinded, Claire had vanished. The Germans approached, binoculars in hands, guns loaded, dogs on leads growling, but there was no girl in a beret with them. Yann turned to see that Rozenn, Luc and the boat had gone too.

Claire must have run up into the graveyard. Instinct pulled him after her, but he feared making any sound that would draw German attention to his sister's hiding place. But perhaps she'd already left the cemetery and was running back home, terrified? He needed to warn Maman and Papa about what had happened.

He ran back towards the rocks and clambered up to the path. As he reached the track to the house a van rumbled up from the lane. He threw himself down behind the bushes. Uniformed Germans hammered on the door.

His parents were dragged out to a black van. 'A male believed to be your unregistered son was seen on the cliffs,' a German told Papa.

Papa looked him directly in the eye. 'My son left for Paris weeks ago.'

Yann put a hand over his mouth to silence himself. Revealing himself now would be the worst thing he could do for them. Another German emerged from Yann's outbuilding holding a piece of paper.

'Interesting,' he said. Yann's final drawing. He hadn't burnt the French mice gnawing the factory cables while the German foreman rat turned his back. He'd left it on his desk for Rozenn. He swore at his own folly.

The van bumped its way up the lane. A second vehicle arrived and two local policemen sealed up the door. 'This all seems unnecessary,' the first one said. 'The Boches didn't even catch anyone on the beach. If there was a boat, it got away.'

'The good doctor was hiding an unregistered prisoner of war,' his companion replied. 'Who was publishing Resistance material.'

'So what do we do for a doctor now Guillou's gone?'

When they'd driven off, Yann crept down the lane into the village. A roadblock. *Merde*. He scrambled over the wall into the field, too scared to use his torch, running bent over, until he was on the cliff footpath. Was Claire still down there, terrified, hiding among the gravestones?

Pinpricks of lights flashed below. Two field-grey uniformed men were visible, shining their torches. Sweat ran down his back. Yann waited another hour. No shouts. No screams. She'd gone.

Dawn. His leg muscles cramped and shaky at first, Yann ran the length of the footpath back to the *longère*, stopping every hundred metres to check over his shoulder. Nobody in the outbuildings. He passed the donkey field on the way to the lane leading back down to the village. Perhaps Claire was hiding behind a wall, too scared to reveal herself. 'Claire,' he called softly.

Nothing. Fully light now. If he stayed in St Martin they'd pick him up. There was nowhere he could take Claire. Her best hope was that Maman and Papa had succeeded in persuading the Germans that he'd left the zone and they knew nothing about any activity on the beach. It was safer for them all if he went away.

As for Rozenn, he didn't know what to think about her.

He did what he ought to have done weeks earlier: pulled the silver compass out of his pocket and set a course south.

⁂

Weeks, a month, passed. He walked through fields and forests, hiding from police and Germans, begging or stealing food, until he reached one of the rivers marking the border with the *Zone Libre*. A farmer showed him the best place to swim across one morning while mist lingered on the water and deer drank.

Three years of hiding out in farm buildings and railway yards, in groups that came together and parted as the war progressed and people died or vanished. Yann learnt to use plastic explosives. And a dagger. He woke drenched with sweat and shaking, haunted by his abandoning of Claire in Brittany and leaving that cartoon in the outbuilding for the Germans to find.

The war ended.

❧

Yann sat in a Red Cross agency in Paris with an official, looking at a file. He'd tracked his parents from a prison in Rennes, to another in Paris and from there to a holding camp in eastern France. They were released in early 1943, he saw – in what kind of condition? – his father sent to work in a German military hospital in St Malo. In August 1944 bombs had dropped from planes and battleships blasted the old port.

The official flicked through a list of casualties. His finger paused.

'It's them, isn't it?'

The official nodded.

'Claire?'

'Not on the list.'

As a result of his work with the Resistance, Yann had friends among the Americans. They were generous with rations. He exchanged a tin of ham for an old bicycle and an orange for a map.

Before he left the capital, Yann wondered about visiting the Guillou apartment to leave a letter for Rozenn, in case she'd survived. But he didn't know what to say to her. And he couldn't face the apartment.

He pedalled north-west, passing through Versailles and the wheat fields they'd looked out on when they'd left Paris for Brittany by train in 1941. American military planes sat on runways at Dreux airport and jeeps shot past him on the roads. There were frequent diversions: roads still damaged, bridges still blown up.

It took more than two weeks to reach St Martin. Yann arrived to find the door to the *longère* still sealed, Maman's vegetable garden overgrown with spinach and weeds. He discovered a few early apples and hazelnuts and devoured them. The door to his outbuilding was unlocked. A few of his pencils were trampled into the earthen ground and Yann retrieved them. Everything else – clothes he left behind the night he went to meet the boat, books, even his improvised keg weights – was all gone.

Yann cycled down to the quay and asked the fishermen if they knew where his sister was. But when he told them who he was, one of them spat at him. 'Someone told the Germans about the boat landing. Luckily the boat got away. But you escaped. How was that?'

'Why would I tell the Germans? They arrested my parents.'

A fist caught him on the side of the jaw. Before he could return the punch a blonde girl pulled him aside. 'Don't.' She led him over the beach and up the steps to the cemetery, looking over her shoulder. 'You're asking too many questions.'

'They think it was me who betrayed the operation?' he asked her. 'It doesn't make sense.'

The girl shrugged. 'Everyone in this village was in the Resistance, according to them. And anything that went wrong was a collaborator's fault. You were an outsider, easy to blame.'

'It must have been Luc who told the Germans.' Yann'd had three years to run through his logic. 'He was the only other person apart from Rozenn who knew about the landing.' The girl looked sideways. 'You don't want to believe it, do you?'

'I'm going to forget you even mentioned that name.'

'All right, but, really, why do the locals think it was me?'

'You were seen on the cliffs talking to Germans, handing over papers.'

'That was just a silly cartoon I—'

She brushed off his explanation. 'I can't stay here talking to you any longer. There's something more important you need to know. I took Claire to Madame O'Donnell. She lived there safely until just after the war.'

The blonde girl, Martine, she said her name was, told him how a diphtheria outbreak claimed Claire. Yann made a sound that was half cry and half laugh. 'My father took her out of a convent in 1941 because of a diphtheria outbreak.'

'*La pauvre*. Perhaps it was what God intended for her all along.' Martine crossed herself. 'I'd tell them it wasn't you who was the traitor, but they'd just say I was a whore for the Germans and can't be trusted. I was lucky they didn't shave my head.'

He touched her hand briefly. 'Can you tell me anything about Rozenn?' He still found it hard to say her name.

'She and Luc disappeared. We think they must have gone to England in the boat. I couldn't see much from where Claire and I were hiding in the cemetery, but perhaps they panicked and took your place.'

❧

He could apply to Papa's lawyer for money to cover the voyage and set himself up in America, but it might alert Rozenn. And he still couldn't face her. He told himself it was because he was still angry with her but really it was because he was angry with himself.

❧

A Jewish woman he'd helped when she was sheltering in a farm-house near Lyons reappeared in Paris. 'No debate, you're having this to help you set up in New York.' She pushed bank notes across a café table.

❧

From the ship's deck the skyscrapers of Manhattan framed the sky like a work of art. Before they even docked Yann decided to become John Gardiner.

❧

At first all he found was a job in a warehouse, long hours, low wages. At night he slept in something resembling a dosshouse. Maman would have had a fit. On Claire's saint's day he went to Mass and lit a candle. Mourning her was straightforwardly painful. Thinking about the others was too complicated for now.

❧

When he could afford paper and pens he drew: cards for birthdays and Christmas, Valentine's, anniversaries, Easter, graduation, bar mitzvahs. Americans loved their cards. Sometimes a newspaper took a cartoon or two. Two years after his arrival the *New York Herald Tribune* syndicated one of his comic strips and paid him more money than he had ever dreamt possible. A studio on Broadway approached him and at last Yann found himself working on animations, just as he'd imagined himself years ago, sitting in his outhouse in Brittany.

❧

Decades passed. He picked up a Sunday supplement and saw a photograph of Rozenn: 'French Female Architect Building in

Helford'. He scrutinised the photographs of the house on a small Cornish creek. In one of them Rozenn, now a woman in her prime, elegant, dignified, sat on a jetty with a small boy. Yann read on: *Rozenn Caradec, whose husband Luc died last year . . .*

So she'd married Luc. The traitor. How could she? Did she even care about what Luc had done?

But, Yann's more rational side reminded him, Rozenn was the only one in their family who'd actually done anything concrete to get him out of Brittany. Anyway, Rozenn could justifiably accuse Yann himself of a number of poor choices.

He looked more closely at Rozenn's house: a replica of the *longère* in St Martin? A memorial to her family? That last meal, when they'd all been together and Maman had brought out the food she'd saved from Paris. It had been so bittersweet. Yann had felt the house embrace them all. Rozenn must have felt the same way and she'd carried that feeling to England with her.

❧

More years raced by. A chance came to fly to London for the premiere of *Treasure*. He extended the trip and found his way down to Helford village, the closest settlement to Rozenn, leaving the car a mile or so away and winding his way along footpaths and lanes to Rozenn's creek.

From time to time he patted the silver compass in his jacket pocket. He didn't need to use it that afternoon: his feet led him in the right direction. The water sparkled azure, grey or even yellow as the light changed. She'd landed here, confused, scared, and this water and light gave her comfort. It connected her to St Martin. That was why she'd built here.

He reached the house. Vue Claire. He gasped out loud: the name was like an electric shock. The house was beautiful, so reminiscent of the *longère* in its wide lines, though with a stronger outline. A home that had been planned rather than evolving through centuries. Just as you'd expect of Rozenn. And although coastal, this location was less exposed than the cliffside original in Brittany, as though Rozenn had craved the cover of trees and valleys.

A Golf GTI sat on the drive. Rozenn was at home. He could knock on her door. His hand wouldn't connect with the metal knocker. Suppose he was still angry? Suppose she was, for his years of silence? Suppose the reunion ended in more bitterness? It'd been more than fifty years. Too long. Not long enough.

He bought a ticket for the night ferry from Plymouth to Brittany, heading east from Roscoff when he reached France. In St Martin he parked on the lane leading out of the village towards the *longère*. There were still donkeys in the field, he noted. Claire would be pleased.

An elderly couple sat in deckchairs in the front garden, bushes and weeds growing almost around them. They glowered at Yann and he didn't like to ask if they owned the house themselves and would consider selling it.

Why did he even want to buy it? The family had barely lived there for a month in 1941. How was it that the place dripped with memories?

❧

Another decade and then another passed. Since the 1990s the money from *Treasure* had bought him a Californian life he still found hard to believe was his. Yann reran a conversation with a Los Angeles doctor. 'You're old but in remarkably good shape. We can buy you months, perhaps even a year . . .'

Wheeled into the anaesthetic room, images of Rozenn on the beach flickered through his memory. This separation had gone on too long.

The operation and the chemotherapy ridded him of cancer but also of his strength. More years passed with him incapable of crossing the Atlantic. He should have knocked on her door in Cornwall all those years ago.

He was in his nineties now. Sometimes the doctors looked at him, a single, childless elderly man, as though wondering why he carried on with it all. He knew why. There came a point when he accepted he was as strong in body and mind as he would ever be. He picked up the fountain pen he preferred for writing. Email might have its place, and even this old man had mastered it, but for this first communication with Rozenn, there was something comfortably solid about the feel of the pen in his hand. Writing the letter was hard at first, and not only because of his stiff fingers. By the time he finished it he felt exhausted but somehow younger too.

Would she reply? But she telephoned him. The first call wasn't a success: thousands of miles between them making the conversation, even though it was in their native tongue, stunted, painful. They both kept saying they were sorry and the echo on the line repeated their words over and over again so there was no space for anything other than an endless apology. They tried another call a week later and conversation was more fluid. Rozenn told him about her son Marc and two granddaughters. They laughed together at their memories.

'You knew,' Yann asked her, feeling they had to speak of the serious things too, 'that it must have been Luc who told the Germans about the boat landing?'

'I worked it out before we even docked. But I made myself forget. We had to register, get ration cards. Luc joined up and eventually went away to fight. I found a job.'

Across the ocean and mountains and plains Yann nodded.

'When the war ended everyone was gone: Maman, Papa, Claire and you. Only Luc came back to me. And I loved him.' She sounded like a young girl when she said the last bit. 'I didn't want to think too hard about what had happened on that night. For years that approach of mine seemed to work.'

Her voice cracked over the line. 'Despite all Luc's business success he was haunted. He never wanted to return to Brittany, said Marc and I were all he needed. He didn't even like talking about St Martin. Then one night, when, as usual, Luc'd had too much Courvoisier, he let something slip about a brother, Benoît, I never knew he had. Benoît was a communist and had been arrested before I met Luc. Once the Germans invaded Russia French communists were in more danger. I remember the evening Luc found out about the invasion. He was on edge but I didn't know why. It all came out years later. Luc told the Germans about the boat landing to save his brother from the firing squad.'

A pause before Rozenn continued. 'That must have been why he tried several times to persuade me not to go with you to meet the boat. He knew it was dangerous. Claire saved us by distracting them with the torch.'

'Why did you both get into the boat?'

'Because of me. Apparently I was drowning.' She explained how the oar struck her head, how Luc leapt into the sea to pull her out, instinctively pushing her towards the boat to save her, then climbing in himself, perhaps frightened and simply wanting to be out of danger.

'I missed that bit,' Yann said. They both laughed, darkly at first and then more easily.

In their last call Yann talked more about the *longère*. 'You know I bought it back in November?' They'd already discussed his plans for renovation. 'I thought there would be more time, that you and I could perhaps spend a few weeks there in summer.'

Rozenn was silent.

'I know, I know. I was deluding myself with daydreams.'

'You always were a dreamer.'

'And you were always the practical one. You and I are far too old, too sick to see the house again. But I would like to leave it to your family.'

'I was going to leave Vue Claire to Marc, but my son is a prosperous man. My granddaughters have always loved the house and I wondered about leaving it to them jointly.'

'What about a house each instead? Which granddaughter should have which house, though?'

'Morane is the one who loves to transform houses, to make them the most beautiful they can be.'

'So she would love a house that is not finished? The *longère* is now apparently habitable but does not yet have that final touch. And the garden is in a state.'

'Good. Morane needs a project she can throw her heart into. She needs to work until she is too exhausted and too happy to brood. And if she could rent out the house when it is finished, it would help her finances.'

Rozenn had already told Yann about Morane's boyfriend emptying their bank account to fund his addiction.

'It would be hard work for her. Is she up to the task, Rozenn?'

'She is a Guillou woman.'

They both laughed. The laughter was the last memory they would have of one another's voices.

35

The sound of hooves outside jerked me from the reverie I'd fallen into after reading Yann's book. Lise: on her horse, a small rucksack on her back. I went to the door to greet her. She tied the bay's reins around a bough of the oak, and swung the rucksack off her back. 'I bought you food.' She kissed me on the cheeks. 'And wine. I assume you're staying here now?' She smiled at my puzzled face. 'News travels, even from the discreet office of the Tanguys. Apparently you are the missing heiress. It's like one of your Victorian novels about lost wills and inheritances.'

'Come inside.'

She removed her helmet, leaving it on the doorstep, and followed me, looking around quizzically. 'This is better than I feared, but you still have a lot of work to finish it.'

'That's the real gift Yann left me.' I explained briefly about my job. Lise looked interested. 'Projects like this just absorb me.' I paused. 'I love working on houses like this.'

'It's good to love your work.'

Lise sat down at my table, pulling provisions out of her bag: bread, milk, salad, coffee, cheese, a bottle of red wine.

I opened a cupboard and found wine glasses. Lise raised an eyebrow. 'A little early, but why not?' She sipped the wine I poured her, looking around. 'It will be beautiful, *non?*'

'I've been given something I didn't even know I was yearning for. Just a few days ago I couldn't imagine how I'd ever be happy again. But I think I will be, here.'

'I sense hesitancy?'

'It sounds silly but I just wonder if I deserve it?'

'Don't worry, you can still inflict some purgatory on yourself.' She looked out of the open front door. 'Dealing with French bureaucracy. And taming that jungle out there.' She stared more fixedly outside. 'You have visitors, Morane.'

Joséphine was approaching, a man in his thirties with her. I went out to meet them and she greeted me with kisses to my cheeks. 'This is my son, David.' She gave him a gentle shove.

The man nodded, extending a rough-skinned hand to me. His faded jeans, navy crew shirt and weathered skin made me wonder whether he was a fisherman or farmer, some kind of outdoor worker, anyway.

'David has something to say to you.' She turned to her son.

' . . . *désolé*.' I could barely make out his words. Joséphine was blushing.

'David was the one who painted that word on your door.'

'I cleaned it off, Madame,' he mumbled. 'I'll treat the wood where I went at it too hard.'

'*Mat ar jeu*, David.' Lise stepped out and kisses were exchanged. 'You'll make good on the door, I know.'

'*Oui*. And I will tell the people in the bar that they are wrong.'

'And you will help Madame Caradec here settle into the village?'

'*Bien sûr*. I will help her with her garden. And on market day I will buy her a drink in the bar and introduce her to my friends. And I will make sure she gets the best fish.'

'*Bon*. Because we have all had enough of this nonsense,' Lise said. 'I don't want to send my father up here in his electric wheelchair to sort it out.'

David turned pale and muttered something about not troubling *monsieur le juge*. So Louis was a retired judge? No wonder he'd been so good at pushing me along an inquisitorial route when we'd met.

'*Non*,' Joséphine said, sounding scandalised. 'You can rely on us, Lise.'

David smiled at me shyly. 'I think people will like you, Madame.'

He shuffled away to pat the neck of Lise's horse.

'My son has always been easily led.' Joséphine sighed. 'Good at outdoor work but not at this.' She tapped her head. 'I was ashamed but not surprised when I found out he'd painted that word on your door. But strange as it sounds, people do listen to David when he gets an idea stuck in his head. Probably because he doesn't have very many of them.' She shrugged at my shocked face. 'I'm his mother, I can say it.'

Lise laughed. 'If David tells his friends you're *sympa* you'll be overwhelmed with fish and cider, Morane.'

'I'm not sure I'd deserve too much benevolence. My family isn't entirely absolved of betrayal.'

The two women looked at me.

'It was actually Luc who betrayed the boat landing,' I said.

'Luc Caradec.' Joséphine sighed. 'One of the secrets my mother never told me. How did you find this out, Morane?'

'Yann left something for me inside the house. My grandmother knew too but she didn't tell us. Perhaps she was ashamed.'

'It's hard to find a family where nobody was compromised in those years,' Joséphine said quietly.

'My father always knew Luc and his brother were playing a dangerous game, between them too close to the Germans and the communists.' Lise picked up her helmet. 'It's time to let the whole story die down. It's been over seventy-five years, after all. I must

305

ride back now. My father will be wanting to know how you're getting on, Morane.'

'I'll come and see him as soon as he's stronger,' I said.

'You look as if you are making yourself at home.' Joséphine
cast an amused glance over my shoulder. I realised that the opened
bottle of wine was visible on the table. My mobile trilled. I looked
at it. A message from Gwen.

David held the bay while Lise mounted. 'Will you come for a
ride with me tomorrow, Morane? My grey mare needs exercise. At
home we have a track that is not open to the public. I never meet
anyone when I ride there.'

I was about to snap a refusal at her. But I stopped. Lise was
promising I would not encounter cyclists, cars, or silently approaching joggers who might startle a horse.

'I'd like that,' I said, stunning myself with how much I wanted
to get back on horseback. 'Good way to see the local countryside.
And if he's up to it, I'd still like to sit down again with your father.'

'Papa is itching to ask you all kinds of questions. Brace yourself
for the full inquisition.'

With a wave she rode off, the other two walking with her. I
watched until they vanished up the lane and then turned back to
look at the house, *my* house.

Something waved gently outside one of the front windows: a
golden rose, survivor of one planted years ago, perhaps. I now knew
what I wanted to call my house: Rozenn was the Breton for rose
so the name was even more appropriate. Maison Rose, a match for
Vue Claire. The two houses would never be identical, were probably
never meant to be. Rozenn had created her house on the Cornish
creek using her memory of this property, a memory clouded with
guilt and longing and a kind of defiance, a refusal to let the past
bring her down. And she'd instinctively known that this was where
I belonged. How she must have suffered as she struggled to explain

it all to me before she died. Yann must have died within days of her. If I hadn't come to Brittany, how much longer would it have taken for the lawyers to track me down and tell me about my inheritance?

Gwen and I would decorate and furnish our houses very differently. Even though we were sisters who'd grown up under Rozenn's influence, we were distinct personalities with distinct tastes. That was as it should be.

It might take me some months, possibly even a year, to finish the refurbishment of Maison Rose. Jean had told me there was a sum of money left over for me to complete the renovations and decorate. When finished, I'd probably have to rent the house out for as much of the year as I could to boost my income. No doubt French bureaucracy and Brexit would tie me up in knots while finishing the interior and taming the garden exhausted my body. And I'd have to find a way to manage my business in the UK at the same time as I worked on this place. Maison Rose would be no easy inheritance but one that couldn't have been more perfect for me.

I remembered that I hadn't looked at Gwen's message and took my phone out of my back pocket.

Can I come and see the house and meet Lise, Louis and Joséphine, handsome Jean and all the others?

Book the ferry, I really want you to see the house! I answered. I sent the message and felt a little peculiar: I was acting the host, the giver of hospitality. The mobile trilled with a response from my sister.

There's something else. Rozenn kept a spare back-door key under a pot and someone must have taken it and made a copy. She brought her own key inside when she fell ill and wouldn't have known. Quite a few people locally have been burgled recently and the police think it was all done the same way. I'm so so sorry for letting you think it was your fault, Morie. I'll ring you later to grovel some more. I was going to wait a few more weeks to tell you but there is another reason for my terseness.

I've been horrifically nauseous for a few weeks now, could barely leave the house, but am finally feeling better. At first I was blaming it on too much clotted cream. But you can probably guess you're going to be an aunt. XXX

Rozenn's great-grandchild. How delighted she would have been. I felt pleasure, too, flowing like honey through my veins.

No need to grovel, I texted back. *Just come over as soon as you can! This won't be perfect until you and your little bump are here too.*

I pulled at a strand of bindweed in what had once been a narrow flowerbed in front of the house and heard a sound that had me puzzled for a second. It was me, I was whistling, a most unmelodious sound: one I hadn't heard myself make for months and months.

I laughed to myself and tugged at the bindweed so that the whole strand, roots and all, came out in my hand.

ACKNOWLEDGEMENTS

As always, I couldn't have managed without the support of my husband, Johnnie, and my critique partner, Kristina Riggle. Thank you to both of them. My continued gratitude also to the team at Lake Union, especially to Sammia Hamer, Dolly Emmerson, Nicole Wagner and Bekah Graham for their ongoing support. Celine Kelly's editorial advice inspired me to write the best book I could. Melissa Hyder and Sadie Mayne saved me from myself on many occasions as we polished the manuscript.

Thanks also go to the staff at the Bartlett Maritime Research Centre at the National Maritime Museum in Falmouth, Cornwall, for alerting me to several very useful books and papers when I was there in June 2019 researching the background to this book.

ABOUT THE AUTHOR

Photo © 2018 John Graham

Eliza Graham spent biology lessons reading Jean Plaidy novels behind the textbooks, sitting at the back of the classroom. In English and history lessons, by contrast, she sat right at the front, hanging on to every word. At home she read books while getting dressed and cleaning her teeth. During school holidays she visited the public library multiple times a day.

At Oxford University she read English literature on a course that regarded anything post-1930 as too modern to be included. She retains a love of Victorian novels. Eliza lives in an ancient village in the Oxfordshire countryside with her family. Her interests (still) mainly revolve around reading, but she also enjoys walking in the downland country around her home.

To find out about Eliza's new releases, sign up for her newsletter on her website: www.elizagrahamauthor.com. She's also on Facebook: @ElizaGrahamUK and Instagram: @elizagraham1.